FIRE'S FOLLY

Book One of the Gods' Lands Trilogy

DEAN RICHARD KAYLER

Publishing Services provided by Paper Raven Books LLC

Printed in the United States of America

First Printing, 2023

Paperback ISBN: 979-8-9875138-0-4
Hardback ISBN: 979-8-9875138-1-1

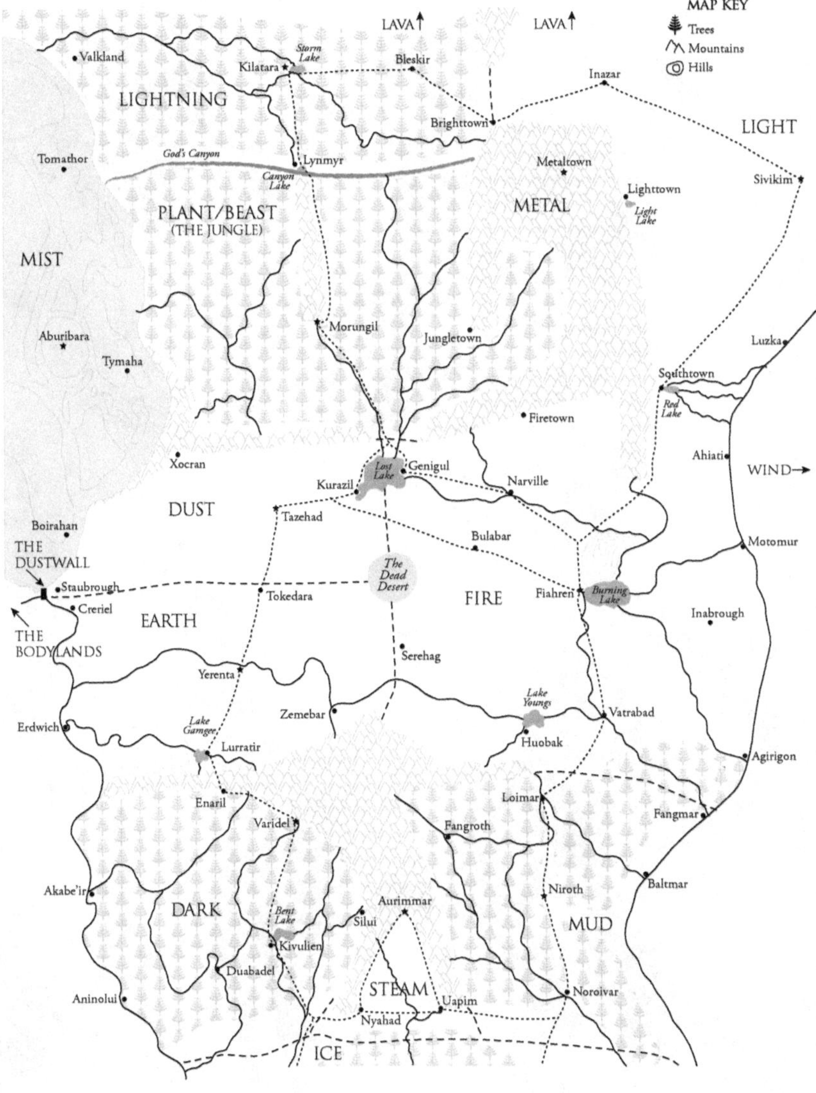

MAP KEY
Trees
Mountains
Hills
LAVA
LAVA
LIGHT
Valkland
Kilatara
Storm Lake
Bleskir
Inazar
LIGHTNING
Brighttown
Sivikim
Tomathor
God's Canyon
Lynmyr
Metaltown
Lighttown
Light Lake
Canyon Lake
PLANT/BEAST
(THE JUNGLE)
METAL
MIST
Luzka
Aburibara
Southtown
Red Lake
Tymaha
Morungil
Jungletown
Ahiati
Firetown
WIND
Xocran
Lost Lake
Genigul
DUST
Kurazil
Narville
Tazehad
Boirahan
Bulabar
Motomur
THE DUSTWALL
The Dead Desert
FIRE
Fiahren
Burning Lake
Staubrough
Inabrough
Creriel
Tokedara
EARTH
THE BODYLANDS
Serehag
Yerenta
Lake Youngs
Zemebar
Vatrabad
Erdwich
Lake Gamgee
Lurratir
Huobak
Agirigon
Enaril
Loimar
Fangmar
Varidel
Fangroth
Akabe'ir
Baltmar
Niroth
DARK
Bent Lake
Aurimmar
Silui
MUD
Kivulien
Duabadel
STEAM
Noroivar
Aninolui
Uapim
Nyahad
ICE

To my friend Rey

Without you,
this book would have taken twice as long to write,
and been only half as good.

ACKNOWLEDGEMENTS

A few words of gratitude to the people who helped this book come to life. First are my family, close and extended, who are too many to list here, but all of whom have always been great and encouraging about me pursuing my dreams. And especially my parents, who were endlessly supportive of me from the very start. So a big thank you to my mom and dad. All my friends as well, who encouraged me through the years, but especially my roommate Kim, who spent many hours in the creation of this book listening to my wild, and often random, ideas of things that could be and shouldn't be, despite how rarely my ramblings probably made any sense. A special thanks again to my friend Rey, who helped with every aspect of this book: from worldbuilding to creating characters, figuring out the plot and telling me when something just wasn't working. I don't know how things would have turned out without him, but I doubt this story would be nearly as good. And finally to the team from Paper Raven Books, who helped turn this messy little project into a real, quality novel. My editors Kate, Brian, M.A, and Stef. The project managers/coordinators: Brandy, Heather, Karen, Megan, and all the rest who have helped to make this a reality. Thank you all!

CONTENTS

PROLOGUE

He was nervous. Or was he excited? Both? Probably both. In nearly 80 years of life, there were few times where Anderas Anto, the great prodigy of Fire, had ever had cause to feel nervous before a fight. When he was merely 15 years old, he had fought in the battles against the Earth church as they attempted to retake the city of Serehag, shortly after his uncle had been made lord of the city. Thanks in no small part to the actions of the teenage Anderas, his uncle was still lord of Serehag, and Earth had learned to fear the name Anderas Anto. After all, how many Descendants in history had managed to defeat a Blessed in battle, forcing them to retreat? That had been the greatest fight of Anderas' life, now almost 70 years ago. In all that time, with all that he had done and accomplished, his name was now known throughout the world: Anderas Anto, the greatest Descendant alive! And yet he still hadn't received a Blessing. But now he finally had his chance.

Finally, finally, after all this time, after a lifetime that was already longer than most people even lived, Anderas was in a situation where even Soleil, the annoying High Priest of Fire who was always so reticent to give him his well-earned Blessing, could deny him a Blessing no longer. The Demon from Wind was coming to Ohena, and Anderas was there to stop him.

He wasn't the only one there, of course: not even the great Anderas Anto would be enough to stop the Demon by himself. How many Blessed had failed to kill him already? How many Descendants, Awakened and Unawakened alike, had that monster slain in his rampage across the world? There was a reason that he had been given the moniker of 'Demon' after all. A half-forgotten reference to mythical monsters from long-dead beliefs. So no, Anderas was not alone. Not by far. First there were the soldiers, hundreds of them. Not much was really expected of them, truth be told. It was no secret, at least not among the nobility, that Fire's soldiers weren't exactly the best of the bunch. The Firelands were simply too big and too short on manpower to afford the time to train them properly before they were sent off to guard the borders. But they would serve their purpose nonetheless: they would slow down the Demon. He would cut through them like an Earth mole dug through the ground, but the sheer number of them would at least slow him down.

Then there were the Descendants, like Anderas. Well… not quite like Anderas. There was no point in being humble about it. 27 Descendants there were here at Ohena, sur-rounding the town in secret, all of them Awakened, naturally (Unawakened Descendants would barely be of more use against the Demon than a common soldier, but far more tragic to lose), but none of them even close to Anderas' prowess with their God-given magic. Some of the Descendants were older, some younger, and some roughly the same age as Anderas, but he outshone them all. Drastically. He had long since learned to stop being humble about that fact.

And finally there were the Blessed. Three of them, even. The last time three Blessed had been sent to handle a single problem had been during the last great Bodylands Horde (and more than three had been sent for that nightmare, naturally). To have sent three Blessed to deal with a single man? It was overkill. There was no other word for it but sheer, mind-boggling overkill. Even Anderas could only best a single Blessed by himself, and even then only the weaker, stupider ones. To send three Blessed to deal with one man? And to add 27 Awakened Descendants and hundreds of soldiers? This was a force to conquer a city with, not ambush a single man!

And yet here they were, hiding on the edges of Ohena, inside the buildings that they had commandeered to ensure that the Demon would cross into the depths of the town and be surrounded on all sides, escape impossible as he was crushed by the weight of hundreds of soldiers, over two dozen Descendants, and three Blessed. And in truth, it was likely only the Blessed who would matter here, for they were taking no chances with the Demon. When he arrived, when they were ready, the Blessed would burn the man to ashes before he even had a chance to react. There was no person alive, other than the Gods themselves (who really didn't count, seeing as they were Gods), who could survive the onslaught of three Blessed at once.

Anderas could understand it, at least in part. He had heard all the stories, all the rumors surrounding the Demon, after all. Honestly, he had trouble believing most of them.

But if they were even half true, then Soleil's paranoia was understandable, if still overkill. When dealing with a being who had caused as much death and destruction as the Demon from Wind, who had killed countless Descendants and even survived facing Blessed and escaped, there really was no room for error, no benefit to holding back. The man had to be put down. And Anderas was there to do it. He didn't even have to strike the killing blow. Hells, he didn't even need to get involved at all, as the Blessed would likely end the Demon in the first few seconds of conflict! But simply his being there, at the Demon's death, regardless of his involvement, would be enough to finally force Soleil's hand and get him his Blessing! Even if it wouldn't for the other 26, he was Anderas Anto, and everybody there knew that this was the event that would finally push him into the ranks of the Blessed! He knew that that worried some of his more craven allies, the ones who believed the outlandish tales of the Demon, so much so that they didn't even believe that the Blessed would incinerate him in moments! Those faithless few were afraid that, if the Demon somehow evaded the opening salvo, their greatest asset (aside from the three Blessed) would stay out of the fight, wouldn't risk his life and inevitable Blessing against such a fearsome foe. They really should know better. Anderas hadn't gained the reputation he had by being a coward, by taking the easy route. No. If by some impossible means a fight did occur, he would fight side by side with his allies, his friends, his soldiers, and he would see the Demon dead even if he had to tear that monster's head off with his own two hands to do it. The Demon would die today.

A whisper passed through the air, and the already-silent room that Anderas was hidden in grew tense: that was the signal. The Demon was approaching! Anderas peeked through the wooden slats of the window he was hidden behind, invisible to any outside of the house he was in. He, like the other 26 Descendants, were hidden along the very outermost buildings of their trap, while the three Blessed were hidden in the very innermost, the three closest to the town's central square. The soldiers were arrayed all around and between them.

From his limited view through the window slats of the street, the road that had been deemed most likely for the Demon to come from, Anderas saw a lone figure calmly walk into view. He felt his pulse race—this had to be the Demon! He matched every description they had of the man, as vague as they were: average height, all alone, entire body hidden within the depths of a worn, dull, dark cloak, head and face hidden within the hood of said cloak. This figure, so calmly strolling up the street of the small town, matched that lackluster description entirely.

As the Demon passed the house he was hidden in, Anderas wondered if this really was the Demon. He was walking unerringly toward the town square, seemingly unbothered by how much quieter the place was than how it should be. The residents had not been told the truth of why they were there, not wanting to cause a panic that could have alerted the Demon, but the whole town had known something was happening. It was impossible to avoid, what with hundreds of soldiers and dozens of nobles descending on the town and commandeering buildings like they had. The whole thing had left the town eerily quiet, as the people went about their business in a rush, none loitering to talk and laugh as was normal in such a place. Was the Demon unaware of how strange the quiet was? Or had he not even noticed it, lost in his own head, perhaps? From all of the horror stories that had been told about the Demon in the few short years since he had first appeared, Anderas doubted that the man wouldn't have noticed such an unusual atmosphere. So was this strange figure so calmly strolling actually the Demon? Anderas hoped it was. Else some poor traveler was going to be killed in his stead.

As the figure reached the very edge of the town square, Anderas felt a brief spike of power resonate in his mind. That was the Blessed—which one he didn't know or care—signaling them all to be ready. All of the Descendants there could feel that spike of power, a signal weak enough that only those who wielded the same God's power could feel it. Whatever he was, the Demon was no Fire wielder, so it would be impossible for him to have felt the signal. One more step, and the Blessed would attack, killing the man in an instant.

From his vantage point, Anderas would swear that, just for a second, the stranger had hesitated when the signal went out. But whether the figure had or not didn't matter, as his foot never actually stopped moving, and it stepped down, bringing him off of the rocky street and onto the cobblestone of the town square. The moment that step brought his body forward, fire erupted from three separate sources around the square! Massive pillars of fire, each one wider than a man was tall and burning so hot that they were melting the very rocks beneath them, shot through the empty air and collided on the lone figure!

Anderas stared in awe as he felt the sheer power erupting in front of him. This was what it meant to be a Blessed! Anderas might have had a skill with his magic that surpassed even most of the Blessed, earned through decades of devoted practice, but even he couldn't compete with the raw power that a Blessed wielded. Even at his distance, he could feel the heat pouring off of the flames. The Demon was most certainly dead: Anderas had seen him caught within the flames, surrounded by them so that even had he time to try and escape, he had nowhere to go to avoid them. No one could survive in the center of that much power. What an anticlimactic end to the being that had come to haunt the dreams of the entire world.

As the flames died out, Anderas kept his eyes on their collision point as best he could, despite the immense light that such flames produced. He wanted to see if any part of the Demon had survived such immense power or if even the monster's bones had been vaporized in the assault. He wouldn't be surprised if nothing was le—

His breath hitched, and he felt his heart skip a beat. That was impossible! The light had messed with his eyes, and now he was seeing things! That was the only explanation! He couldn't—couldn't—be seeing reality right now! He blinked, and blinked again, as his vision never changed. Anderas looked on in horror as the Demon, standing amongst the melted, steaming cobblestones looking not so much as singed, began to laugh.

"Go! GO! GO!" someone screamed, snapping Anderas out of his shock as all around him his soldiers began charging through the door, a sight that was replicated across the entire square and down each street that led off it. In mere moments, the nearly empty streets and square of the town had been filled with hundreds of soldiers and dozens of Descendants. Anderas had let the mass of bodies pull him along and out the door, still trying to make sense of what was happening. How—how!?—had the Blessed assault not left so much as a mark on the monster!?

Screams filled the air as blood went flying. Through the mass of soldiers between him and the Demon, Anderas caught glimpses of his target. The beast whose hood was somehow still on his head—hiding his face from them—was moving almost faster than Anderas could believe, a longsword in one hand and a strange curved blade in the other. They were practically flying through the air as the man spun, parried, and slashed, desperately trying to stay alive amidst the hundreds of enemies surrounding him. Had Anderas not been in such great shock, he would have smiled: whatever this monster was, he would be brought down by sheer numbers. One man could survive against hundreds, but not without God-given powers of his own. And if the Demon did have any sort of power, if he was some special weapon from Wind, he would have used them already. However he had survived the Blessed fire, solid steel would bring him down.

So assured in that fact, in seeing the Demon fighting as a mere man who would be brought down like any other, Anderas didn't feel any urgency to participate himself. He had no skill with any sort of martial weapon, and he was too far away, with too many of his own soldiers between them, to use his flames without burning his allies along with the Demon.

XVIII

So he would be content with merely watching as the Demon went down in blood and steel.

Or not. One of his Descendant brothers had worked his way to the front of the crowd surrounding the Demon, and fire was already springing to life in his hands. No doubt his fellow Descendant had decided he wanted the glory of killing the Demon himself. No matter. So long as the Demon died, Anderas couldn't care less who struck the final blow. He watched on eagerly as the fire shot out of the priest's hands, straight at the Dem—BOOM! The priest's fire exploded in a massive ball of force and heat, burning through the soldiers as Anderas was picked up by the force of it and thrown backwards down the street, landing in a pile with his soldiers.

Groaning in pain, a sensation that Anderas rarely felt, he slowly pushed himself up, trying to stop the ringing in his ears. What in the Hells had happened!? He looked down to get his footing and saw the blank eyes of a soldier with a broken neck staring back at him. Gods, she was young! He grit his teeth and looked away, pushing himself fully upright as he staggered sideways, into the wall of the street. As the ringing in his ears began to lessen, it was replaced by different sounds: screams, crying, laughter? Anderas looked up, at where the Demon had been, and he choked on a breath: what in the Hells was HAPPENING!? The town was on fire! The buildings nearest to the explosion, one of which was where Anderas had been hiding, were destroyed! The entire wall was rubble, and at least two buildings had collapsed completely! And everywhere was fire, burning buildings and people alike! Everywhere there were people, soldiers and civilians alike, running around as flames quickly consumed them, dropping to the ground as their legs and bodies gave out on them, burned away to bone and ash!

Through the flames and the ash and the smoke, Anderas could make out a figure spinning and jumping, sword and curved blade in his hands, cleaving through every person he came across: soldiers, merchants, and children! And in all this fire and death and destruction, as he reaped his way through panicking soldiers and civilians, the monster was laughing! He was laughing as though he were experiencing the greatest joy of his life! As Anderas stared on in uncomprehending horror, the Demon laughed as his strange curved blade cleaved the head off of a Fire priest in her ornate robes. An Awakened Descendant. Slaughtered as though she were nothing.

What was happening? WHAT WAS HAPPENING!? Anderas couldn't understand! This didn't make sense! How was the Demon doing this!? Where were the Blessed? Anderas stumbled forward, trying to get closer, trying to see… something! Anything! There! One of the Blessed had been hidden there! In that building! Where was the building!? Anderas stared uncomprehendingly at the wreckage. A Blessed had been in that building, and the building was gone. The whole block of buildings beside and behind it were gone. All that was left were piles of stone and burning wood, fires running rampant, burning through every building with a speed of which only magic flame was capable. Where were the Blessed!? Where were the Descendants? Why wasn't anyone taking control of the fires, stopping their rapid spread through the town and its people!?

He stumbled over a body and almost collapsed in horror when he looked down at it. He couldn't tell if it had been a man or woman, so burned it was, but even deeply charred, those were unmistakably the clothes of a noble, a Descendant, very similar to the ones he himself was wearing. That wasn't possible. That. Wasn't. Possible! A Fire Descendant could not be burned, not by normal flames! Only magical flames, empowered by a Blessed or Descendant, could hurt a Fire Descendant! What was happening!?

An enormous crunching sound whipped Anderas' head up, his eyes shooting to the source: the lord's hall, the largest building in the town, home to whichever Descendant ruled it, was crashing down before his eyes! Screams resounded from inside its flaming, falling halls. How many people, how many civilians, were trapped in that building, crushed or burning to death in the same hall that they had hidden in for safety? Dozens? Hundreds?

His eyes slid to a figure standing alone inside of a—what had once been a street. Even in his cloak and hood, Anderas could tell that the Demon was watching the hall collapse on the people inside of it, and he was laughing! The Demon was laughing as innocent men and women and children died brutally in the destruction he wrought! Anderas looked around, desperate to find somebody, anybody, that he could rally! Soldiers, Descendants, the Godsdamned Blessed! Anybody! They need to come together, to organize, to slay this monster that had destroyed this small, peaceful town!

There was nobody. Everywhere he looked, he found only the dead and dying. Civilians, slaughtered like vermin. Soldiers, who had fared little better. Even Descendants were sprawled everywhere, cut or stabbed or burnt, all dead or dying.

Hundreds, maybe even thousands, of people, slaughtered within minutes by this madman. What few survivors there were, at least that Anderas could see, were running away from the town, as fast as they could go, many limping and stumbling as they tried to flee. And the Demon was after them. The monster was no longer laughing, at least not that Anderas could hear, but he was prancing about in clear glee as he continued his wanton slaughter, cutting down every person he came across. Injured or healthy, running or hiding, he did not discriminate, merely dancing from one person to the next as he slew them all.

Anderas felt an anger, a rage rear up inside him, like nothing he had ever felt before. He had an order, a duty, to put down this monster before him, who was so happily slaughtering even innocent people. He called his fire to him, ready to strike out with all of his skill and power at the monster, and pulled back at the last second, just as the immense power he had gathered was about to leave his palms. *No*, he thought, dread warring with his wrath. Whatever, however, the Demon had done it, the Gods' magic had failed before. It was a Descendant's magic that had exploded, saving the Demon from the crushing weight of hundreds of swords and spears and axes, killing countless and throwing Anderas clear out of the fight. It had been Blessed magic—Blessed!—the combined might of three that had not so much as scorched this creature's cloak. For the first time in his long life, Anderas couldn't trust in his magic. For the first time in his long life, Anderas' magic had failed him, for even he was burnt and singed from that explosion, a pain that he had never felt before. Never thought he even could feel before.

XXII

For the first time in his life, Anderas bent down and picked up one of the many swords lying around, one that seemed undamaged, as far as his ignorant eyes could tell. It didn't seem cracked or broken or warped; the blade still looked sharp. It felt awkward in his hand, and he couldn't tell if he should hold it in one or two, but that didn't really matter. The Demon was an expert fighter. He had seen as much when the man wasn't immediately sliced to pieces despite being surrounded by hundreds of weapons, all aiming for his head. Anderas had never so much as wielded a sword before; he barely even knew how. He had barely ever paid attention to how others wielded the weapon that he, like all Descendants, had considered beneath him. There was no chance, none, that he would slay the Demon. He knew that, with a surety that he had never felt before, one that ran deep into his bones. But he was Anderas Anto, the prodigy of Fire, the most respected man in the country, and he would not dishonor himself now, not after a lifetime of service to his church and his God. He had been tasked with killing the Demon from Wind, and he would see his charge fulfilled, or die trying.

CHAPTER 1

Cheers resounded around the arena as a spray of gore erupted out of the man's back. His opponent withdrew his spear, whipping the length of hardened bone to fling the blood off. Tala clapped along with the rest of the crowd, although he was doing so halfheartedly. What else did they expect to happen? The now-dead loser was an ordinary man, some poor bastard taken from… somewhere. Tala hadn't been paying attention when or even if they had announced the man's origins. He had fought well enough, though, that he had probably been a soldier instead of a criminal or escaped slave. Maybe from Mud? Tala had heard that tensions on that border had been increasing lately, and skirmishes were becoming more common. It didn't really matter, though: however experienced a fighter the man might have been, he had had no chance of surviving that fight. Not when his opponent was a Bone Descendant. That had been the Bone wielder's third fight in a row—all against ordinary people—and the man didn't have a scratch on him.

Not that it's easy to even put a scratch on a Boney, Tala thought. Even an Unawakened Bone Descendant like the man in the pit could grow a nearly impenetrable armor of hyper-dense bone around themselves, making them exceedingly difficult to hurt. The fact that they could grow and form weapons out of their own bones—like the bone spear that had just been used to finish that last bout—and kill anyone with little more than a touch only added to their terrifying might.

As the loser's corpse was dragged out of the arena by some slaves, Tala looked around at the crowd. The great arena of Fiahren, the capital city of the Fire Country, was filled to the brim with excited, bloodthirsty spectators. Rich and poor alike were taking the day to enjoy the bloody combat, eagerly anticipating the 'special' bout that had been promised to them by the Church earlier in the week.

Many had thought that the vaunted surprise was the Bone Descendant currently standing in the middle of the pit. The announcement that morning that such a person would be fighting had brought a level of excitement to the packed arena that Tala hadn't seen in years, not since the last time they had had a Descendant fight. Although that had been an Earth wielder which, while still rare to see, was far less of an exotic treat than the Boney.

As special as having a Bone wielder fight was, though, the man had won his bouts far too easily to be the Church's lauded 'main event,' and his consequent victories certainly weren't a surprise, at least not to Tala. He had heard the horrifying tales about the people who came from the Bodylands, and the man down in the arena could probably fight for days without suffering a single injury. It could take an army of normal folk to kill a Descendant, especially one from the Bodylands. The Church wouldn't have made such a big deal over something so simple as having a man like him fighting a bunch of normal people. They had been relentless in advertising their surprise. There had been criers on every street all week reminding people about the mysterious special event, and they had even gone through the trouble of hanging up posters around the city. The sheer number of slaves they must have needed to create that many posters—and plaster them around the entire city—had to have been enormous. It was slightly past noon. The sun was high in the sky: the main event—whatever it was—would be soon.

Tala's eyes wandered over the seats until they landed on the Church's private section: a series of lavish, plush, comfortable-looking boxes that dominated their section of the arena, draped with fine cloth and filled with luxurious furniture. The only seats in the entire coliseum that actually had coverings to shield the occupants from the burning sun or rare bout of rainfall. Only the Church's ranking members and the nobility (which were often one and the same) were allowed to use those boxes. Everybody else was stuck sitting on the plain, open, uncovered stone benches that encompassed the rest of the seating around the arena. Another sign that the big surprise was much bigger than a single Boney: usually, a majority of the private boxes sat empty, dim, lifeless, and wasting space.

Today, though, they were all full, men and women of power and privilege enjoying the day's blood sport in cool shade as servants and slaves rushed in and out, bringing them food, drink, and whatever else they desired. Not a single one of the boxes was empty. There had to be something really special for that to happen: even the few other times Tala had seen a Descendant fight in the arena, there were usually some boxes left empty. For people who had fought against such beings on the battlefield, watching them fight in the arena didn't hold nearly the same level of entertainment as it did for the masses.

Tala could see into most of the boxes with ease, his own seat being in a reserved—if much less opulent—section. Despite his being a mere apprentice, his position as a Researcher at the world-renowned Fire Institute, along with his parents, meant that Tala was granted many perks and privileges rarely enjoyed by the common folk. One of those privileges was guaranteed seating at the arena, in a reserved area close to the Church's own section. The Institute's reserved seating area was the only part of the entire arena that wasn't filled to the brim with spectators. It was fuller than Tala had ever seen it before, but the overwhelming press of bodies so obvious everywhere else was absent there. It wouldn't surprise him if half of the Institute wasn't even aware that there was a special event going on: some of the Researchers spent so much time at the Institute, so focused on their studies and experiments, that he wasn't positive they even remembered that they had homes outside of its august walls. Gods knew he and his parents had slept there often enough when engrossed in some study or other.

Enjoying his ability to stretch out and relax unlike the rest of the audience, Tala looked over to the Church's boxes to see if he could identify some of the nobility that were present.

Although he had met none personally, most of them were well-known figures in the city who he had seen at one point or another. The main attendee who had caught his attention from the moment he sat down was, naturally, Lord Soleil: the High Priest of Fire and right hand of the Fire God, the man in charge of enacting and enforcing their God's will upon the world. The most powerful (human) person in the country sat in his grand box with a swarm of personal attendants flitting around him. And from the bobbing of hair at the man's waist that Tala could just barely see over the balustrade, it seemed that the glorious leader of the Church of Fire was enjoying himself immensely.

Along with the High Priest, Tala could recognize at least seven other Blessed in attendance, each showing various levels of enthusiasm either in the combat below or in the men and women that they were enjoying in their 'private' boxes. The only one of the Blessed—or any of the other nobles for that matter—that Tala could see who wasn't engaging in such activities was one he thought he would probably never fail to recognize in any circumstance: Anderas Anto, one of the most decorated, beloved, and dangerous members of the Fire Church. Fire's favorite son sat quietly in his not-quite-a-throne, calmly watching the Bone Descendant below. Unlike the other boxes, there was little to no movement around him; his attendants stood quietly at his sides, the very picture of regal dignity.

Tala's eyes flicked uninterestedly over the other nobles present, men and women who—under normal circum-stances—he would be excited to see. Compared to those two, though, they were hardly worth mentioning: Soleil, the man who had been High Priest for over 200 years, and Anderas, the most famous Blessed alive despite his relative youth of being just under 100 years old. There had to be something truly special planned for those two to be present. Wondering what it would be like to meet either of those men, Tala leaned back in his seat, enjoying the coolness emanating from the Ice wolf pelt he was sitting on. It was a hot day—like it so often was in the Fire Capital—and the eternal chill that emanated from the pelt of a wolf from the Icelands far to the south felt wonderful beneath him. Another one of the many perks he had access to as an apprentice Researcher.

As he enjoyed the soothing chill of the pelt, the noisy crowd around the arena fell silent as a torrent of flame shot out of the High Priest's box: a searing red stream directed toward the center of the arena where it began to spiral upwards in a flaming helix towards the clouds. All eyes turned towards the source to see Cacawari, the arena master, standing at the front of Soleil's grand box.

"My dear people!" Cacawari cried, his voice echoing throughout the arena. "We have witnessed great feats of combat here today, men and women who have fought with admirable bravery and valor! Who have lived and died through strength and wit! But coming up next is a *very* special fight, the type of battle we rarely get the chance to see! For it is not just a barbaric Boneman who has come to our fine city to show us his martial prowess, no! For we have with us today a rare treat indeed! From the frozen wastes far to the south, fighting for us today, a Descendant! Of! Ice!"

His words sparked a flurry of shouts and frantic conversation all across the stadium as the people's excitement rose to a fever pitch. An Ice wielder! Most—Hells, none!—of them had ever thought that they would get the opportunity to witness such a rare Descendant fight. Tala sat back with his eyes wide as his mind raced through what little he knew of the Ice wielders from the south… Which was actually barely anything, he realized. They could control ice and cold—any fool knew *that*—but he knew nothing of the specifics of those abilities. The Icelands were on the far south of the Continent, past the treacherous terrain of the Mudlands, so Ice wielders were practically unknown in the Firelands. Tala couldn't help but wonder how exactly the Arena, or the Fire Church in general, had gotten their hands on an Ice Descendant!

"Yes, yes!" Cacawari called out, his good cheer audible in his voice. "We haven't had an Ice wielder fight in our arena in well over a thousand years! But we are not a heartless people, and we won't force this poor Boney bastard into facing such a foe when he's still exhausted from his earlier fights! So to give him some time to rest and recover, our grand finale shall begin in a half hour's time! And as for you, dear folks, I would suggest using this time to pay a visit to the betting booths! A fight such as this could make one rich!"

As he finished his speech with a final flourish, the crowds immediately rose up and began rushing to the back wall of the stands, where the betting booths lay in a ring installed in the very stone of the stadium. It was only small windows cut into the stone that made them accessible to the crowd. All around the arena, the betting booths were swarmed with eager gamblers; even the booth set at the back of the Institute's section had a small crowd swarming it.

Tala stayed seated, forcing himself to refuse the temptation of joining the frantic stampede of betters. He wasn't one to gamble unless he felt sure of the odds—which barely even made it gambling—and he simply didn't know enough about Ice users to feel comfortable in predicting the victor. So instead of joining the mob of gamblers, he looked around for a food vendor, intent on instead using his money to buy himself a treat to enjoy as he watched what he was sure would be a truly memorable fight. Hells, it would probably be the greatest fight he would ever see!

After returning to his seat with a snack of fried fish and roasted chickpeas, along with a nice cup of wine, Tala settled in, eager to watch the battle between Descendants. He wasn't the only one as the seats around the arena that had been emptied in the rush to place bets were rapidly refilling with their excited patrons. Cacawari had announced that the fight would begin in just a few minutes.

He looked down at the Boney who was sitting quietly in the middle of the pit: the man was still covered head to toe in his bone armor, with his spear lying across his lap. His calm demeanor was a stark contrast to the hate and ferocity he had shown up to then.

Not for the first time, Tala wondered what it must be like to be an arena fighter: forced to fight to the death for the amusement of others. It was an open secret that, despite what the Church claimed, most of the arena's fighters weren't there by choice. They were often soldiers and citizens or—on rare occasions such as this—Descendants, who had been captured from the neighboring nations, with Earth and Mud naturally being the two most common. Where an Ice Descendant had come from was still a complete mystery to him.

The Boneman, though, was much less of a puzzle: the Church of Fire had quite a few Bodyland Descendant slaves, and most of the noble families had at least a few of their own as well. Most likely, this Boney had been a slave who rebelled in some way—possibly attempted to escape—and had been sent to the arena as punishment. Whichever family he had belonged to was likely paid quite handsomely for him too. Although where a possible former slave had learned to fight like this man had was another question. Nor how such a ferocious fighter—if he was indeed an escaped slave—had been captured in the first place: everyone knew that Bodyland Descendant slaves were to be executed at the first sign of trouble, regardless of how many generations of their ancestors had been born into slavery. The devastation caused by the Bodyland Hordes in the past, along with the reputation that the rare beings like the Bone Merc had cultivated, meant that there could be no risk for mercy for such people. The Church wouldn't even risk them being allowed to live as slaves if they weren't so incredibly useful.

As Cacawari called for the fight to begin, amongst truly raucous cheers from the crowd, one of the great iron gates set into the wall of the pit rose open, and out of it, a great bank of fog slowly emerged. Tala's eyes narrowed as he peered into the fog, trying to spot the Ice user he suspected was hiding inside it. If nothing else, the use of an obscuring fog bank to hide inside promised good things from the Icey: it was a clever tactic, and in the great heat that always pervaded the

Fire Capital, it could not have been an easy thing to create, meaning the Icey must have some decent skill. As Tala spared a glance at the Boney, he saw him crouched low, bone spear held in a tight grip as he also tried to find his opponent hidden within the chilling fog.

A fog that slowly crept further and further into the pit, creeping over the ground and crawling along the walls like fingers of deadly ice reaching to ensnare and kill whoever was unlucky enough to be caught within their grip.

The crowd fell silent in eager anticipation, not wanting to miss a moment of what was about to happen. Suddenly, with no prompt or warning, the Bone wielder leapt backwards as a spray of small but sharp bone spikes shot out of his empty hand and into the fog. In the silence of the arena, the thudding of the knives impacting the stone wall echoed, not one having scored a lucky hit on the elusive Ice wielder.

The fog continued to spread as the Boney fired more and more spikes blindly into it. Sounds of the crowd murmuring in irritation began to drift through the arena: this was not what they wanted to see! They wanted an intense, violent, bloody clash between two super-powered beings, not this game of cat and mouse where they couldn't even see both combatants!

While Tala understood their annoyance—and a part of him shared it as well—he couldn't really find it in himself to blame the Icey. Bone wielders were some of the most feared people on the continent, due in no small part to the infamous Bone Merc. Only a fool would try to fight one head-on. He wondered how much further the Icey would be able to extend the fog, though: it was a hot day as usual in Fiahren, and the air was dry, meaning just maintaining such a large fog bank must have been an exhausting effort, to say nothing of making it grow!

His prediction that the Icey would have to change tactics soon came true as the fog bank stopped spreading and, if anything, was already beginning to shrink. Silence once again encompassed the arena as all present could feel the change in atmosphere: the real battle was about to begin.

The Boney had also noticed and was no longer blindly throwing his sharpened bones into the fog. Instead, he was warily watching it, waiting for his unseen opponent's next move. It came so suddenly that by the time Tala had even registered what had happened, it was already over: a swarm of small ice needles shot out of the fog, each one hitting the Boney and shattering uselessly on the dense bone armor with which he'd covered himself. Without hesitation, the Boney had immediately returned fire with a spray of small bone spikes where the needles had come from, leaving only dull thuds against the stone wall.

The fight settled into another silent stalemate, but Tala could see that the fog bank was steadily shrinking. The Icey wouldn't have much longer to hide in it, and their only attack so far had shown that if they wanted to win, they would need to use much heavier, or trickier, attacks to get through the Boney's armor.

As the crowd tensed in anticipation, the fog bank suddenly shot forward like a spastic cloud, engulfing the Boney within its frozen depths. Forbidden as he was from studying the Gods or their gifted powers, Tala still couldn't help but wonder just how the Icey had pulled that move off. Using cold to create fog was one thing, but making it move like that—fast and condensed and controlled—seemed more like something a Mist wielder would be able to do, not an Ice wielder! He was snapped out of his semi-heretical thoughts as odd thumping sounds rang out, sounds that Tala could only assume were caused by collisions between hardened, weaponized ice and bone. After a rapid series of thumps, a guttural roar rang out, and a figure charged out of the fog at an immense speed before smashing into the wall on the far side of the pit.

It was the Boney, whose armor had been frozen and then shattered into tiny pieces upon his impact with the stone wall of the pit. Completely fine despite the collision that Tala was sure would've broken every bone in *his* body, after hitting the wall, the Boney spun around and quickly began growing a new set of armor around himself. Strange, unnerving growths of bone sprouted through his skin on various points of his body that slowly began growing to cover him. He raised his once-again bone-encased left arm an instant before a sword made of ice slammed into it. Holding onto the other end of the sword was the ice wielder, giving Tala and the rest of the audience their first look at her.

Similar to the Boney, the Icey wore the garb of an arena fighter: a simple set of cloth shorts and ragged shirt, with no other accoutrements. Unlike the man, though, she had ripped the bottom half of her shirt off and tied it around her mouth and nose, so that only her eyes and short-cropped hair were visible. In response to her sudden attack, the Boneman punched a bone-encased fist, covered itself in small bone spikes, right at her bare abdomen.

As his fist made contact, the girl exploded into numerous shards of ice, forcing the Boney to cover his exposed, vulnerable eyes. In his moment of blindness, the girl attacked him again—silently—from his left side, grabbing onto his bone helmet and trying to freeze his head through it. She couldn't do it fast enough, though, as his helmet erupted with a layer of bone spikes which, longer and thicker than those he'd used on his glove, pierced straight through the Ice girl's hands.

With a cry of pain, the girl dropkicked the Boney in the side of his ribs and launched herself away. The moment she landed, she stomped on the ground, a web of ice expanding across the sand and dirt outward from her foot. Within seconds, it had raced forward towards the Bone wielder, freezing the ground as it sped over it. The man jumped backwards, wary of getting caught in whatever she was doing. Instead of extending the ice further towards him like Tala had expected, she instead stomped the ground again, pulling all of the ice and frozen sand and dirt back, where it shot up into the air, creating a large wall of ice between them. The Boneman—whose helmet had shattered but was already in the process of reforming—charged forward with his head down, smashed into and through the ice wall, and rammed straight into the woman who, again, exploded in a blast of ice, covering the Boney in a frozen layer and eliciting a pained roar from him.

Tala was watching the fight in amazement, his food long forgotten beside him. While the man was ridiculously strong and fast, the woman was faster, having dodged the Boney's charge and created an ice clone in her place in the mere second it took for the man to break through the wall and reach her.

Unless the wall had been a trap and she'd planned to have him hit her clone all along? Either way, that was the first thing she had done that had undoubtedly hurt the Bone wielder.

Suddenly appearing behind the Boney—who was rapidly regrowing his armor once again even as he turned—the Ice girl created a barbed chain of ice that she launched at the man's back. Where was she getting the moisture for these frozen creations in the heat of the arena? *Blood,* Tala realized, noticing the distinctly red tint of her ice. *She's using the blood that was soaked in the sand from the earlier fights as a catalyst. That's how she froze the ground and turned it into a wall.* It was a brilliant tactic on her part; a way to counter the severe disadvantage she was at by fighting in such a dry place. Still, the realization surprised him: he hadn't been aware that anyone other than a Blood wielder could manipulate the substance in any way. Unfortunately, he'd have to keep that realization to himself, though, lest the Church find out he had learned that and accuse him of heretical research. They really were too strict about certain things.

The blood-infused ice chain struck the Boney in the back, just to the side of his spine, where his bone armor was still in the process of forming and very thin. The spiked barb that was on the end of the ice chain broke through the thin layer of bone and stabbed itself into his flesh, ripping an agonized roar from the man's throat. The Ice wielder immediately yanked back on the chain which, instead of ripping its way out of the man, pulled him with it, making him fly backwards through the air to her as she formed an indistinct icy mass over her free hand, clearly intending to use blunt force on the airborne Boney where everything else had failed.

In an impressive display of pain tolerance and ability, however, the Boneman spun around in midair and slammed his arm down onto the ice chain, shattering it into pieces. He hit the ground once before using his momentum to roll to his feet, where he took a moment to glare at the Ice woman. Panting heavily, his bone armor grew and covered the gaping wound and barbed-ice spike still stabbed in his back. He didn't stop there, though. His bone armor continued to grow all around his body, thicker and thicker and covering every inch of him. Tala looked on, wondering just what the man was planning: his armor was getting so thick, so large, that it was going to be more of a hindrance than a help to him. It was already resembling a giant ball of bone more than a person at this point.

From the corner of his eye, Tala saw movement come from the Church boxes. Sparing a glance over, he saw Anderas Anto, Fire's favorite son, stand and move to the front of his luxurious box. He was staring at the rapidly growing bone ball with a light frown marring his features. As Tala watched, he lifted his hand, and an orb of fire sprouted to life in his palm, hovering just an inch above his skin. Tala wondered what the Blessed man was doing, but he just stood there, still and unmoving as he glared at the bone ball, the fire flickering innocently over his palm.

Keeping one eye on the most celebrated person in the country, Tala returned his gaze to the events happening in the pit. The ball of bone was still growing in size, and the Icey didn't seem to know what to do about it. She had already ran up to it and tried to freeze it—like she had done earlier to the Boney's helmet—but her power wasn't strong enough to overcome the Bone user's focused power on… whatever he was doing. At her failure to freeze—and presumably shatter—the giant bone ball she had opted to retreat to the other side of the pit, as far away from the Boney as she could get while she waited for him to finish whatever he was doing.

The audience watched with bated breath, just as confused as the Ice woman. As Tala looked around to see if anyone had any idea of what the Boney was doing, his eyes once again fell upon Anderas, who was still standing just as before: staring at the bone ball with what Tala could only read to be displeasure. Whatever the Boney was doing, the Blessed man seemed to know what it was, and he didn't seem very happy about it.

Suddenly, a thunderous crack resounded around the arena, and Tala's head jerked around towards the bone ball, the source of the noise, just as Anderas shot his hand out, and the flame he had been holding launched forward. Tala's eyes shot wide in fear as the giant bone ball cracked again before exploding, launching millions of tiny shards of bone in every direction. At the very moment Tala thought for sure he was going to die, pierced through by a countless number of small shards of bone, his vision was engulfed in a flash of red and orange as an intense heat washed over him.

His mouth was too dry to swallow as he looked in astonishment at the massive, swirling disk of fire that was covering the top of the pit, shielding the audience from the deadly storm of bone that would have slaughtered them all. He slowly panned his eyes over to Anderas, one of the most lauded Fire Blessed alive, who had his arm outstretched as he commanded the massive, spinning, superheated shield of Fire.

Somehow the man had known what the Boney was doing and had prepared to shield the audience from becoming collateral damage in his attack. Tala's mind boggled at the sheer level of power and control the man must have had to have formed that flaming disk in time to prevent a catastrophe. In a mere moment, he had managed to create flames hot enough—and/or somehow *dense* enough—to stop what must have been well over a million empowered bone shards in their tracks!

Despite the heat, a shiver ran up Tala's spine at seeing the Blessed's abilities on full display. That was the power held by those who had been Blessed by a God. Fighting down his primal terror towards the man who had just saved his life, Tala turned back to the pit as the great flaming disk died down. His mouth opened in awe as he saw the state of the pit: every single inch of the place, from the stone walls to the sand-covered floor, was covered in bone. Small, sharp, numberless shards of bone. It looked less like a pit for fighting in than it did the mouth of some giant beast with a billion teeth, ready to consume the whole world.

As he scanned the pit, his eyes fell upon a strange protrusion on the wall. Puzzled, he stared at it before his eyes widened in shock as he realized what it was: the Ice woman, struck by so many bone shards that she was almost indistinguishable from the wall she had been stuck to. His eyes shot to the other side of the pit, where the Boneman had been, only to the see the man down on one knee, panting heavily and looking like he was moments from fainting, a large protrusion of bone still covering his back where the woman's ice chain had torn into his body. Tala watched as the Boneman slowly raised his now-naked head and looked at the audience he had nearly slaughtered. Tala could see the man frown as he took in the lack of devastation. In what Tala could only describe as a disappointed manner, the Boney turned his head towards the Church's section of the arena. His eyes met Anderas', who stood there calmly staring back at him before—with a resigned nod that Tala thought might have been one of begrudging respect—the Boneman collapsed, completely spent from the battle.

With his form lying still on the ground the crowd, who had been watching in silent awe up to that point, erupted in cheers at the battle they had witnessed and its explosive finish.

Cacawari stood at the front of the High Priest's box, arms held out wide with a large smile on his face and yelled over the cheering crowd. "And the Boneman takes the victory! What an amazing fight! What power, what speed, what strength! And what an ending! And let's hear it for the great Anderas Anto! Whose swift action saved many of us here from sharing in that girl's fate! To our victor! And to our hero, ANDERAS!" The arena master led the audience in cheering for the exhausted champion, who was already being carefully carried out of the pit by slaves. As Tala looked at the Blessed who had saved them all, clapping along with the rest, the crowd began to shuffle out of the arena and he saw as the Blessed's smile began to fall as a strange look filled his eyes.

CHAPTER 2

Tala stepped out onto the street for his morning walk to the Institute, enjoying the still slightly cool, mostly morning air. He really had overslept. It was good he didn't have anything demanding his attendance today, so it didn't really matter what time he actually got to the Institute. As he strolled through the streets of the city, his mind was still back at the arena and the battle between the two Descendants.

He knew the basics of how a Descendant's abilities worked: they could control and manipulate whatever element an ancestor of theirs had been Blessed with. Awakened Descendants had greater control, greater power, and more varied uses with their element than their Unawakened counterparts. That was just about the extent of the knowledge that the Church allowed people to have, even Researchers. He wondered what a fight between two Awakened would look like; the fight in the arena was crazy enough. He could barely imagine what it would have been like had the two Descendants been Awakened! Not that he would likely ever see such a thing: the Fire Church would never allow the Awakened of other Gods to live (Dust wielders the exception, of course), not even as slaves. They were far too dangerous. And the day he saw two Blessed get into a fight would likely be the day he died. Such battles could level entire cities if they weren't careful! One of the many reasons that Blessed were rarely seen on the battlefield anymore.

A cold chill went up Tala's spine as he remembered what had almost happened in the arena, even from an Unawakened, and he sent a silent thanks towards Lord Anderas for saving his—and everyone's—lives. Had Fire's favorite son not been there, it was likely that Tala and the thousands of others in attendance would have been killed. He still had no idea how the man knew what the Boney was doing. None of the other Blessed there had seemed to know, and as far as Tala was aware, Anderas had never encountered a Bone wielder before. Although that wasn't really saying much: unlike most Blessed, Anderas had been far from idle in the decades since he had received his Blessing, and Tala probably knew about less than half the things that that man had done in his vaunted life.

But the last Great Bodylands Horde had occurred over 200 years ago, well before Anderas had even been born! Perhaps he had recognized the move from stories he had heard? But High Priest Soleil hadn't seemed any more familiar with the Boney's actions than anybody else, and the High Priest had fought against the last Great Horde! It was one of the events that had distinguished the man so much that he had been named High Priest when his predecessor died! Tala had to shake his head in bemusement. Just one more mystery to add to the living legend that was Anderas Anto.

Still, he wondered how many of the other spectators in the arena had truly understood just how terrifying that fight had been. Not just in what abilities the two Descendants had displayed, but in all the things that they *could* have done, even as 'mere' Unawakened.

Tala absently swore as he pondered the 'curse of knowledge,' as one of his mentors at the Institute called it. The rest of the audience didn't understand how terrifying those two fighters had been. As an apprentice Researcher, Tala had learned enough history (albeit highly edited history, which his teachers hadn't even pretended to be otherwise) to know how much damage had been wrought by the Blessed and Descendants in the earliest days of the Churches. In the first few millennia after the Gods descended from the heavens, the unrestrained wars between the Churches and their burgeoning nations had almost wiped out humanity altogether! But few people knew about that these days, about how much devastation could be caused by the Empowered.

Even if research into the Gods was uncompromisingly forbidden, simply having an education meant that Tala could understand the abilities of the Blessed and the Descendants better than most any other folk could. He knew that to create fire there had to be heat and fuel (even if the Gods' chosen cheated by using their magic as their fuel). He knew that to create ice and ice constructs, there had to be something physical to freeze and form, even if that was just moisture in the air (or blood in the sand, apparently). He knew that somebody who could manipulate bone, and apparently grow a near-endless supply of it, was a ridiculously dangerous person.

Given the events of the last day, part of him was wishing he didn't know these things. His dreams last night had been full of ice and fire and blood and bone, bringing to horrifying life the stories he had heard of those ancient great wars that had occurred in the early days of the Gods' rule. The tales he had heard of the horrors that came out of the Bodylands when their Hordes assaulted the Dust Wall. Ordinary people like him were powerless in the face of such beings. If even an Unawakened Descendant one day decided to kill him, he knew that there would be nothing he could do to stop them. Curse of knowledge indeed.

As he strolled through the streets that he'd walked all his life, Tala shook his morbid thoughts away and turned his mind to the world around him, replacing encroaching fear with the wondrous joy that was the city of his birth, basking in the smells and sounds and energy: the sheer *vibrancy* that was his city. He caught the scents of cooking meat, and had to force himself to keep walking. Food native to the Firelands, although it carried the risk of spontaneously combusting if not handled carefully, was undeniably delicious when cooked properly. But there was no point wasting money on food when there would be a whole buffet at the Institute just waiting for him.

Gritting his teeth as he attempted to distract himself from the tantalizing smells of various foods and baked goods, Tala let his mind wander to the buildings that surrounded him. Fiahren, at least so far as he had heard, was an entirely unique city in the world: A chaotic sprawl of great, winding buildings that reached unflinchingly into the sky with no rhyme or pattern behind them, an eclectic mix of old and new and sometimes *ancient* designs and materials that varied drastically from one building to the next. The Church of Fire claimed that it was the first and oldest city in the world, the first of all the Gods' capitals in the mortal realm. The God of Fire had ruled from Fiahren since the Gods first descended from the heavens. The sheer chaos that was the layout of the city stood as testament to just how old the city was: one could tell when entire districts had been built sheerly by how drastically they differed from the districts beside them. There were few other cities in the world that changed so dramatically, so *chaotically*, throughout.

Hunger lay long forgotten as Tala mused about all the different cities that he had heard about in the world. Even if they weren't nearly as great as Fiahren, he would love to see them one day! Experience just how different they were for himself. It was too bad that Researchers were rarely allowed out of the country: they were considered high-value targets for the other nations, especially to kidnap. Any Researcher might have knowledge that could greatly strengthen one of the other nations, greatly harm Fire, or both. Even Dust and Metal were considered potential dangers where a Researcher was involved, despite their nigh-permanent status as neutral parties in the world. Maybe he would follow in the footsteps of Researcher Admani, who, after years of trying, had managed to convince the Church to let him travel the world in secret to study (and spy) on the different nations. It was unfortunate that the man's research was highly classified, an act that many Researchers openly disagreed with. But when the Church ordered a subject to be restricted, even the Institute would acquiesce, regardless of their opinion on the matter. It would likely be many years still before Tala would be allowed to access the official records of Admani's journey.

It wasn't all bad, though: even the Fire Church couldn't contain information spread through word of mouth, and Researchers loved to talk. Much of what Admani had seen on his travels was well known inside the walls of the Institute, including many noteworthy aspects of the cities he'd seen throughout the world. For example, only Fiahren utilized a massive pipe network to supply water, heat, and steam throughout the city. How any city could function without a pipe network simply boggled Tala's mind.

His eyes naturally turned to the numerous pipes that crisscrossed the walls and upper alleys of Fiahren like a web of metallic blood vessels, providing life to all areas of the city, big and small. Tala, like all denizens of the Fire Capital, had learned early on in his life that the pipes were *not* things to play with. But like any resident of Fiahren, he had long ago learned which pipes were safe to touch, which ones would provide a nice, comfortable warmth (and were great for drying wet clothes on), and which ones could sear flesh off the bone with nary a touch.

Although the pipes were generally safe, he had heard tales of what sort of horrors awaited a person if they were near a pipe that broke, either by chance or through their own idiocy: explosions of steam that could blow apart a wall as easily as a person (or a few), water so hot that it could boil a person alive, or even just cold water shooting out at such pressures it could pierce through somebody like a bone hot-knife through butter. And while they were (mostly) cautionary tales told to children to keep them from playing on the pipes, occasionally, an incident did occur somewhere in the city that gave a brutal reminder to its occupants that the dangers of the pipes were very real.

Despite the hidden dangers that Tala knew lurked within the innumerable pipes that crisscrossed his city, he had always found their constant weaving and winding to be a rather beautiful and comforting sight. To those who knew what to look for, the pipes could serve as a roadmap for the entire city, and following the right pipes could take someone anywhere they wanted to go, even if they were otherwise hopelessly lost (an easy thing to be in such a large, chaotic city). He had often thought that he would enjoy life as a member of the piping guild, but he had been born the son of two Institute Researchers and so had practically been born on the track to becoming a Researcher himself. Not that he could really complain, though: it wasn't a bad job by any metric, and it was a highly coveted position within the city.

There were few careers—outside of joining the Church of Fire itself, of course—that were treated so well by the Church. As a researcher, he was even immune to conscription; a perk he was more than fine with, as he had no interest in becoming one of the nameless soldiers that were constantly being sent to fight and die in the never-ending skirmishes that occurred on the nation's borders. He had no desire to be drowned in mud or swallowed by the very earth beneath his feet, thank you very much! And the less said about what could happen to him at the border of the Jungle, the better! Or as a victim of the Wind Raids, although it had been over 20 years since those had stopped, to everybody's continued relief.

He truly didn't mind the prospect of becoming a full Researcher at the Institute: having practically grown up there, he was well aware that its image of being a strict and disciplined place only for the best of the best was rather… inaccurate. The truth was that the Institute was a very casual, laid back, and actually rather fun place to be. It was filled with eccentric folk who might one day study the paths that the moons took through the sky and the next be trying to tie little sticks to the feet of ants to see if they counted their steps (they did!). Although the number of tiny burns that that particular Researcher had gotten by irritated Fire ants made him question how worthwhile his study had actually been.

Tala wasn't even sure what that Researcher was planning to ever do with that knowledge, but that was the way of the Institute: study what you want (so long as the Church allows it) and share with the Church anything you happen to discover. Having spent so much of his life at the Institute, Tala had long ago come to the conclusion that the real reason it had garnered the reputation it had was to trick the Church. Trick it for what, he wasn't really sure, but whenever Church officials came by (about every few months or so), the entire place would flip like a switch, and everybody would act like the 'dignified, no-nonsense professionals' that they were so often believed to be. His parents had told him once that because the Church owned the Institute (like they did everything else in the country), they liked to see its workers behaving 'appropriately,' so the Researchers would act like that out of respect.

One of the Researchers had once told him, though, that it was a practice started in the early days of the Institute (many thousands of years ago) to keep the Church from interfering quite so much with their research. He had never really understood the purpose of that—seeing as all of their research went to the Church anyway—and the Church still interfered quite a bit regardless. He'd lost track of how many times he'd heard his parents complaining about the Church stopping their research on something or refusing to let them even begin studying something else. He could recall four separate instances during his life when his parents had requested to study the great desert to the west and its strange phenomena, only to be completely rebuked. He had no idea why his parents cared so much about it, or why the Church was so opposed to it. According to them, it was just a lifeless desert, too dangerous to study and with nothing of interest in it, but his parents obviously disagreed. Of course, his parents were rather eccentric in their own right, so their interest in the desert probably wasn't actually anything special anyway.

As Tala passed through a small, semi-hidden alley tucked between two buildings, he couldn't help but grimace as he passed a small child asleep on the ground, tucked away as far out of sight of either entrance as he (she?) could be. Whatever circumstances had led the child to sleeping on the streets, they couldn't have been out here for long, and wouldn't be for much longer. There were no beggars or street urchins in Fiahren: the guards always found them in the end. Judging from the size and androgyny, the kid couldn't be more than eight years old, 10 at most, meaning if they were lucky, they would be 'adopted' into the Church. If they weren't lucky, they would simply be conscripted into the army and sent to one of the borders. If they were *really* unlucky, they would simply be turned into a slave. A noble or Church member might even take a liking to them, and they would become a personal slave, and Tala wasn't sure if that would be a better or worse fate than being a general slave; he had heard some disturbing horror stories about what could happen to personal slaves.

As Tala exited the alley and continued his walk home, he passed a small cadre of guards, almost alerting them to the child in the alley before snapping his mouth shut and continuing on. He knew it was his duty to help keep the city clean, but the thoughts about what would likely end up happening to that child kept him from following through with it. He kept an eye on the guards as they approached the alley, this side's entrance just as hidden as the other's, and relaxed slightly as they passed right on by. Let the child have a few more hours of peace before their life was no longer their own.

A faint prickle went down Tala's neck as he thought that, suppressing the urge to look around for somebody watching him. For all the abilities that the Gods had 'gifted' to the world, mindreading was not one of them, at least as far as he was aware, so there was nobody who would ever know about Tala's heretical sympathy for the (likely orphaned) child. *All* of their lives, everybody's in the whole of the Fire Country, belonged to the Church of Fire. Even so much as thinking of that child's life as being its own was heresy, but Tala couldn't help it. He had never truly been able to attune his own sense of self as 'belonging' to the Church, nor that of anyone else's. His parents had always been rather… unenthusiastic when teaching him about his place in the world and how he lived only to serve the Church of Fire and, through it, the God of Fire.

It wasn't like it was really that big of a deal, though, right? A few stray thoughts here and there, a couple minor opinions that didn't quite corroborate with the Church's doctrine; that was okay. It's not like he ever actually acted on or promoted, or even *talked about*, any of those beliefs. He certainly wasn't a *Dissident*: that heretical group of madmen and terrorists who actively fought against the Churches and the Gods. The people who thrived on death and destruction, who devoted their lives to tearing down the Churches and overthrowing the Gods! Tala couldn't help but shake his head at *that* idea: overthrow the *Gods*! Really! Madmen for sure: the Gods couldn't *be* overthrown! They were the Gods! They created the world and humanity, and they could just as easily snuff it out if they so wanted. The Dissidents were fools, the lot of them.

Like most people, Tala wished the Dissidents would just go away. They brought nothing but pain and suffering to the world. How many noble men and women, honest, good, true followers of the Gods, had died at the hands of the Dissidents? Killed by assassins' blades or from sabotage and destruction? Rumor had it that even the Demon from Wind had been working with the Dissidents before he died, and that man-demon-beast-*thing* had brought a level of death and destruction to the world not seen since the great Blessed wars of old, that rivaled even the worst of the Great Bodylands Hordes, and he had accomplished all that *by himself!* Nobody who would ever deign to work with a monster such as that could ever be considered *good!*

So no, Tala thought, *a few little heretical thoughts here and there aren't that big a deal. I'm a loyal servant to the God of Fire. No way in any of the Hells would I ever be a Dissident.*

As he walked, Tala attempted to distract himself from thoughts of the Dissidents by turning his ears to the city criers calling out the news of the day. His steps faltered as a crier called out a piece of news that shocked him: apparently, a Dissident cell had been discovered inside the city a few days before and had been promptly executed. *Good,* Tala thought, even as he felt a chill go up his spine. A Dissident cell, *inside the city*! How horrifying was that? At any moment, those people could have gone on a rampage, sowing death and destruction as they were wont to do. He knew *in theory* that there were Dissidents in the city, and probably more than just the one cell, but to have it confirmed wasn't a happy thought. It was much more pleasant to just pretend that they only existed elsewhere, a threat that lay outside the great walls of the city that kept them safe. The crier had said nothing about how the cell had been found, which was hopefully a good thing. Any news at all of the Dissidents was usually accompanied by tales of the death and destruction that they wrought.

Feeling just a bit less safe than he had before, Tala's footsteps sped up without his conscious knowledge. The Institute was one of the securest places in the city, maybe even more so than the Gods' palace itself, and he was feeling a renewed desire to get there as fast as he could.

CHAPTER 3

The first thing Tala did once he reached The Institute was beeline directly to the mess hall, where he grabbed himself a sumptuous breakfast, greeting a few other Researchers and apprentices he passed and taking his food to a table where a few of his friends sat, fellow apprentices like him, joining into their conversation.

"…'cause there are some diseases that require a Blood mage to cure, right? So she thinks it could be an alternate way to cure those, without having to rely on the noble's Blood slaves."

"What's this, then?" Tala asked, taking a bite of fruit.

"Eilidh. Apparently, she thinks there's a way to clean people's blood of diseases without needing to use Bloodies," Elio answered him skeptically. "Lick here won't stop going on about her."

"It's Liekki." The shorter, auburn-haired girl glared at him. "And she's right! We're still figuring out how to separate the good blood from the bad, but if we—*when* we do, it could completely change how we handle diseases! People wouldn't have to beg the nobles anymore!"

"If it's a blood-based disease. If it's something else, it won't do much good, though, right?" Tala pointed out.

"Still! Blood diseases are some of the worst anyway!"

"Tell that to those people with that one that makes their flesh rot away! That's pretty damn nasty!"

"Or that one that makes people not feel pain. They don't realize when they get injured until it gets infected and they have to have their limbs amputated."

"Or that one that—"

"Alright! Enough! I get it!" Liekki cried. "You all suck! Blood diseases are still a big deal, though!"

"Fair enough." Tala nodded and grinned at her, making her glare back at him. "So how would cleaning blood work anyway?"

"I don't know. We're still figuring that part out. Eilidh thinks there's a way to pump blood out of the body, clean it, and then put it back in, though."

"Gods! That's nasty! How would you do that without killing them?"

"We wouldn't take it all out at once, moron! It would be a process, a bit pumped out, cleaned, back in, more out, cleaned, et cetera."

"Huh. Honestly that sounds like shit a Blood mage would do. You sure your precious Eilidh isn't doing some Arcane Research up there?"

"Fuck off, Elio." Liekki threw a boiled egg at his face, which the boy caught in his mouth with a grin.

"Hey, don't joke about that shit," Tala chastised him, glancing around the room. "If the wrong people even hear a whisper about that, we'll all end up in a dungeon for 'interrogation.'"

"Oh lighten up. Nobody gives a shit in here. Hells, half the people in this place would do Arcane Research all damned day if the Church would let us. And you're one of them!" He pointed at Tala accusingly.

"Yeah, well, it's still stupid. Especially right now. Didn't you hear? They caught a Dissident cell in the city a few days ago."

"Wait, really?" chirped Fintan, wide-eyed.

"Yeah, the criers were talking about it. Apparently, they torched the whole cell."

"Gods! I mean, I know they're, like, everywhere. But for them to have actually been *here*. Just—Gods!"

"Do you think there are more?"

"Probably. They're like cockroaches. Worse, they're like Beast cockroaches! Even if you step on them, you don't know if they'll just get back up and keep scurrying around!"

"Eww. Do Beast cockroaches really do that?"

"I don't know. Does the Jungle even have cockroaches?"

"…"

"I have no idea."

"Well, thanks. Now I'm going to have nightmares about giant undying cockroaches."

"Always happy to help!" Elio smiled cheekily.

"Mmm. Well, Tala, tell us about the fights yesterday! What was the big surprise the Church kept going on about?"

"Right!" Tala perked up, eager to discuss the Descendant battle with his fellow apprentices, even if that discussion would border on Arcane Research. He described the Bone wielder and the first few (rather boring) fights, before going into graphic detail about the fight with the Icey.

"Damnit! You got to see Anderas use magic? Now I wish I had gone!" Liekki cried.

"Aww, is Miss Eilidh not enough for you anymore? Do you wanna trade her up for Daddy Anderas? Become his… something wife. How many wives does he have?" Elio asked.

"None," Tala answered instantly, ignoring Liekki's burning face. "He's never taken a single wife. Or husband. Nobody knows why. He wasn't even using anybody at the arena yesterday, and all the rest of the nobles were."

"Gods. I don't get it. A man like that could have literally anybody he wants. What do you think, Lick, wanna try your hand at becoming the first Mrs. Anto?"

"Fuck off, Elio!"

He laughed but continued. "I guess he's just not really in a rush. He does have centuries after all. I wonder what he gets up to in private, though? Shining image like him, I bet he's got some real nasty secrets!" Elio leered.

"Down, boy." Tala laughed. Even if Anderas was just more private about those things than most, Tala doubted the man had anything really bad hidden away. He was the golden child of Fire; he wouldn't have become that if he had any truly deep and dark secrets.

"Well on that note," Fintan said as he pushed his plate away and stood. "I've got to get back to work."

"Where are you working these days?" Tala asked.

"I'm still over in mil-tech." The boy grinned, utterly failing to hide how pleased he was.

"Really? I'm surprised they even let you back in there. Didn't you just spend a week in bed with a Boney trying to piece your ribcage back together?"

"Ahum!" Fintan coughed. "Well, yes, but I'm all fixed up now. That was just a small mistake. Had the wrong ratio in the powder. And they patched the wall up already too!"

"Fine, fine. Off you go! Play where we mere peasants aren't even allowed!" Tala waved him off with his nose in the air. Fintan laughed and left, shoulders slumping at Tala's parting shot. "And don't blow yourself up again this time!"

They laughed as Liekki also stood, going back to keep helping Eilidh try to work out her blood-cleaning idea, leaving just Tala and Elio.

"So what are you doing today?" Tala asked as the other boy slowly mopped up some last bits of egg yolk with sweetbread.

"Nothing special, just back to the air works." Elio shrugged.

"Again? You really think you lot can figure out a way to make a ship fly?"

"Why not? Paper flies, especially if you fold it right. It can go pretty damned far! What are you working on today?"

"I don't know, really. Might go play around with those far-eyes from Wind again. I heard that those wannabe Researchers up in Light figured out how to make stronger versions and were even able to look at the moons up close!"

"Man, you believe the weirdest stuff sometimes! How would the idiots in Light figure out something that we haven't?

And what's the point of looking at the moons closer? What are you expecting to find, little people dancing around up there? Some secret moon city or something?"

"It does make some sense. Not the moon people, you moron, but Light making more progress with the far-eyes. I mean, light is literally their element. Get a couple Descendants to help out and they could probably make far-eyes that could see across the world."

"Yeah, right. I think that'd count as Arcane Research if they did that."

"Oh. Shit, you're right. Damnit."

"Tala, Tala, Tala." Elio shook his head, grabbing Tala by the shoulder. "Always so careful about that sort of talk, but can never get it out of your head."

"Shut up."

"I'm just saying. I know you, man. You probably spent all of yesterday thinking about those Descendants you saw fight, right? How do they do that? What else could they do? You can fool everyone else, but you can't fool me. You're a Dissident at heart, my man. I'm so ashamed!" Elio broke down into fake tears, sobbing comically into Tala's shoulder. "It's alright! I understand! You can't help being a dirty, filthy, child-murdering heretic! I still love you, you disappointing monster!"

"Yeah, well, I hate you!" Tala grumbled, pushing Elio off of him. He hated that he couldn't even deny his friend's accusations that he had been thinking about those Descendants', and Anderas', abilities all day. Although he also hated that his friend would compare him to the Dissidents. That was just uncalled for.

"No you don't!" Elio chirped happily, moving on from his 'heartbreak' as though it had never happened. "Seriously, though, you should join me up at the air works. We could really use you, man, and it'd be better than fiddling with those toys of yours!"

"Nah, I'm good." Tala waved him off. The idea of building an airship was appealing, but they were still too early in the process of even guessing at 'how' for him to waste his time on it yet. Better he continue his research into the far-eyes. He had accidentally discovered the other day that when the far-eye was held at the right angle to the sun, it created a beam of intense heat that could start a small fire, and he wanted to play around with that a little more.

What if I could use the far-eye to power a large steam spinner? Keep it heated without needing to tend a fire? Tala thought to himself as he got to his own little workspace, lighting a small fire under the steam spinner that he was working with.

Grabbing a nearby piece of paper already half-full of notes and a graphite stick, Tala sat down and watched as the steam spinner slowly began to move. It was a funny little contraption, the steam spinner: it consisted of a hollow metal ball, about the size of a fist, with two tiny little curved pipes coming out of it directly across from each other. When half-filled with water and heated by the small flame that Tala had ignited underneath it, the water would turn to steam and exit out of the pipes, making the ball spin. It was one of many little contraptions that Tala had picked up, hoping to find inspiration for his own ideas.

While the steam spinner was little more than a toy, Tala had hoped that he could discover something greater about steam power from it, but so far had been disappointed: since the spinner's creation, steam power had become a major force behind the industries of Fiahren, and the great pipe network had already been fully renovated to send steam throughout the city, a process that had taken centuries. Tala was certain that even more could be done with steam—he had sheets of paper covered in calculations and drawings of different types of steam spinners he had imagined, from small ones like he had to giant ones larger than any person—but so far he hadn't been able to come up with anything truly special.

And that was what Tala was ultimately hoping to discover: something great. Something new and amazing that would change the world, that would be revolutionary! Something that would see his name forever emblazoned on the walls of the Institute like some of the great minds before him, men and women who had made history with their inventions and discoveries, helping the Church of Fire become the strongest in the world! Such a discovery could earn him not only wealth and fame, but potentially even a title! A place of nobility! And Keahi would become a proper family name instead of just an unused tail to his own name! Instead of Tala'Keahi, he could be Tala of House Keahi! Something truly spectacular could even earn him a Blessing! It had happened before, if rarely: the great Anderas Anto himself was the descendant of a Researcher who had earned a Blessing for his creation of Fiahren's first plumbing system, a system that had eventually evolved into the great pipe network! Even today, there was Ishaan, one of the oldest Blessed currently alive who had been a Researcher himself before he had discovered how to utilize steam to further strengthen Fiahren's already prestigious industrial complex, reestablishing Fire's waning dominance as the greatest power in the world.

And as had become the norm for Tala when he had a day to focus on his own projects without having to be anywhere else, the time passed quickly, and far too soon, he found himself looking at the quickly dimming sun out the window. Putting aside his work, Tala stood up and stretched, feeling his muscles pull from far too long spent sitting in a chair hunched over a desk. He looked at his desk and considered following his parents' example of just staying at the Institute overnight. He would just be back here tomorrow, after all, and the Institute had more than enough space for him. Sighing, Tala shook his head and began heading down to the mess hall, intent on grabbing a late dinner before heading out. He didn't live all that far from the Institute, and sleeping in the peace and quiet of his own bed in his own home would be far more pleasant than sharing one of the many sleeping rooms in the Institute with an unknown number of other people. Plus, with tomorrow being another day all to himself, he could sleep in as long as he wanted without the risk of being woken up prematurely. He'd return to his work in the morning. Or early afternoon. Whenever he got up.

ság# CHAPTER 4

Tala had walked the route between his home and the Institute more times than he could count, for nearly as long as he could remember. So despite the general labyrinthian layout of Fiahren, Tala had long since stopped needing to pay attention to find his way there. Which was particularly good on days like this, when he slept in far too much and, despite it being early afternoon, was still feeling a bit disoriented at being awake, and so was mindlessly shambling back to the Institute while being barely aware of where he was going.

And because it was usually such a peaceful walk, he was quite startled when, suddenly and with no warning, he heard a door slam open down one of the alleys. Not an uncommon occurrence in other parts of the city, but in this section of it, at this time of day? It was enough to break him out of his early afternoon fugue and glance down the offending alley, curious as to who was causing a commotion at this time of day but not truly expecting to see anything important. Perhaps somebody had simply drunk too much too early? His eyes widened in shock when he saw that, just down the alley, a tall man was holding a young girl, perhaps a few years younger than Tala, against a wall by her throat. Her feet were barely touching the ground, sliding back and forth as she tried to gain a solid footing. From her clothing, Tala could tell that she was a courtesan, and he watched as the man said something to the terrified girl. He was about to turn back towards one of the main streets to call some guards when the man suddenly smacked the girl, hard, across the face. Had he not been holding her up, Tala was sure that she would have collapsed from the blow. He pulled her back and slammed her against the wall, before raising his hand in what looked to be preparation for another strike. Before he had time to think about what he was doing—or if this was even a situation that he *wanted* to get himself involved in—Tala found himself striding down the alley yelling at the abusive man.

"Hey! What do you think you're doing?"

The violent man stopped moving for a moment and stood there completely, unnervingly still, before slowly turning his head to look at Tala, as did the girl choking in his grip. Though she couldn't fully turn her head to look at him, Tala noticed that her eyes, despite bulging out in fear and suffocation, looked less hopeful at the appearance of a possible savior as they did downright shocked. Like she couldn't believe that someone was coming to her rescue. The man though looked less shocked and more… bemused, like he was surprised that somebody would object to his wanton violence. Swallowing with too-late apprehension at the situation he suddenly found himself in, Tala did his best to put on a brave face and quickly tried to think of what to say.

"I-I don't know what's going on here, but if you don't let her go and leave right now, I'm going to call the guards on you!" Tala bit out, hoping that his voice wasn't shaking quite as much as he thought it was: he was an academic, a thinker, damnit! Not some warrior hero who could fight off a clearly disturbed man! To his great despair, instead of letting go of the girl and backing off like Tala had so desperately hoped, the man holding her started to snicker, which quickly turned into full blown, uproarious laughter. The man—who Tala was growing increasingly certain was completely insane—began laughing so hard that he dropped the girl as he bent double, holding his stomach with both arms. Tala hoped that the girl would have the sense to get up and run away, but all she did was sit still on the ground, staring in utter fear at the psychotic, laughing man.

Tala's eyes were quickly flitting back and forth between the laughing man and the girl, hoping that she would look at him and get his silent message to run away, a course of action that he was also desperately wanting to take. All of a sudden, the laughter stopped, cutting off so abruptly that Tala thought he had gone deaf for a moment.

The psychotic man stared at Tala before standing to his full height. Tala couldn't quite stop himself from taking a step back in fear: he hadn't realized it from a distance, but now that he was close, he could see that the man was quite a bit larger than he was. He stood a good two heads above Tala and had muscles that were quite a bit larger and significantly more well defined than Tala's own. Tala only had a second to process how much of a mistake he might have made in getting close to the man before, without warning, one of the man's arms suddenly struck out, backhanding Tala across the face. The sheer force of the blow, combined with Tala's complete unpreparedness for it, caused him to get knocked off his feet, tumbling down and hitting the wall of the alley. He lay on the ground, disoriented both from the shock of getting hit and the pain coursing through his face. He was dazed enough that he didn't notice the man walk up to him and, as he climbed to his knees, didn't even realize the man was there until he felt a sharp pain in his gut as the man kicked him, hard, sending him sprawling again.

Wheezing and engulfed in agonizing pain, Tala looked towards the man who had so casually beaten him down. He was still standing where he had kicked Tala, with his hands in his pockets and an amused smirk on his face. As Tala looked him in the eye, he saw a cruel malice there, and a deep shiver ran down his spine: he felt like a small animal staring into the maw of a hungry predator, one that enjoyed playing with its food.

Winded from the kick, Tala blindly reached his arm up the wall, eyes never leaving the monster in front of him, and when his hand found one of the many pipes that ran along the alley's wall, he gripped it, using it as a hold to pull himself to his feet. As he struggled to rise, he watched the vicious man slowly step towards him, pulling his right hand out of his pocket as he sauntered forward. He held his hand up in front of his face, and with no warning at all, it burst into flame.

Tala's eyes shot wide open as the yawning sense of doom that he had felt ever since first confronting the man crashed down on him in overwhelming despair. To be able to conjure up fire on a whim like that meant that this man was an Empowered. Just like the Descendants he had watched fight the day before. Without prompting, his earlier thoughts echoed in his head: those Descendants existed on an entirely different plane than ordinary people. Either of them could have fought and killed hundreds of people like him without trouble. Now—now Tala was the one facing down a Descendant. In some random back alley in the middle of the Fire Capital, he had challenged a man who could kill him as easily as a fly. It didn't even matter if he was an Awakened or not; there was nothing Tala could do to defend himself! And as his eyes flickered from the flaming hand to the eyes of its owner, he knew, in that instant, that this man was going to kill him.

His hand instinctively tightened on the pipe that he was holding himself up with as he fought to keep from panicking. If he had any hope of surviving here, he needed to think: think of some way of convincing the man to let him go, or think of a way to distract the man so he could escape. He couldn't just try to run for it: he was too weak and out of breath from the kick for that. If he made a break for it, he knew the man would easily catch him. He briefly considered trying to fight, but the flickering flames quickly disabused him of that notion. He had just seen the other day what kinds of things a person such as this was capable of! He also had no weapons or tools to use, while all the Descendant had to do was touch him with that flaming hand for the fight to be over. Hells, he didn't even need to touch him: he could just summon a burst of fire, and he could fry Tala where he stood! The only reason he hadn't yet was because he was toying with him, and Tala could tell from the evil glint in the man's eyes just how much he was enjoying himself, and that nothing that Tala could say would convince him to let him go.

All of these thoughts flickered through Tala's head in a moment, but his rampaging mind ground to a screeching halt when the flame-wielding man took a step towards him. He stepped back out of reflex, knowing that trying to run away would be futile but not being able to help himself when facing down certain death. Standing tall and proud in the face of death was easier in the imagination, it seemed. He couldn't run, couldn't fight; he couldn't even beg for mercy. Still gripping the warm pipe in his hand, he took another step back as the man stepped forward again, sauntering forward a step at a time, savoring the fear he could probably smell on Tala.

Tala's mind once again made the comparison of a vicious predator, one who knew it had won and was savoring the final moments of fear in its prey before it went in for the kill. As his hand slid along the metal tube in his grip as he took another step back, he felt it pass over a lever on the side of the pipe. A lifetime spent living in the Fire Capital let his mind immediately supply him with the knowledge: it was a steam pipe he was leaning on, something he had already figured out by its (normally comforting) warmth, and that the section of pipe he was leaning on was a temporary replacement—likely due to damage on the original section of pipe—and was being used to keep the steam flowing until the more durable and permanent piping was either fixed or replaced.

He was about to dismiss that useless knowledge when he suddenly stalled in realization. He, like all kids of the Fire Capital, had been warned to be careful around temporary pipes, easily recognizable by their off-coloring, because they were much weaker than the normal pipes and could be dislodged quite easily, to often disastrous consequences. The levers on the ends of the pipe section were used to block off the flow of whatever was inside for a short amount of time while they were being switched out.

An unexpected yet most welcome ray of hope suddenly shone within Tala as he fought against his instincts to keep backing away from the Descendant before him. Exerting an iron will he hadn't even known he had, Tala forced himself to stand still while the psychotic monster approached him. With as much subtlety as he could, Tala grabbed the lever and shut off the steam flow in the pipe, knowing it wouldn't take long for the pressure to build up very, very high. He sent a quick prayer to the Fire God—the irony of doing so not lost on him—that his plan would work. For all his (technically forbidden) knowledge about the Empowered, he had no idea if Fire Descendants could actually be burned—or even be hurt from heat at all—but the shock of the steam should distract the man long enough for Tala to escape. He hoped.

Feeling like his heart was going to burst out of his chest as the man's flaming appendage got ever closer, Tala slipped as much of his hand as he could around the other side of the temporary pipe, leaning on it like it was the only thing still keeping him on his feet. As the Descendant closed in on him, he could see the spark of victory in the man's eyes, shining in anticipation as he closed in for the kill. Leering over Tala, the man slowly leaned over and stretched his arm out, blazing hand sedately heading right for Tala's throat.

Mustering all the willpower he could, Tala braced himself to do the one thing he could think of that might allow him to survive this hellish situation. And as the flaming fingers reached towards him, he struck. With a yell that was really little more than a groan, Tala wrenched the end of the pipe off of the wall and pointed the opening right at the Descendant's face. The pipe came off easier than Tala had been expecting, and in an instant, the now-open end of it had been pulled right in front of the man's evilly grinning mouth. With a desperate pull, Tala raised the lever, releasing the steam that had been building pressure deep in the pipe. The sudden explosion of steam that shot out almost made Tala drop the pipe, and he barely held on before remembering that dropping it and running away now was exactly what he wanted to do. Unable to see or hear the man before him in the explosion of steam, Tala dropped the pipe and began to turn around, preparing to run away before the man could get his bearings from the face full of high-powered steam. As he began turning, though, the steam was already dissipating, giving him a brief view of the Descendant before he escaped. What he saw made him stop mid-turn, falling on his butt as he lost balance, something he barely noticed as he stared in mute horror at the scene in front of him.

The pipe lay drooped on the wall, still spewing steam (albeit much more calmly now) at the ground. Next to the pipe lay something that took Tala a few seconds to truly process what exactly it was he was seeing: lying on the ground just a few feet in front of him was the man who had just been about to burn him alive. Except the man was missing his head. Lying right in front of Tala was the now headless corpse of his would-be killer. As he stared at the gruesome sight, he vaguely noticed that surrounding the body—and covering almost the entire alley—were large splotches of blood and what looked to be chunks of brain. And skull. And skin. Some with hair still on it.

Tala stared at the gruesome scene, uncomprehending of what had happened, as his mind—sluggishly at first but gaining speed rapidly—began trying to work out what had happened.

High-pressure steam. Shot straight into the man's face. Against a normal person, it would have been a brutal attack: the speed and heat of the steam would have seared skin, burned hair, possibly severely damaged the eyes. A devastating, likely incapacitating, horribly painful method of distracting someone. Against a Fire Descendant, the effects were more uncertain: would the heat actually cause damage or pain to a Descendant? Would just the water vapor and speed of it be enough to hurt? Tala didn't know, so he had just been hoping that the explosion of steam would have disoriented the man, obscured his vision, surprised him long enough for Tala to escape. Ordinary person, Descendant, Awakened or not, Marked, any of them should have survived that. In agonizing pain? Perhaps. But survived, nonetheless. So why, *how*, had this man died? Not just died, but had his head exploded? That shouldn't have even been possible!

…His mind whispered the answer, and Tala tried desperately to ignore it. It couldn't be that, that was impossible!

Perhaps the man had some sort of… some sort of disease that weakened his body? *Impossible,* his mind whispered back to him. Any Descendant who could walk around the city freely like that would have belonged to one of the noble families, who had Bodyland slaves that could cure any such ailment.

Water and air. Water as air, his mind whispered. He shook his head, trying to clear those insidious thoughts away. There had to be another answer! Normal person? No. His usage of Fire meant he was an Empowered. Marked? No. Even if he was one, it wouldn't explain him dying, wouldn't explain his head being splattered around the alley. They were barely different to ordinary people, really! Descendant, Awakened or Unawakened, same issue: neither held abilities that would explain such a thing. Steam couldn't explode flesh and blood and bone like that. Maybe if it was being controlled by a Steam user, but Tala certainly wasn't one! Maybe if there were Flesh and Blood and Bone users nearby who had weakened the man's body, but that was absurd! They had to be touching their victims anyway! But if steam itself couldn't do that, it meant either that that wasn't steam in the pipe—which it very obviously was—or that the man's head wasn't made of flesh, blood, and bone. Except that it clearly was, as it was those exact things that lay scattered around the alley. And on its walls. And on him. Not lying in a cone-like pattern behind the body like one might expect from such a one-directional explosion, but in a near circle around it, splattered on *everything!* The only explanation was that when the steam hit his head, his head was no longer made of normal body things like blood and flesh and bone. But there was only one kind of being that

Tala was aware of who could change the very composition of their body like that, either at will or as an automatic response to harm. Except that was impossible: they couldn't be killed, not by an ordinary person like him! But only Blessed had the ability to alter their body so completely like that. Sure, Unawakened could control their element, and maybe cover their body with it, and Awakened could do even more, but only Blessed could literally turn their whole body into their element! *Air and water.* A high-speed blast of air and water—of steam—into the face of a person who would automatically turn into fire to avoid harm. *Air and water.* If his head had turned to fire when the steam hit, it would have blown the fire apart. Scattered the flames all around the alley. But a Fire Blessed's flames would return to where they belonged—that's part of what made them practically invincible! How did you hurt somebody whose body couldn't be damaged? Slash a sword through a Fire Blessed's head and their head would turn to fire and reform exactly as it was once the sword had gone through. *Air and water.* Blessed were almost immortal: they lived for hundreds of years easy, and only another Blessed could kill a Blessed. Even for Awakened Descendants, it was almost impossible to kill a Blessed. It could take dozens, maybe even hundreds, to kill one single Blessed, and even then most of them would die in the effort! *Air and water.* The only beings stronger than the Blessed were the Gods themselves, and they didn't even really count! *Air and water.* The steam made his head turn to fire; the steam scattered the fire; the scattered fire would have returned; the steam would've re-scattered the fire as it tried to return; the fire would have turned back into head: bone and blood and flesh; the pieces of head would be scattered around the alley, scattered like fire in front of steam. There was only one explanation.

Tala had just killed a Blessed.

He stared at the headless corpse lying in front of him, eyes unseeing as he failed to find any other explanation. He, Tala, an ordinary, normal person, with no special powers or training or anything, had just killed a Blessed! It was impossible, but he had done it. The still corpse lay as a gruesome testament to the fact that he had just done the impossible. And had done it by accident to boot!

He was startled out of his shock by a sudden, distinctly female cry of "WHAT!?" He looked away from the body towards the girl that was still sitting in the alley, but she wasn't the one who had cried out. No, she was staring at the headless body like she couldn't believe it was real. Tala could empathize. Looking away from her further down the alley he saw—for the first time—a small squad of guards who were looking at the scene with mouths agape, like they also couldn't believe what they were seeing. He numbly thought that they must not be very good guards if their reaction to a crime was to just stare dumbly at it. Suddenly, two cloaked figures dropped down into the alley. Tala stared at the new arrivals dumbly, still too shocked by what he had done to properly register their arrival. Wasting no time, the two figures rushed towards Tala, who just sat there as they approached. As they reached him, one of the figures bent over and grabbed his arm, pulling him roughly to his feet. Not letting go of his arm, the figure began pulling him back up the alley, away from the guards who were just starting to move. Stumbling from the rough handling, Tala was forced to run along with the two mysterious figures, body moving but mind still reeling over what had just occurred. What he had just—impossibly—done!

CHAPTER 5

Tala ran through the back streets of the city harder than he had ever run in his life, mostly due to the tight grip that the cloaked figure had on his sleeve. If he tried to so much as slow down their frenetic pace, he'd get yanked onward, almost tripping them both a couple of times before he gave in and just focused on trying to keep pace with the mysterious pair. They weaved through a veritable maze of winding streets and alleys, narrowly avoiding crashing into anybody they passed. So distracted was he from trying to process what had just happened, what he had just done, that he wasn't really paying attention to where they were running: his thoughts consumed by what they were running from. It wasn't until his legs began to ache and his lungs began to burn that he was brought back into the present, where he realized that he had just fled from a dead body: the dead body of a Blessed; a dead body that he had created. And he was running on the (almost literal) heels of two cloaked and hooded figures who had appeared out of nowhere right after his gruesome deed and dragged him (more literally) away from the scene.

As these thoughts came pouring into his head, he dug his heels into the ground, intent on stopping their chaotic charge to Gods' knew where. He needed answers from these two strange people who had stormed in from nowhere. He failed to consider that suddenly attempting to stop when running at full tilt—especially when being held onto by someone else running all out—was not a great idea. Tala's sudden attempt to halt their momentum ended up with both him and the cloaked figure tumbling head over heels and finally landing in an unseemly pile tangled up with each other.

He groaned as he lay there, eyes closed and body aching from more than just the run now. He opened his eyes and looked around to see the other cloaked figure—the one not groaning on the ground along with him—just standing there, staring at them. Or he thought the figure was staring anyway. He couldn't see any of their face as it was hidden in the dark depths of their hood, the only exception being a darkly stubbled chin just barely visible. Probably a man then; good to know but not exactly the information he was wanting.

Tala looked down towards his feet where the other figure was slowly getting up. The figure's hood had fallen down in their tumble, and he blinked in surprise as he saw that it was a woman: a girl about his own age, with dark, shoulder-length, silky hair pulled into a braid behind her head and light olive skin that was fairly similar to his own pale-brown hue.

As she rose to her feet, she shot a glare at Tala, who realized that he had been openly gawking at her. With an embarrassed cough, he looked at the other figure again, who hadn't moved a muscle as far as Tala could tell.

"What the Hells was that about?" the girl demanded, still glaring at Tala as she ran a hand over her hair.

"I—umm—sorry about that," Tala said awkwardly, scratching the back of his neck in embarrassment before he remembered exactly why it was he had sent them tumbling. "Wait, no, I mean. Ugh!" He bit out in frustration. He shot a quick glare at the still man standing just a few feet away, getting the distinct impression that the bastard was laughing at him despite having neither moved nor made a sound.

"Okay! Just—I mean—who in the Hells are you? Why the Hells are we running away? Why did you grab me!? Oh Gods, I—I just killed a guy, I JUST KILLED A BLESSED! And I ran! There were guards there. There were guards, right there! WHY THE HELLS DID WE RUN AWAY? WHO IN THE HELLS ARE YOU PEOPLE!?" he burst out, the reality of the situation finally starting to sink in. He had just killed a Blessed! *It was defense. It was self-defense!* He started ranting over and over again in his head. They wouldn't have arrested him for it, not when that psycho was literally seconds from killing him! Sure, he'd probably have to explain things to the Church, but they'd understand, right? It was an accident! An accident done in self-defense!

The girl sighed and gave a look that Tala couldn't quite discern to the still-hooded man, who turned his head towards her, then back towards Tala, before his hands came up and pulled his hood down. Shaking his short, wavy, brown hair out as the hood fell stood a rather plain-looking man. He had long, dark stubble on a lightly tanned face and looked to Tala to be around his father's age. After dropping his hood, he held his hands up halfheartedly, palms facing out towards Tala in a non-threatening gesture. Tala thought it would have been far more placating if the man's face wasn't completely expressionless, and his dark eyes weren't looking at Tala quite so intensely.

The strange man stared straight at Tala, locking eyes with him without changing expression. The two stared at each other in silence, with Tala growing more and more uncomfortable with each passing moment. The silence was broken by the girl grumbling under her breath as she gripped the bridge of her nose, breaking Tala out of his stare.

"Look, I know that this all must be a lot to deal with, but we really don't have time to waste," she said in a tight voice. "We need to get you somewhere safe before they start looking for us, okay?"

Tala shifted uncomfortably. Something in him wanted to trust the girl, but he was far too uncertain of what was going on to just blindly follow them like this.

"Just—just tell me who you are and why you're doing… this!" He gestured around them randomly.

The girl clenched her jaw before taking a deep breath and speaking with forced calm. "We'll explain everything when we get there, but we need to move, now!"

"No!" Tala retorted. "I'm not going anywhere until you explain who you are and why the Hells I should trust you!" He glanced towards the man, hoping that maybe he would give Tala the answers he wanted, but the odd man wasn't looking at him anymore; instead, he was toying with his sleeve, trying to rub something off of it. The sheer lackadaisical attitude of the man contrasted starkly with the intensity of his female companion, making the whole situation seem even more surreal to Tala.

The girl huffed and rubbed her temples. "Okay, short version, then we leave, got it?" she grit out, glaring at Tala again. Tala stared back before giving a quick, stilted nod in response, having no intention of keeping his not-word if he wasn't satisfied with the 'short version.' "That man you killed? That was Ignis Fatus, of the Fatus family." Tala's eyes shot wide at hearing this, and his heart began beating even faster in his chest as his palms began to sweat. He knew of the Fatus family: they were one of the most powerful families in the city, in the whole of the Fire Country, with more Blessed in their ranks than any other family! "You have an idea of what that means. Good. You just killed a prominent member of the Fatus family. They're going to want your head on a spike. And worse, he was a Blessed. Which means the Church is going to want you dead too. So to be blunt, we're your only chance of survival right now. Now can we go?"

Tala felt his heart seize up as his mind went back over everything that happened. The now-named Ignis' (Gods! How had he not recognized the man?) treatment of that girl in broad daylight, with a cadre of guards in plain view doing nothing about it. He had known, afterwards, that the man was a Blessed, but he hadn't really thought about the implications. About who the man might actually be. Had been. Shaking his head, Tala stumbled backwards, hitting the wall behind him and sliding down it. If... if he really had just killed a Fatus—and a Blessed one at that—his life was over. Even if the family didn't, the Church would hunt him down and kill him, he was sure of it! Not even his position at the Institute could save him! Accident, self-defense, none of it mattered! It was stupid of him to even pretend that things would have been okay had he not run away!

"Who, who are you? If—if what you're saying is true, then why'd you get me out of there? Why are you helping me? Who the Hells are you?" he asked with a shaky voice split somewhere between panic and desperation. The girl sighed again before glancing up and down the alley. Seemingly content, she looked back to Tala and spoke in a solid voice.

"We're with the Dissidents. We were following Ignis all day and we saw what happened. We're helping you because you, some random kid with no powers, just killed a Blessed. And if the Church—if any of the Churches—get a hold of you, well, we don't want that to happen. And believe me, neither do you."

If Tala thought that things couldn't get any crazier than they already were, he was sorely mistaken. The Dissidents! He almost laughed at the sheer lunacy of it! Of course they were with the Dissidents! Who else would have helped him but a bunch of crazy terrorists and fools? Gods, this day couldn't get any worse! He had to get away from them before anyone found out who they were! Just being associated with them like this could get him executed! Except, Tala realized with a cold sense of dread, he couldn't. He was now a wanted man, an enemy of the Church of Fire who would be hunted down and killed. If he was lucky. Just like them. It didn't matter if he was accused of being a Dissident now. He had already committed a greater crime than they ever had.

The Dissidents would soon be the only people in the world who might even consider helping him. He knew that what the girl was saying was true: They were his only chance of survival now. He took a deep breath and shook his head, trying to clear it of the panic that was threatening to overwhelm him. As he looked up at the girl who was now standing in front of him, she held her hand out. Tala gave it an intense look before, with a furrowed brow and locked jaw, he reached up and took it, letting the girl pull him to his feet, which she did with a grim smile. Once he was up, the girl—whose name he realized he still didn't know—clapped him on the back once before turning away and pulling her hood up again. The man gave him one last blank stare in the eye before also turning away and pulling his hood up as well.

"Let's go," the girl ordered. "We've got a safe house near here that we're heading to. Once we're there, we can figure out what we're going to do next." And with that said, the two of them took off running again, albeit at a far slower pace this time, with Tala, after one last shake of his head, following right on their heels.

As they continued their jog through the back alleys of the city, Tala's head was spinning, and he was having some trouble keeping his footing straight. In only a few minutes his life had gone from being rather ordinary, if privileged, to… well, he wasn't sure how to describe it now.

They were brought to a halt as the man suddenly stopped running right before a corner and held his hand up by his head. Tala stumbled to a halt a few inches from him, with the girl stopping far more smoothly by his side. The man turned around to face the two of them and lowered his hood, speaking in a low voice. His tone was odd, sounding almost like he was bored. "We're coming up on a main street. Walk casually, stay together, don't arouse suspicion." The sheer contrast between his words and tone of voice made Tala pause for a moment, having to go over the words again in his head just to make sure he had actually understood them properly.

As the girl also lowered her hood, Tala couldn't quite stop himself from glancing at her face for a few moments. She didn't seem to notice his look, but he thought the man might have, for he gave Tala another dead-eyed stare before turning around and facing the corner that they were about to round. After a moment's wait, he stepped around the corner, followed by Tala and the girl.

As Tala walked around the corner, he caught sight of the busy street just ahead and felt his heart once again begin to pound painfully in his chest. He noticed that both of his new companions were walking as casually as could be, as though they were just random people out on the street and not wanted criminals: fugitives who would be interrogated, tortured, and killed if they were caught. He tried to emulate their relaxed posture but was far too anxious to pull it off: his knees were locked straight, his back was so rigid it hurt, his hands were clenched so tightly at his sides he could feel his nails digging into his skin, and even his breathing was fast and ragged. They hadn't even reached the main street yet—it was still a few feet away—and he knew that anybody who looked at him would be able to tell in an instant that there was something wrong. The girl beside him bumped her shoulder into his, giving him an odd look between a smile and a glare.

"Relax. Take a few deep breaths and let your muscles untense. Walk like you're just going home and aren't in any hurry," she told him. He swallowed and nodded to her, trying to smile but managing only a pained grimace. He looked ahead again and tried to follow her advice: deep breath in, deep breath out, repeat. He felt his whole body unclench as he focused on his breathing, his gait becoming much more natural. "See? Much better."

For just a moment, Tala felt his whole body seize up in fear. Suddenly, being out in the open with hundreds of people all around, he had a sudden urge to panic: his thoughts were spiraling out of control almost before he could even process having had them. Pulling together what tattered remnants of willpower he could still grasp, he forced himself to take a deep breath, and another, and another, as he let his legs carry him. They turned right and started walking down the street, where he saw a guard patrol coming their way: six men and women in standard guard uniforms with swords at their hips. A spike of panic shot through him; the guards were coming right towards him! To arrest him and bring him to the Church! As his pulse quickened and his vision began to blur, the guards walked right on by the trio without sparing them a second glance. He let out the breath he hadn't realized he'd been holding, to the amused look of the girl beside him. He did his best to ignore her as he had the flippant thought that at this rate he was going to give himself a heart attack before the Church even learned that Ignis was dead.

He decided to focus his attention on simply following the strange man as he wound his way through the street, expertly navigating the crowd as they slowly but surely made their way down and across the busy thoroughfare. Right as they reached the opposite row of buildings, the man quickly ducked into another alley, followed closely by Tala and the girl. Tala let out a sigh of relief now that they were out of the busy Main Street. It was somehow easier to forget just how much trouble he was in when he wasn't surrounded by hundreds of people.

The man continued on down the alley unperturbed before stopping mid-step as a noise made itself heard over the ambient sounds of the busy city: the deep, gonging ring of the city's bells carried through the alley, echoing off of the many buildings as the sounds of the city dipped to a low hush. Despite having spent his whole life in Fiahren, it took Tala a few seconds to place the meaning of the bells: they didn't sound like the usual clock strikes that rang every hour. With a plummeting sensation in his stomach, he realized what these specific bells were for: they were a warning to everybody that the city was going into lockdown. That something had happened and everybody was to get inside and stay there until the bells rang again, signaling the lockdown was over.

For a few moments, Tala wondered what had happened to send the city into lockdown before he realized—with bone-chilling terror—that the bells were probably for him. He had killed a Blessed. Catching him would be a top priority for the Church, one worth even locking down the entire city to accomplish!

The man seemed to have come to the same conclusion as Tala, for he turned to the two and, with a strange look in his eye and tone in his voice, said "Run." And with no further warning, he turned again and sprinted down the alley, with Tala and the girl hot on his heels.

They weaved their way through a few more back alleys at a dead sprint, with Tala nearly tumbling more than once at the quick turns that he was having to make following the surprisingly agile man. He had just enough time to realize that—despite spending his entire life in the city—he was now hopelessly lost in the endless maze that was its incredible sprawl. With ever-growing concern as to where he was being led, Tala nearly stumbled when the man barely a few feet in front of him came to a quick stop. He turned towards one of the walls of the alley and with a quick glance around banged a fist in a strange pattern onto a few of the bricks in the wall. He then just stood there, staring at the wall as though expecting something to happen.

Tala was just about to question what they were doing staring at a blank wall in some random alley when part of the wall suddenly swung inwards. Tala's eyes shone as he realized that he was looking at a secret door! A face poked out of the darkness of the hidden doorway, one of a rather jovial-looking man despite the suspicious look currently on his face. He looked at the man standing in front of the doorway, then glanced at the girl before his eyes passed over Tala, narrowing slightly in an expression Tala couldn't quite place. The new arrival looked back at the first man, rolled his eyes, and stepped aside, gesturing to the three to enter the dark, hidden doorway.

CHAPTER 6

Gazin downed another mouthful of… whatever it was he was drinking. He really hadn't cared what Og poured him, only that it was strong. The burn of the liquor as it poured down his throat and into his stomach was a small relief from the headache that was forming. Gods! He cursed in his head, finishing off his second glass of whatever he was drinking. He should've known better than to let Vail and Serala go out alone! It was such an easy mistake to make: Serala had grown into such a fine young woman, smart and cunning and skilled and capable, that it was easy for Gazin to forget just how like Vail she could be!

He should have pushed for Ilan to go out with them. Ilan was many things, most of which were a mystery even to Gazin, but the man was a calming influence. He was great at keeping those two out of trouble, although how he managed that was one of the many mysteries about him. But he was also a giant of a man, one of the largest Gazin had ever seen even in his almost century-and-a-half of life, which made staying inconspicuous quite difficult for him. And when spending a day tailing a Blessed, staying inconspicuous was of the utmost importance.

But it could have been done! There were ways that Ilan could've stayed hidden while keeping the other two in line! And had they done so, had *he* pushed for the safety net that was Ilan to accompany those two today, then maybe this wouldn't be happening! Maybe *the Gods-be-damned bells wouldn't be ringing*! Gazin knew that whatever had happened to send the city into lockdown, Vail and Serala were involved. Some of the others doubted, and even now the whole room was broken into little groups discussing what might have happened, wondering what could send a city such as Fiahren into lockdown. Even if the others doubted, Gazin was certain, 100 percent, undeniably *positive* that whatever had happened, those two were right in the middle of it.

And he wasn't the only one. After the bells had sounded, and the shock of it faded and all the members of their eternal rebellion that were present began trying to figure out why, Gazin had seen in it the faces of a few of the others. As the many frantic conversations flowed over and around him, Gazin had looked towards Ilan, who was staring blankly at the wall. He had a look equal parts annoyance and exasperation, and Gazin knew that the man was thinking the same thoughts he was. It had been a surprise to many in Hagan's safe house that Ilan had willingly stayed behind when Vail and Serala left, Those Three so rarely being apart from each other that they had become collectively known as 'Those Three.' That had been what had convinced Gazin to not push for him to join them on their stalking of Ignis: Ilan knew those two better than anyone else alive, Gazin himself included, so if he thought they would be fine without him, Gazin would trust in him. As would Hagan, although the master of the safe house had been far more uncomfortable doing so.

And their host was clearly of the same mind as to who was responsible for this unexpected turn of events. The moment the bells sounded (a few moments after, really; even Hagan had been surprised to hear them ringing) the man was running out of the room to close up his store in the front of the building. And as he returned to the luxurious lounge where over two dozen Dissidents were in hiding, Gazin heard him cursing out Vail and Serala under his breath.

Gazin knew that Hagan hadn't wanted to request Those Three to come to the city, and had waited as long as he could before doing so. But the situation in Fire Country, inside Fiahren especially, had been getting worse over the last year. Their operations were facing more and more challenges, before beginning to fail outright. It had been Gazin who finally convinced him to call in Those Three before things got even worse.

Gazin looked around at his fellow criminals as they talked and wondered if maybe Those Three hadn't been... overkill. In that room, hiding away, were some incredibly skilled and dangerous people. With this group here, they probably could have solved their issues in Fire and Fiahren themselves. There was a leak or spy somewhere in the Dissidents, that was a certainty. But it had taken a whole year for one of their safe houses to be raided. With this group of people, they could have found the problem and solved it without needing Those Three. Probably. Maybe. The involvement of Ignis Fatus certainly made things more complicated, though. Blessed always made things more complicated. Well, it was too late now. Whatever madness those two had created, they would deal with it when they got back to the safe house.

With a look at his empty cup, Gazin contemplated getting a third refill of whatever Og had given him when a hollow knocking resounded through the room, dulling the din of conversations. Someone was knocking at the hidden back entrance of Hagan's safe house, and there were only two people who it could be. With a tense jaw, Hagan left the room through the back door that, as far as the Church knew, led to nothing but his private living areas. No need for the Church to know that one of their most trusted traders had a secret door back there that he used to smuggle Dissidents into his place. Although seeing the look on Soleil's face if the high bastard of Fire ever learned that fact would almost be worth the ensuing immolation they would all suffer.

The bit of humor was swiftly replaced by seriousness as Vail and Serala were shuffled into the room, and then replaced again by confusion when a third figure followed them. Gazin turned a critical eye, well trained after over a hundred years in the cause, onto this unexpected newcomer.

Researcher was his first thought: the clothes were both too casual and too well made to be anything but. *Apprentice Researcher.* The lad was too young to be a full Researcher: he'd wager the boy was no older than Serala. Maybe a year or two younger, like Lito and Alina. So probably just on the cusp of becoming a full-fledged Researcher. *Not one of us.* The lad clearly wasn't a Dissident: the poor boy looked to be fighting off a bit of shock, his light brown face shiny with sweat and his short, curly hair matted on his head. He was looking around with wide eyes, clearly not expecting to see such a nice lounge, nor one so full of people. Gazin held back a sigh, not looking forward to hearing this story: the city in lockdown, Vail and Serala bringing some random Institute youth into what was probably the most secret and protected safe house in Fiahren? All signs were pointing to a disaster far worse than anything any of them had imagined.

Hagan brushed past the stunned lad, turning to glare at Vail with all the venom he could muster. "Vail, what in the Hells is going on? And who the Hells is this?" he demanded while gesturing towards the boy.

Vail took a deep breath before speaking loudly in a disinterested voice. "Ignis is dead. I don't know who the kid is."

A sudden stillness engulfed the room as everyone stared at the man, or the boy beside him, in shock. Gazin was no exception, eyes flitting between the two as his enhanced brain tried to piece together some semblance of sense from what he'd just heard. A Blessed, a particularly dangerous and skilled one at that, was dead. And it had something to do with this unknown kid. Vail and Serala seemed fine, something that Gazin doubted even they would manage if they had somehow been responsible, which meant that the kid had killed him? But, other than clear signs of shock and physical exhaustion, the boy seemed fine too. There was a bruise beginning to form on his cheek, but that looked more like someone had hit him, not the kind of injury one would expect from a Blessed's involvement.

For all the improvements Gazin had made to himself, to his brain so that it would be faster and all around *better*, he found himself stumped as to what the Hells was going on, his thoughts swirling in a whirlwind of confusion. Indeed, it was Ilan who actually broke the silence that had consumed the room. A testament, perhaps, to how used the man was to dealing with Vail's utter bullshit.

"How?" he asked in that soft, deep, powerful voice of his.

"The kid blew his head up with a steam pipe," Vail responded simply, half-heartedly pointing a thumb towards the lad.

"Umm… care to elaborate on that, Boss Man?" Nuri piped up from on his stool at the bar, the affable smuggler doing a decent job of not looking like he had just fallen half out of his seat.

Instead of Vail, it was Serala who answered him, the girl, as usual, showing herself to be the far more responsible of the two. "We can give the details later, but right now we need to move. We've got to get him out of the city. Now. Hagan, how many bolt bags do you have?"

"More than enough," Hagan answered weakly. "Plenty for whatever you're planning."

"Wait!" the boy blurted out, finally seeming to catch up to the conversation. "What do you mean about getting me out of the city? I can't just—just up and leave like that!"

Vail turned to the boy and stared at him. Even though Gazin couldn't see his face, he could picture it well enough in his mind: blank face, blank eyes, blank everything. The boy's nervous shifting only confirmed that was indeed the look Vail was giving him. Poor kid.

After a few awkward moments, Serala spoke quietly to him, her words easy to make out for everyone in the dead silence of the room. "Look, I know this is all really sudden, and it sucks, but if you stay in this city, you're dead. Even we won't be able to hide you here forever. Hells, as long you're in the Fire Country at all, it'll only be a matter of time before you're caught. So we're going to get you out, into another country, so you'll at least be out of reach of the Fire Church."

The boy looked down, clearly conflicted. Gazin felt pity for the poor kid. Serala wasn't wrong, but she could have said that in a much kinder way. Although, for her, that probably was the kinder way. The fact that the lad was considering her words instead of rejecting them on panicked instinct spoke well of him. Perhaps it was a Researcher thing? Gazin had never really spent time with any of them before.

The lad's head suddenly shot up with wide eyes. "My parents! What about my parents? Won't the church go after them too?" Good lad, Gazin mourned. Even in this unthinkable situation his first thought was for his family.

"Yeah, they will. Who are your parents? What are their names? And where are they? They should still be there with the city in lockdown."

"Um, Edana and Moelo. They're Researchers at the Institute. They should be there."

Vail tilted his head minutely to the side, giving the boy that same blank look. Did he not know that the lad was a Researcher? How exactly had they met? Serala though took it in stride, turning towards Hagan, who had a look of deep thought on his face. "Moelo? As in Moelo'Keahi?" Hagan asked.

"What? Yeah. You know my dad?" the lad asked in surprise. *Naive*, Gazin realized. Researcher or not, the boy was clearly sheltered if he didn't understand just how important Researchers and the Institute were to the balance of power in the world. Hagan probably knew the name of every single person to enter the Institute in the last decade, be they Blessed or slave.

"Something like that," Hagan responded. "That'd make you Tala'Keahi then, huh?"

"Tala. I just go by Tala. Wait, what? How do you know that? What?" The boy's head was clearly spinning. Was he really that unaware of the position he'd been born into?

"Knowing things is my job, kid. And your parents aren't exactly nobodies now, are they? Anyways, Og? Can you get them out?" he asked of Og behind the bar.

The well-dressed man nodded. "Absolutely. It should be a trifle."

"Good, get to it then. We need to hurry."

With a nod Og walked around the bar and left through one of the doors in the room. As he left, Serala turned back to the lad, Tala. "Okay, Og's gonna get your parents out. Anybody else we need to worry about? Siblings, grandparents, anything?"

Tala shook his head. "N-no. It's just me and my parents."

"Good. Now then." She turned back to the room. "Vail, Ilan, and I are taking him out of the city. With the whole place on lockdown, it's too risky for us to stay here anyway. Alina, you're with us. Nuri, can you get us out?" she asked.

Despite the seriousness of the situation—and his earlier, less than flattering thoughts—Gazin had to stifle a chuckle and fond smile. He liked seeing Serala like this: strong, confident, commanding. It was such a difference to that young, terrified little thing gripping onto Vail's leg when they first met all those years ago. Gazin had grown quite fond of that young child, and had come to see her as something akin to a grandchild. When Vail had finally left with her in tow, Gazin was immensely worried about what would become of her. It made him feel good to see the young woman she had grown into.

Nuri, in his ever-present, beloved duster, stared at the floor with an intense look on his face. Gazin worked with the man enough to know that he was going over every single route he knew of out of the city and every single challenge each one might present. A lovable idiot he might seem, but Nuri was one of the best smugglers Gazin had ever met. After a few moments of silence, he looked back up. "Yeah, yeah, I can do that. We're gonna have to go through the Undercity, though. Ain't no way we're getting the kid out any way else. Though having the princess along will make it a lot easier." Gazin couldn't help but roll his eyes at the nickname. Childish as it was, that nickname had really stuck onto the poor girl. If only Alina would listen to his advice, she might eventually rid herself of that hated epithet.

Serala nodded, either oblivious or—more likely—uncaring about the heated glare that Alina shot at Nuri. "I figured as much. Okay then. Gazin, we'll probably end up needing you at some point, so you're with us too."

Gazin gave her the kindest smile he could muster, given the circumstances. "Of course. I'm with ya, lass." He would have joined this little adventure regardless. His abilities would likely be sorely needed in the weeks to come, and there was no way he would miss this even without them. If this lad, Tala, had discovered a way to kill Blessed, Gazin would do whatever he could to make sure that he survived to share his knowledge.

"I'll come too. I figure I can be good for something." That was Lito. Gazin didn't even need to look to know, despite not knowing the boy all that well. If Alina was going, Lito wouldn't be far behind. He'd heard good things about the lad, though, and he really was something of a package deal with Alina, so Gazin wouldn't complain.

"I will join you as well. I am of little use around here." Dunlop. That was good. Keeping the Tala boy safe would be much easier with Dunlop around. Keeping them all safe would be easier with him around.

Eight people. That was a good number. Enough to protect the boy, with a good variety of skills. Eight very skilled, very dangerous people. Gazin glanced around quickly, double checking who was present. There was no one else there who he thought should join. Too many people would create more problems than they would solve, and there weren't many others here who could stand on the same level as this forming group.

Serala clearly agreed, for she gave a final, solid nod before turning to Hagan again, prepared to speak. Before she could, though, another voice cut in: it was light and feminine but held an air of strength and power to it. "I think I shall come along as well."

The room turned as one to stare at the speaker: sitting in a high-backed, velvet, regal-looking chair sat Caida. Despite the eyes on her, she sat relaxed with a small smirk and sipped from the goblet in her hands, staring confidently at Serala.

That was a surprise. While Caida was one of the few other people who Gazin thought could be particularly helpful in this situation, he hadn't expected the woman to be interested. She was a woman who was accustomed to ease and luxury, not a perilous journey running from the full might of the Fire Church. The full might of all the Churches, soon. Although, now that he thought about it, perhaps her interest wasn't such a surprise. She hadn't gotten to where she was by taking things easy, despite her appearance. She contributed an entirely different type of danger than the rest of them, after all.

"Caida. I wouldn't think a desperate flight through the wilds would interest you," Serala said in surprise.

"Perhaps not normally," she replied with an amused tone. "But a little discomfort is a small price to pay to keep this boy safe." She gave Tala a look that sent a shiver down his spine, much to Gazin's amusement. He would have to warn the lad about her at some point, or she would eat him alive. "Besides, my particular skillset could be of great value to you, and I doubt either Alina or you, dear, could quite manage that role in my absence."

Gazin almost snorted at that, and was glad he didn't. Alina was about as uptight of a person as he'd ever met, and Serala was, well… her skills certainly didn't lie in the same sphere as Caida's did.

Serala, however, didn't seem to care about the not-quite-insult. If she even realized it had been made. Even Gazin couldn't tell if she was aware of it or not. She really did take after Vail in some ways. Regardless, she just nodded in acquiescence before speaking again. "Alright. We should be good. Hagan, can you get the supplies?"

Hagan gave a nod in response and strode through the room towards another door, gesturing for a few of the people he passed to join him as he left.

Serala turned to the room once more and spoke to the people who had agreed to join them. "Hagan will cover all of our basic necessities. You all go grab whatever else you need and meet us in five minutes in the store room. I'm going to go help Hagan and tell him about today. He's going to need to know the details. The rest of you be careful. This city's going to be dangerous for a while now. You," she pointed at Tala, "go with Vail." And without waiting for a response, she strode towards the door that Hagan had gone through. Vail, without responding or in any way acknowledging what she had said, turned and went through another one of the side doors. With a start at the sudden movement, Tala hurried after him. Gazin sighed again and stood with a small stretch. He only had a few minutes to get his things together. Best get to it. If he survived, he had a feeling this was going to be a journey that he would never forget.

CHAPTER 7

Tala wasn't entirely sure what this place was. It was large, clearly. A dark hallway that had a staircase in it, some sort of large lounge area that had comfortably fit a few dozen people inside it, and now this well-lit hallway, with bright windows set high in the wall and many brightly burning candles spread throughout. There were also decorations adorning the length of it: paintings and tapestries of incredible quality. Had the lounge not been evidence enough, this hallway was a clear sign that whoever owned this building (that Hagan fellow, perhaps?) was a very wealthy person. As Tala followed Vail, he wondered what such expensive items were doing in a Dissident safe house; it seemed like an odd display of wealth for an organization that likely needed all the money it could get. Or was it a cover? Making a place that looked too nice to hide criminals inside it? Tala toyed with these thoughts until Vail opened another doorway set at the end of the hall.

This room was some sort of store room, filled with crates and boxes, some sitting open while others were shut tight. One open crate seemed to be filled with wine bottles, of which a few were missing. Another looked to be filled with blankets.

Vail continued through the room to a door on the other side, opening and entering it without pause. Tala followed, wondering where the man was taking him. As large as the buildings in Fiahren tended to be, they were usually split up into smaller, separate rooms, not one big assortment like this. How did they stay hidden from the Church in such a place? As he entered the new room, he stopped short in surprise: the room was full of weapons! Arranged in racks on the walls and tables and stands throughout the room were swords of various sizes and designs as well as axes, spears and other polearms, bows, daggers, and shields. There were enough weapons in the room to equip hundreds of soldiers! What in the Hells kind of place was this? Tala turned to Vail with wide eyes, hoping for an explanation of why they had so many weapons just lying around, but the man was looking at an array of swords on one of the walls, completely oblivious to Tala's silent question.

After waiting for a bit, Tala decided to just ask the man.

"What is all this?" he asked, his voice a bit higher-pitched than he had intended.

Vail half-turned around to look at Tala, showing him the same blank expression that the man always seemed to have.

"Weapons."

With his answer given—and none of Tala's questions actually answered—Vail turned back to examining the swords.

Bemused and slightly annoyed, Tala tried again. "I can see that. I mean why do you have so many of them? What if the Church found out?"

This time Vail answered without turning. "They aren't mine. They're Hagan's. And they don't care."

With mounting frustration and feeling like he was trying to squeeze water out of a rock, Tala continued his questions.

"Okay. Why does *Hagan* have so many weapons? And why wouldn't the Church care? The man practically has his own armory here!"

"Because it's his job. He's a merchant. This is the weapons room of his shop."

Tala sighed to himself. Still, as little as Vail had told him, it was enough for him to figure out the important bits.

If Hagan was a merchant with a large supply of weapons—weapons whose possession and sale were heavily monitored by the Church—and the Church didn't, or wouldn't, care about him having so many, then that must mean Hagan was an independent, trusted merchant. A trusted merchant would naturally be very wealthy and could easily afford a building as large as this one clearly was, as well as all the decorations and the private bar. Such things would even be expected for such a person to have!

And if he was a member, or even just a supporter, of the Dissidents, then they could feel safe in his care. The Church wouldn't take a second look at anybody the man vouched for, especially anybody he trusted enough to stay with him. So long as he was never suspected of actually having ties to the Dissidents, the man was essentially above the law, and the Church wouldn't take a second look at whatever company he held or any questionable items that might find their way into his hands.

Tala couldn't help but be impressed with Hagan's cleverness. And his audacity: he was providing a safe haven for Dissidents in one of the very last places the Church would ever bother to look for them, and was using the Church's very own authority to protect the people they hated! He wondered how often the man had dealt with Church members without their being aware that their sworn enemies were staying in the very same building!

Vail interrupted his thoughts. "You know how to fight, right?"

Tala blinked at the sudden question, before shaking his head negative. "No, I've never been in a fight, or been taught how."

"So you can't use any weapons?"

"No."

He heard Vail hum in… acknowledgement? Displeasure? The noise was oddly lacking in intonation. "We'll need to work on that then." With that, he walked over to a box filled with leather belts. "We don't have time to get you better clothes." He pulled out a belt from the box and held it up for Tala to see. It was covered in buckles and loops, and along with the part that went around his waist, there was a strap that looked like it went over a shoulder. "Put this on."

Tala recognized the item as a combination baldric-belt, but he had no idea how to actually wear the thing. He said as much to Vail, who just gave him that same blank stare in response before speaking.

"This part goes around your waist," he said, holding up the belt. "This part goes over your shoulder." He held up the baldric before passing the whole thing to Tala, who mutely took it. Tala thought that he should be feeling panic, shock, despair, something along those lines. Instead, this man he was dealing with made him unable to feel anything other than a growing irritation.

As Tala donned the baldric, Vail stepped over to a variety of knives and daggers and, after looking at them for a few seconds, grabbed three along with their sheaths. Next, he turned back to the swords, where he grabbed one after only a moment of looking along with the sheath underneath it. He brought the weapons over to Tala with a brief explanation.

"These are daggers. Use them for close combat. This is a hunting knife. Use it for skinning animals, cutting food, or close combat. This is a sword. Don't use it until you're taught how. When you are taught how, use it for stabbing or cutting. It does both."

Tala hesitantly took the weapons and went about trying to place them in his belt as Vail stepped back, giving him an… entirely blank look.

"That'll do for now. Let's go," Vail said as he began walking back the way they had come. Tala followed, trying to adjust to the awkward feeling of the weapons now hanging at his hips. Vail strode down the hallway, stopping midway at a door which was already opened. He walked through it with Tala following close behind to see that the new room that they had entered looked remarkably similar to the store room that they had just passed through: crates and boxes lay stacked and scattered about in no discernible pattern.

Upon their entry into the room, the occupants all turned to look at them, ceasing the quiet conversations they had been having. Serala spoke up from where she had been sitting on one of the crates. "Good. Everyone's ready then. Alright. Nuri will take the lead. Do what he says. Alina, stay behind him and be prepared to cover us if needed. Dunlop next. You," she pointed at Tala, "stay in the middle. Gazin, stay with him. Lito and Caida next. Ilan, Vail, and I will cover the rear. Stay together and keep quiet. Keep an eye out for any problems. It will be best if we can get out of the city without anybody knowing about it." She paused for a moment, looking at all of the tense faces. She gave a single, solid nod before focusing on Hagan. "Get it open then."

Tala watched as Hagan and Nuri—who spun around with a dramatic flailing of his leather duster coat—turned to one of the crates near them and pushed it off to one side. He stared blankly at the spot the box had been, seeing nothing but bare floor. Hagan crouched down, pulling out a small metal object from a pouch at his waist and, after fiddling with it for a few moments, put it to the floor. Tala couldn't quite see what he did, but a few moments later, Nuri had seemingly grabbed the very floor and lifted a square of it up, revealing a trapdoor, which Hagan promptly grabbed and swung all the way open.

Despite his anxiety, Tala couldn't quite help grinning: a real trapdoor! With a quick look back at the room, Nuri climbed down the hole, on what Tala assumed must be a ladder. The next to go down the hole was Alina. Following her was Dunlop. He had a strange-looking wooden round shield slung across his back and otherwise seemed to be covered in weapons. Before he descended, Tala was able to count a sword, an ax, two oddly curved short swords, half a dozen knives, and a bow and quiver full of arrows.

As Tala stared in surprise at the disappearing form of the walking armory (how did the man carry so much when he was shorter than Tala?), Serala walked up next to him and nodded for him to climb down next. He took a deep breath and with shaking hands approached the trapdoor. He looked down at the hole in the floor and saw that there was indeed a metal ladder leading into the darkness. After a moment's hesitation—and a quick look up at the people still waiting on him—he sat down on the edge of the hole, grabbed the ladder, and began his descent.

As the darkness enveloped him, he tried to take deep, even breaths. He wasn't claustrophobic by any means, but he had no idea how long the fall would be if he slipped off the ladder, the all-consuming void beneath him giving no hints as to how deep it went. As he slowly climbed down, he noticed that the air was growing increasingly stale, so much so that he could almost taste it, making his dark descent even more unpleasant. Unable to see in the inky blackness, he used his feet to feel out the rungs beneath him as he carefully worked his way down. The only indication he had that he wasn't alone in that stale, black void were the sounds of movement coming from the others both above and below him: hands and feet lightly impacting the metal in a staggered rhythm. He wanted to stop, take a few moments just to compose himself, but he didn't dare: if he stopped moving, or even moved too slowly, the person above might step on his fingers, making him lose his grip on the ladder and plunge into the depths below.

To distract himself, Tala tried to recall all that he knew about their destination: the Undercity. While he knew of the Undercity, he, like most people, had never actually been down there. From the things he'd heard, its name was a bit of a misnomer, as it wasn't truly a city: it was simply a place for prisoners and slaves to work the great furnaces that supplied so much to the city proper. Heat, water, and steam were pumped throughout the entirety of the Fire Capital from the Undercity, through the massive array of pipes that extended from the Undercity's depths to all corners of Fiahren. The same steam, the same pipes, that Tala himself had used not even an hour ago to kill a Blessed.

Shaking his head to pull himself out of *that* train of thought, he refocused his mind. From what he could recall, the only real entrance, or exit, to the Undercity from outside of the Fire Capital itself was the place known as the Wretch's Gorge: a short but deep chasm that extended to the south of the city into the Fire Plains. Heavily guarded with steep walls and little foliage, it was nigh impossible to escape from the gorge, which was why it had served as the main 'residence' for the workers of the Undercity for thousands of years. Given that the gorge was the only exit from the Undercity outside of the walls of Fiahren, Tala wasn't sure how they were planning to escape, but he hoped they weren't going to try and use that route. He was certain that would be doomed to failure.

So lost in his thoughts, Tala almost missed it when Nuri called for the group to stop. Pausing to listen, he heard a 'thump' come from below as Nuri called up that he was at the bottom. A few moments later, a small light rose up through the darkness. Peering down, Tala saw the flickering flame of a torch being held in the hands of Nuri. As those below him renewed their descent, eager to reach solid ground, Tala had to force himself to keep pace and not just jump off the ladder where he was. Keeping an eye out below him, he followed Alina as she reached the ground and stepped off to the side. A few moments later, Serala was on the ground beside them as they waited for the rest of the group to dismount.

Looking around, Tala tried to get his bearings. Underground was obvious, but the place the ladder led to looked to be no more than an old, small, empty square room. Four stone walls surrounded them with no discernible markings except for the wall directly in front of the ladder, which had the outline of a large, rectangular shape on it with what looked like some sort of hand grip carved into it. Tala stared at the (presumed) hand grip, mind whirling with thoughts. How old was this secret entrance to the Undercity? Had the Dissidents built it in, or had they merely discovered it somehow?

It was clearly an old room, even if the ladder was in good shape. Tala figured Hagan must keep an eye on its condition in case it was needed quickly, like now. But to have what must have been a hidden room in the Undercity that extended all the way up to a shop in the middle of the city proper, and a ladder that ran the whole length? Tala was gaining a new understanding of how the Dissidents had managed to survive for so long.

As the final figure, Vail, dropped to the ground, he crouched and fiddled with the bottom of the ladder. After a few moments, he gripped the rung in front of him and rose with force. The ladder shot up into the darkness, the sound of metal on metal reverberating throughout the chamber. Tala's eyebrows rose, impressed. A retractable ladder that long was not something he had expected.

As the echoing clang of the ascending ladder finished reverberating around the room, Serala gave a nod to Nuri, who stepped up to the outline in the wall. The man gripped the indent in the stone and pulled, causing the stone doorway to slowly swing open. The stone made a grumbling sound as it moved, but Tala was surprised by how quiet it was: they must keep the door maintained as well as the ladder. Was it sheer paranoia-based preparation, or was this a route that was often used?

Nuri halted the door's opening with just enough room for a single person to slip through the gap. He poked his head through and—after a few seconds of looking around—pulled it back. With a nod, he pulled the door open a bit more, enough for the largest of their party to fit, and then walked through the opening himself. Immediately, Alina followed, with Dunlop, the man clothed in weapons (was that a mace on his belt?), right behind her. After a beat of stillness, Tala felt a nudge from Serala. Taking her meaning, he took a steadying breath and followed after, trying to keep his footsteps light so as not to make too much noise. He had a hard time telling if he succeeded due to the rapid beating of his heart in his ears, drowning out whatever noise his feet were making.

While he hoped that he was doing a good job at appearing calm to the others, inside, he was a mixture of emotions: terrified, excited, and still in a minor state of shock, he was aware. Everything that day had happened so fast that he had—more than once—entertained the idea that he was dreaming. Everything seemed to have a heightened quality to it: the darkness was darker than it should be, the sounds louder, the flickering torchlight behind him burning brighter than any fire he had ever seen before. It was even brighter than Anderas' giant flame disk! If it wasn't for the slight burning of his muscles after climbing down such a long ladder, and the exhaustion still present from their earlier run through the city, he would have easily believed that everything that had happened was merely a figment of his sleeping mind.

But it was all real, and whatever he might have wished, it was happening right then and there. Trying to pull his thoughts together, he slipped through the opening in the wall behind his new companions. What he found was… more darkness. Only a small bit of light was filtering in from the torch on the other side of the doorway, enough for him to vaguely see the shapes of the others in the darkness standing just off to the right. He moved over to stand with them as the rest filtered in behind him. As Vail came through, once again at the end and carrying the torch, he had one hand gripping something on the stone door, which slowly closed shut behind him.

With the torch now on the other side of the door, Tala could see that they were in some sort of hallway: stone blocks encased the walls, ceiling, and floor running in both directions. Looking back at the wall they had come through, there were no signs whatsoever that it was anything but a bland, uninteresting stretch of stone wall. If nothing else, these Dissidents were great at hiding their secret doors.

During his quick look around, Vail had approached the figures of Nuri and Alina at the front of the group, and—to Tala's surprise—instead of giving the torch to Nuri, who was supposed to be the one leading them through the Undercity, he instead handed it off to Alina before sidling back to the other side of the cluster, alongside the massive man who must be Ilan. As Tala wondered why Alina had been given the torch, he was caught by surprise as she lifted her empty hand, made an odd sort of sideways cupping gesture towards the flames, and then in a fluid motion extended her arm out with her fingers splayed wide.

While there was no change to the flames themselves, the hallway before them suddenly grew not quite bright, but visible enough to see, as though the very stones themselves were illuminating the path before them. Seeing his clear surprise, Serala spoke up next to him in a whispered voice. "She's an Awakened Light Descendant. It's why we wanted her along. After Nuri, she's our best chance at getting through this place unnoticed."

He could only nod dumbly in response. Even having spent his life in Fiahren, in the very Capital of the Fire Country, he had only rarely seen Fire Wielders using their magics; Soleil and Anderas' displays earlier in the arena were rare and exciting events. Even rarer still, though, was witnessing wielders of the other elements: the Descendant fight between the Boney and Icey was one of the only times in his entire life he had seen other magics worked. Even Dust wielders weren't allowed to use their magics inside the city! A Light Wielder—an Awakened one at that—was not something he had ever expected to see.

Holding his hand up in a 'wait' signal, Nuri began to creep forward through the stone hallway with Alina shortly behind him. As they moved, the dim light resonating around the hall fluctuated with them. Despite carrying the torch, the source of the light, the bend in the hall that they were heading towards never got any brighter, remaining just as dark as it had ever been. Watching this, Tala couldn't help but be impressed at Alina's skill. True, he didn't actually know how difficult it might or might not have been to bend light around them in such a way, but to see a moving torch burning bright yet casting no discernible light around it was still quite a sight. He suspected that the only reason he could see them—or even the torch itself—was because she was letting the light filter backwards for the sake of her companions. He wondered what it must look like from the other direction: if he were to stand in front of those two, would he see nothing but a pitch-black hallway? A chill ran down his spine: that was likely the exact scenario that had killed so many in the past.

Just before the bend in the hallway, the two stopped, and Nuri made some sort of gesture towards Alina. She nodded and made a hand flourish in response. Tala blinked as Nuri's already-shadowed form seemed to grow hazier until he could barely even tell that a person stood there at all! Watching carefully, Tala thought that he could see the strangely… missing form of Nuri move to the corner of the bend. Tala figured that he must be scouting ahead: looking to see if there was anyone around the corner, he had Alina hide his form so that if there was anybody, they wouldn't be able to see him in return.

A few moments later, Alina gestured towards the group in what Tala assumed was an 'all clear,' and they began quietly making their way forward. Before Tala had even begun to move, Alina stepped around the corner, presumably with the hidden Nuri, to continue scouting ahead. Despite having taken the torch out of their sight, the corridor was still awash in that strange glow.

Deciding to focus on just following the man in front of him instead of looking at the confusing lighting, Tala continued to creep through the hallways with the rest of the group as they followed the twisting path of light through a maze of stone corridors. He now understood just why Nuri and Alina had been recruited for this little adventure rather than left to volunteer like the rest: there were so many twists and turns that they would all have gotten hopelessly lost. And without Alina to work her magics, it would have been easy to run into somebody. It was no wonder that Light produced exceptionally skilled assassins if they could perform tricks like this. At least according to the rumors Tala had heard.

But her light magics didn't cover the sounds they made, so why hadn't they run into anybody yet? All they had encountered so far was the faint echoing of different sounds, too distorted for Tala to identify, that had started to increase in both volume and frequency. Were they getting lucky, or were they just in an old, unused portion of the Undercity? From the dust on the walls and floor, Tala had a feeling it was the latter. Given that the Undercity was supposed to be as large in area as Fiahren, if not even larger, he supposed it made sense that much of it went unused. Although that begged the question: why make it so big in the first place? He couldn't even imagine how much time and work it must have taken to create the entirety of the Undercity!

It wasn't much further when, as they rounded another corner, they found Alina and a now fully visible Nuri waiting for them in a short stretch of hallway that only had one bend in it, not even 20 feet away from where they stood. Tala could tell that the noises he'd been hearing were coming from around that bend: he could make out what sounded like the clanging of metal, whooshes of air, and a general clamor of all sorts of other noises that he couldn't quite place.

As the rest of the group came around the corner and huddled around the two, Nuri spoke in a hushed voice that was a strange mixture of a whisper and a yell as he struggled to stay quiet but still be heard over the roar of noise coming from around the corner.

"We're about to enter the Under proper."

What exactly did that mean? Had they not been in the Undercity all this time already?

"It looks like things are still normal down here, so that's good. We're gonna need to sneak around the sides until we reach the northern corridors. That means left."

That was good. If they were going north, that meant they probably weren't going to try to escape through the gorge to the south. Of course the Dissidents had secret exits.

"It's going to be tricky, but stay close together. It'll make it easier for the princess to hide us all."

Tala noticed Alina's mouth tighten at the nickname, but besides that, she made no other indication of her displeasure.

"It probably won't matter too much, but do try to stay quiet, just in case."

Having said all he intended to say, Nuri turned around and began to creep once again to the corner of the hallway and into the 'Undercity proper.'

CHAPTER 8

As she passed around the corner, Alina couldn't quite help the widening of her eyes and a small gasp escaping her mouth as she got her first ever look at the fabled 'Undercity' of Fiahren. The only word she could think of when she saw it was 'large.' Ahead of her lay a massive, cavernous room stretching back farther than even she could see, despite how brightly lit the whole thing was. A countless number of truly massive furnaces lay neatly arranged in rows running up and down the cavern. A dizzying number of pipes crisscrossed through the air above the furnaces, going up into the darkness or straight down into the floor. She had heard tales of the Undercity, but they hadn't prepared her as well as she had thought for seeing it for herself.

And all around the massive cavern were people: a few thousand at least, and those were just the ones she could see! She could make out the workers easily: the slaves and prisoners who were brought down there to feed and maintain the furnaces. Most were wearing little more than tattered rags, and even at a distance, Alina could see that many of them looked malnourished even as they performed their demanding tasks. Some of the workers were in groups at giant bellows to pump air through the furnaces, while others were shoveling coal from massive piles near each furnace into their burning maws. Spread throughout and around the workers were the many guards of the Undercity, who were monitoring the workers and ensuring that none were brave—or stupid—enough to try to escape or sabotage anything. Each guard was equipped with at least a sword and a whip, and even in the few seconds that Alina watched them, she saw that many were quite liberal in using their whips to either motivate or punish the workers.

Spread at intervals throughout the room, patrolling between the furnaces, were what must have been the 'Illegitimates': bastard Descendants born out of affairs or 'unworthy' partners who were sent to the Undercity as youths to hide their forebears' 'shame.' Seeing them here stuck in this hot, dark cave, being treated barely better than slaves, made Alina have the rare feeling of pride in her own country before ruthlessly squashing it: Light deserved no good thoughts from her. But even still, she couldn't help but feel that a life in the Shadow Sect was better than *this*. Even if they had harsh lives since birth, and didn't officially 'exist' in the world, and were mostly used as disposable assassins that the Light Church could deny having any knowledge of if they were caught. Okay, perhaps the Shadow Sect wasn't much better, but *still!*

But Illegitimates were treated terribly no matter what the country. With abilities too useful to kill, but births too shameful to acknowledge (despite how many there were), they were destined for lives of misfortune. Unless the Dissidents got to them somehow. And these weren't all Illegitimates down here either: Alina knew that Fire used the Undercity as a punishment for Descendants who had angered their superiors somehow.

It was a brutal, if effective, solution that the Fire Church had come up with millennia ago: the risk of a furnace exploding or causing some other disaster was minimal when there were people around who could completely control the flames with nothing more than their will. Arguably a better method than how Light handled problematic Descendants: sending them to the front lines of the endless war with Lava to die in 'glorious' battle.

Looking up, Alina saw large, round structures atop each furnace that must be the great water pools. They were fed from pipes carrying water from either the Burning Lake at the eastern edge of the city or all the way from the ocean further east. The pools were in many ways the source of the Fire Country's power in the world: the water from the lake was heated and then pumped through the pipes up into the city where it could be used by the residents for all manner of things. The ocean water was boiled into the steam that was carried to many of the city's factories and other industries. It was steam power that had assured the Fire Country of continental dominance. They'd used steam-powered factories to mass-produce weapons, tools, and war machines on a scale well beyond what the other nations were capable of, even the Steam nation itself, ironically enough. Not that their dominance had really mattered for the last few hundred years. The borders of the Fire Country had long ago spread to the point that even with their technical superiority, it was all they could do just to keep them secured. If it wasn't for the stabilizing influence of Southtown on the border between Light and Fire, Alina knew that Light would have pressed that weakness until the lines of Fire broke. She had heard her family wistfully talk about that exact scenario many times in her youth. Although they never could give her a proper answer when she had asked what Light would do if Fire sent one of their infamous Blessed like Soleil or Anderas to defend their land. How Fire continuously created such dangerous people was still a mystery to her.

Shaking herself out of her thoughts before the others noticed, Alina quickly turned her attention to the rest of the group, embarrassed at how she had let seeing the Undercity enthrall her. Thankfully most of them seemed to have been just as enraptured by the sight. Her momentary distraction hadn't caused a lapse in her magic, either. Not that she thought it would, of course—even hiding a group this size within a bubble of her power was a simple task for her—but she couldn't be careless: in the depths of the Undercity like this, if they were discovered, they were dead.

Nuri slowly led them to the left, keeping as close to the wall of the large cavern as he could. As little as Alina cared for the man, she couldn't help but hold a grudging respect for him: the smuggler, for all his playfulness and idiocy, was an expert at his craft. Despite the tenseness of their situation, he moved with a calm certainty that Alina doubted she would ever be able to emulate. She had a feeling the man was doing it more for the others' sake than his own, though. Lito and Tala were clearly drawing a source of comfort from Nuri's nonchalance. And she was certain that that's exactly what the smuggler was intending. The man was far more intelligent and observant than his usual irritating behavior suggested. Even she felt more relaxed, to her chagrin.

She glanced back at the rest of their group, her ego hoping that it wasn't just the three of them who were finding comfort in the annoying smuggler's behavior. Much to her frustration, the others seemed tense but as calm as ever. She wasn't surprised. They each had years', if not decades', more experience, but it still rankled her pride. Especially Serala, who was looking more bored than anything, as though this whole affair was barely worth her time. She didn't know much about Serala, but the girl couldn't be more than a few years older than Alina. Alina was a prodigy! She had been groomed her entire life to become Light's version of Anderas Anto before… everything had happened! So why did she always feel like she was coming up short? Serala was leading a group of some of the most dangerous people in the world, Alina being one of them, to protect a boy who had killed a Blessed, and yet Alina was only here because she was useful!

Alina shook her head, hard, dispelling those unwelcome thoughts before they grew stronger. She knew where they would take her if she entertained them, and she hated that place. She was Alina, prodigy of Light, and she would not fall into that pit of despair when there were people relying on her to keep them safe!

Thankfully, a proper distraction came in the form of another opening in the long wall. They had already passed a few, and each one had required her to exert more power to keep the group invisible from the many guards and workers that surrounded them. And even better, instead of passing it like the others, Nuri had cautiously looked around and gestured for the group to follow him. Finally, their slow, terrifying crawl along the walls of the great chamber was over!

Alina placed herself off to the side of the corridor's entrance to ensure that each of them was covered in her magic as they escaped the cavern. Her eyes followed Dunlop as he passed through the opening, but he suddenly froze just past the threshold, nearly making Tala crash into him. Confused, Alina and Tala both watched as Dunlop slowly turned back towards the cavern. Following his suddenly intense stare, the two also turned back toward the furnaces, only then noticing that the atmosphere of the great chamber had changed. Instead of the busy, ceaseless activity that had before engulfed it, the chamber now stood almost completely still and silent, the only sound and movement being the roaring dance of the furnace flames and the marching steps of a troop of guards that had just entered the cavern from one of its larger entryways.

Alina's jaw clenched tight as she looked at the new squad of guards that had entered and in her peripheral vision could see that her companions were also staring at the new arrivals. The biggest cause of concern, though, wasn't the new guards so much as it was the figure at their head: dressed in ornate red-and-gold robes that almost looked like flickering flames themselves stood a pale man who was talking to one of the Underguards. As he spoke, he gestured to the sides, and the guards behind him began to split up and march through the room, clearly searching for something.

There was only one reason that Alina could think of for why a Fire Priest would be leading a troop of guards around the Undercity and ordering them to search. Out of the corner of her eye, Alina saw Dunlop grab Tala and quietly pull him forward into the corridor, quickly followed by the rest of the group, Alina on the heels of Vail and Ilan. She walked backwards, turning all of her attention to keeping the illusion of an empty hallway in place as the group hurried away from the great chamber.

Once they were all deep in the hallway, out of sight of any guards in the chamber, Alina rushed past the others to rejoin Nuri at the front, and without delaying any further, they all hastily began making their way down the new hallway. Instead of their former way of progressing, with Nuri and Alina scouting out each turn in the path while the rest of the group followed at a distance, now the group was staying right on their heels. Alina could feel the power of her magic thrumming through her veins as she used all of her considerable skill to scout out each bend and break in the endless hallways before they approached them.

To make matters worse, the corridors they were now in were not quite as forgotten and unused as the ones they had been in before, so despite their newfound haste, they were occasionally forced to stop at some junctions and wait for the way ahead to clear of people. Alina used every trick she could to hasten their departure and could feel the drain on her power as she sometimes had to bend entire corridors around to disorient Underguards and stop them from finding the group. While they could have simply killed anybody they came across, they had neither the time nor the means to dispose of any bodies, and any sign that they had escaped through the Undercity would only cause them more problems in the future.

As they ran, they started passing through halls with strong wooden doors set into the walls. Rooms for the guards or workers, perhaps? This deep in the under, it made sense for them to have lodgings nearby instead of going to Wretch's Gorge every night.

She resolutely turned her mind away from the other purpose she knew those rooms would serve. And as they passed a door that some careless guard had left open, she was careful to turn her head away so as not to risk seeing. In doing so, she was able to catch a glimpse of Tala moving towards the door and peeking inside as he ran past.

Idiot! she yelled silently. He had just risked being seen! Or was he just some sick bastard hoping to catch a glimpse of some guard's leftovers?

Tala recoiled back from the door, stumbling and almost falling as his momentum carried him onward. Had Gazin not firmly grabbed him and forced him to continue moving, Alina was sure he would have collapsed on the ground then and there.

Just a fool, then. A naive, idiotic fool. The boy never would have reacted like that had he known, or in any way expected, what she knew he had seen. Was he really that naive? She knew that the Researchers of the famed Institute of Fire existed as an entirely separate class. But were they really that *sheltered*?

As they continued their frantic journey through the Undercity, the hallways once again became unbroken lines of stone, with the occasional door set throughout. The signs of use also faded as they went, with layers of dust on the walls and floor growing thicker and the only light once again coming from Alina's manipulations.

Despite the safety they were now in, far away from the activity of the central cavern, the sense of anxiety and panic that they were feeling had yet to abate. There was no way of knowing how long it would take for the Undercity to be searched, or how thorough the guards would be: for all they knew, they were planning to search from the outside in, and there were guards not a minute behind them or, worse, just around a corner in front. So they kept their frenetic pace, racing through the maze as quietly and carefully as they could.

Suddenly, Nuri skidded to a stop, halfway down some dank, bland hallway, and started examining one of the walls. After a few moments, he found what he was looking for, and he pulled out a dagger, which he slid into a small gap between two of the stones. He toyed with it for a few moments before a quiet click sounded out, and a small section of the wall swung open, leaving a little hole extending from the ground to just about waist height.

With an audible sigh of relief, Nuri turned to the group and gestured towards the hole. "Everybody in," he said in a voice that belied both relief and exhaustion. Alina stood by him, twisting the light so it bent into the opening. She passed the torch she had been carrying to Dunlop, who took it and dropped down to all fours and began crawling into the hole. The rest of the group began filtering in one at a time after him, crawling on hands and knees.

After only a minute or so of crawling, she followed the others out of the tunnel and stood up. Looking around, she saw that they were in another cavern, though this one was much, much smaller.

Taking the torch back from Dunlop, she drew on her power and, with a few graceful flourishes of her hand, expanded the torch light out again, brightening the small cavern up. It was completely empty, bare of anything of note except for another passage (this one large enough to walk through, thankfully) extending out directly opposite from the tiny one they had just crawled through.

"Well, let's keep at it," came Nuri's tired voice, as he started walking towards the passage. "We can't stop yet, but at least we don't have to run or sneak around anymore." To his credit, the smuggler at least tried to sound cheerful.

CHAPTER 9

The group trudged through the passage in a tired silence, the relief they felt at no longer being in danger of discovery evident in their slumped forms. The flickering dimness of their ambient lighting, caused by Alina's exhaustion, was an apt symbol of how they were all feeling.

For his part, Tala was just trying to keep up with the steady pace of the rest. He desperately wanted to ask for a break, a few minutes at least, to sit down and recover some strength. But as tired as he was, he could see in the faces and body language of the others that they were all feeling the same. He had no idea where they were, but if none of the others were suggesting they rest, then they must not be safe enough. He was tempted to ask how much further they had to go but couldn't quite muster the energy for it, instead resigning himself to enduring the increasing burning in his legs as they trudged onwards.

Eventually, as he started to think that he couldn't continue without some sort of break, the dirt tunnel opened up into another small cavern. Very similar to the last, this one was also mostly empty but had some small signs of use: a hole ringed with stones in the center that was likely meant as a fire pit, a few discarded scraps of cloth scattered about, and some random wooden stumps sat here and there, most likely for use as makeshift chairs. Most notable, though, was what looked like a door on the far wall of the cave, directly across from the tunnel that they were in.

As the group coalesced in the room, Serala walked up to Nuri and after a short, whispered conversation, turned towards the group. "We'll take a short rest here. We'll have to keep moving soon, though, so don't get too comfortable," she announced.

Visible relief swept through the group, and they broke apart to rest around the cavern. Some sat down on the logs with a groan while others just dropped to the floor entirely. Tala joined those on the floor, dropping down next to the passage they had come from and leaning against the wall, closing his eyes and savoring the feeling of being off his feet.

A few moments passed, and he heard someone sit beside him. Opening his eyes, he saw it was Serala: she was sitting similarly, with her legs stretched out in front and her back and head propped against the wall. She seemed to be handling their long trek better than he was, however, for instead of basking in the break, she was staring at him with a complicated look.

After a few moments of staring at each other, he quirked his eyebrow in a silent question. With a quick glance at the others, none of whom seemed to be paying them any attention, she leaned towards him and asked in a quiet voice, "How are you doing?"

He considered her question carefully.

"I'm, uh, not really sure, to be honest," he eventually said, attempting a smile that barely managed to twitch his lips. "This is all just… so much."

She nodded pensively. "Not really where you thought your life was going, is it? But you're doing well so far. We made it through all right, and it should be a lot easier from here."

He nodded, not really sure what to say to that. They sat for a few moments in silence, before a question that Tala had dreaded asking worked its way from his lips.

"What about that woman?" At Serala's confused look, he elaborated. "In that room back there. In the hallway. There was a woman lying on one of the beds. She was naked, bloody, and her eyes… her eyes looked *dead*. But she was breathing. What—what was that?" he asked, his voice shaky.

Serala frowned at the floor as she gave a deep sigh. "She's no one. Just one of the slaves."

"How can you say that?" Tala demanded, appalled at her nonchalance. "That, she… she's a person!"

Serala turned her frown to him. "She's also a slave. That's what happens to slaves: Fire, Lightning, Mist, everywhere! They're property, to be used however their owners see fit. One of the guards took a liking to her, maybe even a few, so they did what they wanted to her! And if she's really as broken as you say, then they'll throw her in one of the furnaces, same as the rest. What did you think happened to slaves, down there or anywhere else?"

"But that was… that was horrible! How could anyone do that? How could anyone *let* someone do that?"

Serala raised a brow at him, before shaking her head and mumbling something about 'capital' under her breath. "Because that's how things are. That's how the world works: the powerful get to do whatever they want, especially to those beneath them, and there's no one lower than a slave. And there are a lot of terrible people out there who are more than happy to abuse that fact. You were an Institute Researcher, right? Along with your parents? You've spent your life with privileges, protections, that most people never get, so you've never really seen how horrible people can be. Especially the Churches: they have absolute power, and no one can—or is even willing to try to—stop them. Any friends you've ever had, who weren't with the Institute or something else that protected them? They have spent every day of their lives having to worry about getting drafted into the army, or catching the eye of some noble or Church member and being enslaved. Or even just mildly annoying them and being enslaved or killed. What happened to that woman you saw? Yeah, it was horrible. But those kinds of things are *common*. They happen every day, everywhere, and can happen to *anybody*, at any time. You've just had the good fortune to never have had to face that, or worry about it happening to you. Until now, that is: you've managed to do something that no position in the world will keep you safe from." She ended her impromptu speech with a slight smirk at him, one that Tala couldn't have returned if he wanted to.

He fell silent as he thought about what she said. As a kid, his friends had always been more scared of the Church than made sense to him. Sure, he had a healthy respect for Church members, but he'd never felt particularly *scared* of them. They were the ones who had devoted their entire lives to ensuring the rest of them became the Favored in the afterlife! He had never understood how anyone could be scared of such people! Was this why, though? Had he really been as sheltered, as oblivious, as she was implying? Even if it was in service to the Fire God, being ripped away from everything you've ever known and loved to become a slave or soldier was a terrifying prospect.

Something she said rang through Tala's head, spurring him to ask a question he'd wondered about since he was a child and had first heard about the Dissidents.

"Is that what you all are fighting for then?" At her silence, he continued. "You said that no one can or will stop them—is that what you all are trying to do? The Dissidents? Stop them all from abusing their power? The Church says that you all are heretics; heathens who have forsaken the Gods for your own selfishness in this life. Are you just trying to stop the Churches from abusing their power?"

She shifted awkwardly, avoiding Tala's eyes. "Something like that. The truth is most of us have our own reasons for fighting, some better than others. But we do all agree that the way things are, the way the world works right now, isn't good. It needs to change, and since change like that is the last thing the Churches want, nobody is willing to even try to make it happen. So, for most of us, we're just trying to make things better. Even if that means fighting a war against the whole world."

Tala stared at her. That was… that was actually rather admirable. Nothing like the evil, self-serving, psychotic,

delusional monsters that the Church spoke about. He wondered if it was actually true; he could tell there was something
she wasn't telling him. Was she lying about all of it, or was
there just something she was leaving out? She didn't seem evil.
None of them did, although that wasn't saying much, seeing
as this was his first real conversation with any of them. But
she and Vail *had* risked themselves to save him after—after
what happened. And they certainly weren't responsible for
that woman in the room. If he had ever seen evil, then that
was certainly it.

But what did that mean? If the Dissidents were actually
good, and it was the Churches that allowed things like that to
happen, did that mean the Churches were evil? Were they lying
about more than the Dissidents? He felt his breathing start to
get tight, his palms start to sweat, and shook his head, clearing
it of those treasonous thoughts. But what did it even matter?
He'd already killed a Blessed—could he commit greater treason
than that? Right, wrong, good, evil, none of that mattered
right now. It was an accident. He was just trying to do the
right thing, and now he was trying to survive. It didn't matter
if the Dissidents were good or bad; it didn't matter what was
true and what wasn't. He just needed to survive. He didn't need
to know their whole agenda for that! At best it didn't matter,
and at worst, it would just complicate things that didn't need
to be complicated. Feeling calmer now that he had come to
that conclusion, Tala chose to push the conversation towards
what *did* affect him.

"So what exactly is the plan then? Right now, I mean?
Other than just getting me out of the city? And the…

country?" He trailed off, still wrestling with the idea of leaving the Fire Country.

"Well, I can't say for sure. I don't think we really have that much of an actual plan yet. This all kinda happened pretty fast for us too. But for the moment? We'll probably head to Southtown."

"Southtown?" he asked, recalling what he had learned of geography in his time at the Institute. "Isn't that the Metal city at the Red Lake? On the border of Fire and Light?"

She stared at him in surprise before smiling slightly with a small shake of her head. "Right, Researcher: you're actually educated."

"Okay... And why are we going there, exactly?" he continued after a few moments.

"Well... We're north of Fiahren now, so going south would mean going around it, which would take too much time and be too risky. And Mud is where most criminals run to hide anyway, despite the Wild Guards, so even if we did manage to get around the city, they'd be watching for us. East is the ocean, and even if we got a boat, it's all Wind territory, and they aren't the most... accommodating to strangers. West is the desert, which is a no, and if we tried to go around it, it'd be either Earth or Dust, and both of those borders are too heavily monitored for us to sneak you through. And word will definitely get there before we do, so they'll be looking for you. So we're stuck going north, which is the Jungle, Plant and Beast territory, but that border is too small and well-guarded to easily sneak through. Normally, we'd go to Firetown, since it's closer and a Metal-controlled city, but they're already on high alert for Dissidents right now. So instead we'll go to Southtown, since it's the easiest way to enter either the Lightlands or the Metal Mountains at the moment. And since the city is also controlled by Metal, and they're strict on neutrality, it'll be easier to not only get inside the city but hide ourselves there. At least for a short time."

"A short time? We won't be staying there?"

"No. Even though it's controlled by Metal, Fire has enough influence there that it won't take them long to find us if we stay too long."

"So what then? We go from there to Metal or Light?"

"Yep. Metal most likely between the two. They're a lot easier to deal with than Light, and with Alina with us—well, I don't think she'd be particularly willing to go to Light anyways." She trailed off at that, with a glance at Alina who was sitting primly on a log and chatting with the only other guy in their group who was around Tala's age, Lito.

"Oh." He wasn't sure what to say to that. He had wondered what a Light Descendent, an Awakened one at that, was doing in the Fire Country. Or as part of the Dissidents. He had a feeling her story probably wasn't a very happy one. "So is that it then? Get me set up in Metal? Or would we keep going north? To Lightning or somewhere else out of the Fire Church's reach?"

The look she gave him at his question sent a chill down his spine. It was completely empty, eerily similar to the blank expression that Vail always wore but with just a hint of… something else in it. Whatever it was made him fear what she was going to say. "You aren't getting 'set up' anywhere," she said bluntly.

"What? Why not? I thought that's what this was all about!" He gestured frantically to the rest of the group, the cave they were in, and everything. "Getting me out of the Church's reach! I'm sorry, but I don't want to join you! I don't want to spend my life running and hiding and fighting with you all! I'm sorry, but I don't! That's not me! I'm a researcher, a-an academic. I'm not a fighter or a rebel or a—a *heretic* or anything like that!"

Despite his protests, the look on her face didn't change. "Sorry, but it's not that simple. It's not even that we're going to force you or anything. But there simply *is* nowhere safe for you to 'settle down' and live a normal life. Not even in Lightning. Not even all the way up in Lava or if we turned around and brought you all the way down to Ice. You don't *have* to stay with us, or join or fight with us, if you really don't want to. But no matter what you do, you'll be running and hiding forever. As long as you're alive, anyway."

His head was spinning. What was she talking about? All he had to do was get away from the Church of Fire, wasn't it? Getting into another country and settling down might not be *easy*, but he wouldn't be hunted there, right? Especially somewhere far away like Lightning or Lava that didn't even share a border with Fire?

"But I just have to get out of reach of the Fire Church, don't I? As long as I get across the border, get deep into another country, I'll be fine!"

"It's not just the Church of Fire that's going to want you. You killed a Blessed! Every Church is going to be after you, simply because of what you represent. The Blessed are the chosen of the Gods, and it's important to the Churches that they're seen as invincible beings. For an ordinary person to kill one? None of them can accept it. They *have* to kill you. And they're all going to hear about you."

"But how would they know I'm me?" he asked, desperately clinging on to the hope of still living a more peaceful life. "I can change my name, grow a beard, shave my head, I can become a completely new person! Surely if I'm in another country, I'll be safe!"

She kept shaking her head. "Because the Fire Church will find out everything they can about you. They'll have drawings and descriptions of what you look like, and they'll pass those on to the other Churches. And the Churches are good at finding people no matter how much they change."

"What? But how would they get pictures or descriptions of me? Wouldn't the Fire Church want to keep it a secret from the other Churches that a Blessed died?"

"No. Quite the opposite in fact. They aren't friends by any means—they'd still happily murder each other given the chance—but they do work together sometimes. Take Earth for example: the only times in history they've ever played nice with Fire is when a Horde from the Bodylands manages to break through the Dust Wall and spill into the continent. Or when there's an incident involving us: not much gets the Churches to play nice quite like Dissidents. But what you've done? That's something new. Even we have rarely ever been involved in a Blessed's death, and we've been around about as long as the Gods have. But you: an ordinary person, who just happened to kill a Blessed out of nowhere, after standing up to him for abusing a young girl?

"Your very existence is a threat to their power, all the Churches' power. You're living proof that the Blessed aren't as invincible as they seem, that the Churches don't have the absolute power they like to pretend they do. They need your head on a spike, paraded through the streets, to prove to everybody that you were just a fluke. They'll probably even claim something like you were secretly a Blessed sent as an assassin, just to maintain the image that only a Blessed can kill a Blessed. But they can't do that as long as you're alive. The Churches can't be publicly caught in a lie like that, and as long as you're alive, they can't make any of those claims for fear of you showing up and proving that they lied. That'd hurt them, and they know it."

It was the calm, matter-of-fact way that she spoke that broke Tala. He desperately glanced around, hoping that someone would contradict her. That's when he noticed that their formerly private conversation was in fact being followed by everybody.

"But what about the Gods?" he asked aloud to the group. "Doesn't—*everything* come back to them? How am I more important to them than their fight for the throne?

"And what about the afterlife? This life doesn't matter. It's just a chance for us to prove we're worthy of receiving eternal bliss after death. And the whole point of the Churches fighting each other is because those who followed the victorious God will be elevated above the rest of humanity for eternity?

"How can I be more important than all of that? So important that they'd work together to find me? Even if they kill me, I'm not a heretic! I serve the Gods as much as anyone! And I've served the Fire God loyally my whole life! I didn't know he was a Blessed; I didn't even know someone like me could *kill* a Blessed! It's all just a misunderstanding! I'll still be allowed into the realms of heaven! And if the Fire God wins, I'll still ascend as a Favored! Just because I'm trying to survive doesn't mean I've forsaken the Gods! Or turned on the God of Fire! I'm just trying to *live!*" he finished desperately, pleadingly, as though his words would reach the Gods, the Churches, and his actions would be forgiven.

"Then why not just have me kill you now?" The question was asked calmly, casually, as though speaking of murder was no different than speaking of the weather. Tala's head whipped to Serala in shock, his eyes wide and mouth agape, only to see her looking back at him with half-lidded eyes, flipping a wicked-looking dagger in her hand.

"It'll be quick. Painless. You'll barely even realize what happened before your life is over. If you're right, then none of this matters anyway, so why not? You'll be welcomed into the heavens and spend eternity awaiting the Gods' little game to be over so that you might ascend as a Favored. It would be a lot nicer than spending the rest of this life running and hiding, wouldn't it?"

Tala stared at her in horror. He saw there, in those bright, beautiful, green eyes, that had so attracted him earlier, nothing. Apathy. She was serious; he could feel it. For the second time that day, Tala stared into the eyes of his own death.

CHAPTER 10

Silence echoed through the cave, as all others present watched the two of them. The silence dragged on, as did the stillness, even the dagger lying still in her hand. Eventually, she moved, the single motion of one eyebrow arching up as she spoke a single word.

"Well?"

The word jolted Tala out of his shock.

"No. I—I don't want to die."

She began flipping the dagger again. "Why not? If all of that is true, then why don't you want to die? Especially right now, quick and painless? I can promise you that it'll be a better death than you'll get at the hands of the Churches."

"I just—I just don't! I don't—I don't know why! I just... *don't*. I'm not ready to die yet!"

She opened her mouth to speak, but he cut her off, acutely aware of the dagger as it flipped through the air, landed in her palm, and flipped again.

"But just because I don't want to die, *yet*, doesn't mean I'm wrong! There's nothing wrong with wanting to live a bit longer! It doesn't mean I've forsaken the Gods or anything!"

"Fair enough," she responded casually, tucking away the dagger with a shrug. "But what about us then? We've forsaken the Gods. Not all of us maybe, but most of us at least. I have. Am I to be damned to the Hells for eternity? Are all of us? Do we all deserve damnation just for trying to make the world a better place for the living?"

"That's what they say. The Churches. That you're heretics, that the Gods will forsake you in the afterlife just like you've forsaken them in this one."

"Maybe that's better. Better than worshiping Gods that would use us. Like that girl you saw back there. Besides, how do you know any of that's true anyway? The Churches lie about how slaves are treated, about how invincible the Blessed are. What makes you think they're telling the truth about this?"

"The Gods!" Tala nearly screamed at her. "Even if some of the things they say are lies, the Gods are proof that this is true! Their very existence is the proof! How else do you explain their existence? All-powerful beings that are immortal and invincible! That can't be hurt or even *die*!"

"Lies," came a voice, instantly securing the attention of the room as all heads, all eyes, shot to Vail, despite his having only spoken the single, monotone word. They all sat silently, staring at the man, waiting for him to say more, but he just stood there, leaning against the wall, with the same blank face he had had every time Tala looked at him.

After several moments of silence, Tala spoke. "What do you mean 'lies?'"

"All of it. It's all lies."

...

"What's 'all of it?'"

Vail let out a breath that might have been a sigh. The man was impossible to read.

"Everything about the Gods. Almost everything. They do seem to be immortal, and they have absolute control over their element. But the rest? Their whole 'story?' It's all lies."

"But—what? What other explanation is there? Doesn't the very existence of the Gods *prove* their story? Why else would they have left the heavens? Or formed the Churches? Or allowed thousands of years of war without ever actually getting involved and *doing* anything beyond creating the occasional Godsdamned Blessed?" Tala finished with a shout.

Vail shrugged absently. "I don't know." Tala waited for him to elaborate, but as Vail yawned and closed his eyes, leaning back against the wall again, Tala was reminded of the frustrating conversation he had tried to have with the man when he was getting his weapons. He looked around to see Gazin, Ilan, and Serala all had either their heads in their hands, or had their eyes closed and jaws tensed in irritation. The rest of their group seemed as bemused as Tala as to Vail's behavior.

"Okayyy…" Tala started, taking a deep breath to try and calm himself down. "Then *how* do you know that they're lying?"

"Because the Gods can be hurt. And feel fear," Vail said with his eyes still closed, with such nonchalance that Tala thought he might've imagined it.

Tala stared at him, channeling the man's usual blank face as utter, baffled bemusement overtook whatever else he had been feeling. "And how do you—"

"Let me stop you there, laddie," came another voice from the cave. Tala looked over to see that it was Gazin who had spoken. The short, flame-haired man glanced at Vail with a complicated look that Tala couldn't even begin to decipher before focusing again on Tala.

"We'll be in here a week at this rate, so let me speed things along, eh? The whole 'Gods can feel fear' thing? I don't know about that, but that they can be hurt? That's the truth. Tell me, lad, what do you know about Marks?"

Tala blinked at the non-sequitur, his head spinning. He took another deep, calming breath and tried to answer the man. "I… not a whole lot, really. I mean, I know they are special tattoos that can give people specific powers? Something to do with the Gods blessing the ink used or something? I know they aren't common and that the Churches are really strict on keeping the means of their creation a secret."

"That's about all the important stuff right there." Gazin nodded. "But there's one very specific aspect of the Marks that the Churches keep very, *very* secret. You see, lad, it's not that the Gods bless the ink or anything like that. They are made with regular old ink, mixed with a few certain herbs and stuff, and a few drops of the key ingredient: blood. Gods' blood, to be exact."

Tala blinked. Then blinked again. He stared blankly at Gazin, feeling like he was imitating Vail. He looked around to see the others watching him curiously, waiting to see how he would react. Except Vail, who was cleaning his fingernails with a knife and seemed entirely focused on his task.

"What?"

"Yep," piped up Nuri from where he was lounging on a log against the wall. "Gods' blood, kid. You want a Fire Mark? Get some ink, get the rest of the junk, get some blood of the Fire God, mix it all together, and find someone to put it on you. 'Course, the tattooist has to be at least a Descendant, or have one with them, to make the Mark proper. Otherwise, it's just a fancy tattoo at best, or lethal at worst. Even a little bit of Gods' blood is full of power, and if it's not properly attuned or whatever, it's liable to kill you. Messily. But the important bit here is that Marks are made with Gods' blood, and if Gods can bleed, they can be hurt, and if they can be hurt, they can be killed. That's that logic you Researchers like there."

"That... actually makes a lot of sense. Wait a minute." Something Nuri said caught his attention, even over everything else. "What do you mean 'can be killed?'"

He sat there in silence as he watched them all awkwardly shuffle in place.

"Okay. You—you all are *actually* trying to kill the Gods. Wow, okay then. Right... because that's totally possible. It's not like they're *fucking immortal Gods* or anything. Do you—know how to kill them? Is there like a—like a *plan* or something? Some sort of God-killing weapon or something?"

"Not really," Serala sighed defeatedly. "But like Nuri said: if they can be hurt, they can be killed. So we know it's *possible*, just not really how to do it. And we have ideas, things that *may* work, and we're always looking for new ideas. But until we have something we're positive *will* work, we can't risk trying. Even getting near the Gods is almost impossible. So we're waiting: waiting until we're sure we have a way that will work. And once we're certain that we *can* kill them, that's when we'll strike. We'll kill one, or as many as we can, and show the world the truth about the Gods. And once people see that, we can finally begin to free the world from their tyranny, and from the Churches. If we show the people that everything is a lie; that everything that they, their friends and families, have fought and died for is a *lie*? It could start a revolution."

Tala sat back, stunned into silence. A revolution? Overthrow the Gods? *Kill* the Gods? A world without the Gods, without the Churches. Not because one had 'won' the throne and they all left, but because they weren't immortal, weren't invincible, and had all been killed? What would a world like that be like? Tala thought back to all the stories he'd heard growing up: not the ones the Church told, at least not about *their own* God, but the stories he'd been told in hidden whispers by some of the Researchers at the Institute. Of the horrors that had been committed by the other Gods and Churches: about the experiments that the Institute's researchers had been forced to conduct on people in the past. About their treatment of slaves, both their own people and those captured from the other nations. All the things that the other Churches did, that the *other* Gods allowed, which was why the Fire God was the one who *deserved* the throne, because he didn't allow such horrible things to happen.

Except he did. Tala had seen that firsthand in the Undercity, with clearly starved and beaten people being forced to work the furnaces. The woman he'd glimpsed in that little stone room, to say nothing of the countless others he hadn't seen. And he thought about himself: how he had lived as a law-abiding and innocent civilian, still barely more than a kid, who was now a hunted man simply because he had tried to stop a stranger from beating a girl in the streets. And his parents, hopefully still alive, who had spent their lives working towards the betterment of their city, their country, in absolute service of their God, and were now forced to flee, like him, leaving everyone and everything they had ever known, lest they be tortured and killed. He didn't know if he would ever see them again, or ever know if they were even still alive. He felt his heart speed up and his chest tighten, tears threatening to spill out of his eyes as he struggled to take a breath. He didn't know what to do! Everything he had ever known was being turned on its head! The Gods, the churches, his own place in the world! He might have gotten his parents killed! By the very people that they had spent their lives serving! He pulled his knees up to his chest and dropped his head between his elbows, hands grasping at his hair. He closed his eyes and in the darkness focused on his breathing: In. Hold. Out. Repeat. It was a trick his mother had taught him when he was young, the night after his first time ever seeing a fight at the arena, when he had awoken in a panic from terrible nightmares.

As his breathing evened out and his pulse slowed along with his racing thoughts, he brought his head up and opened his eyes, looking around again at those who were there with him. Vail, who was still giving him that creepy, blank stare. Serala, whose eyes were no longer empty like they had been before but were now filled with some sort of emotion Tala couldn't identify. He looked over to Gazin and Nuri and Caida and the rest who were all watching him carefully, clearly waiting to see how he would respond. He tried to think of what that response would even be. He felt stilted, jarred, like his mind, which was moving so fast before, was now having trouble formulating even the simplest of thoughts. He opened his mouth, and closed it, and opened it again, not sure what he was going to say but determined to say something.

"So," he began, voice cracking. "I'm about to become the most hunted person in the world. The Churches *may* have been lying about everything. The Gods may be false. I'm probably going to be damned for eternity just for *saying* that. And my best chance of survival is to stick with people—heretics—who have made it their lives' missions to *kill the Gods*. Do I... do I have that right?"

"Aye, lad. That about sums it up," Gazin said, giving Tala a sympathetic half-smile.

"Fuck... do I... I don't really have a choice, do I?"

"Not if you're serious about staying alive you don't. Sorry, lad."

Tala could only give Gazin a weak, sick-looking grimace in response. He felt like crawling into a hole and crying.

After another minute of silence, in which Tala tried not to faint or get sick, and the rest of the group just looked at him in pity and sorrow, Serala stood up and dusted herself off. "We've rested long enough. It's time we got moving again. Nuri, if you would?" She gestured towards the lone door in the wall.

"You got it, Boss Lady," Nuri responded; his voice somber, devoid of its usual good cheer. He swept his feet off the stump he'd been using as a footrest and, with one last concerned look at Tala, moved to the door set into the wall.

CHAPTER 11

nderas leaned against the wall, arms folded as he calmly surveyed his peers, watching as they spoke and yelled over each other in a frantic cacophony of voices. Twelve Blessed, some of the most important and powerful people in all of the Fire Country, in all of the world, packed together in one little room, biting each other's heads off. They just couldn't play nice with each other. One of the many reasons that such meetings were so incredibly rare. So rare that very few had ever even occurred in Anderas' 100 years of life. In fact, this was the first time since he had become a Blessed that such a meeting had been called. The last time Soleil had summoned all the Blessed like this (all those present in the city, that is) had been over 20 years ago, when he had received word that the Demon from Wind had been spotted inside their borders. Anderas hadn't been present for that meeting, of course, having been still just a Descendant at the time, but the consequences of that meeting he was all too familiar with. The fall of Ohena, the disaster that had 'earned' him his Blessing.

And now a meeting of the Blessed had been called again, to the surprise of everyone involved. None of them had expected it, Anderas himself included. There were no monsters from beyond the borders of the map terrorizing the world right now, no signs of another Bodylands Horde, no great tensions between nations. Well, no more than usual, at least. Anderas doubted even he would live long enough to see the day that the countries weren't actively all trying to kill each other. In fact, the world was experiencing a rare moment of (relative) peace.

And yet, here they were. All the Blessed currently in Fiahren, arguing with each other in the most opulent meeting room in the palace, waiting on High Priest Soleil himself to arrive. Most of them had no idea why they were even here, which was the (current) topic of their argument. The few who did know were easy to pick out: the first was Ishaan, one of the oldest and most respected Blessed in the world. The former Researcher was sitting quietly by himself in a chair at the side of the room, observing the others much like Anderas himself was doing. Anderas had gotten to know him quite well over the years, and despite his age, the crotchety old man would have been making himself heard whether the others wanted him to or not.

The next was Sulien, one of the more mysterious Blessed. The strange man was always playing his own game, and even Anderas often had trouble figuring out just what his goal was at any given time. Even now the eccentric and irritating man was actively participating in the heated discussion, despite Anderas' certainty that he already knew exactly why they all had been called there. His spy network was extensive and efficient after all, as Anderas well knew.

And then there was Egan and his daughter, Adena. The head of the Fatus family was engaged in a quiet yet furious discussion with his daughter; the pure, malicious rage emanating from the two gave Anderas no doubts that they were aware of what had happened earlier that day.

The last was Anderas himself, of course. His own spy network might not have been quite as large as Sulien's was, but it had yet to fail him, although for a few moments earlier in the day, he had thought it had. He had been just as surprised as anybody when the city's bells had sounded, and had had just as little idea about the cause. It was rare that Anderas found himself caught so completely unprepared for something so important, and he didn't like the feeling. When he heard the first rumors that a Blessed had been killed inside the city, he had almost dismissed them: the odds of such a thing happening were astronomical! But he had faith in his network, and when he had confirmed that Ignis Fatus had been killed—*murdered!*—deep inside the city, he had been well and truly shocked. Unfortunately, Anderas still had yet to learn the who, how, or why of it. Although he had a feeling that would be revealed by Soleil fairly soon. The Church had its own methods of learning information quickly when it wanted, methods far quicker than a hidden spy network.

And his expectations proved correct, for when Soleil finally entered the room, Anderas could read on his face that the man was troubled. The High Priest knew something about what had happened, and it was even worse than it seemed.

Anderas frowned, mind working furiously to figure out what exactly could make the murder of a Blessed even worse.

The others in the room ceased their pointless arguments as all attention turned to the High Priest. He sat down behind the ornate desk at the front of the room, reserved solely for himself. An opulent reminder in these rare meetings that, even though they were all Blessed, the High Priest was still above them. A reminder that was lost in the temperament of the spoiled beings in front of him.

"Soleil! What the Hells is going on?" spat out Fintan. Anderas fought the urge to roll his eyes: the man might have once been a terror on the battlefield, but in the centuries since his Blessing, he had become little more than a self-aggrandizing blowhard who always thought himself the most important person in the room.

Soleil looked calmly back at him, the mask of office back on his face, the worry that Anderas had seen nowhere in sight.

"Murder, Lord Fintan," Soleil replied solemnly. Anderas fought back a smirk: even in a scenario such as this, the High Priest couldn't help but add a bit of drama. Out of the corner of his eye, he caught the tensing of Egan and Adena. Soleil would have to be careful if he didn't want to further anger the head and heir of the most powerful family in the country.

"Murder?" Fintan asked, bewildered. "Why in the Hells do we care about somebody being murdered?"

Anderas' eye twitched, and he saw similar indications of annoyance from many of the others, even those who hadn't known what had happened. A Blessed meeting being called over a murder was more than enough for them to piece together the basics themselves. Fintan, though, had never been the cleverest of men.

"Because it was my son that was murdered!" roared Egan, flames erupting around him in his rage.

Despite the fury directed at him, Fintan looked back at his fellow Blessed with disdain, making it clear that he was neither intimidated nor impressed by the outburst. Anderas sighed internally; Fintan was likely the stronger of the two (and certainly believed he was, clearly), but the man believed that his martial strength meant he had nothing to fear from Egan. The damage that the Fatus family head could do to Fintan outside of combat clearly wasn't even a consideration in Fintan's head. How the Avani family was still thriving with him at their head was a wonder. Although Anderas knew that it was really the man's daughter that ran things behind his idiotic back. If that girl could get a Blessing and replace her meathead of a father, Anderas had a feeling that the Avani family would become a force to be reckoned with.

"So?" Fintan asked contemptuously. "What does one of your many spawns' death have to do with us?"

Anderas felt a spike of power come from Adena, but unlike her father, the girl contained herself. She was the one who answered, though, and anger was clear in her voice.

"It was Ignis."

One blink. Two. Anderas could almost see Fintan's mind trying to make sense of that bit of information. He could see the moment the man finally understood what everyone else present had already figured out. Dismissing the father-daughter pair as though they were little more than servants, Fintan turned back to Soleil.

"How!?" he asked, incredulous. Finally, the moron was asking a decent question. Ignis might not have been the greatest Blessed, but he was by no means weak. And he was an incredibly clever person, who had earned his Blessing through cunning instead of battlefield accomplishments, as had started becoming the norm over the last millennia. Regardless, though, he was a *Blessed*. However dumb or unskilled a Blessed was, killing one was still practically impossible without another Blessed to do it.

Soleil sighed minutely as all attention turned exclusively to him again. This was something none of them knew, with the possible exception of Sulien, but as Anderas was still standing at the back of the room, opposite from Soleil, he could only see the man's back, and that wasn't enough to know if the spymaster already knew this as well.

"A steam pipe was used to… disperse his head," Soleil reluctantly admitted. Sharp breaths of shock resounded around the room, followed by silence as they all digested that news. Anderas felt his frown reform as his mind whirled in thought. It was one of the most well-guarded secrets among the Blessed that they weren't quite as invincible as was believed, but the means to actually hurt or kill them were still very rare and specific. The implementation of steam and steam pipes in the city had been deemed a worthwhile risk hundreds of years ago, given how unlikely it was that it would ever actually be used against a Blessed, especially with any modicum of success. How had this happened?

He glanced at Ishaan. The old, old man was the one who had first created the concept of using steam as a power source and had convinced the Church of its worth, earning himself a Blessing when it had proven itself to be an even greater boon to the nation than the man had foreseen. Ishaan, however, looked at Soleil impassively, expression betraying not the slightest hint of what the creator of the steam works thought of his work being used to kill a Blessed.

"Who? Who did it? Was it *them*?" Fintan asked, the disgust in his voice making it clear who he was asking about, as if anyone present wouldn't have known anyway. Only the Dissidents would have the audacity to murder a Blessed like that. Even the other nations wouldn't use such a means; not if it meant risking the secret of the Blessed's not-so-indomitable power.

"No. It appears to have been an accident. According to the guards who were accompanying Ignis, the boy who did it was as surprised as they were."

"You have him then? The boy who killed my son?" Egan demanded.

"No." The word was met with cries of disbelief. "The boy escaped, fled from the scene. Apparently, two unknown persons appeared and dragged the boy off before the guards could react."

"Dissidents!" growled Fintan.

"We believe so. We don't know if it was coincidence or if they were tailing Ignis, but all three have vanished."

"How do you know the boy isn't a Dissident? It seems rather convenient, his killing Ignis and then disappearing with accomplices who just happened to be there?"

"Because we know who he is." Soleil sighed again. Anderas knew this must be what was troubling him so; it had barely been a few hours since the bells had rung, since Ignis had died. Whoever this boy was, he couldn't be some nameless commoner if the Church had already uncovered his identity. "His name is Tala'Keahi. He was an apprentice Researcher at the Institute. His parents have vanished as well, both of them also Researchers."

Oh. That would explain it then. A Researcher had killed a Blessed. This was going to be trouble. Predictably, chaos erupted at the announcement.

"The Institute!?" roared Egan, amid the clamor. "Those Researchers are responsible for the death of my son! I'll all of their heads on spikes!"

"Silence!" roared Soleil, power flaring out like a momentary sun before he reined it back in, the brief display more than enough to cow his subordinates as they all got a glimpse of the man who had fought the Hordes and survived. "We have already begun to interview all people who enter or leave the Institute! We have no reason to suspect that this was a coordinated action, merely an unfortunate accident! We will find the boy, and when we do, you shall have his head! You are to take no action against the Institute itself or the Researchers!"

"Why not?" growled Fintan. "Why are you only interviewing people who enter and leave that damned place anyway? We should go in there and turn the place inside out! Make sure they aren't hiding the boy in that damn fortress of theirs!"

"We cannot do that!" Soleil retorted, frustration visible.

"Why not!?" yelled Fintan. "The Institute has been left alone for far too long! They no longer have any respect for us! We should go in there and remind the lot of them that *they* serve *us*! For all we know, they've been conducting Arcane Research! How else would one of those useless fools kill one of us? I'll burn down that grand gate of theirs myself and torch every person who resists!"

"You're welcome to try, Lord Fintan," came a quiet, aged voice from outside the group of Blessed, cutting through the clamor as all attention turned to Ishaan. "But you will do so alone. And when you fail, on your own head be it."

"What?" roared Fintan. "You treacherous old bastard! You would turn on your own to protect those heretics!?"

"You misunderstand," Ishaan replied, making no attempt to hide his annoyance. "There are more reasons than you know why the Institute is allowed the freedom it enjoys. Should you attack, I would not need to stand in your way. Not even the power of a Blessed can bring down those walls. And besides, you are wrong: they have not been conducting Arcane Research. My agents are careful to monitor everything that occurs within the Institute."

"Wha—bu—" spluttered Fintan, at a loss for words at being so directly challenged by the senior Blessed.

"Explain yourself!" ordered Egan. "What do you mean a Blessed cannot bring down the walls?"

Ishaan looked towards Soleil, the High Priest looking as annoyed as Anderas had ever seen him, but he gave Ishaan a reluctant nod all the same. Anderas was riveted. What were they talking about? He had never heard any of this before. He knew that the Institute was quite possibly the single most valuable asset that the Fire Church controlled, and had always assumed that that was the reason for the many privileges granted to it and its Researchers. Was there more to the story than even he had ever suspected?

"The Institute is old, older than any of you know. As old as the Gods themselves. There are legends, ancient stories known only to those few of us who have been allowed access to such things, that say the reason the God of Fire chose this place, this city, to be his capital is because of the Institute. I do not know the truth—nobody does except the Gods themselves. But I do know, from ancient records of the Blessed wars, that Fiahren has never fallen. This city is the only capital that has never been moved: it was the first city of the Fire God, and has been the only city of the Fire God. No other God has managed to keep their original capital from their first descent into our world, except our own. And possibly the Body Gods. When enemy Blessed besieged Fiahren in those early days, it was the Institute that fought them off, alongside our Blessed ancestors, although how they did so, I cannot say. But when they broke through the walls of the city, they were stopped at the walls of the Institute. Not even an army of Blessed were able to break into that place, and it was in their futile attempts to do so that our Blessed ancestors were able to rally and crush the invaders against those same walls. So go ahead, Lord Fintan, assault the Institute as you wish. But do not expect to meet with success. And remember: the Fire God himself decreed millennia ago that the Institute was never to be treated with hostility by the Church, so whether you succeed or not, be prepared to face His wrath."

Ishaan ended his monologue to resounding silence, as all present stared at him in fascination, Soleil the sole exception. Even Anderas had been entranced by the man's words, having never heard so much as a whisper of any of these things. If nothing else, the look on Soleil's face convinced him of the truth of Ishaan's words: Soleil wouldn't be looking quite so resigned if it wasn't all true. The way that Ishaan spoke, it sounded as though the Institute existed almost as an entirely separate, sovereign entity, one that was merely allied with the Fire God. Although why the Fire God would have agreed to such a dynamic, instead of dominating the Institute entirely, was a complete mystery. It was clear that Anderas, like all the Blessed that came before him, had been negligent when it came to learning about the Institute. That would have to change.

"There you have it." Soleil said tiredly. "Even if we *could* take such drastic action against the Institute, we would likely fail. As it is, the Fire God told me himself when I first took this office that the Institute was not to be interfered with beyond the measures that are already in place. So no, we will take no further action against the Institute for Ignis' death, and we will trust in Ishaan's people to alert us if anything occurs within its walls."

Anderas could tell that none were happy with the decision, but none of them would go so directly against the orders of either Soleil or the Fire God.

"So what do we do then? If this boy who killed my brother is now with the Dissidents, how do we find him? Do we even know if he's still in the city?" asked Adena.

"We have to assume that if he hasn't already, he'll escape the city soon, and plan to flee the country. We'll scour the countryside and reinforce the borders. We've already begun having sketches of him made up that will be distributed to all cities and border posts. Additionally, I'm sending some of you with extra guards and Descendants to help secure the most likely border crossings."

That was a sensible plan. If the boy, this 'Tala'Keahi,' was being sheltered by the Dissidents, it would be almost impossible to find him within the country. Fire was too large and its forces spread too thin. And the Dissidents hadn't survived for millennia by being bad at hiding. The borders would be the best place to catch them. And sending extra Blessed there would work as a good show of force to keep the neighboring countries in line when they heard the news about Ignis.

The biggest problem was that they had no idea where the boy was going. Where the Dissidents would be taking him. As the others began discussing who would go where, Anderas stayed quiet, mulling the problem over in his mind.

The Dissidents had many hidden entrances and exits to Fiahren; he had figured that out long ago. Despite countless investigations of the Undercity over the millennia coming up empty, Anderas was certain that the Dissidents used it for their smuggling. It was simply too large, and too much of it unused, for any search to be reliable. How many secret rooms and passages existed in that ancient maze that the Church knew nothing about? Given the lockdown of the city, Anderas was willing to bet that if the boy really was with the Dissidents, they would—or already had—smuggled him out through the Undercity. But which direction had they gone?

East was unlikely. Not even the Dissidents bothered with the Wind Sea, and even the Undercity wasn't big enough to get around the burning lake. South was equally unlikely, in his opinion: even if the Undercity had secret exits to the south, it would take them too close to Wretch's Gorge, and with the heightened state of alert that Fire was now in, patrols around the gorge would increase dramatically. And even if they did manage to successfully escape south, Mud was the country that criminals flocked to, something the Dissidents would be well aware of. They would know that that border in particular would become almost impossible to pass, despite its size. The bulk of Fire's forces would be positioned there, prepared for the boy to try and flee to where so many other criminals did.

That left west and north. Despite cutting down the possible directions in half, it didn't help Anderas much. Earth, Dust, the Jungle, Metal, Light, all of them would make for decent destinations. He listened with half an ear as Egan and Adena demanded control of the Mud border forces, so blinded by their grief and rage that they were failing to consider that the boy didn't matter; it was the Dissidents themselves that would be too clever to take him there. It never failed to annoy Anderas just how easily his fellow Blessed underestimated the Dissidents.

At least the Shadow Mountains weren't a concern. That range was far too large and dangerous for even the Dissidents to risk. Same with the Desert; it held nothing but sand and slow death. Even the fractions of the great Bodyland Hordes that had entered the desert in the past had never been seen again.

But that still left Five destinations. He needed to narrow that down. Earth? Of the five, that was the most unlikely, assuming he wasn't overestimating the Dissidents the same way the others so often underestimated them. The border with Earth had always been a contentious one, as Anderas himself knew first hand from his time as a child in Serehag. It was hard for anyone to sneak across that border at the best of times, so, while he was positive that the Dissidents had their ways, he doubted they would risk it now when the border would be even more secure.

Dust was a possibility. Or at least, it would be in any other circumstance. No country was willing to risk angering Dust and losing access to their trade networks, so normally, it would be a good place to hide, since Fire hunters wouldn't follow. But with the murder of a Blessed by a normal person, especially one who might be involved with the Dissidents, even Dust would break their neutrality and assist in catching the boy. As much as the Churches tried to keep their collaborating a secret, Anderas knew that the Dissidents knew about it. So they would know that Dust wouldn't be any safer for the boy than anywhere else, which would make the already-unappealing nation entirely not worth the risk.

The Jungle would be a great place to hide the boy, at least for a short time, but getting there would be far too difficult. That border was too small and well-guarded for them to get such a wanted person across. Even if additional Blessed wouldn't be present to make it that much harder, it would be all but impossible to get the boy into the Jungle without drawing the attention of the Jungle itself to them. And the Dissidents would know that they couldn't survive in the Jungle if it knew they were there.

So due north. That must be where the boy would be going. So Metal, or Light? Light would be difficult. Crossing the three rivers or the Red Lake without being spotted was all but impossible. So they would have to go through Southtown. But if they managed to make it into Southtown, Metal would be the better choice of the two from there on anyway. And if the plan was to take the boy to Metal, there were better options than Southtown. The Metal Mountains encompassed almost the entire northern border of Fire, and there were plenty of paths into the mountains.

But not paths that would work to smuggle in a Blessed Killer. The smaller forts and settlements at the base of the Metal Mountains simply didn't see enough traffic. Not once the Metal Church learned of him and went on alert, which they would far sooner than the Dissidents could get the boy there. Which meant Firetown. It was the only settlement that was busy enough to give any hope of concealing the boy. That must be where the Disside—no. They were too cautious for that. Firetown was surrounded by nothing but mountains and the plains of Fire. If something went wrong, they would have no escape. Anderas had spent years studying everything the Fire Church knew about the Dissidents, and they would never back themselves into a corner like that unless they had no other choice. It was that same caution, that same paranoia, that had seen them survive for millennia in a world where they were so helplessly outmatched. It had to be Southtown. They could go from there to Metal or Light, and the city was one of the busiest in the world, being the central trading hub from Metal to the Southern half of the world. It would be easy to sneak a single boy in and out no matter how infamous.

"Lord Fintan, you will lead a contingent to Southtown. Same as Firetown, Metal should be willing to host you in the city given the circumstances, and Elidor should be happy to accommodate given your friendship with the man. It wouldn't surprise me if Light also sends a delegation to the city, so don't antagonize them. We have bigger problems to worry about right now," Soleil told Fintan sternly.

Well this won't do, thought Anderas. He couldn't deny that, potential problems with Light aside, Fintan was a good choice for Southtown as he did have a longstanding friendship with Elidor, the Blessed Lord of Southtown. There weren't many people whose strength in combat the two respected more than each other's, despite their differing loyalties to their Gods. But if he was right and the Dissidents were bringing the boy to Southtown, it was going to be Anderas there to meet them. Not the pompous, egotistical, idiotic Fintan. Anderas had ambitions, and this Blessed Killer was the best opportunity he would likely ever have to achieve them.

"No." Anderas spoke clearly, calmly looking at Soleil. To his credit, the High Priest merely raised an eyebrow back at him in response. "I will go to Southtown."

Anderas couldn't deny feeling a small thrum of pride at the way his fellow Blessed didn't immediately object to his overriding decisions that had already been made. Despite being the youngest in the room by a fair margin, he had already attained a reputation far greater than any of them, possibly even greater than Soleil's.

"Why?" Fintan asked, bewildered as to why Anderas would usurp his posting. Anderas' eyes flicked over to him briefly, and in doing so, he was able to glimpse the faces of most of the others. They were largely looks of surprise and confusion, except for two: Ishaan was studying him intensely, and Anderas did his best not to betray any of his inner thoughts. There were few people alive who could read somebody as well as the ancient ex-Researcher. The other was, of course, Sulien, who was watching Anderas as though he were the main event of some great circus, the creep.

"I believe that there is a strong likelihood of the boy going there," he responded calmly.

"If you think that's where he's going, then I should be the one to go!" Egan demanded.

"Oh? This boy has already proven himself a danger to us, and now it seems that he has Dissidents helping him, which will only make dealing with him even more difficult. Do you really think you would do a better job of ensuring his death than I?" he asked mildly with a small, friendly smile on his face. He couldn't help but be amused at how uncomfortable his question had made the others. Youngest he might be, but they all respected Anderas, whether they wanted to or not. Soleil aside, none of those present could match his magical prowess, and they all knew it. He was *the* Anderas Anto, after all.

"The last time you were sent to deal with such a dangerous person, it didn't go so well, did it?"

Soft gasps were heard from their audience, but Anderas paid them no mind. He stared Egan dead in the eye, betraying no emotion. The head of the Fatus family was paling quickly, his words, said so thoughtlessly in his anger, catching up to him. Adena quickly stepped away from her father, her face even paler than his, eyeing Anderas fearfully, terrified of his reaction to the slight.

He was tempted; he couldn't deny it. Egan might have been powerful, with far more years than Anderas in both life and Blessing, but his mastery over his magic was far inferior to Anderas' own. Anderas could crush him in an instant, before any of the others could hope to stop him. They all knew it. Even Soleil, the High Priest tense, prepared to intervene the moment a move was made, wouldn't be fast enough to save Egan if Anderas decided to kill him. Oh, he was tempted. But he wouldn't survive either. Not with Soleil there. Not with Fintan and Ishaan as well. Anderas had plans, and he would not throw his life away over such a little thing. But he hadn't become *the* Anderas Anto by sheer force of power. He could strike back all the same.

"Indeed it didn't. It is unfortunate that I had not received my Blessing at the time. Perhaps with a *competent* Blessed present, things would have gone differently, wouldn't you agree?"

And just as expected, the fear was overtaken by rage. It wasn't subtle by any means, but Anderas didn't really care. Egan's beloved uncle had been one of the three Blessed who had fled in the face of the Demon, and neither the man nor his family had yet to recover from that shame. It was foolish of Egan to bring that event up, especially to Anderas. Time to twist the knife.

"How is your uncle doing, by the way? Since he isn't here, I assume he must still be the lord of Motomur? Such a... *prestigious*, appointment. You must be so proud of him." Despite his calm and collected appearance, Anderas reveled in the pure rage emanating from Egan. The man's face was almost as red as his flames, as was his daughter's. Or would be, if their flames were actually present. Anderas felt a vicious thrill run up his spine as he used his power to smother both of theirs, keeping their flames from manifesting despite their anger. He watched on, amused, as their anger warred with their growing fear: even for Blessed of the same element, suppressing another Blessed's power was extraordinarily difficult, bordering on the impossible. For him to be suppressing both of them at the same time was a feat the likes of which even Soleil couldn't match. And as the seconds passed, he basked in their growing looks of horrified despair, as they were brutally reminded of just how inferior they were.

"Enough, Anderas!" snapped Soleil, spurring Anderas to release his two compatriots as he languidly turned back to face the High Priest, giving him a respectful nod of acquiescence. That was the most admonishment that Soleil would give him. The High Priest himself had been—almost—as angry as Anderas at Egan's barb, but there was only so much infighting that the man would tolerate, regardless of his personal feelings on the matter.

The High Priest sighed and closed his eyes for a moment before opening them as he once again donned the mask of his office.

"Anderas will go to Southtown. Any objections? No? Lord Egan, Lord Fintan?" Egan stayed silent, glaring hatefully at Anderas.

"No, no. Fine with me!" Fintan earnestly shook his head. For all that the man had let himself go, he still respected power above all else, and seeing Anderas' display of sheer, overwhelming power had cowed the man out of even considering challenging the decision. Anderas almost smirked. Despite how quickly it had occurred, and the complete lack of any sort of indicator as to what had been happening, he knew that every person in that room had felt him use his power to smother the Fatus'. A good reminder to all of them as to just why he was *The* Anderas Anto. Now all he had to do was arrange for his trip to Southtown and figure out how he was going to handle the Metal Church, Elidor, and his advisors.

The door that Tala assumed led to the outside world looked rather out of place compared to the rest of the small cave that they were in. While the walls, floor, and ceiling all consisted of densely packed dirt, with some roots crawling through and poking out, the door looked to have been made out of a combination of stone and metal. There was no handle, but it didn't seem to need one, as Nuri simply put both hands on the left side of the door and pushed, causing it to slowly swing open, allowing dim sunlight to wash into the cave.

Judging from the amount of light, and its color, Tala figured that it must be late afternoon. It was clearly still daytime, as the light streaming into the cave was definitely sunlight, but the color was more reminiscent of dusk: a dim display of mottled oranges and reds instead of the bright yellow that was common for a midday sun. He had been worried that it would already be night by the time they left the Undercity and so was relieved to see at least a bit of sunlight, even if it likely wouldn't last much longer.

He was eager to go outside and leave the dark, claustro-phobic conditions behind. The cloying, stale air of the small cavern was making it far too easy to let the weight of his new reality crush him. Even the dying light of the setting sun would help chase away the oppressive thoughts threatening to consume him. He was also, despite the circumstances, excited for his first foray into the world beyond the walled confines of Fiahren. Like many that were born in the city, he had never left it: everything he knew of life beyond its walls was either the product of rumor or random bits of knowledge he had gained from his time spent at the Institute. He watched with mixed emotions as Nuri poked his head through the gap he had created and looked around before withdrawing it and pushing the door fully open.

As Nuri cautiously ventured forth through the doorway and into the open, the rest of the group rose and followed behind him, hands ready on weapons and senses on full alert in case there was an ambush waiting for them.

Tala followed at the tail end of the exodus, with only Serala behind him. By the time he reached the door, the others seemed to have decided that they were safe, for they were no longer holding themselves tense and prepared. As Tala stepped through the doorway, his first sight of the out-side world was… grass. A sloping wall of grass. He looked around and saw that the door they had gone through was situated in the base of a large hill. Surrounding them on all sides, including directly in front of the doorway, were more hills. They were all covered in a light layer of grass with some trees and brush and large rocks scattered about. He could see the dappled sunlight streaming over and through the hills from the left, which, given the time of day it was, meant that must be west. They certainly were north of the city then: right in the middle of the Burning Hills. Even though Tala had never left Fiahren before, he could tell that much because the Burning Hills were the only hills within days of the city, and, as tired as he was, Tala knew that they hadn't spent *that* long in the Undercity.

He turned to the right and followed Gazin on a small trail that ran around the base of the hill in front of them, walking in a single-file line. The light and fresh air, as well as the novelty of being outside the city, did wonders for Tala's mood. He pushed away the fear and damning thoughts as he marveled at the feel of walking with grass beneath his feet instead of the cobbled stone that made up most of the city's streets. It felt solid still but strange, less firm and unyielding than he was used to. He couldn't help but bend his knees and change up his steps as he walked, experimenting with the strangeness of it all. After a few moments of this, he stiffened as he remembered that he was not, in fact, at the very back of their group and that Serala had followed behind him as they left the cave.

Feeling heat swiftly climbing up his neck, he sheepishly turned and looked at her, to see her watching him in grinning bemusement. He awkwardly mumbled his defense. "I've never left the city before. Grass is—walking on it is… different."

Her confusion left as her smile settled. "You'll get used to it, I'm sure." Tala nodded in embarrassment and turned back around, shuffling awkwardly to catch up to the group.

He followed as they weaved between the hills, large and small, keeping the sun on their left as much as they could as the light continued to grow dimmer and dimmer.

It wasn't much later when, with only a few dim rays of sunlight left, the group stopped in a small stretch of (mostly) flat land nestled amongst the hills. Dunlop, the-man-of-a-thousand-weapons (that was definitely a mace on his belt, with some sort of wicked-looking hammer on the other side), called out that the light was too low to safely continue and they'd make camp there for the night. Gratefully, Tala sank to the ground, exhausted from the long day. He watched as the others, instead of collapsing as he did, started moving around the clearing, sweeping aside rocks and debris and pulling things out of their packs. It took his tired mind longer than he would have liked to realize that they were setting up an actual campsite.

He felt awkward sitting on the side doing nothing while the others were busy, but he had no idea how to set up a camp in the wilds. No one seemed bothered by his lack of contribution, though, and he saw that he wasn't the only one not doing much. The alluring woman who had volunteered for their journey, Caida, was resting as well, sitting on a log that two of the men had carried over from beside the clearing. On the log next to her sat Alina, the *Light Awakened*, who had a small pile of stones at her feet and one in her hand that she seemed intently focused on.

She held the stone in one hand and moved her other hand along it, as though painting patterns across its surface with her fingers. After a minute of this, she placed the stone aside and picked up another one, repeating the process.

Tala watched her odd work, curious about what she was doing as the rest of their companions continued bringing logs to circle a small fire in the center of the clearing. With a loud thump, he saw Gazin and Lito drop another log just beside him. Gazin sat on the log and offered Tala a gentle smile. "Wanna join me up here, lad? It's not much, but it's more comfortable than the ground."

With a nod, Tala half-rose and slid onto the log beside the man, still watching Alina's strange actions. "You know what she's doing there?" Gazin asked him after a few moments. At Tala's negative reply, he explained. "She's enchanting the rocks. When she's done, we'll place them around the perimeter of the camp. They'll keep the light from the fire in so we won't have to worry about anybody seeing it, even if they're just a hill over. Useful bit of trickery she managed to work out. Makes staying hidden in the wilds a much more pleasant experience."

Tala's eyes widened, and he looked at Alina and her rocks with a newfound respect. He'd heard about enchanting before, but it was supposed to be an extremely difficult and rarely used form of magic, especially when done to an object that wasn't already associated with the element being used on it. To be putting a light enchantment on random rocks lying about was no mean feat from what he'd heard.

He shared his thoughts with Gazin, who nodded. "Aye, it's no simple thing what she's doing. But it's one of the perks of having her with us. Even among Awakened, she's exceptionally skilled, especially for her age. She's barely just started her second decade and was Awakened years ago. Most of the great families won't even consider Awakening their members till they've reached their mid-twenties at least. She's a rare talent for sure. You won't find many in any of the nations who can do something like that so easily. She can do in minutes what would take most hours."

"How did she get so good?" Tala questioned.

"Talent and practice." The man shrugged. "She's from one of—well… what used to be one of the most prominent of the great Light families. They're all gone now, though. She's the last one left, but they were a family known for their skill, and she was raised with high standards. Picked up enchanting after she joined us, though. Doubt her family would've considered such a 'menial' skill to be worthy of them."

"What happened to them? Her family, I mean?"

"Politics. Same as anywhere. They put on a show of them noble and Descendent families being united together under their Church and the Gods and all that rot, but behind closed doors, they compete with each other just like anyone. Her family got a bit too powerful, made too many enemies and too few allies. I don't know all the details. It ended with them all dead, though, either killed where they stood or executed later on. She's the only one who escaped."

"Gods," Tala muttered, eyes wide and full of horror as he looked at her. "That's horrible."

"For her, yeah. Not so bad for the rest of us," the man said quietly.

Tala looked at him aghast. "What? How the Hells could you say that?"

"Don't get me wrong, lad," the man replied, holding his hands up in peace. "It is horrible, and I feel for the lass, I truly do. But her family weren't good people. Most of those families aren't, in any of the countries. They're the people we're fighting against." He gestured to the whole clearing. "I know it sounds bad, but their destruction is the exact type of thing we want. Their getting wiped out was a win for us, even if it wasn't our doing that caused it. And we got an exceptionally skilled Awakened on our side out of it; she's probably one of the most talented Descendants alive right now, the Anderas Anto of her generation. Give it a few years and she might even be able to challenge a Blessed. A less skilled one maybe, but still. That lass is probably one of our greatest assets, and she's devoted to the cause. Even if she can still be a bit of a spoiled princess at times, she's worth having around."

Tala asked something that he'd been wondering for a while. "Is that why they keep calling her princess then? Because she acts like she's better than them or something?"

"Mostly, yeah." The man nodded. "From what I've heard, it was worse when she first joined up. Not that you can really blame her; it's how she was raised. Still made her a hard person to like, though. She's actually not that bad now, if you ask me. But I grew up around people like that, so I've probably got a higher tolerance for that sort of behavior than most."

Tala glanced at him sidelong. "Did that happen to you too? Raised in a noble family?"

The jovial man gave a dark chuckle. "Not exactly. I was born a slave to one of the noble families in Earth Country. I was 'in their service' for about three decades before I was freed by the Dissidents. Joined up with them then and there and I've been with them ever since."

Tala gave the man a confused look: he barely even looked to be in his thirties, but he spoke like those events had taken place a long time ago. Gazin, seeing his confusion, gave him a mischievous grin. "Thinkin' I look a bit young for that, eh?" He chuckled. "I'm a Fleshy. Unawakened, but that's not as important for us Bodymages. I'm well over 100 years old now. Closer to 150, really. Spent the last century or so doing what I could to help fight the bastards who made the first 30 a living hell."

Tala stared at him wide-eyed. He'd heard that Bodymages could extend their own lives beyond even the normal extended lifespan of a Descendant, but to see a man who apparently hadn't aged for 100 years was a bit beyond what he'd expected. He knew it might be rude, but he couldn't stop himself from asking, "How long do you expect to live?"

Thankfully, the man didn't seem offended at his question and responded happily, "That's actually a hard one to answer. Assuming I don't end up getting killed somehow, which is quite likely really, given my line of work, it really depends on me." Seeing Tala's confused look, he continued. "Now let's see. You know the average lifespans, right? For most ordinary folk, like yourself, normal lifespan's around about 70 years, right? Varies a bit based on country, city, things like that, but that's the average. Now, most Descendants break 100 years easy, and some even get as far as 200. Most Awakened break 300. Some have even made it to 400. Blessed live 400 years easy, with most making it to at least 600. Some have even been known to make it another hundred or two beyond that, and there have even been some known to live over a thousand years.

"Things are different for us Bodymages, though: our base lifespan's the same as the rest, but our abilities let us keep going even longer. Blood and Bone wielders can usually give themselves an extra one or 200 years, Awakened three or four. Blessed I assume can go significantly longer, but you'd have to go into the Bodylands to learn that. I don't think anybody this side of the Dust Wall knows how long they can live. But us Fleshies, even among the Bodymages, we're a bit special: we can keep our bodies strong and healthy for practically as long as we want, if we've got the skill for it. It's almost unheard of for one of us to die of old age, even us Unawakened. If one of us manages to live long enough without getting killed or intentionally killing ourselves, then we usually end up dying from accidental suicide."

Tala blinked. "Accidental suicide?"

Gazin nodded. "It's all about the brain." The man sighed. "Except for the Gods, all our bodies break down over time, and the longer you live, the faster it happens. The Blessed go the slowest, followed by Descendants, Awakened, and then Unawakened. Bodymages can slow things down even further, if they want to, but there's only so much Blood and Bone can do when it comes to the brain. Us Fleshies, though, we can repair ourselves pretty much indefinitely, fix anything that breaks down, if we even let it get to that point in the first place. We can even keep our bones healthy without too much trouble. But the brain is different: messing with it is uniquely dangerous, and fixing anything wrong with it is difficult, even for us. The older we get, the faster it degrades, and the harder it becomes to fix. So those rare few of us who live long enough, they usually end up dying by trying to fix something in their brain and making a mistake. There's no fixing something that instantly kills you. Even if it just leaves you mentally impaired, that's usually the end. I'm quite good, though, if I do say so myself, so I doubt I'll live long enough for that to really become a risk," he finished flippantly.

Tala sat back deep in thought. He was barely even 18. He couldn't imagine what it would be like to live over a hundred years and still potentially have a few hundred to go! And the man had been fighting as one of the Dissidents since before Tala's own parents had even been born.

"What's that like, then? Having already lived past what most people ever will, and still having so much longer ahead of you?"

The man gave him an appraising look. "Well, it's very different, I can tell ya that. Not many of us that actually go out in the field die of old age. But just the time I have lived has given me a different perspective on things. And people. I've seen some great and amazing people in my time; and some useless, terrible, and evil ones. You're the first civilian I've seen kill a Blessed, though, so congratulations there!" He gave Tala a respectful nod, who ducked his head in an awkward acknowledgement.

The more they talked, the more Tala wanted to ask the man, but he spoke up before Tala got the chance to voice another question. "Oh! Looks like the food's done. C'mon, lad, we could both do with some hot food after today." The man rose and strode over to the fire that had been lit while they were talking. There were a few creatures speared on sticks roasting over it. Tala was surprised; he thought it would have taken longer to hunt down enough animals to feed a group of ten. As he approached the fire, he cautiously sidled up next to Serala to ask her about it. So far he liked the girl, and she had been friendly towards him, but their conversation in the cave, when she had threatened—offered—to kill him still lingered in his mind.

"Dunlop did some hunting while we were setting up," she explained after Tala had worked up the courage to ask her about the food.

He looked over towards Dunlop: the man was cleaning the hides of the animals that were roasting over the fire. Despite being the one who had caught the food, he seemed to have no interest in it, being completely engrossed in his work cleaning the hides.

"Huh. I thought it would've taken longer to catch all that."

"Normally, it would, yeah. But he's incredibly good at it, a natural according to Vail. And Gazin says he's one of the best hunters he's ever seen, and that's saying something."

"Oh?"

She smirked. "Gazin's been around a long time. A compliment like that isn't one he gives often."

As they spoke, they each received a sharpened stick stabbed through a few cuts of meat, prepared and given to them by Ilan. Nodding their thanks to him, they continued their conversation as they sat on one of the nearby logs.

"He told me about that. Over 100 years old already and still hundreds left to go."

"Oh? Is that what you two were talking about?" she asked.

"Mhmm." He nodded. "He also told me about Alina, and what happened to her family."

Her face darkened at that. "Ah. Yeah. You shouldn't bring up that around her, though. Or Lito for that matter."

"Lito? Why not?"

"He's the one who helped her escape when her family was purged. He was spying on her family for us, disguised as a servant. When it all started, he snuck her out and brought her to us. He's stuck with her ever since. One day, she might even realize why." She smirked.

He looked over to where Alina and Lito were sitting on their own log, eating in silence. He noticed that Lito kept glancing at her, though she seemed oblivious. "How long ago was that?" he asked Serala.

She looked up with pursed lips, thinking. After a few seconds, she spoke. "About four years now, I think? We've worked with them a few times. Her talents are too good. Lito's really useful himself. He's good at disguising himself and getting people to trust him. Which is great for information-gathering or assassinations."

Tala nearly choked on the slice of… whatever animal he was eating. He kept forgetting that as nice as everybody here had been so far, they were still rebels and terrorists: topics such as assassination were probably normal for them. Before he could respond, though, Nuri called out to Serala, causing the whole camp to focus on her response.

"Hey, Boss Lady! Now that we're out and everything, where exactly are we headed? S'there a plan or somethin'?"

Serala raised a brow at the man before replying. "For now we're going to Southtown. We won't be there long, though; just enough so we can get whatever supplies we need and any info worth hearing. If things pan out, we'll head into the mountains. We should be able to lay low in Metal for a while. We'll figure out our next move from there."

There were nods from around the camp. Nobody seemed particularly opposed to the plan, or at least willing to voice their objections if they were. As everyone went back to eating and their conversations, Tala sat forward, hunching his shoulders as he looked into the fire. Southtown. Metal. Whatever would be next. Even as loose as the plan was, hearing it out loud made it seem just a bit more real.

Tala sat, silently staring into the fire as he wrestled with his new future, until activity around the camp caught his attention. He looked up and saw that everyone was laying out bedrolls, one each from the packs that Hagan had given them. He looked into his own and found a simple bedroll for himself. Following their lead, he rolled it out near enough to the fire to feel its warmth and lay down, feeling the exertion and emotional stress of the day weighing down on him like a blanket. He drifted off to sleep to the noise of the still-crackling fire and the light of the evening and night moons above. The glistening stars were scattered about them, more visible than they had ever been inside the city.

CHAPTER 13

Gazin frowned in thought as he watched Tala, the Blessed Killer, go to sleep. In all his years, and all his travels, Gazin had never seen nor even heard of a normal killing a Blessed. Even the Demon hadn't accomplished that, although Gazin had always wondered if that had been intentional. He had never understood how that man did the things he did, the annoying bastard being as secretive as he was, but killing a Blessed certainly seemed like something he could have done. But Tala wasn't anything like that.

No, this kid, Tala, wasn't anything special. Not by the Dissidents' standards, anyway. He was clever, sure. Intelligent and wise for his age. Quick-witted and could function decently under pressure, at least for someone so unused to it, but none of that was exactly rare. To make things worse, the lad was kind. He was nice, had a good heart, and believed in doing the right thing. Admirable traits, maybe, but not ones that would serve him well now. He had clearly lived a nice, sheltered life. One where he could grow up to become a nice, kind person. The type of person who would interfere if he saw a prostitute being abused in an alley. The type of person who wouldn't survive long in the life that now awaited him.

Gazin sighed as he tilted his head up, looking at the stars and the two moons. He had been involved in recruiting many different people to the Dissidents' cause over the decades: former slaves, prostitutes, soldiers, criminals, guards, even nobles and other Descendants. All types of people, from psychopaths to (wannabe) heroes, Gazin had helped bring into their endless fight. Tala was the kind that he hated recruiting the most: innocent, naive, kind, *good*. When those types of people joined, it always brought an ache to his heart, for he knew they wouldn't last. Far too often, they died early. Those that survived changed. And Gazin could rarely bring himself to look upon the people that they became. Even after 100 years, he didn't know which outcome he hated more: their dying well before their time, or surviving to become a cruel reminder of the person that they used to be. It was always the kindest people who, when broken, became the cruelest. The nicest who became the meanest. The best who became the worst.

And he liked Tala so far—he really did. He would do his best to keep the lad alive; he was far too important to let him die. But he wished he didn't have to. Tala was in a position nobody had ever been in before, and Gazin was certain that if he was to survive, he would have to change. Change more than anybody Gazin had ever seen. He was certain to die otherwise.

Gazin's eyes flicked over the members of their little group, his enhanced brain easily calling forth everything he knew about each one of them: their first meeting, every conversation they had ever had, every rumor and tale he'd heard, and all of their little quirks and habits he'd observed for himself. This was no motley collection, haphazardly thrown together in a desperate attempt to keep the lad safe. Vail would have never allowed it.

First there was Gazin himself, of course. And he was not too humble to admit that he was likely one of the most dangerous people alive. There was a reason Bodymages were allowed to live only as slaves, after all. And in the centuries since the last great Bodylands Horde, the world had largely forgotten just why Bodymages were so feared. Oh, they all heard tales of the Hordes, but they always focused on the monsters, the abominations, not on the people who created them. If it weren't for the Bone Merc having killed the Demon, Gazin sometimes wondered if the world would have forgotten about the danger of Bodymages entirely, save for those few people still alive who fought against, and *survived*, the last great Horde. As it was, because of the Bone Merc, the world only truly remembered how dangerous Bone wielders were, and Blood and Flesh wielders became remembered as sideshows, and not as the living nightmares that they truly were. So yes, Serala hadn't brought Gazin along simply for his healing abilities, or because she liked his company. That girl was pragmatic to a fault, and he knew she brought him because if things went sideways, there were few people in the world who could protect that boy like he could.

It was a strange experience then, for Gazin, so used to being the most dangerous person around, to be surrounded by people who were as dangerous as he was. Not all of them of course: Lito, as skilled as he was in his own areas, wasn't a particularly dangerous child. He had great potential, but his skills lay in softer arts: deception, information, planning. But the boy had worked hard over the years to at least be able to hold his own in a fight, so at least he would be more of a boon than a liability if things did go sideways.

Nuri was similar, if a bit more dangerous. The man was a thief and a smuggler and all-around rapscallion who would rather avoid combat than face it, but he was no stranger to a fight and could hold his own far better than one might expect. Gazin knew that the playful, amorous, kind-hearted man had left a rather impressive trail of bodies in his wake over the years. There was a reason he and Caida were so close, after all, beyond their mutual love for, well… love. The woman had turned seduction and pillow talk into a proper art form, and had worked her way into the bed and confidence of just about every significant person in Fiahren. She was careful to avoid the attentions of the Blessed, though: even she didn't have a perfect record, and if a Blessed got suspicious or wanted her to become their own 'exclusive' mistress, she couldn't get rid of them quite so easily as she had disposed of her former 'problematic' paramours. Still, it was often joked that there wasn't a person alive she couldn't seduce, and Gazin wouldn't be surprised if that was the truth (barring a few rare exceptions that he knew). So even though she was no longer in her 'lair' of Fiahren, Gazin didn't doubt that her skillset could quite possibly save them all from ruin. Knowledge was power after all. And she had left enough bodies behind that he wouldn't be too worried about her in a fight, either.

So all three of them—Nuri, Lito, and Caida, despite not really being 'fighters'—Gazin would consider exceptionally dangerous people. Albeit in different ways than most might think.

And as for Alina and Dunlop, well, he didn't really even have to think about that. One was an Awakened Light Descendant, a prodigy who even from her earliest years had been expected to one day become the High Priest of Light. The girl had her issues, but she was about as dangerous as any non-Blessed could be. And Dunlop was a former Wild Guard who, even in that legendary organization, had been considered one of the best. An organization of people with such tremendous martial prowess that even the Churches admitted they could threaten Descendants, despite not having any powers of their own. Any person who *even the Churches admitted* could fight one on one with a Descendant and emerge the victor was somebody who could be trusted to handle themselves no matter the situation. Unless they ran into a Blessed, of course. Nothing could be expected from anybody, no matter how great they were, in that situation. Unless they were the Demon or Bone Merc, of course. His eyes drifted over Tala's sleeping form once again.

And then there were Those Three: Vail, who as far as Gazin was concerned didn't even count; Ilan, who he actually didn't know much about, much to his chagrin, although he certainly had his suspicions; and Serala. Poor, dear Serala. Taken in by Vail of all people when she was still so young, so traumatized by what had happened, what she had seen that day. Gazin doubted he would ever not be amazed, and oh so proud, of the young woman she had become. How she had grown despite her trauma, despite being raised by *Vail*. And eventually Ilan, when the giant man had somehow joined their weird little family. And even though she had her quirks—her *Vailisms*, as Gazin liked to call them, such as that episode in the cave where she had—*offered*—to kill Tala, she really had grown into a wonderful young woman. And a few quirks were to be expected of people who lived lives such as theirs. At least she didn't go around slaughtering innocent people for the fun of it, like he had first feared would happen to her all those years ago. So assuming that Ilan was even half as dangerous as Vail and Serala were (which Gazin felt positive of if the man had survived living with those two for so long), this really was one of the most dangerous groups of people Gazin had ever seen. And that was just the nine of them.

His eyes once again turned to the slumbering form of Tala, the boy who killed a Blessed. The lad was in about as deep a sleep as he could be, which didn't surprise Gazin a bit given the day he'd had. He doubted the boy had ever had a day even a fraction as stressful or exhausting as this one had been. And yet, he had done the impossible. A privileged, academic, painfully naive young man had—entirely by accident—done something that would put his name on par with the likes of the Demon from Wind and the Bone Merc. Gazin had heard the quick story from Serala of what had happened, the bare details as much as she knew them, but he was desperately eager to hear the tale from the lad's own mouth. To learn about what he had been thinking when he faced down Ignis and found a way to kill him. Did he know something special? Did the Researchers of Fire have some sort of knowledge about the Blessed and their weaknesses that somehow the Dissidents weren't aware of? It couldn't have purely been just luck; Gazin firmly believed that. It would have happened before if it was that simple, wouldn't it? No, he was certain the boy knew things. Things that had helped him kill Ignis. Things that could help all of them to kill more Blessed. Even if Tala didn't realize yet how the things he knew could be used, just how world-changing his knowledge could be, it was in there, just waiting to be uncovered. Waiting for him to pull it out and create a new world. Gazin would do everything he could to make that possible.

But all of it, the entire new world that Gazin was dreaming of, relied on Tala. The lad had to be kept alive, had to be kept safe, had to be given the opportunity to utilize that knowledge. An almost impossible task with all of Fire, and soon to be all of the world, hunting him down. But if Tala was going to survive the things to come, this little group would give him the best chance to do that. The best chance to survive, to live long enough to become a person who could survive.

Tala would live. He would grow, and he would change. This kind, smart, curious lad who was still so innocent despite being already near full grown would have to grow to become a person he could have never imagined. Change into a man who could survive in this cruel world of theirs. Not just survive, no, but thrive. Grow and change into a man who could, a man who *would*, bring this awful world to its knees. Gazin looked to the sky, to the shining stars and bright steady glow of the moons, and wept. And he couldn't help but wish that little Serala had just slit the lad's throat in that cave.

CHAPTER 14

"Unghh," groaned Tala, as he slowly regained consciousness. He didn't want to be awake; he was still tired, and so very sore. These things, along with the hard, uncomfortable ground that his bedroll lay on, let him know that the events of the previous day hadn't been a dream. That, and the sounds of nature: the singing of birds and the sounds of people moving around him, rustling as they packed up the camp and ate the leftover meat from their dinner the night before.

He groaned again as he rolled over and opened his eyes. It was barely dawn, with streaks of orange and purple racing across the sky, barely illuminating the clearing they were in. It was far too pretty a sight in Tala's opinion, given the sharp contrast with the way he was feeling. At least he hadn't had any nightmares. He supposed he had simply been too exhausted for his sleeping mind to bother with their creation. The things he had done and seen though were already haunting his waking mind. It would only be a matter of time before they invaded his sleeping one too. He was not looking forward to that.

He gave one more groan and painstakingly rose to his feet. His muscles protested in agony, unaccustomed to the strenuous activity of the previous day. He stretched his back as much as he could manage before stumbling his way into joining the people circled around the small fire pit. They greeted him tiredly as he plopped down on a log next to Nuri, who passed him some strips of meat that had been left to smoke through the night.

He tore into the strips, eager to satisfy his empty stomach. It wasn't the tastiest of breakfasts, devoid as it was of any sort of seasoning, but he couldn't really bring himself to care. He'd have to get used to such meals over the coming weeks anyway. It did make him miss the food that was always available at the Institute.

Through tired eyes, Tala examined the rest of the party, vaguely curious as to how they were handling the morning. Vail, Serala, Ilan, and Dunlop all seemed to be fine: they were already wide awake and moving around the camp, removing what signs they could of having been there. From what little he knew of them, he figured that they were used to long, hard days of travel. The rest of the group were circled around the fire with him, each looking different degrees of tired, although all of them still looked a fair bit better than Tala felt.

As the others finished eating, they broke from the circle to continue the effort to pack up the camp. Tala was not far behind. He didn't have much to gather for himself, just the bedroll he had slept on, the cloak he had used as a blanket, and the weapons that Vail had given him before they left, which he had removed to sleep.

Eventually, the camp was fully cleared; with all the logs having been moved back out of the clearing and the small fire pit dismantled and covered with dirt. To his untrained eyes, the clearing looked as though no one had ever been there, and he hoped that the illusion wasn't merely due to his inexperience.

As they were making their final preparations to leave the clearing and continue their journey, he noticed that Gazin was standing behind Caida, with his hands on her shoulders and eyes closed. When he removed his hands and opened his eyes, she rolled her shoulders before smiling at him. He nodded back and made his way over to Tala, who gave him a quizzical look.

Answering his unspoken question, Gazin explained. "We've got a long day ahead of us, lad. I can get rid of that soreness for ya. Just stand still there. It'll only take a moment."

Tala did as bid, and Gazin rested his hands on the back of his shoulders. He could feel a wave spreading throughout his muscles, simultaneously burning hot and freezing cold. He wasn't sure whether the feeling was pleasant or not, but the aching soreness of his body began to recede, and in less than a minute, he was feeling almost as good as new, with only a small amount of easily ignorable ache left.

With a huff of laughter, he turned around and spoke, stretching his neck as he did. "Thank you! That's so much better. Almost all the soreness is gone!"

Gazin nodded, pleased with his response. "Good. I left a little bit: it'll help you get used to it faster, and you can't always rely on having someone like me around to do this sort of thing. The others don't need me to do this at all, 'cept for

Caida, 'cause she doesn't normally go in for this sort of travel. Nuri tried to get me to do it for him, but he doesn't need it: he's just a hedonistic bastard. Give it some time, though, living like this, and you won't be needing it either."

Serala called to them, and they moved over towards where the group was starting to filter out of the clearing, resuming their trek northeast. There was no trail to follow, so the group just followed in a loose line whoever was at the front. Mostly they were being led by Nuri, who seemed to be quite familiar with the hills that they were traveling through, and Dunlop, who was particularly good at finding paths either through or around some of the more difficult bits of terrain.

Tala usually trailed at the tail end of the group. Being the most unfamiliar with traveling through the wilds—or at all, really—he had the most trouble with navigating and keeping his footing in general, but especially in the more treacherous areas, which caused him to go slower than the rest. Caida seemed to be the next least experienced, often staying only shortly ahead of him, but clearly still more used to it than he was.

On occasion, Dunlop, Serala, or Ilan broke off from the group and scouted ahead, letting them know if there was anything of note in their path. Sometimes, they would return with a small sack or two filled with nuts, berries, or eggs, which would cook in their shells when shaken hard. They could've used some salt, in Tala's opinion, but given the circumstances, he couldn't bring himself to complain: the only reason they even had access to foods that could cook themselves was because they were still close to Fiahren, and well within the range of the Fire God's ambient power. The further they got from the seat of the Fire God, the rarer such things would become.

While trying to peel off a particularly stubborn piece of shell, Tala stumbled over something, barely keeping his feet thanks to a quick hand from Gazin. Gazin often stayed with Tala, keeping a watchful eye and giving him occasional advice on where to step so that he didn't trip and fall or brush against a dangerous plant. While Tala had studied fire nettles at the Institute, he hadn't recognized the agonizing plant growing in the wild, and if not for Gazin's assistance, he would have spent the rest of that day with a burning pain all along his arm. Gazin was clearly experienced at trekking through the wilderness, and his assistance went a long way in keeping Tala safe and on pace with the rest of the group.

Despite the hardships of traveling through such unfamiliar terrain, a part of Tala was enjoying the experience. As someone who had never left the walled confines of Fiahren, his experience with nature was limited to the gardens at the Institute and stories he had heard growing up about the outside world. To be out in it was like a dream come true: with the sounds of birds and critters hiding in the brush, the tinkle of water from the streams they passed, even the smell of the air was different. Even if the circumstances that had led him there were less than ideal, Tala was having a hard time not feeling at least a little happy on their journey.

As they made camp the second night, it was decided that Tala needed to be taught how to properly wield the sword and daggers that Vail had given him, for while every member of their company would do their utmost to protect him should the need arise, the ability to defend himself would likely become necessary. So it was on that eve, nestled deep within the Burning Hills, with the evening sun shining down upon him, that Tala found himself, with Lito surprisingly at his side, facing a stern-looking Dunlop, in what would be his first conversation with either of them.

"Vail says that you have no experience with weapons or fighting. Is that correct?" Dunlop asked him, in a tone that sounded more like he was making a statement than asking a question.

Despite being slightly taller than the stern-faced man, Tala felt rather small. He barely stopped himself from asking how exactly the man had gotten any information out of Vail as he nodded stiffly and responded, "Er, yeah, it is."

"..."

"..."

"Yes? …Yes, Sir?" The man continued to mutely stare at him, showing no indication that he'd heard Tala speak. Tala shuffled uncomfortably, shooting a glance at Lito beside him. He had no idea why the other young man was there, but by the way his jaw was tensed, he seemed to be fighting a smile.

Eventually, Dunlop spoke again, his tone still unchanged, making his question again sound like a statement. "Then exactly *how* did you manage to kill a Blessed?"

Tala rubbed the back of his neck in embarrassment, getting the feeling that he was going to be hearing that question a lot in the future. "I, uh, I kinda blew his head up… With a steam pipe…"

"Yeah, Vail told us all that back at Hagan's. He's asking how that even happened," Lito chimed in.

So Tala explained to the two what had happened, and how he hadn't been trying to kill the man as much as just survive him. He hadn't even known he was a Blessed until his head exploded! At the end of his short tale, Lito was looking at him like he couldn't quite believe what he was seeing, but Dunlop was staring at him with a pensive gaze. Eventually, the stern man spoke again.

"Alright. You have good instincts, and can think clearly even when your life is in danger. That is good." He nodded before continuing. "For the time being, if you are at risk of being killed or captured, use that to survive rather than depending on weapons that you are only just learning. Using that sword before you have properly learned how will make it more dangerous to you than to your enemy. Understood?"

Tala nodded, before catching himself and speaking. "Er, yes… sir?" he answered, still not sure how he was supposed to respond. Dunlop just stared at him again before speaking.

"For now, I am going to teach you the most basic aspects of swordplay. Take out your sword."

Tala did as he was told as Lito joined him. Dunlop began to instruct Tala in the 'basic stance' he should use when wielding his sword. Once he was satisfied, and with a quick glance at Lito beside him, he told them to copy his movements. He took out his own sword, drew it back and above his head, and brought it back down in one swift motion. He did it three more times, each time facing a different direction, before sheathing his sword and turning back to face them.

"That was a basic strike. For the next few days at least, you will practice that strike whenever we set up camp for the night. I will tell you when to stop. Begin."

Blinking at the sudden command, Tala fumbled with his own sword for a moment before trying to copy the strike as Dunlop had done. Next to him, Lito also performed the move, but much more smoothly than Tala. Dunlop stepped up to him, corrected his grip and footing, and stepped back, nodding for him to try again. After a few strikes and corrections, the man seemed satisfied with his form and stepped aside, sitting down on a nearby log facing the two. After continuing to practice the strike with no input from Dunlop, Tala spoke up to get Lito's attention, wondering why the other boy was practicing with him when he seemed to know what he was doing.

"'Cause I can still be better," he answered. "And it never hurts to practice the basics." Tala nodded thoughtfully.

"Why isn't anyone else practicing with us then?" he asked after a few more strikes done in silence.

"I don't really know," the boy responded. "This is my first time working with most of them. I guess sword fighting just isn't really their thing? It's not really mine either, to be honest. But I'd like to get better, and there aren't many better than Dunlop to learn from."

"Really?" Tala questioned. "What's so special about him?"

Lito paused for a moment, before continuing his practice. "Right, you're completely new to all this. Well, he was a Wild Guardsman, down in Mud, before he joined us. They're some of the best fighters in the world, and Dunlop was one of their best. Even learning the basics from someone like him isn't a chance that I'm going to get often. I'm not gonna pass that up."

Tala fell silent. The Wild Guards were a renowned force for good reason: the country of Mud was one of the most sparsely populated in the world, mostly due to the fact that it was largely made up of uninhabitable wetlands. Even the dryer areas of the country were mostly covered in dense forests, except for some of the mudflats on the coast. Despite the danger, it had become a common destination for criminals, as the landscape made it easy for them to hide and almost impossible for any pursuers to catch them.

The Wild Guards were a special force that the Mud Church had created to hunt down the many criminals that tried to hide away in their country. They were unrivaled at surviving in the dangerous, inhospitable wilds of their home, and excelled at all forms of fighting. It was said that there was no weapon that a Wild Guard could not use, and that there was nothing that they could not use as a weapon; a pile of leaves was more dangerous in a Wild Guard's hands than a sword in any civilian's. They spent most of their lives alone, traveling the untamed wilds of their country in solitude, endlessly hunting the criminals hiding there who preyed on the travelers, traders, and small villages scattered throughout the country.

One of the most unique things about the organization was that Wild Guards served exclusively as an internal force: they only hunted criminals hiding within the country's borders, and never engaged in the fights and skirmishes that occurred with the neighboring nations. Nobody knew why the Wild Guards stayed out of such conflicts, or why the Mud Church let them. They could easily turn the tides of a battle. It was rumored that Wild Guards were such great warriors that they even posed a threat to Descendants! As such, though, Wild Guards were almost never seen by anybody outside of the deep wilderness of Mud Country, and the rare traders in Fiahren who had encountered a Wild Guard when passing through Mud could often get free drinks for days as they regaled eager listeners of their (likely highly exaggerated) encounters with the almost mythical figures.

Tala glanced over at Dunlop, who was still sitting on the log facing them. What was a man such as him doing in Fire Country? Or as a member of the Dissidents? The warrior's eyes stayed fixed on the two of them as they practiced their strikes, but in his hands was a small knife and what looked like a weirdly shaped block of wood. Tala realized that the man was whittling, and despite never once looking at the wood or knife in his hands, he seemed to be doing an expert job of it. Tala shifted his eyes forward and focused again on his sword strikes, hoping they'd be allowed to stop soon as his arms were really starting to hurt.

After they had finally finished their practice for the night, Tala went to Gazin to ask if he could use his fleshmancy to alleviate the pain and blossoming soreness in his arms. To his displeasure, the man refused, stating that it would be better for him to let them recover on their own for the night, but that in the morning he would treat them, along with any soreness he had from their day of travel again. The Flesh wielder explained that much like the soreness caused by travel, the weakness in his arms would only make him stronger, and removing it would slow down his progress immensely. The only reason he would acquiesce in the morning was because having Tala in good form would help them travel faster, which was more important than helping his combat fitness. After all, the ability to swing a sword wouldn't make a lick of difference if a Blessed caught him.

Despite the terrifying nature of their adventure, once he got over the novelty of it, Tala found the journey itself to be rather boring. Long, exhausting days of hiking through the hills followed by painful, exhausting evenings of training in only the most basic of sword arts, followed by nights of troubled sleep. Still, there were some perks to it all; Tala found himself forming a fast friendship with Lito, who practiced swordplay with him every night.

He learned that the young man had been born and raised into the Dissidents in Light Country, and that due to his natural talents at infiltration, he had volunteered to become a servant of Alina's family to spy on them when he had still been little more than a child. The boy was a quick learner with a good memory and had easily adopted the type of behavior that was commonly found in 'good' servants. After entering into the service of the Aurels (which had apparently been Alina's family name before they were destroyed), he had quickly and easily become a valued and trusted servant in their household. He was the one who had brought Alina to the Dissidents after her family had been massacred, and had been watching out for her ever since.

When questioned about why he had stuck with Alina for so long, Lito blushed and mumbled out a string of excuses, much to Tala's amusement. After that, Tala kept an eye on the two's interactions, and, much as he had expected, the boy certainly seemed smitten with the deposed and seemingly oblivious (former) noblewoman.

This in turn had spurred Tala into speaking with the Light-wielding prodigy herself. Ever since that first night when he had learned about her history, Tala had wanted to speak to her, though not for the same reasons. While their backgrounds weren't exactly similar, she had also been born and raised in belief and service of the Churches' stories of the Gods and, much like Tala, found herself in a situation where joining the Dissidents had been necessary simply as a matter of survival. What Tala wanted to know was what had convinced her—a noblewoman and Light Descendant—that what the Dissidents said was true: that the story the Churches told of the Gods was false.

Having that conversation with the girl had proven to be more of a challenge than Tala anticipated. Most of their days were spent hiking through the hills, traveling through the most wild and untamed regions they could so as to avoid any Fire patrols that might be searching for them. Maintaining any form of conversation during this time was difficult, and with the importance it held to Tala, he had to wait until the evenings after they had set up camp. With his evenings largely consisting of sword lessons with Dunlop and Lito, though, his only real opportunity to ever speak with her was during dinner, or in the short span of time between to the end of his lessons and sleep.

CHAPTER 15

Alina took a deep breath, enjoying the peace and quiet as she relaxed. A log in the middle of nowhere might not exactly have been the pinnacle of comfort, but she had long grown used to life on the move. Still, it was sometimes hard not to miss the plump, luxurious chairs and cushions that she had grown up with in her family's mansion. Not for the first time she wondered what had happened to that giant pillow that her father had had made for her fifth birthday: it was so big that even now, as a fully grown woman, she could have lain across it and barely reached the edges. She hoped it had burned. Better that than seeing one of the *traitors* take it. She lived for the day she could return to the city of Light and slaughter the lot of them. She could do it too; a few more years, maybe, and she would be able to strike down even her former idol: that bitch Annelore.

And she was certain now more than ever that it could be done. She was a prodigy, the likes of which hadn't been seen since Anderas Anto himself had been a child. That boy, Tala, didn't have so much as a single Mark, and he had killed a Blessed. She was an Awakened who had been *fated* to kill Blessed, trained since she was a child to join the endless war with Lava and kill their Blessed. It was no secret that her mother had intended for her to one day ascend to the position of High Priest of Light. She would be appalled now to see that her daughter, who she had such high hopes for, was now more likely to murder the High Priest than replace him. At least her father might have approved.

She took another deep breath, pulling herself out of her memories and back into the present. Even now, years later, she still fell into those thoughts far too easily. Lito needed to hurry up and return. He was good at keeping her mind focused on the now, and not on what was or would be. She felt the usual stab of guilt in her stomach before ruthlessly shoving it aside, much like her mother had taught her to as a child. Lito liked being around her! He did! It wasn't her fault that she had trouble with other people. If he didn't like her company, he could have left her long ago. He didn't stay with her out of pity. They were friends. It didn't matter if he was her only friend; one was enough. *No, stop it!*

She gritted her teeth. She had long since learned to smother that voice in her head, the one that made her question her friendship with Lito. He would never abandon her. She didn't know what she would do if he did, but it didn't matter because he never would!

She took another deep breath, closing her eyes and listening to the sounds around her. Bugs grew active in the dimming light along with the sounds of her companions as they moved around the camp. The familiar *shing* of Dunlop sharpening his sword. Or axe. One of his knives, maybe? That man had far too many weapons. She didn't know how he carried them all. She liked Dunlop, though. He was one of the few people who treated her just as he did everybody else. No sneering whispers, no looks of pity, no attempting to sleep with her as so many did. He treated her awkwardly, since she wasn't a weapon and couldn't talk to him about weapons. Still, she would take his awkward attempts at politeness over everything else she had to deal with.

But Gazin and his poorly disguised pity, Nuri and his endless attempts at 'seduction' or whatever he called those cheap attempts to bed her, Caida and the jests about her 'prudishness.' Vail and Ilan were… alright, she supposed. Ilan was much like Dunlop, always polite, but far more… absent. Less willing to actually engage in conversation. Not that she had ever tried very hard: the sheer size and *presence* of the man was intimidating even to her, a girl who had been raised among Nobles and Blessed. And the less said about Vail, the better. She had worked with Those Three before and wasn't confident the strange man even knew her name. She would have been insulted by his clear apathy if she didn't find it slightly relieving, as it kept her from ever having to interact with him.

Serala was—alright, she supposed, but something about that girl was *off*. Even aside from the slight envy Alina sometimes found curdling in her gut when Serala so effortlessly took charge of people. Serala was always friendly enough, neither cruel nor pitying, but ever since they had first met years ago, she couldn't help but feel a fear about that girl. Something deep and inexplicable. At first Alina had thought it was something wrong with herself, perhaps some lingering bits of envy, but then she had seen how… how *wrong* Serala could be. Like that time in the cave, when she had 'offered' to kill Tala. There was something in that girl that was deeply broken. And despite Alina's status as an Awakened, despite her training, skill, and prodigious talents, something about Serala scared her.

She was still forming an opinion of Tala, though what she had concluded was resoundingly negative. The boy might have killed a Blessed, even without any powers of his own, but over the last week, she had caught him looking at her more and more often. She was almost impressed that the boy hadn't propositioned her yet, despite Lito's presence to deter him. Most people she met tried to bed her within a day. A few days at most. A week showed impressive restraint on Tala's part, although it wasn't going to help him succeed where any of the others failed. She simply Was. Not. Interested.

And it looked like a week was the limit of the Blessed Killer's restraint, as she opened her eyes to see him determinedly marching over to her with a tense look on his face. She sighed and raised her face to him, fully prepared to turn him down, Blessed Killer or not.

She watched the boy hesitate as he got close, clearly off put by the look on her face. Really, it wasn't even a strong look! It was just cold haughtiness, one of the first looks she'd been taught as a child; single raised eyebrow, chin tilted slightly up, very simple. Her opinion of the boy fell even further: he had killed a Blessed, and yet he was intimidated by a look children were taught?

They looked at each other in silence for a few moments before the boy finally swallowed and spoke up.

"Do you mind if I, um, ask you something?"

She couldn't quite help her expression from shifting into one of bored annoyance. Her mother would have been appalled at her lack of control, but it didn't really matter. She didn't have to wear pretend faces anymore, not amongst these people. And 'bored annoyance' sent the message she wanted to get across anyway.

"If you must."

"Right. Well… I was just—I was just wondering what made you believe them that the Churches are lying about the Gods and the afterlife and all of that?" He spoke out in a rush, nearly tumbling over some of the words in his haste.

She stared at him, feeling a faint expression of surprise spreading on her face, although she had plummeted far past caring already. This was not what she had expected. "Oh. I thought you were—never mind." She shook her head. From his very first words, the 'conversation' Alina had anticipated was thrown out the window. This was something else entirely. She wasn't even sure how to handle this sudden, new conversation. Where was Lito? Trying to hide her sudden discomfort, she fell back on politeness, trying to buy time as she rapidly tried to think of what to say. "Would you like to sit?" She gestured to the empty space on the log next to her. He nodded jerkily and sat down on the log, turning to look at her. She looked back at him in silence, a slight frown marring her brow.

"I'm sorry," he started. Good; if he was talking, she didn't have to. She could think of what to say. "That was—I just—it's been hard, you know? My whole life, I've been taught that serving the Gods is all that matters and that we'll all be rewarded in the afterlife for it and all that. But you all seem so certain that it's all a lie, and I just… I just want to know what makes you all so certain. I mean, what they told me back in the cave kind of makes sense, but how do you *know*? How can you be so certain that the risk of being wrong is worth it? I mean, if you're all wrong, that's eternal damnation! I know—I'm *learning* that the world isn't exactly a good place. I mean, I knew it had problems, but it's way worse than I ever thought. I get wanting to make things better, but if that means being damned for all of eternity, is it really worth it?" He finished with a gasp, having said all of that in a single, rambling breath. "Forget how things should be, or what's right or wrong. How do you *know* that it's false? How did they convince you?"

"They didn't," she answered with a shrug. That was an easy question to answer, at least. Tala stared blankly at her, in a decent imitation of the way Vail did, actually, although Tala's look wasn't quite so empty. Oh. He wanted more of an answer. Alright, that wasn't hard. "I learned the truth about that a long time ago. Well before I joined the Dissidents."

Tala blinked. "Oh. I thought…"

"What? That the truth was some great secret known only to us—the Dissidents?"

"Uhh… kinda?"

She sighed. How was she going to explain this? Why couldn't he have asked Lito during one of their training sessions? "Technically, it *is* a great secret. And the Churches are very… brutal about keeping it that way. But it's more well-known than you would expect. Specifically, I imagine most—if not all—of the Blessed know the truth, and at least some of the Descendant families. That's how I learned it."

"Oh." Tala hesitated, but Alina continued. If she was going to explain these things to the boy, she might as well tell him everything. It would be easier that way.

"We aren't supposed to know. Descendants, that is. But my father told me. He was a Blessed. When I was younger, he told me about his Blessing, when he met the God of Light. It was supposed to be the greatest moment of his life: meeting his God, earning Her blessing. Instead, when Aurandiel—the High Priest of Light—took him to the God's chambers, he said that the Goddess was a mess: she was naked, covered in filth, with a chamber full of naked slaves and servants, and a half-empty syringe sticking out of her arm. She was barely aware he was there; Aurandiel practically had to force her to Bless my father before pushing the rest of the drug into her, after which she collapsed onto one of the slaves.

"He had spent his whole life in her service, only to learn that the God he worshiped was a drug-addled despot, who cared about nothing more than having sex and getting high. The whole 'competition for the throne' was meaningless: even if it was true at one point, she didn't care about it anymore. The whole country was—is—under the control of the Church, not for some greater purpose but because they like having absolute power. They can do whatever they want, and the God of Light is nothing more than a source of power and a story to control the people.

"The rest of it I learned after joining the Dissidents. I don't actually know if the competition for the throne is a lie, or if they've all just forgotten or stopped caring about it. I don't really even know any more if I believe that the Gods have any sort of control over the afterlife, or if there's even such a thing as 'eternal damnation.' Even if it does exist, I don't think the Gods care enough anymore to condemn any of us to it no matter what we do. What I do know is that the Gods don't deserve being worshiped. At least not anymore. Even if they once did, they don't anymore."

She finished her impromptu speech with a level of hatred and passion that she rarely allowed to show. She couldn't help it, though. Talking about the 'beloved' God of Light always brought out these things in her. Her family had served loyally for generations, and that addled, useless God had done nothing as they were all slaughtered!

"What about your father? What did he do after he learned all that?" The hesitation in the boy's question made her shoot a glance at him, and she could see on his face why it was there: Tala knew about her family. Had Lito told him? Or was it Gazin? Perhaps Serala. Did the other girl even know about Alina's past? She couldn't say for sure, but she suspected that she did. Those Three always seemed to know everything. It didn't matter, though; she wasn't going to bite his head off for asking about her father. She had come to terms with it all a long time ago.

"He did what they all do. He embraced it. As a Blessed, he could do whatever he wanted, when he wanted, with no consequences as long as he didn't oppose the Church. Even if his life before had been built around a lie, he decided it didn't matter. Who cares what's true when you have absolute power?

"The ironic thing is that he told me so that I could embrace it sooner. He was already approaching his second century of life when he was Blessed, and I was born a few decades later. He wanted me to embrace my place in the world and enjoy my position as a Descendant without having to waste hundreds of years of life in service to a useless God. It was already too late for my older siblings: they were already too entrenched in everything they had been taught and grown up believing. They didn't believe him when he tried to tell them the truth. So he told me as early as he could, in the hope of at least having one child who lived for themselves and not devoted to an unworthy God. Even if I never became a Blessed, being a Descendant from such a *prestigious* family was more than enough. For all that prestige helped them," she couldn't help but mutter. "My mother didn't believe him either. Or she just didn't care, I don't know. Despite my father's insistence that I enjoy my life for myself, she wanted me to be great. She wanted me to become the High Priest of Light one day. I can remember them fighting about it, although I can't recall the details. I think they settled on my becoming High Priest eventually anyway, although for what reason I don't know.

"Whatever their reasons, instead, I ended up joining the very people who are trying to get rid of the Gods themselves! Sometimes I wonder what they would think of my life. If they would be proud of me..." She trailed off, staring off in the distance, looking not at the landscape but at the ghosts that existed only in her memories.

She shook her head and focused back on Tala. "Anyway, that's how I know that what we're doing is right, and that the Churches' stories are all lies. I don't know if Vail is right that the Gods can be killed or feel fear, but they can be hurt so it makes sense. And even if they can't, the Churches and the Blessed and everyone else can be, so I think it's at least worth trying. Even if we can't get rid of the Gods themselves, we can keep them hidden up in their towers, drugged into complacency as we make a better world right under their feet."

She took a deep breath, feeling the warm, dry air of a Firelands night pour into her lungs. That had been more than she had intended to say. A lot more. She wasn't sure why she had gone off on such a tirade; she rarely spoke of her parents these days. And she hadn't given voice to her inner worries about what they might have thought of the person she had become since her earliest days in the Dissidents, when Lito would hold her as she cried herself to sleep at night, and comfort her when the nightmares of her family's demise plagued her dreams. She thought she had moved past all that!

Oh, right. Tala was still there. The Blessed Killer was staring at her wide-eyed, clearly having expected her sudden diatribe about as much as she had. Well, he had wanted to know about why she believed in the Dissidents and their goals. Now he knew. She fought down a blush. Once she had begun speaking, she just hadn't been able to stop herself! She hoped he wouldn't be cruel about it, hoped that he would forget about all the extra things she had accidentally told him, about herself and her family. He didn't seem like the type who would use it against her, but she had already clearly misjudged the boy, thinking that he was interested in her, that he wanted her for her looks. In her defense, though, that was why most people tried to speak to her!

Feeling doubly embarrassed, she tried to mask it by asking if he had any more questions. He simply said no. As he left her alone again on her log, going to sit in deep contemplation next to the fire, she felt a strange mix of relief and disappointment at his departure. Despite her embarrassment, there had been something nice about having another person to talk to, somebody who wasn't judging her for her family, pitying her for her past, or simply trying to get into her bed. She loved Lito—she always would—but it had been nice to feel, even if just for a moment, that she had another friend.

CHAPTER 16

Tala awoke the morning after his talk with Alina with his thoughts in a confusing jumble. For one thing, he had seen that the girl had some serious problems. Whatever she had been expecting, he wasn't sure, but she looked at him as though he were a bug entirely unworthy of her time. She was surprised when he asked her about what the Dissidents had told him about the Gods, but quickly warmed up to the conversation. From the way she had carried on, she seemed like somebody who spent far too much time alone in her own head without other people. He had known some Researchers who were similar: people who would hole themselves up for days or weeks at a time, working on their own projects in isolation. When they finally emerged, it was impossible to get them to stop talking, like they were desperate to make up for all of the words that they hadn't said while they were alone.

Compared to them, though, Alina's case seemed much more tragic. She almost always had Lito around, and often spoke to him, but otherwise, the girl was practically a mute.

Only ever having a single person to talk to couldn't be easy. And the way she had gotten lost in herself when she began speaking about her family? To be blunt, Tala was concerned. He was growing closer with Lito and Serala, so why not befriend Alina as well? After all, the four of them were all roughly the same age. It made sense for them to be friends in his mind. Especially since they would all be stuck together for the foreseeable future. Since he didn't really have anything else that he could contribute to their group, some companionship with a person who clearly needed it was the least he could do.

The other big thing on Tala's mind that morning when he awoke was something that Alina had mentioned. According to Alina's father, the God of Light had been doing drugs. That led him to the question of *what in the Hells kind of drugs could even affect the Gods*!? He was still struggling with the concept that the Gods could even be hurt! Even if what he had been told about Marks was true, that was a far cry from envisioning the Gods succumbing to the effects of drugs! The Gods were an entirely different type of being that lived by different rules! Hells, they created the rules!

So what about drugs then? Even if the Gods could bleed, somehow they were immune to all other forms of harm: they couldn't be hurt by fist or sword or magic; they couldn't be affected by drugs or alcohol or poison. So then what had Alina been talking about? What had her father *actually* seen when he met the God of Light? Alina said that the God of Light had been naked with a syringe in her arm. Maybe that was how they extracted blood for use in Marks? But that meant that a God's skin at least could be pierced. Which meant they could be hurt. Was it something they could choose? Could the Gods choose to let something hurt them? Choose to let a syringe pierce their skin and draw their blood? Choose to let drugs or another substance affect them? But wouldn't that mean—

Tala cut himself off, shaking his head and climbing to his feet. He was starting to think in circles and was only going to give himself a headache. He'd already learned the hard way that, for all of Gazin's wonderful skills as a Fleshy, he couldn't help much with headaches.

As he began his day, the questions Tala had about God-affecting drugs stayed in the back of his mind. He didn't get the chance to ask anybody about them for a while, though; a long day of trudging through the Burning Hills (which, like many things in the Fire Country, didn't resemble their name at all) wasn't very conducive to engaging in conversation. Despite the hills' proximity to the Fire Capital, they were largely untouched, with the northern road out of the Capital passing just west of the hills and splitting off to the west and northeast. It made the hills a relatively safe place to escape the city, but it also made traveling through them a slow and at times dangerous prospect. Without Nuri, who was clearly familiar with traversing the hills, and Dunlop, whose experience in the wilds of Mud Country made him an excellent trailblazer and hunter, even in unfamiliar lands, Tala expected their journey would have been much slower and harder.

It was in the evening again, as usual, that Tala finally found his chance to ask somebody about the drugs that had been plaguing his thoughts all day. After working with Dunlop on sword forms for a while, the man finally deemed him capable and sat off to the side as he usually did, whittling little pieces of wood and keeping an eye on Tala and Lito to ensure they didn't make any mistakes. After a few minutes of silent practice between the two, Tala spoke.

"So," he started. "I was talking to Alina, and she said something that I wanted to ask you about."

Lito stumbled in his practice. "What? When did you talk to Alina?" the boy asked, looking at him, shocked.

"Last night, when you were getting water. I just wanted to get her thoughts on, well… everything."

"And she actually talked to you? Like, you had a conversation? Or did you just ask a few things and she told you to fuck off?"

Tala blinked, not quite sure what to make of that last question. Alina certainly wasn't the friendliest person he had ever met, but she didn't come across as being quite *that* rude. "Uh, no. Or yes, we had a conversation, no, she didn't tell me to fuck off. Is that a normal thing for her?"

"Oh, sorry." Lito sounded embarrassed. "Never mind. It's just… she doesn't really talk to a lot of people. It's not her fault! Not really. She just… well, she has a complicated past. Not really used to people being friendly, y'know? And most of the time, when people talk to her, it's 'cause, well, you know, she's, uhh… kinda really pretty, y'know, so people are usually trying to—uh, well, y'know."

Tala blinked again, staring at Lito as the boy blushed and stammered his way through that disaster of an explanation. For a boy who seemed so confident most of the time, and had snuck out of camp on more than one occasion for some fun with Nuri and/or Caida, he really became a mess whenever Alina was brought up. Tala found it amusing and more than slightly odd, considering just how much time the two spent together. Fighting the urge to laugh at the poor boy, Tala decided to spare his feelings and press on.

"Yeah, I know about her past."

"Oh, uh, good. That's good," Lito said, nodding, seeming more than happy to move the conversation on. "So what'd she say that you wanted to ask about? And just so you know: she's not interested. If that's what you were wondering."

Tala gave him a sideways look, not sure if he should be amused or offended at Lito's sudden and vehement insistence of Alina's interest in him, or lack thereof. He decided to just ignore it.

"Not that." From the corner of his eye, he saw Lito relax and had to stifle a laugh. "No, she told me about her dad, though, about when he got Blessed. She said that the God of Light was on drugs. I mean, a God? On drugs? I didn't know that was even possible."

"Ohhh." Lito nodded. "I get it. You didn't know?"

"Nope. Care to fill me in?"

"Yeah, sure. It's not really all that exciting, to be honest. It's kind of an open secret, both among us and the Nobles. Well, the Blessed and Descendants at least. I'm not really sure if the normal nobles know about it. Basically, they're kind of like Marks: mixing Gods' blood with certain other chemicals creates a drug that the Gods can use to get high. Has to be other Gods' blood, though. They can't get high using their own. I don't know why. So the Churches make the drugs and trade them to each other. It keeps the Gods happy and out of their way so that the Churches can do whatever they want without interference. Not really sure how different things actually are, though. According to some of the old stories I've heard, things weren't really much different before the God drugs were discovered and the Gods became complete shut-ins. That was thousands of years ago, though, so I don't really know the truth of it."

"Oh." Tala wasn't really sure what to say. It made sense, in the same way that everything he learned these days made sense, which was to say barely at all. "Sooo the Gods are all drug addicts. Why not? Guess that's a thing now."

"It was always a thing. You just didn't know about it," Lito stated. Tala resisted the urge to whack him. "And I don't really know if it's all the Gods or not. Most of them at least. Nobody, not even us, knows what's going on with the Body Gods, or anything that's happening beyond the Dust wall. I can't imagine Wind has access to Gods' blood, unless they stole some in the raids somehow. Nobody's heard from Water in thousands of years. And the Jungle hasn't been part of the trade for centuries, maybe longer. I'm not sure why, but I've heard some weird things about the Jungle Gods. 'Course, there are always weird rumors coming from the Jungle, so I don't know the truth."

"Weird rumors? Like what?" Tala asked, curious about what Lito had heard of the Gods of Beasts and Plants.

"Just some weird rumors. More about the Blessed than the Gods themselves." He shrugged. "Apparently—and I have no idea if it's true—but apparently, there are actually quite a lot of Plant Blessed, and very few Beast Blessed. And the circumstances around their Blessings are apparently really weird too. The to-be Beast Blessed disappear for a while. Weeks, months, sometimes even years, and nobody has any idea what happens to them. And then one day they just appear again, as Blessed. And some don't ever return at all. It's weird."

"Hm." Tala grunted, unsure what to make of it. "I've heard that Beast Blessed can transform into any animal they want; maybe it takes time to get used to that? Maybe turning into an animal is easy but turning back into a human is the hard part?"

"Maybe. I have no idea. I don't even know if any of it's true, remember. We hear weird things from the Jungle. That's not even the weirdest. Apparently—and I really doubt this is true—but apparently, behind the palace of the Plant God, there's a giant tree. According to rumor, that tree is actually the Plant God himself! Apparently, a few thousand years ago, he got tired of eternal life spent doing nothing and turned himself into a giant fucking tree. Apparently, the Church is really protective of the tree and doesn't let anyone near it. They say that's why the Jungle grows like it does, and why once it takes over an area you can't get rid of it: because it's the Plant God himself keeping the Jungle strong and alive through his roots or something."

"..."

"Yeah, I know. Like I said: we hear weird things from the Jungle."

"Yeah. I guess so. Hey, Dunlop?" Tala turned and called to their teacher, who had been silently carving his wood the entire time. Even though the man didn't seem to be paying any attention to them, Tala was sure that he had heard every word that they had spoken; the former Wild Guardsman had incredibly sharp senses. "Do you know if any of that's true? About the Plant God or the Beast Blessed?"

The man looked up with a blank expression, hands never stopping or slowing in their whittling. "I don't. I've never been to the Jungle."

"Oh." Tala shrugged, slightly disappointed.

"I have heard that the Plant Church harvest the fruits from that giant tree, and eating those fruits is how they become Blessed. If it doesn't kill them instead."

"Oh," Tala repeated, glancing back to Dunlop, who had gone back to focusing on his whittling. He couldn't tell if he had been joking or not. The man was a strict teacher—a strict person in general, really—but had a cunning, subtle humor about him that made it hard to tell when he was joking or not.

"Has anybody here been to the Jungle?" Tala asked to both of his current companions, curious if he might be able to confirm any of these wild rumors. Dunlop merely glanced up at him silently, but Lito answered.

"Not that I know of. Gazin may have—he's been around long enough that I wouldn't be surprised. Otherwise, Those Three probably have, but good luck getting answers out of them." The boy finished with a snort.

"You really don't know anything more about Those Three?" Tala asked Lito after a minute of thinking.

"No. I've already told you everything. They showed up one day to our safe house in Light, and everybody instantly acted like they were in charge. It was weird. I mean, I was still a kid at that point. So was Serala. Ilan and Vail were leading, not her. Well, mostly Ilan, but Vail was a bit more… I don't know, present? Back then. He was still weird, just not quite as much as he is now. I tried to ask about it, figure out who they were and why everyone was acting that way, but no one would tell me. I'm not sure most of them even knew themselves; but Anwar—he was the master there, like Hagan—he treated them like they were in charge, so everyone else just kind of went along with it. And when I asked him about it, he made it clear it wasn't my business. Even after Alina joined and we started working with them on occasion, he refused to tell me anything about them beyond 'just follow and do whatever they say.' It's even why we were in the Fire Capital that day you came in: Alina and I were in Earth when the master of our safe house there got a message saying Those Three were going to be working in the Fire Capital and requesting he send Alina to be backup just in case. The man didn't even hesitate to send us over. It's been years since I first saw them, and I've never managed to figure out who exactly they are, except that everybody who does seem to know follows them without question."

Tala nodded along as Lito retold the story, having heard it all before from the first time he asked the boy about Those Three. He'd asked Caida, Nuri, and Dunlop as well, and they told him similar things: they didn't know much about Those Three, except that they would often show up without warning, completely take over, and then vanish as soon as they were done.

The only member of their group who seemed to know anything more about Those Three, apart from the three in question themselves, was Gazin, but when Tala questioned the man, he had blatantly refused to speak on it, stating that their business was their business, and it wasn't his place to spread it around. A strange stance for such an obsessive gossip to take, but Tala had utterly failed to get any more information out of him.

As Tala and Lito finished their training for the evening and joined the growing circle around the small fire for dinner, Tala looked over the three. Vail sat across the fire from him, staring blankly at his food as he ate, looking about as bored as any man Tala had ever seen. Ilan, per usual, sat next to him, silently enjoying his meal and seeming perfectly happy with the figurative distance that existed between the two and the rest of the group. Serala sat down next to Dunlop and engaged the man in a conversation that Tala couldn't quite overhear. His eyes lingered on her for a few moments longer than they should have before he tore his gaze away. For all the mystery surrounding the girl, Tala had found her company quite enjoyable and rather liked talking to her. Although he sometimes had to fight off a shiver as a chill ran down his spine when he remembered their conversation in the cave, and the blank stare she had worn when she offered to kill him.

Tala turned to Gazin, who was next to him, and struck up a light conversation with the man, even as his eyes flickered back to the strange girl a time or two.

He went to bed that night with the mystery of their three de-facto leaders swirling in his head, wondering if he should take the risk of asking Serala about the three of them the next time he got the chance.

When he next woke, he felt Dunlop's strong, callused hand covering his mouth.

CHAPTER 17

Tala's attempted gasp as he woke was stillborn, stifled by Dunlop's hand. His eyes shot wide open in a panic as he tried, and failed, to breathe. Dunlop relaxed his grip, allowing air to pass under his hand and into Tala's heaving lungs.

"Quiet! Be quiet! We have to move—they're near!" The man spoke softly, urgency clear in his voice.

Tala's eyes traveled to Dunlop's own, the words meaningless as they tried to pierce through the sleep and sudden panic clouding his thoughts. They stared at each other until Tala's brain finished processing just what the man had said, spurring a renewed sense of panic in Tala as he shot up.

"What? Where? What?" Thankfully, Dunlop was able to make sense of the meaning behind Tala's jumbled words.

"A scout found us. Ilan dealt with him, but we have to go. Now." Dunlop was already moving even as he spoke, grabbing Tala's pack and bringing it to his feet as he began rolling up Tala's sleeping mat. Tala looked around the camp in the dim light of the moons and stars, the fire having already been killed, to see the dim forms of the others in the process of clearing out the camp, doing a far hastier job than usual.

Tala rolled off his mat so Dunlop could finish packing it. He then shoved the whole thing into Tala's arms before going to help the others. Tala stumbled to the hastily concealed remains of the fire pit where he saw everyone else converging. Looking around, he saw that three were missing.

Feeling his heartbeat grow even faster, he grabbed Lito by the arm, catching the boy's attention. "Serala, Alina, Nuri, where are they?"

"Scouting. Nuri and 'Lina are checking the path ahead. Serala's checking the perimeter."

Relaxing slightly, Tala released his grip on the boy. That was okay; that was good. His heart was still beating out of his chest, but at least none of them were hurt. He turned to see a faint light blinking in and out between two of the hills before hearing Dunlop's quiet tone.

"That's the signal. Let's go."

With that, the former Wild Guardsman, short sword and round shield held at the ready, began making his way towards the blinking light, followed by the rest of the group. Tala glanced behind him to see Vail and Ilan taking up the rear, but there was something wrong with the dark silhouette of the giant man. Glancing back as he walked, Tala tried to figure out what was wrong with Ilan. After a moment, he realized that the man was carrying a person over his shoulder! Tala's heart skipped a beat before he remembered Dunlop's words.

"A scout found us. Ilan dealt with him." Tala swallowed as he realized that the body Ilan held must be the scout.

Why were they taking him, though? Was he alive? Were they planning to interrogate him later? Or was he already dead? Tala turned back forward, not sure he really wanted to know the answer.

As they reached the gap in the hills where the light had come from, he was relieved to find Nuri and Alina waiting for them, the latter likely having been the source of the light trick, for Tala could see no other light source with them. Dunlop didn't stop moving as he passed them, the two scouts merging seamlessly into the line. Tala looked around, trying to spot Serala, making sure they didn't leave her behind, but the girl was nowhere to be found.

He turned to Gazin, who was by his side, intending to ask about her, but the old man anticipated his question and spoke before he could ask.

"Don't worry about the lass." Gazin spoke softly and calmly. "She'll meet up with us later."

Nodding with his worries only slightly assuaged, Tala focused on following the others. He was able to move far easier than before. After having spent weeks traversing the hills, he had gotten somewhat used to traveling through the wilds, but this was the first time they had moved during the night, and Tala was finding that he was far less confident in his footing when he could barely see where he was stepping, or where he was going. Their slower speed helped him keep pace, but every crack of a twig or crumple of a leaf that he stepped on made him cringe; silence was paramount right now, and he was bad enough at moving quietly during the day.

As they snuck through the dark valleys of the hills, Tala couldn't help but curse himself. His reaction to being awoken had been dismal, wasting precious time as he panicked and processed what was happening. Two weeks of peaceful, uninterrupted travel had made him complacent, relaxed. It had been easy to forget the situation he was in: a hunted man, probably one of—if not *the*—most wanted men in the country, soon to be the world. He had been a fool to forget just what that meant, a fool to think that he was safe in the hills just because nothing had happened yet. *Of course* there were soldiers scouting the hills! The Burning Hills were a huge, wild range stretching for dozens of miles to the north and northeast of the Capital, a natural place for fleeing criminals to run to, even if it was in the opposite direction of Mud Country. It was a miracle that they had lasted these past few weeks without encountering soldiers!

Or perhaps less of a miracle than it might seem, Tala thought as he looked at the others and couldn't make out even the faintest of footsteps. The sheer silence that accompanied their passage greatly impressed Tala.

Another thing that impressed and frightened him was Serala's appearance. One moment the girl was absent, and the next he saw her walking right next to Dunlop, whispering quietly into his ear. Her sudden, silent appearance rattled his nerves, causing him to watch their surroundings with a new paranoia in case the enemy was similarly skilled.

Whatever Serala told Dunlop when she returned must have been important, for the man swerved hard to the right, changing their path to due east. Shortly after, the group came to a stop as Dunlop signaled to Ilan, who began climbing up one of the hills. Tala watched him climb, curious why he was still carrying what Tala now knew was a corpse.

As Ilan approached the top of the hill he stopped, close to the peak but not quite high enough to be seen against the glow of the night sky. After standing there for a few moments looking around, the large man turned and dropped the body he was carrying. The group watched as it tumbled down the hill, bouncing off rocks and roots before coming to a stop on a bush only a few feet away from Tala. Even in the dim light, Tala could see that the body was now properly mutilated: the limbs were resting at strange angles, broken bones were protruding from the skin, and half the head seemed to have caved in.

Tala turned away in horror, fighting the urge to vomit. He wanted to ask why, but he feared that if he opened his mouth, he would be violently ill. He felt a calming hand begin to rub his back and turned to see Gazin.

"Keep it in, lad. It'll be alright, but you can't be getting sick, not right now."

The incredulity Tala felt helped him to subdue the waves of nausea. Those were not the comforting words Tala had expected to come from the man. As Ilan slowly made his descent down the hill, Tala swallowed a final time and spoke in a heavy whisper to Gazin.

"What was that? Why—why did he *do* that?"

"To hide our tracks, lad." Tala stared uncomprehendingly at the man, prompting him to elaborate. "The man got lucky, got close enough to find us. So Ilan killed him, broke his neck. But some random dead scout is a dead giveaway that we were there. But this?" He gestured to Ilan and the hill and the dead scout. "Makes it look like he slipped in the night, fell down the hill, and broke his neck in the fall. It's gruesome, aye. But it keeps us safe. He died by accident, not murder; no reason to send more hunters this way."

Tala merely nodded in response. It made sense, Gazin's reasoning, but he still felt ill about it. Killing a person in defense was one thing, but carrying and mutilating a corpse like that just to cover their tracks?

As Ilan rejoined the group, they began moving again, sneaking their way through the darkened hills, hopefully moving away from those who were hunting them. But as the dark of deep night began to slowly grow lighter and lighter as dawn approached, Tala couldn't help but envision the broken bones and twisted neck of the poor soul who had gotten just a bit too close.

CHAPTER 18

A few days after their midnight escapade, having turned to traveling northward, the hills began to grow smaller and smaller, eventually giving way completely to the flat, empty grassland that made up the great Fire Plains. They set up camp just inside the hill range, earlier than usual. Tala sat on one of the slopes, staring out at the great nothing before him: a massive sea of grass, waving gently in the evening breeze, unbroken as far as the eye could see.

It was easy to pretend, when looking at that great expanse, that there was nothing else beyond the grass: no mountains to the north, no ocean to the east, no desert to the west, just grass stretching out until the ends of the world. *Peaceful,* he thought. *Boring too, probably.* It was strange to think that the idea of a peaceful life sounded boring; he had spent the last few weeks in fear of his life, traversing the wilds and constantly on the lookout for soldiers hunting him. Like most kids, he had always dreamt of adventure, of traveling the world and seeing what mysteries it held. Yet the last few weeks, where he had been on an adventure of sorts of his own, all he had wanted was to go back to his old, peaceful life.

Maybe boring would be better, he thought as he remembered all that had happened: the fear he had felt when Ignis was bearing down on him, the terror and claustrophobia while running through the city and sneaking through the Undercity afterwards. The blank eyes of the woman in the room and the broken, mutilated body of the scout. A boring life held none of that; none of the guilt and fear and nightmares that had been plaguing him more and more lately. It was almost enough to convince him to stop right there: build a little shack in the hills on the edge of the plains, get Dunlop to teach him how to hunt and live in the wilds, and spend the rest of his days quietly with a view of that peaceful vista to greet him every morning.

Until the day it would all go up in flames. Literally. Probably sooner rather than later. Even in that remote location, far away from the roads and cities, he would be found. The Church of Fire would scout every single hill looking for him, even if it took them years. So would the others: Metal, Mud, Ice, Mist; all would be hunting him eventually. He would never be safe in one spot. He was doomed to a life on the run.

Tala heard the sound of shuffling behind him and turned to see Serala sitting there, looking out over the plains as he had. She had a calm, peaceful look on her face as she stared out at nothing, and not for the first time, Tala was struck by her beauty. As dangerous, capable, and downright scary as she could be, in moments like this, Tala couldn't help but feel drawn to her.

"Watcha thinkin' 'bout?" The sudden, casual words took a few seconds to register. For a moment, he was tempted to tell her the truth: that he was admiring her beauty, but he quickly disabused himself of that notion. He could still see her blank, apathetic look when she had offered to kill him. And he could still easily recall the night when Nuri pushed his (attempted) flirting with her a bit too far and a dagger that Tala hadn't even seen her draw was sticking the crotch of his pants into the log they were sitting on. Nuri complained the next day that she'd shaved some hair off, and it would take him forever to groom things back into place. Caida still hadn't stopped teasing the man over his 'lopsided' appearance.

Well aware of just how dangerous the girl beside him was, and fully unaware of just how she might respond to *his* flirting, Tala elected to simply say that he had been thinking of how peaceful the plains looked.

Serala nodded calmly. "Mm. Let's hope they stay that way."

"How will we hide out there? Keep them from finding us?" As peaceful as the plains looked, they also provided no cover, no places to hide as far as Tala could see. With unobscured vision for miles, he didn't know how they would even try to stay hidden unless they had Alina use her magic to cover them. As skilled and powerful as the girl was, he doubted even she could manage to do that, not for weeks on end.

"We won't," she said simply, seeming entirely unbothered by their vulnerability. "If we get spotted out there, we'll have to fight, no running or hiding for us. We should be fine even if that does happen, though. As long as it's not a Blessed that finds us, but I doubt any of *them* are scouring the countryside. That kind of work is below them," she finished with an amused scoff.

Her nonchalance at the idea of having to fight off trained soldiers, maybe even Descendants, helped calm Tala's nerves somewhat. He wasn't confident in his fighting abilities yet; despite daily training with Dunlop and Lito, he had still only first gotten his sword a couple of weeks ago. The others—most of them at least—seemed to be experienced fighters. Tala was confident that even if he could be of no use, the group wouldn't have much trouble. Not with a Wild Guardsman, a Flesh Descendant, and a Light Awakened on their side.

"Well, that's good then. I'm not really ready to face down a Blessed again. Ever. Like *ever*, ever," Tala said half-jokingly. He really did never want to so much as *see* a Blessed again as long as he lived. His one up-close-and-personal experience with such a being was more than enough for one lifetime, even if by some miracle he had managed to walk away.

"What? You don't want to fight a few more? Maybe take a handful of grass and shove it down their throat? Choke them to death with your Blessed-slaying prowess?" she asked, laughing. She really had a nice laugh.

"Gods, no!" Tala laughed. "…Would that even work?" he asked after a few moments, curious.

"What? Choking one to death with grass? No, I'm pretty sure it wouldn't. Then again, before you came along, I didn't think you could blow one's head up with a steam pipe. At least not to the point of actually killing them, so what do I know?"

Tala laughed, but her answer did spur another question out of him.

"So you've never… you know? Killed a Blessed?"

"What?" She laughed, eyeing Tala like he was crazy. "Gods no! Are you crazy? What do you think I am? I've never even heard of a normal person killing a Blessed before. Why do you think your doing it is such a big deal?"

"Well—I mean… I just thought that, y'know: you're the Dissidents! I figured if anyone would have killed one at some point, it'd be you lot."

"Yeah, no. We had theories that maybe it *could* be done, and how we *might* do it. But no. Off the top of my head, I can only even think of a handful of Blessed who have actually been killed in the last… what? Two, three decades? It's not exactly a common thing to happen outside of open war."

"Well, how'd they die? Those other Blessed?"

"Hm?" She pondered his question. "Well, aside from Ignis, I think the most recent one was down in Steam. I'm not sure what happened, though. Rumors say it was a Dark assassin, but even a Dark Blessed would have trouble killing a Steam Blessed, and normal assassination methods don't really work on Blessed. Or I thought they didn't; we've been reevaluating what we thought we knew about Blessed after what you did. 'Course, Dark magics don't really work like the rest either, so who knows? Even we don't really have a good understanding of everything Dark wielders can do. That whole country is weird.

"The others killed have all been up north. The head of the Aurel family a few years ago when they were wiped out. Otherwise they've all been in the war between Light, Lightning, and Lava. That's been going on for centuries and is usually the only place Blessed are killed. In the last few decades, I think about half a dozen have been killed there? One each from Light and Lightning, and four from Lava."

"Four from Lava? That's a bit imbalanced, isn't it?"

"Mhmm. All from the same Light Blessed too."

"What? Really? Who?"

"Anna something. Annalise, maybe? Annelore? I don't remember. She's become known as 'the Blessed Slayer' now, though. It's actually how she earned her Blessing, see: a few decades ago, a Lava Blessed was pushing hard into Light, so naturally, Light sent a Blessed of their own to counter him. The Light Blessed was killed, but the Lava guy was so weakened that an Awakened Light Descendant who was there was able to finish him off. Earned herself a Blessing for it, and instead of staying in the capital to 'serve the Church,' she decided to keep fighting Lava. I'll give her credit for that, at least: she didn't take the Blessing and become a lazy piece of shit like most of the Blessed do. But yeah, since then she's beat back about a dozen different Lava Blessed and killed three more of them. From what I've heard, she's about the only thing keeping Lava at bay these days, so they've stopped trying to invade Light quite so much and are focused more on Lightning instead. So if you ever get the chance to kill her like you did Ignis, take it. Her death would be a disaster for Light.

"But anyways, yeah, aside from your killing Ignis, those are the only ones I'm aware of to have been killed in my life-time and then some."

"That's really it? Eight others in 20 years?"

"More like 40 years. What did you expect? They live for hundreds of years easy and rarely ever participate in anything actually dangerous to them, so they aren't exactly dying very often. Honestly, they might even become less active over the next few years. A Blessed being murdered out of the blue in the heart of his own capital city? It's bound to scare them a bit. Hells, it's not even been 30 years since the Demon scared them into hiding, and he never even killed one. Now you show up and do kill one? I bet some won't even leave their mansions for the next decade if they don't have to."

"Scare them? Into hiding? Are you serious? Blessed scared because of me?" The very idea of Blessed being scared because of Tala was such a ridiculous idea he couldn't help but laugh at it.

"They're nearly invincible. You'd be surprised just how strongly they might react to suddenly having to face the prospect of getting killed. Why do you think they rarely join the battlefield? Other Blessed are the only thing they've ever really feared, so they do whatever they can to avoid having to face them. Even Lava rarely have Blessed go out to fight, and they've been in a constant three-way war with Light and Lightning for centuries. Most of the Blessed are cowards.

"The only real problem for us are the ones who aren't, or who are too confident in themselves to be scared. They're the ones who might try to actually hunt you down. Blessed like Anderas Anto and Anne-whatever-her-name-is. Or like Levina and Torben from Lightning, or Kier, Goran, and that third one from Earth—Avani, I think? Ivek and Horst from Plant. Hells, even Elidor will come after you if he learns you're in his city, one of many reasons we won't be staying long in Southtown.

"Unfortunately, most of the Fire Blessed will be sent to hunt you down whether they want to or not, which is why getting out of this country is so important. Only good thing about it is that most of them won't actually *want* to be the one who finds you, in case you kill them too, so they won't be looking very hard."

Tala couldn't quite stop the keening whine that escaped his throat. "But I *can't* kill them! Any of them! Ignis was a fluke! If he hadn't been toying with me, if he hadn't been a *Fire* Blessed specifically, if I hadn't been right next to a pipe seam, if I'd have been even a second too slow, I'd be dead, and none of this would have happened!"

"Yeah, probably." She shrugged. "But it did happen. And no one is going to know or care about all those details. All they know or care about is that you—an ordinary, mundane person—killed Ignis—a Fire Blessed—in the middle of the city. If you did it once, who's to say you can't, *won't*, do it again? So they'll want you dead, and some will even have the guts to do it themselves."

Tala hung his head, rubbing his eyes with his palms.

"You'll probably become an urban legend even. Tala: the boy who killed a Blessed. Stories will be told about you a thousand years from now." She was laughing again, her amusement at the concept clear. Tala couldn't quite stop a small grin from forming despite the horrible topic. There was something appealing about the idea of becoming a legendary figure because of a moment of good-hearted idiocy.

"That doesn't sound too bad. Tala: the Blessed Killer," he joked. "Almost makes me want to do it again. Secure the legend, you know?" Except he really, really didn't.

"So am I really the first? Nobody—no normal person—has killed a Blessed in all the thousands of years? 'Cause, to be perfectly honest, it wasn't really that hard. And it was an accident."

"Accident or not, you may have just started a whole new era in the world. Certainly a new era for the Dissidents; our greatest adversaries aren't quite as untouchable as we thought. In a few years we might even manage to kill one ourselves, now that we know for sure it can be done."

Tala just shook his head, feeling more than slightly overwhelmed at what she was describing. He was—he had been—a nobody. Maybe slightly more privileged than most, but still nobody really important. He still felt that way, which made the idea of his being a legendary figure all the more ridiculous.

"It just seems so weird. Making history. Gods!" He shook his head again. "It feels like we should be talking about somebody else. Like the Bone Merc or the Demon from Wind. The type of people who the Blessed *have* a good reason to fear. Not somebody who just got lucky like me."

His self-deprecating laugh slowly died as he looked at Serala. Her smile had turned into a grimace, with a tense jaw and drawn brows. "Yeah, well, you're not them. You can be better. Make your own, better legend."

He stared at her confused; where had this come from? Why did the sardonically cheerful Serala suddenly become so… whatever this was? Before he could get his thoughts together enough to ask, she stood up and spoke.

"We should get back to it. You don't want to miss your training with Dunlop." And with those words, she stormed off, leaving a very confused—and slightly concerned—Tala sitting behind her.

As Tala returned to the camp, which was just on the other side of the hill, he was immediately beset by Dunlop to begin his training for the evening. As he and Lito worked through their forms, he played over his conversation with Serala over and over in his head, trying to figure out just what had caused the sudden shift in her mood. He couldn't figure it out; had it been slowly occurring and he just hadn't noticed, or had he said something he shouldn't have? Eventually, he gave up trying to figure it out, resolving to simply pay more attention the next time they spoke.

For her part, Serala seemed to have gotten over her sudden bout of… whatever it was, and she was going about the camp like she usually did. At least, if there was anything different in her behavior, Tala couldn't tell. He was glad that whatever had happened didn't appear to have angered their enigmatic leader. As he went to sleep that night, though, the nightmares that he was slowly growing used to were dotted with fields of sharpened bone skewering everybody in sight and entire sections of some distant city collapsing at the hands of an unknown, demonic being.

Tala woke to the sun slowly pouring over the tops of the hills. His strange dreams fled his conscious mind, leaving him with little more than an unsettled feeling in the pit of his stomach.

CHAPTER 19

The first day that they left the safety of the hills was the worst: each of them was on edge, expecting at any moment to see a parade of horses come over the horizon, or even just a patrol of foot soldiers that had, for some reason, ventured so far out into the wilds. If they were seen, there was nowhere to run or hide: their only option would be to stand and fight, a situation that Tala was less than eager to experience. Their best chance to avoid a fight would be to spot any such patrols first and have Alina cover them in an illusion to hide their presence, a solution that was far from perfect in such an open landscape.

The first few hours were especially wretched for Tala, whose heart was constantly hammering in his chest as his head swiveled every which way, looking out for any signs of other people. Eventually, the constant fear exhausted him, and he stopped his paranoid searching. His aching neck played a large part in his decision to trust that his far more experienced companions would notice anything worth worrying about far earlier than he would.

Once the general paranoia that the group felt at being so exposed finally wore down, the changing terrain helped to brighten their moods considerably; walking over soft, flat, grass-covered plains was far easier than trudging through the treacherous hills where they rarely got more than a hundred feet at best of flat surface. The pain and aching soreness that Tala had grown used to was absent when he awoke their second morning in the plains, making him almost giddy for the rest of the day, to the great amusement of the others. The easier sleep that he found on flat ground helped immensely.

It was a few days into their trek over the plains, a journey that thankfully had been uneventful so far, that they came upon the southern flows of the Horseshoe River, named as such because of the large, horseshoe-like shape it made when coming out of the Metal Mountains on its way to the Burning Lake. The river was a welcome sight to the group as, besides a chance to properly wash themselves and their things, the banks were strewn with trees and bushes, a welcome bit of foliage after days spent in the vast emptiness of the plains. Although it was earlier in the day than they usually stopped to make camp, the group almost unanimously decided that they would take the chance to rest and clean both their bodies and their clothes in the gentle flow of the large river. They took shifts in cleaning, going three at a time so that the majority of them would be prepared to act if anybody happened upon them.

The three girls took their turn in the river first, at Caida's insistence. While the woman was handling their wilderness adventure better than Tala (and better than most of them had expected her to from what Tala had heard), she was still a woman who liked her comforts and at the prospect of a proper bath refused to wait any longer than necessary, dragging Alina and Serala along. Both girls were perfectly happy to accompany her.

Shortly after the girls had begun bathing, Nuri tried to sneak off to watch them, to nobody's surprise. What did surprise Tala, though, was who stopped the man: as soon as he began sidling off to the side of the camp, in the general direction that the girls had gone, he had caught the eye of Vail and instantly sat down and struck up a sudden and rather one-sided conversation with Tala. When Tala looked at Vail, though, the man was wearing his usual blank face and absentminded gaze, staring off at nothing in the distance. Still, though, Tala couldn't help the strange feeling that the man was watching Nuri, and the uncharacteristic awkwardness in Nuri's behavior made Tala think that perhaps he was right. It made Tala wonder if there was actually something about the strange man worth fearing, or if it was merely his mysterious reputation that caused people as untamable as Nuri to submit to him.

After the girls finished their bathing, Tala took his turn in the river with Nuri, Lito, and Dunlop. Unlike his three companions, though, Tala stayed in the shallows at the river's edge as he had never learned to swim, nor ever even been in a proper body of water like the Horseshoe River. The deepest waters he had ever been in were the bathing pools at the Institute, which even at their deepest only reached his chest in height. Dunlop stayed near Tala, silently washing himself in the shallows. Nuri and Lito, however, happily swam out into the river and enjoyed the chance to relax in the deeper water, diving and floating as they enjoyed their warm, sunlit break. After cleaning themselves, the two laughingly waved goodbye to Tala and Dunlop and swam a ways down the river, ducking behind a clump of trees and bushes where Tala couldn't see them.

After he had finished, Dunlop gave Tala an even nod and climbed out of the water, slowly ascending the bank. Once he reached the top of it, he gave a hard look around and, seeing the utter emptiness of the plains surrounding them, seemed satisfied with Tala's safety. The man disappeared from Tala's view behind the bank, but he knew that he wouldn't be very far away; the former Wild Guard would never leave Tala exposed to danger, even if there was no danger around.

Tala slowly finished washing himself in solitude, enjoying the peace and quiet. He appreciated that Dunlop had the consideration to give him space. For the last few weeks, ever since he had killed Ignis, he had constantly been surrounded day and night by his new companions. For the most part he didn't mind: they were all there to protect him, after all, and he quite enjoyed their company (with the notable exception of Vail and Ilan, both of whom he had barely interacted with at all). But still, being around people every moment was tiring, and Tala found himself taking advantage of opportunities to be alone whenever he could.

He was far enough away from where they had set up camp that he couldn't hear the rest of the party unless he really focused. He sat down in the waters and, following advice that Nuri had given him earlier, took a deep breath and slowly stretched his body out. Taking deep, even breaths, he closed his eyes and let himself gently drift on the water. Tala couldn't help a smile from forming. It had been a long time since he'd felt so relaxed and at peace.

Much sooner than he would have liked, Tala opened his eyes. He would have loved to spend the rest of the day floating in that blissful river, but he couldn't. Vail, Ilan, and Gazin still needed their turn to wash, and the sun wouldn't stay up forever. Nuri and Lito had already finished up and left the river. Tala appreciated that they had done so quietly, letting him continue basking in peace undisturbed. He knew they were still nearby on the bank anyway, probably with Dunlop.

And he might need their help, Tala suddenly realized. He had been so relaxed, and the water so calm, that he hadn't noticed that he had floated out into the middle of the very wide river. He struggled to keep his breathing deep and even, and to not begin flailing in panic: he didn't know how to swim, and the water was deep enough that if he stopped floating, he would surely drown. Forcing himself to remain calm, and too embarrassed at letting himself get into such a situation to call for help, Tala began trying to slowly make his way to the shore. With his arms still spread out wide in the water, he began making little flapping motions under the water with his hands, hoping that they would generate enough force to direct his floating back to the shoreline.

Far sooner than he had expected, Tala found himself in the shallows again, standing up in the water in confusion: he had gotten back to shore way too quickly. He might not be very experienced when it came to water, but he was positive it should have taken longer for him to get back to where he had started. He hadn't even drifted *down* the river; he was literally in the same exact spot he had started! Looking around in confusion, Tala let out a startled cry and stumbled backwards, falling down in a big splash: right at the water's surface, hidden beneath some bushes that were growing out over the water, there had been a pair of eyes watching him! Human eyes!

Tala's expectations of the other's proximity proved true as all three suddenly burst through the brush with weapons drawn: Lito and Dunlop with swords in hand and Nuri wielding a pair of gaudy yet sharp-looking daggers. They quickly scanned the area for threats before looking to Tala in confusion.

"Somebody's over there! Under the bush!" Tala gasped out, pointing to where he had seen the eyes as he scrambled up and out of the water. With a serious frown that looked out of place on the man's usually laughing, mischievous face, Nuri waded over to the bush that Tala had pointed at and quickly brushed it aside. Finding nothing, the smuggler pushed his way through the bushes until he was out of sight. Tala waited with bated breath, Lito and Dunlop standing guard in front of him with their swords at the ready. It wasn't long before Nuri returned, daggers sheathed and giving them a relieved smile.

"There are no signs of anyone. You probably just saw a bullfrog or something, kid," Nuri chuckled.

"What?" Tala asked in disbelief. "No! Those were eyes! Human eyes!"

Nuri just laughed. "Relax, there's nobody around. Your mind's just playing tricks on you. You saw a frog or a fish or something, and the surprise messed with your head. It's understandable with everything that's happened to you."

Tala frowned. Was he right? He was certain he saw eyes, wasn't he? Tala's certainty was waning; he was questioning himself now. Could they have been the eyes of some random, curious animal that he'd mistaken? "I… maybe. I guess, yeah. I just… I thought it was a person."

"Hey, no harm, kid. Better to be safe than sorry, you know?"

Tala nodded, still uncertain. He grabbed his clothes from where he had hung them on a nearby tree to dry. After he had dressed and they were walking back to camp, Nuri gave him a pat on the shoulder, seeing the conflict still on his face.

"Kid, seriously, don't worry about it. You're far from the first person to mistake an animal for a person watching them."

"Really?"

"Yeah, it happens. Especially to people dealing with a lot of fear and stress. Whatever you saw ain't something to worry about, though, so just forget about it, eh?"

"So you do think I saw something?" Tala asked, not sure why it was so important to him that they believed he had at least actually seen something.

"Sure, kid. Like I said, it was probably a frog or something. Or Hells, maybe it was a River Ghost!" The man finished with a laugh as he walked off into the camp.

Tala blinked. "River Ghost?" he questioned, turning to Lito, who just sighed.

"Don't listen to him. Those are just a myth. He loves fucking with people about things like that."

"Oh, okay. But what are River Ghosts? I've never heard of them."

Lito sighed again. "Supposedly, people have sometimes seen things in rivers and lakes and such. Faces in the water, eyes watching them from bushes, voices in the dark, stuff like that. Every once in a while, you'll hear a trader or soldier or somebody talking about it in a tavern. They say they're the ghosts of people who drowned there or something. Like I said, though, they're just a myth. It's just people like you who mistook a frog or something. Or had too much to drink. Or just bullshitting because they want a spooky story to tell."

"Oh. That makes sense, I guess."

"Yeah. Hey, Gazin!" Lito greeted the Fleshy as they sat down beside the man. "What do you know about River Ghosts?"

The Fleshy turned to them with a raised eyebrow. "River Ghosts? Why you asking about them?"

"Tala thought he saw eyes in the river, and Nuri brought it up. I told him they were a myth."

"Aye, lad, he's right," Gazin said to Tala. "I've been up and down the world for over a hundred years, and I ain't ever seen no ghosts, river or otherwise. Nuri just likes those kinda stories, says the world's more interesting with a bit of mystery to it. Don't listen to him."

"Alright." Tala laughed. "What other stories does he believe in?"

"Oh Gods, lad, don't get me started. That man's got a head of fluff. Let's see: there's the Far Shore, the Moon People, the Skeleton Soldier, the Carnival of Blood, River Ghosts, the Feral God, the Ice Maiden, all sorts of shit. And none of them I've ever seen hide nor hair of. They're just stories people like to tell to scare each other in the dark or entertain kids. Don't think too much on them."

Tala nodded in affirmation, with a small nostalgic smile. He'd heard some of those stories as a kid, and, while he didn't believe them, he liked Nuri's take a bit better than Gazin's. Even if they were all fantasy, Tala agreed that the world was a bit more interesting with some mystery. And even better when those mysteries were abstract, faraway things, and not the mystery of how he was going to survive with the whole world hunting for him. He went to sleep that night staring up at the two night moons, fondly reminiscing over the stories he'd loved as a child.

The morning after their stay at the riverside was marked with quite the surprise for most of the group. They were discussing over breakfast how they should cross the river, whether they should try to ford it or if they should risk following it for a while to see if there was somewhere nearby where it would be easier to cross. Serala had been silent during the conversation, watching with an amused air as they debated ideas. Once they had finished breakfast and had to decide on a course of action, she had stopped all discussion by simply stating that they already had a way across and to not worry about it. Tala could see that he wasn't the only one who didn't know what she was talking about; they were all looking at her with various levels of confusion. Even Gazin didn't seem to know what Serala meant, and the man almost always knew at least something about… well, everything.

Apparently feeling disinclined to share more than that cryptic tidbit about their plans, Serala began moving to clear up the camp, with the rest of the group slowly following as they wondered what exactly the enigmatic girl had planned.

Once the camp was cleared, Serala walked down to the bank of the river with the rest of the group following her in silence, sharing in a mutual curiosity. To their further confusion, Serala stopped at the top of the sloped bank and simply looked back to Ilan, who merely nodded and strode forward to stand beside her. Tala shared a quick glance with Lito: what were they up to?

The giant of a man and the much smaller girl simply stood there for a few moments, staring out across the river at the shore on the far side. Then without warning, Ilan slapped his hands together once before slamming them on the ground. Immediately and with a great rumbling from beneath their feet, a great earthen slab began to grow out from the ground, stretching out across the river until it reached the bank on the far side to form a massive, earthen bridge.

Tala sighed. At this point, the large man's possession of Earth magic barely surprised him. He was already in the company of a Flesh Descendant and a Light Awakened. Adding an Earth wielder to the mix was… well, completely ridiculous, truth be told. Tala sighed again before looking to his companions.

They were clearly having a bit more difficulty accepting Ilan's Earth wielding: they were each staring at the large man with various degrees of shock. Even the normally stoic Dunlop was looking at the man with calculating eyes, and the always-reserved Alina had her mouth open and eyes wider than Tala had ever seen.

He looked back to Serala to see her glance back at the group, failing to keep a mischievous smirk off her face. Tala felt a grin of his own form; she had definitely been planning this for days. A call from her to 'get moving' broke the group out of their Ilan-focused trance, and they began crossing the makeshift bridge: hesitantly at first but gaining confidence as it felt firm and strong beneath their feet.

After they had all crossed, sans Ilan, with Vail bringing up the rear, they looked back to see Ilan begin crossing the bridge himself. As he walked, the bridge began to shrink, becoming narrower and narrower until the giant of a man was walking across little more than a string's width of magically reinforced dirt. Tala didn't know if the man was keeping himself on the sliver of bridge through magic or through his own sense of balance and finesse, but he was impressed either way.

Once the Earth-wielding giant had crossed, the slim remains of the bridge crumbled away, falling into the river.

Once the group began walking again, Tala approached Serala, his curiosity getting the better of him.

"Is he a Descendant too?" he asked her in a quiet voice, not needing to specify who he was asking about.

She shook her head. "Nope. He's a Marked," she answered casually.

"Oh." That actually was a little more surprising to Tala: Marked were pretty rare and usually kept under heavy control by their respective Churches. For a Marked to have joined the Dissidents had to be a rare occurrence, probably almost as rare as an Awakened Descendant like Alina. "How, uh… how did he end up with you?" he asked her hesitantly.

She walked on in silence for long enough that Tala began to think she wasn't going to answer. "It's not really my story to tell," she eventually said, though in a more somber tone than Tala was used to from her. "But he used to be a Stone Knight. You know of them?"

Tala's head shot to her before turning to look at the massive back of Ilan. Of course he had heard of the Stone Knights! They were the Earth Country's greatest warriors: each one a devastatingly skilled fighter who could best dozens, if not hundreds, of the Fire countries soldiers by themselves! Only the best, most distinguished soldiers from the Earth army's ranks were accepted into the Stone Knights, and, according to rumor, as a part of their knighting they were given an Earth Mark of their choosing to make them even more powerful. Stone Knights who further distinguished themselves were rewarded with even more Marks! It was said that they could even beat a Descendant in single combat, and the best of them could even defeat Awakened! And unlike the mysterious and aloof Wild Guards of Mud, who were said to be capable of similar feats of combat, the Stone Knights actually fought against their neighboring nations! He'd even heard that some of Earth Country's Descendant families were first founded by Stone Knights who had distinguished themselves to such a degree that they had earned the Blessing of their God! A non-Descendant earning a Blessing was an incredibly rare event in any of the countries, Earth included!

He wanted to ask her further about the man, about how one of Earth Country's most celebrated warriors had become a member of the Dissidents, but he knew she wouldn't answer.

Not her story to tell. That probably meant that he would have to ask the usually silent man himself if Tala ever wanted to learn that story. A man with whom Tala had exchanged maybe a dozen words with in the weeks they'd traveled together. *Still,* he resolved as he looked out over the once-again-unbroken plains of the Fire Country stretched out before him, *that's a story I'd like to hear one day.*

CHAPTER 20

A week after they had crossed the Wandering River, Tala finally caught his first sight of the mountains: something he had been eagerly anticipating. His first view of them was somewhat disappointing, though, as they were little more than hazy, faint shapes in the distance, barely visible over the horizon. Having grown up exclusively within the walled confines of a city that was built upon the flatness of the Fire Plains, the closest that Tala had ever come to seeing mountains were the Burning Hills that they had passed through.

Over the next few days, he constantly brought his eyes to the blurry shapes looming larger in the distance, waiting for the moment he would be able to make out any details. From the maps he had studied back at the Institute, he knew that eventually he would be able to see the mountains up close: what he was seeing was merely the southern tip of the Metal Mountains that extended down into the Fire Plains. The way the mountains curved up and around meant that as

Tala and the group moved further north on their approach to Southtown, they would become more and more visible.

For all the joy that the mountains brought to Tala, though, they also raised tension in the group: once they passed the tip of the mountains, the risk of being discovered rose considerably. If they were discovered, they would be trapped in an ever-shrinking box with almost no chance of escape. It didn't help that they would eventually have to join a road that ran through the plains long before reaching Southtown: if a group as large as theirs suddenly appeared in the city without having been spotted by road patrols well ahead of time, it would draw a lot of unwanted attention. Not many people traveled through the wilds instead of on the roads where there were plenty of small inns and villages.

The dangers of *not* being spotted on the road approaching Southtown was something that Tala hadn't considered. It was only after Alina had explained to him one night that he understood how different things had become now that all of Fire Country was looking for him: every road was patrolled, big and small; even the countryside was being scoured in an effort to find him. That meant that any travelers would be noted and reported. So a group showing up at a city with no warning would be found extremely suspicious. So now they were in a rather strange predicament: join the Fire Road late enough to be spotted and reported to Southtown, but early enough so as to not appear as having joined the road from nowhere. And then spend what would likely be a week on the road without exposing their true identity. It sounded like an impossible task until Alina explained that whenever they did encounter soldiers, she would be forming a minor illusion around him so that he would look like someone else entirely, hopefully preventing them from being discovered. Apparently, she had already decided on what look she would be giving him and actually *giggled* when describing how she would be giving him pale white skin and freckles. The trick wouldn't hold up to scrutiny from a Blessed, who could feel when magic was being used, even by those of different Gods, but it would work with everyone else.

The bright side of their scheme was that they wouldn't have to join the Fire Road until they were almost in sight of Southtown: instead they were going to travel the Coastal Road that joined the Fire Road about a day out from the city. Their plan was to claim to be Dust traders that had come from Mud up the eastern edge of the continent. They even had an official Dust Trader emblem to help sell their story, much to Tala's exasperation.

One of Tala's concerns was their lack of horses: Dust traders often had mounts of some kind or another, to carry either themselves or their goods if they didn't have carts to do the job. When he asked Serala about it, she explained that if they were asked about it, they would claim to have lost their horses in Mud. Apparently, it was fairly common for traders to leave their mounts at a trading post when entering the Mudlands. There was only one true, unbroken road that ran through that country, and it only reached the capital and some of the largest cities. So traders who were planning to visit the other areas often left their mounts at special trading posts when entering the country, and retrieved other mounts that had been left by other traders when leaving the country. Due to the problems in the Fire Country, it was rather commonplace that traders could not find mounts and so had to cross on foot.

"Problems in Fire? What problems?" he had asked.

"Border sprawl, basically," she answered, which didn't really explain anything to Tala.

"Yeah, I guess they wouldn't really advertise their issues to the people." She chuckled. "Alright, well… basically, the Firelands are too big to maintain the borders. And they have more borders than any other country: Mud, Earth, Dust, the Jungle, Metal, and Light. Even Wind technically. And those borders all have to be constantly maintained and reinforced so that Fire doesn't lose any territory. The borders of Dust and Metal are easier, since there's no real risk of either trying to take land, but they still can't ignore them. And even though Wind Raids haven't happened in decades, they have to keep a watch on the entire coastline just in case. Basically, Fire doesn't have the resources to do it, but they also refuse to cede any land. So they're spread thin and doing everything they can to hide their weakness. One of their strategies is to take every pack animal they can for the army, either to haul supplies or to let patrols move further and faster. While they won't risk angering Dust by taking their animals, it's hard to find good pack animals for sale anywhere in Fire. So saying we just couldn't find any animals to use? It's been a common story for years. Nobody will think twice about it."

"I… I had no idea things were so bad. I mean, they're always talking about how we're the strongest country and so on. That's a lie too?"

"Ehhh, kinda." She wiggled a hand in a sideways up-and-down motion. "As a whole, Fire is one of—if not *the*—strongest countries. It's just spread too thin. If a full war broke out between Fire and any one of its neighbors, Fire would win hands down. But they would have to pull soldiers and resources from the other borders to do so. If one of those countries took the opportunity to attack, Fire could end up losing a lot, way more than they're willing to risk. That's why Fire hasn't actually gone on the offense against anyone in hundreds of years and has focused entirely on defending its borders: it's all they can really afford to do. It's probably a logistical nightmare trying to sweep the country for you. That's probably why we've had such an easy time of it: they just can't afford to put as many resources in as they need to find you. Good for us, and terrible for them," she finished with a happy laugh.

Tala tried to share in her humor, but it was half hearted at best. Even if he was swaying to the cause, Fire was his home. He didn't want to see it hurt.

"How do they manage then? If we—*they*—are spread so thin, how have they managed to keep the other countries at bay?" he asked.

"With a lot more difficulty than they acknowledge," she japed. "Mostly it's just that they've focused on utilizing their strengths to defend themselves. There's a reason that that Institute of yours is so highly valued: the inventions and ideas that are created there have kept Fire ahead of the other countries for millennia. Most of them have created their own versions of the Institute to try and even the field, but yours is the oldest, the biggest, and still easily the best. Some of the things they come up with there are pretty amazing, like the plumbing network in the cities. Like that steam pipe you used to kill Ignis. That was created by the Institute. Even Steam Country itself hasn't managed to fully recreate Fire's steam-powered industry, although they are getting pretty close. I think they have some wounded pride that Fire uses steam better than they do. More than anything, though, it's the military branch of the Fire Institute that accounts for your strength despite the weakness of your army. Fire has some nasty tools that they use to defend the borders. As a whole, the Fire army is probably the poorest-trained in the world: Fire focuses less on the training of its soldiers and more on just getting them in place as fast as it can."

Tala felt a mix of emotions at her words, mostly pride and a bit of anger. He had grown up hearing the Institute's praises sung, but it was nice to hear an outsider confirm just how great it was. Tala had very little experience with the military branch of the Institute (Mil-Tec, as the Researchers called it) as his parents had made sure to keep him far away from the areas where they developed and experimented with weapons, studied military strategy and tactics, and even (according to rumor) practiced and experimented with torture and interrogation. He knew the things that came out of that branch were one of the reasons the Institute as a whole was given so much power and privilege. On the other hand, though, to hear that his country's army was so poorly thought of did rankle his sense of national pride, convoluted as it might have been these days.

"So that's how Fire has kept the other countries from seriously attacking it? The Institute? That's it?"

"No, not entirely. It is a big part of it: the Fire Institute is internationally renowned and its reputation helps, as do all the things it creates, but it's not enough by itself. The other main power that keeps Fire safe are its Descendants and Blessed."

Tala gave her a look. "Isn't that kinda… *every* country?"

"Well, yes." She laughed. "But also no. To go with its size, Fire has the most Descendants and Blessed out of any country, even more than the combined number of Beast and Plant in the Jungle. Only the Bodylands have more, but they… don't really count." Tala nodded at that; not much was known of the lands beyond the Dust Wall, but the sheer number of Blood, Flesh, and Bone Descendants who were always part of a Horde spoke volumes to how many must exist at any given time in that nightmare place.

"And unlike the army," Serala continued, "Fire Descendants are well trained. Both by their own families and by the Church. So unlike the army—where the average soldier is considered less dangerous than one from another country—the average Descendant or Blessed is considered more dangerous. There aren't many Descendants or Blessed out there who would be willing to face down a Fire equivalent one-on-one. There's a reason the neighboring countries only place some of their strongest Blessed in charge of their closest cities to Fire. On top of that, Fire has been known to produce some particularly exceptional Empowered, people so powerful that the very threat of them can sometimes keep the other countries in line. I'm sure you've heard of Anderas Anto, right?"

At Tala's nod and snort of assent, she continued. "He's the most well-known Blessed in the world right now. He might even be the strongest one alive. The Fire Church certainly por-trays him that way." Tala merely nodded again as he thought back to that day in the arena when the man saved the entire coliseum audience from a gruesome death as though it were no more difficult than swatting a fly. "Well, apparently, a few years ago, Earth was starting to push Fire harder than usual. Anyway, Earth was being a bit too aggressive, so Fire sent Anderas to Serehag again as a precaution. Earth found out and stopped their push entirely. The very threat of him made the entire country back down. Not many Blessed in the world could do that. Especially with Earth: they hold a special hatred for the Fire Country, and they've wanted to reclaim Serehag since Fire took it back over two centuries ago. Had any other Blessed been sent, I doubt they would've backed down. Fire knows what they're doing. I'll give 'em that. Fucking Soleil." She finished with a muttered curse towards the High Priest of Fire, clearly unhappy with just how well the man had managed the apparently precarious situation that the Fire Country had been in for centuries.

"It makes sense that Earth would be afraid of Anderas," Tala said, deciding to ignore her abuse towards a man he had been raised to practically worship. "I mean, he survived fighting the Demon, right? He was the only Descendant who survived that mess."

"Right. That." Serala's words came out dry and cold, her good humor vanishing for an instant before slowly returning as she spoke again. "But I was talking about something from longer ago, when Anderas was younger than we are. His uncle was—still is—the lord of Serehag and brought a young

Anderas with him when he took lordship of the city. There was a lot of fighting with Earth going on at the time. They were making a serious effort to retake the city, and that was how Anderas first started to make a name for himself. And became a particularly hated enemy of Earth."

"Oh." Tala had never actually heard that story about Anderas. He wasn't surprised, though. Fire's favorite son was almost 100 years old, so if that had happened when he was a teenager, that meant it had happened over 80 years ago. More than long enough for most people to have forgotten a story about a man who had so many other, more recent accomplishments.

"So that's it then? The Institute and a lot of really strong Empowered? That's the secret to Fire's great strength?"

"Yeah, pretty much." Serala shrugged. "It also helps that most Descendants and Church members are required to learn from the Institute. Usually, I think Researchers are hired to teach them, right?" Tala nodded. He had known quite a few researchers who had been 'forcibly volunteered' to act as teachers for some Descendant kid or other. It was an almost universally hated job in the Institute despite how much the Church tried to make it sound like the greatest of honors. "The Fire Church realized just how powerful education can be a long time ago, and the power of a properly educated ruling class is something a lot of the other countries have been very slow in learning. Good for Fire, bad for all of the neighboring countries who are constantly being outsmarted by Fire."

Tala had never really considered the importance of education in the Gods' war. He was still surprised by just how little people outside of the Institute really knew or understood about the world they lived in beyond the basics of their city and their job. Most people didn't even know how the pipe network that ran through their city worked: they just knew that 'it did,' and somehow that was enough for them. He had found that even the ability to read was rare outside the Institute, and the only people who could do any sort of math beyond the most basic were traders and merchants. Although he knew that many gamblers developed their own strange ways of performing more complicated mathematics.

Their conversation continued, and the topics ranged from the types of things he had learned at the Institute, to where and how she had learned all the things she knew. Apparently, the Dissidents valued education highly, and Vail had made sure that whenever they were at a safe house, Serala was taught as much as she could be by whoever had something to teach. The rest of that day flew by for Tala, who thoroughly enjoyed walking and talking with her.

Thankfully, the next few days that they spent moving toward, and eventually joining, the Coastal Road passed without incident, there being no signs of other people on their approach. With the easier ground to walk on, Tala found himself often engaging the others in conversation as they traveled, sometimes talking to them one-on-one and sometimes in small groups. A few times, they even ended up having large discussions amongst the entire party—sans Vail—where even the silent Ilan would occasionally participate with a word or two.

The enjoyable days (in Tala's opinion) didn't always go quite so serenely, though. Two days after crossing onto the Coastal Road, they had their first encounter with a patrol of soldiers. It went smoothly, although Tala spent the entire time in a sort of panic-induced haze, barely aware of what was happening as Nuri and Caida spoke to the soldiers, and both parties went on their way with a shared laugh.

And it was only two days later that Tala found himself in a daze for an entirely different reason, for they had just passed the remains of a town that had been destroyed in the Wind Raids and subsequently abandoned. It had been common—in the days of the increasingly frequent and aggressive Wind Raids—for the smaller towns and villages along the coast to be completely destroyed, the buildings ruined, burned or otherwise broken, and all the people killed or taken by raiders. Most of those settlements had ended up like that nameless one that they had passed: abandoned and forgotten, crumbled, decaying monuments to the horrors of the Wind Raids. Even though the raids suddenly and inexplicably stopped 20 years prior—about six months before the first appearance of the Demon from Wind—there were still few people willing to risk resettling the coast, and those few who were either brave enough or desperate enough to do so usually ended up in the cities where they had a greater level of protection if the raids ever began anew.

Tala spent the rest of that day in a quiet daze as he thought about the horror that the people of that small town must have felt the day the raiders came for them: seeing firsthand the savagery that the raiders were known for and knowing that they were doomed to become their victims. He also thought about the people who lived: the poor souls who had been taken by the raiders back to the Wind Islands, presumably to become slaves.

It was another few days of travel before the mountains came into view again, still hazy and indistinct in the distance, but there were clearly more of them than the first time. Tala eagerly kept an eye on them until they were stretching far to the heavens above, looming over the party like silent giants. Tala had a hard time taking his eyes off them. It took only a few more days before the great walls of Southtown could be seen.

As they approached the city, it seemed that they were in luck, for the guards at the gate didn't seem to be any more numerous or alert than one might expect, giving only a cursory check of people before allowing them into the city. After all of the fear and worry Tala felt about approaching the city, it was nice to see that something was actually going their way. As their group approached the front of the line, and were given no more difficulty than any of the others had been, Tala gave a sigh of relief as he stepped through the gates and into the great trade city of Southtown.

CHAPTER 21

Tala's first impression of a city other than Fiahren was… weird. He couldn't think of a better word for it. Where the capital city of Fire was an enormous, tightly packed, sprawling metropolis with massive buildings that blocked out the sun and often stretched entire blocks, Southtown was none of those things. He knew it was actually quite a large city, stretching all the way from the banks of the Red Lake right up into the Metal Mountains. But it *felt* small! It was so *open*! He had thought that being in the confines of a city again would be comforting, but he had clearly underestimated just how different the city of his birth would be when compared to the other cities of the world. He had always heard of the differences, but seeing it now still took him by surprise.

The very buildings themselves were odd: most only being two or three floors tall! They were short enough that Tala could see the sky in every direction! And they were placed so… *uni-formly*! The street ran straight ahead, no curves or bends! And the alleys and streets branching off of it looked like they were the same; all coming off at right angles in even intervals. The streets themselves were so wide that the merchants in their stalls were spreading their goods *out* over tables instead of up on racks and shelves! Why was there so much space?

And the city was rather dull-looking in his opinion: the brown wood and gray, white, or black stone with which the buildings were built were on full display. Where was the color? The bronze and copper pipes crisscrossing the walls and alleys overhead? The vast array of tones from the paints or cloth or scrap metal that people would use to decorate their own sections of their buildings to create a mottled, patchwork explosion of sheens in a chaotic dance of expression! This city was just… drab! It felt almost lifeless in a way, despite the great number of people milling about and the endless calls of the merchant hawkers.

He had often heard travelers complain that Fiahren was overwhelming. He never really understood what they meant, but thought he might be experiencing the reverse. He felt like some large bird could just swoop down and grab him at any time! Or worse, that a Blessed just could pick him out where he stood!

And where were the pipes? He looked around in con-fusion before remembering that Fiahren was apparently the only city in the world that utilized a massive network of pipes to distribute water and steam to its residents and that, other than some lesser networks in a few of the other Fire cities, pipe systems like that were entirely uncommon. Denizens of the other cities in the world didn't have such easy access to water or heat or any of those easy luxuries that he had enjoyed in his life. He hunched his shoulders and thanked the Gods that he had been born in the Fire capital.

He followed as Nuri led the group through the streets, eventually stopping in front of one the larger buildings: wide and long and four floors tall. From the sounds of revelry coming from within—and the sign hanging over the door that read The Whistling Weasel—he guessed the building was an inn. As it was getting quite late in the day, Tala was hoping that they would be staying there for food and rest: a proper meal and bed sounded heavenly after the many weeks spent out in the wilds.

He tried not to get too excited as the group went inside and he saw that it was indeed a tavern: the ground floor was a large, open space filled with chairs and tables with a bar on the far end. Serala subtly pushed him over to a pair of long empty tables along one wall, which they were followed to by the rest of the group. Pushing the tables together, they sat around in exhausted relief as they motioned for one of the servers.

They ordered a veritable feast of food and ale and upon its arrival dove into the array, each one displaying a different level of poise and desperation as they enjoyed their meal. Their weeks in the wild and relief at their easy entry into the city caused them to be more relaxed than they had been since the day their adventure began.

As they finished, they basked in the relaxed atmosphere, sipping at their drinks. The exception was Nuri, who, upon finishing, had approached the bar and began speaking to one of the women working there. After a bit of back and forth, and much blushing on her part, he withdrew a money pouch and handed her a small pile of coins, to which she handed him in return a few iron keys attached to small wooden tags.

He returned to the group and placed the keys on the table, five in total. They would be staying there for the night, and possibly the next few days depending on how long it took them to get prepared for the next leg of their journey. Gazin took one of the keys and, with his usual friendly smile, told Tala that the two of them would be sharing a room, which Tala didn't mind. It certainly beat rooming with Nuri, who had already returned to flirting with the barmaid. The smuggler would likely be 'sharing' a room with Caida, although Tala wondered if either of them would even be using their room, as she had also wandered off and joined a small group of people at a table on the far end of the room.

Tala wasn't sure where those two got their energy from, as he and the rest of the party were more than happy to retire to their rooms for a good night's rest, but he figured they probably knew what they were doing. Despite his lax and playful attitude, Nuri was a surprisingly responsible man (when needed) with an incredibly clever yet devious mind. That aside, he often reminded Tala of a horny puppy more than anything else.

Caida was similar, except she was far more composed and gave off an air of sensual mystery instead of playful excitement. Despite her soft, graceful persona, Tala found the woman particularly terrifying. He knew that her role in the Dissidents was that of a seductress and assassin. Apparently, her victims rarely had the presence of mind to keep any secrets hidden after she was finished with them. When she didn't have a target, the woman simply enjoyed plying her craft on whatever poor (fortunate) soul caught her attention.

The others in the party gradually dispersed for the night. As Tala entered his room, he gratefully collapsed onto one of the two beds. It felt strange to be lying on a proper mattress after sleeping in the dirt for so long, but he happily allowed sleep to claim him before Gazin had even gotten settled on his bed. Just having close walls and a roof made him so comfortable that not even the fear and paranoia of being a fugitive could keep him awake.

He awoke the next morning feeling more refreshed than he had since his adventure began. Stretching slightly, he got up and rolled his shoulders, embracing the lack of stiffness or soreness he felt. He greeted Gazin who was already awake, sitting on his bed sorting through his pack. The man greeted him back and informed him that the rest of their group was already awake and had gone down to the common room for breakfast.

The two went down to join the rest of their party, who were already enjoying an array of food that had been placed on their tables. Some had already finished eating and were just relaxing, chatting quietly with each other. Even Nuri and Caida were there, having already returned from their night's activities.

As Tala and Gazin sat down and helped themselves to some breakfast, Serala leaned forward and spoke, immediately gaining the attention of the rest.

"We've been lucky so far, but we can't get too comfortable. We need to gather information and supplies quickly and get out of the city before anything does happen. Nuri, Caida, did either of you learn anything useful last night?"

They both nodded, but Nuri was the one who spoke up. "A bit, yeah. Apparently, over the last week, there's been some activity up in the lord's district and at the embassy quarters for both Fire and Light. Both embassies have brought more guards in, and a lot of soldiers have been brought into the city by Metal. Nobody we've spoken to so far seems to have any idea what's going on, but there haven't been any rumors of Descendants or Blessed from either country entering the city, so it seems like it's just the force buildup we were expecting."

"Good." Serala nodded. "For now, we'll stick to the plan, but try to learn as much as you can about what's being done with the extra soldiers. Lito, I want you out too. Dunlop, Alina, and I will get supplies. Meet back here for lunch and we'll see if anything's changed."

There was agreement around the table, and those that Serala had named got up and left to begin their tasks. Tala stayed at the table, slowly eating as he thought about what he'd heard. Vail and Ilan had also stayed behind and were simply sitting in silence like usual, sipping at some tea. Once he finished eating, Tala asked Gazin what the four of them would be doing.

"Sitting quietly in our rooms, lad," the Fleshy told him. At Tala's frown, he elaborated. "We can't have you wandering around the city, just in case somebody recognizes you. Enjoy the chance to rest. We three certainly will." He finished with a nod towards the others as he rose and gently shepherded Tala back to their room.

"You three are staying here just to protect me, right?"

"Aye. It's just a precaution, though. We don't expect anything to happen," Gazin reassured him.

"Mm. I guess… I'm just wondering: if something did happen, what would we do?" Tala asked.

"Ah, a good thing for ya to know. Well, if any guards or such did come up here for us—and it came down to a fight—Vail and Ilan would take care of them. If they couldn't for some reason, they'd hold them off for you and I to escape. They'd follow when they could. If that happens, we'll try to get out of the city and into the Metal Mountains if we can, or into Light if not. If neither works, we'll make our way to a Dissident hideout in the city and either hole up there or have whoever's present help us get you out of the city. It doesn't sound like they know we're here, though, so that's pretty unlikely."

"A hideout? Why aren't we staying there already?" Tala questioned. If they had one of those already in the city, wouldn't it be a lot safer than staying in such a public place?

"There's a couple reasons for that. First is appearance: we openly entered the city and as a decently sized group. If we suddenly disappeared, it could raise questions; they're already looking for something suspicious. And it could draw attention to the hideout, not something we want to risk unless we have no other choice. You'd be surprised how effective a disguise like this can actually be, 'hiding in plain sight.' It's a favorite tactic of ours, and for good reason."

Tala nodded thoughtfully; that all made a good deal of sense to him. "And the other reasons?" he asked.

Gazin got a dark look at his question, darker than any Tala had seen on the Fleshy's face before. "We can't be certain how safe hiding there would actually be. What do you know about that Blessed you killed, Ignis?"

The question surprised Tala. "I don't really know anything about him. Why?"

"Do you know why Vail and Serala were there to save you that day?" At Tala's shaken head, he continued. "They were following him. He's been… he *was* leading a special inquisition force for the Fire Church, hunting down Dissidents, and with great success. He was far more successful than he should've been.

"Something was—*is*—wrong, so Those Three went to Fire to investigate. A bunch of us—including most of us in this little group here—were sent to Fire as backup for them, just in case. Tell me, lad: can you think of a possible reason for these problems we've been having?"

Tala had already come to what he thought was a likely conclusion before Gazin had even asked. "A traitor. Or traitors. Right?"

Gazin nodded solemnly. "Aye. We don't know who, how many, or where they are, but somebody's been leaking our business to the Fire Church. We don't even know if there are actual traitors, or if some people have just been careless or compromised, but it's a problem. One big enough for Those Three to handle themselves. Since Ignis was the head of the Church's inquisition force and was personally involved in their operations, we thought he might be in direct contact with the leak and so thought following him would be our best chance to learn more. Of course, you destroyed all our plans; ours and the Church's both.

"Oh, don't be looking like that, lad!" he exclaimed upon seeing Tala's face, the guilt evident upon it for having messed up their plans. "That man's death was worth having a hundred traitors. Any Blessed's is. We already told you that you've done more for our cause with that one act than most of us will ever do. That's no exaggeration, lad, so don't feel bad for it."

Tala nodded, his spirits picking up at the words. He understood how significant it was to have killed a Blessed, but he was only beginning to understand its impact on the Dissidents.

"The biggest pity is that you didn't kill more of them," the man continued. "One Blessed death, especially by a civilian such as yourself, will cause problems for all the Churches, but it's still only an isolated incident. It hurts them and greatly helps us, but they'll recover. If multiple were to die like that, though, well, then we'd really be seeing some chaos!"

At Tala's conflicted look, the man hurriedly spoke to him. "Not that you should even think about trying such a thing again, lad! It's a miracle you even survived facing a Blessed, much less killed one! If you ever see a Blessed again and even think they so much as looked at you weird, run as far away from them as you possibly can! You already gave us the miracle of several lifetimes. You don't need to do anything else now but stay alive!"

It would be a lie for Tala to say he had never considered what he would do if faced with another Blessed again, though. He knew the most realistic answer to that question was 'die,' but he couldn't help imagining other outcomes. Especially since his life had now become one where encountering another Blessed was likely. That wasn't a thought he enjoyed.

After a few hours spent in the confines of their small room, a knock sounded at the door, and Serala's voice came through, telling them that they were back and were going to start lunch downstairs. Eager for a chance to leave the room, they both happily rose and followed Serala down to the common room, where all of the rest except Nuri and Caida were already sitting and talking.

They sat and started eating, joining in on the conversation about what to expect once they were inside the mountains, when Nuri entered and hurriedly joined them at the table.

"I think we should leave sooner rather than later," the man interjected abruptly as he sat down, looking more concerned than Tala had ever seen him. "Something is going on in this city. I couldn't find out what, but there are way more soldiers here than there should be."

Serala nodded solemnly as the earlier conversation ceased, and a tense feeling overtook the table. "We heard something similar. It doesn't seem like they know we're here, though. Still, staying in the city is too much of a risk now. We've got everything we need, so we'll leave in the morning."

The rest of the party nodded. Tala felt his gut tighten and tried to reassure himself; the others seemed concerned but more due to the risky situation that they were in rather than any actual danger.

"Where's Caida?" Tala asked aloud, curious but not too concerned since nobody else seemed bothered by her absence.

"Probably still out doing her thing, no need to worry," Nuri reassured him with a grin. "By now, she's probably enjoying herself in some magistrate or other official's bed. If anybody can find out what exactly is going on here, it's her."

The rest nodded at his words, and Tala returned to his meal. While he didn't know the woman well, that did sound like something she would do. So it was of great concern to them all when she appeared a short time later, looking far less composed than usual, and hurried over to them.

"We have to leave. Now," she demanded, sounding far more commanding, and afraid, than Tala had ever seen her before. This was apparently a rare occurrence in general, for even before she had reached them, the others had tensed up in anticipation.

"Explain," Serala ordered in a commanding voice that sent shivers up Tala's spine. He couldn't tell if they were good or bad.

The seductress shot a harried glance over her shoulder at the rest of the room. There was only a light lunch crowd, and none of the patrons were nearby or paying any attention to them. She leaned in and spoke in a haggard whisper-shout. "It's a trap! The whole city is! Getting in so easily, they knew we were coming here! They've already shut the gates and are clearing the streets! And…" She trailed off and gulped, sending a pitying look towards Tala that sent a distinctly bad shiver up his spine. "There are Blessed in the city!"

CHAPTER 22

Tala felt his gut tighten painfully as his breathing stuttered. He barely registered what it meant that the gates had been closed; his attention was on the fact that there were Blessed. In the city. That shouldn't be. They were there for him. He wouldn't survive facing another one.

"Blessed?" Serala asked, voice tight. "Other than Elidor?"

"Yes, but not of Metal. Both Fire and Light were allowed to have a Blessed enter the city. They're here now, and I only know of two people alive that could cause them to let other Blessed into the city. And I'd know if the Bone Merc was here."

"Here's the plan," Serala said. "Get your things. Check the windows. Not you." She pointed to Tala. "Then meet back here. We might still be able to sneak into Metal. If not, we make for Light. If we get separated, make for Gemtown if we're in Metal, and Lutecin if we're in Light. We'll meet up there. You know where they are?" she asked Tala, who frantically shook his head.

"Doesn't matter. Stay with at least one of us at all times. We'll get you there. If it comes to a fight, don't. Just run. Now move!" she commanded the group, who began to hurry up to their rooms to do as told. Except for Vail, who simply leaned back in his chair and sipped some tea, looking entirely unconcerned as he tilted his head back and stared up at the ceiling. Tala shook his head as he turned back to the stairs, desperately trying to control his breathing and stay calm as he followed the others up.

He rushed into his room and grabbed what few things he still possessed and had left in there, Gazin ahead of him peeking through a slight gap in the windows wooden shutters before closing them fully. "We're clear. Didn't see anyone," the man said as he hurriedly grabbed his pack and followed Tala back into the hallway and down the stairs.

"Report. Anything?" Serala asked.

"Nothing on our side," Nuri said. All the others responded negatively as well.

"Good, we may still have time. Nuri, lead us to an entrance into Metal."

"No." The voice came out of nowhere: calm, confident, strong. Tala looked towards Vail. The man was still sitting as calm and relaxed as ever, but his eyes were pointed at Serala with a focus, an intensity, a *presence* that Tala had never seen before.

"What? Why not?" Serala asked in a baffled voice.

Vail sighed and drained the rest of his tea, setting it down on the table. "If they let Blessed into the city, if they've closed the gates and cleared the streets, we'll never get into Metal. The mountains are too far from here, and they'll be locked tight. Too tight even for Nuri."

Tala glanced at the smuggler, expecting some sort of response from the man, but he was simply staring at Vail in shock, a look reflected on the faces of all the others except Serala, Ilan, and Gazin. Tala wasn't the only one who was surprised by Vail's sudden behavior.

"We'll make for Light," the enigmatic man continued, seeming entirely unbothered. "The north gate is the closest to us. If we can get through it before any Blessed shows up, Ilan can collapse it, and we'll be free. We'll steal and drive off the horses at the stables outside the gate so they can't follow." Vail stood up as he spoke and brought his arms together over his head and bent backwards in a stretch before shouldering his pack. Vail lifted his sword a few inches in its sheath, making sure he could draw it smoothly. "Get ready to run. And fight."

With that said, the man began walking towards the door, still carrying himself as casually as though he were going for an afternoon stroll. Ilan followed just a step behind, his giant sword now casually slung over one shoulder instead of across his back. Tala, along with the rest of the group, stared after the man, too surprised to follow, until Serala called for them to move and they all jolted towards the door.

As Vail poked his head out the door and looked around, Gazin grabbed Tala's arm. He looked to the shorter man, who was staring at him with a rare intensity. "Listen, lad. There's going to be fighting. Probably a lot of it. You stay out of it, okay? Stay with me or Dunlop. Or with Alina and Lito if we're fighting, which is likely. They'll keep you safe. But stay away from Those Three. You won't survive close to them."

The man finished by lightly shoving Tala towards the door, which he went through with his head spinning. He was more than happy to stay out of the fighting: even if he was confident in his swordplay or other fighting skills (he wasn't), he didn't want to have to fight. To kill. The broken body of the poor scout that night in the hills flashed through his head. Ignis had been an accident; Tala had never intentionally killed somebody before and didn't want to now. He would stay with Gazin or Dunlop or Alina like he was told. He didn't care if it was cowardly: he didn't want to have more blood on his hands.

CHAPTER 23

As the group shuffled out of the inn, Alina saw that the streets, while not quite empty, were devoid of the usual crowds that had been there before. The people outside seemed scared; they were moving quickly with their heads down, and even as she watched, she saw some slip inside buildings up and down the street. Most of the merchant stalls that were in sight were empty; the few that weren't had their owners hastily packing away their wares.

Alina and the rest of the group mimicked the behavior that they were seeing: heads down, tightly packed, walking fast. It seemed to work as they passed a small quartet of guards, who were harassing some merchants into packing up their stalls faster. From the corner of her eye, Alina saw the guards give their group a suspicious look over before dismissing them as they turned a corner.

The street they had turned onto was wide and completely empty. Nuri led them in a hasty not-quite-run down the empty street when Vail stopped him with a hand on his shoulder. The normally aloof man stared suspiciously at the street ahead of them, silent as his eyes swept the street from side to side. Suddenly, he pulled Nuri back and started walking back the way they came, the rest following him in quiet confusion. After passing a few buildings, he made a quick 'follow me' gesture before he suddenly darted to the right, into a small alleyway.

The group rushed after him, trusting whatever was making him act this way. They ran down the alley in a quick jog, their footfalls echoing in the eerie quiet that had enveloped the city. As he got to the end of the alley, without warning, Vail unsheathed his sword and swung it as he spun around the corner.

A little ways behind him, Alina couldn't see what the man had attacked until a head rolled from around the corner, still encased in a helmet that she recognized as that of a Firelands soldier. As Alina and the rest of the group rounded the corner, they found Vail pulling his sword out of the chest of another soldier, also from the Firelands, with four more already lying dead on the ground in the small, otherwise empty street.

Serala, Ilan, and Dunlop had drawn their own weapons and were now warily looking around, having automatically moved to surround the entrance of the small alley, shielding the others. Alina was glad they were there: despite how small Serala and Dunlop looked compared to the massive Ilan, she knew there were few fiercer fighters in the world.

But they weren't the only ones who had prepared for battle: dear Lito had drawn his own longsword and was gripping it tightly. She wanted to reach out to him, give him some encouragement to help him relax, but held herself back. Now was not the time for such things. She knew that, as tense as he was now, once things actually began, he would relax in that strange way of his. Watching him fight was like watching a dancer dance, and she had to keep her focus to not get lost in his rhythm. Nuri and Caida were also ready, both wielding a pair of daggers. Nuri's were as gaudy as everything else about the man, but they were sharp and well-made. Alina and Gazin weren't holding any weapons, but they were prepared in their own special ways for a fight. Tala gripped the hilt of his sword but had not yet drawn it. That was probably for the best; as skilled as Dunlop was, as much training as he had put the boy through, she wasn't confident enough in his skills yet to let him be involved in any fight. The way that his hands, his entire body, were shaking only further enforced her belief that he wasn't ready.

Vail calmly looked at the group and spoke as he bent down and wiped the blood on his sword, absently pocketing the small coin pouch on the corpse's hip as he did so. "They were preparing an ambush. There's no sneaking anymore. Run."

They ran through another narrow alley emerging onto another, larger street. Unlike the last, however, this one was neither empty nor hosting only a small group of enemies: both ends of the street were blocked off by lines of soldiers, with their backs facing the Dissident group now in the middle of the street. Vail's impromptu change of course had brought them behind and between the ambushes that had been set for them. The quiet of the street, however, had caused their emergence to be quite audible, and more than a few of the soldiers turned around to look at the sudden noise, spotting the fugitive group looking back at them in shock.

After a few moments of the three groups staring at each other, some of the soldiers began crying out, catching the attention of the rest who hadn't turned. The two groups of soldiers reversed direction and began charging towards Alina's party, intending to crush them.

"Ilan, Alina!" Vail barked out. Although she couldn't see what Ilan was doing, she heard the heavy stomp and the loud cracking of stone. From what she had seen of his abilities at the river, she felt confident in assuming that the Earth-Marked man had raised another massive wall of earth and stone to block off his side of the street.

On her end, Alina quickly made a few hand gestures in the air before shoving them out straight in front of her. A brilliant, blinding white light shot out, instantly encompassing all the soldiers on that end of the street. As always, her attack was silent and ended almost as quickly as it had begun.

Unfortunately, the speed at which she had needed to make her move had not allowed her to build enough power to truly weaponize her light, and all of the soldiers that had been hit by it were still there. None were charging anymore, however: instead, they were screaming in pain, hands pressed over their eyes. Even if she couldn't kill them with that move, she could at least take them out of the fight. She would need to be better prepared next time.

CHAPTER 24

With one end of the street blocked off, Vail led them the other way, towards the chaotic mess of blinded soldiers. As he passed by the incapacitated enemies, his sword struck out in incredibly fast, precise motions, felling each person he passed. The others did the same, with their swords and daggers slicing through the unguarded, vulnerable flesh of the soldiers who, still unable to see, had no idea that the attacks were coming.

Tala ran through the gap the others had made in the broken formation, sword still sheathed. He understood the need for such brutal tactics but wasn't yet to the point where he felt he could do such things himself. With the enemy blinded as they were, it wasn't so much a battle as it was a slaughter. He'd enjoyed going to fights at the arena as much as anyone, but this had a distinctly different feel to it. Watching violence from afar was very different than being involved in it.

As they turned a corner, Vail ducked as a sword whistled through the air. Instead of decapitating the man, it impacted on Ilan's sword, the force of the blow not even fazing the massive man, who simply shoved his sword forward in response, smashing it into Vail's would-be killer and knocking him to the ground. Without hesitation, Ilan stomped on the man's head, crushing it under his boot.

In the seconds it had taken Ilan to deal with the man, Vail had already risen back up and sliced two other soldiers across their throats with a single swing, causing them to collapse as their hands tried and failed to stem the torrential blood flow. At the same time, Serala rushed forward, spearing the remaining two soldiers through an eye each, one with the sword and the other with her dagger.

Tala was amazed at the supreme speed and skill of the three, not to mention the sheer brutality of their actions. In a matter of moments, the three had turned a sudden ambush around and killed their attackers. He was also mildly disturbed by Serala's vicious grin. Despite the terrifying situation that they were in, Tala had the distinct impression that she was enjoying herself. The other two—in contrast—wore their normal, neutral expressions, as though the near-death experience and subsequent slaughter were entirely banal events.

He thought the three lines of spearmen that were blocking the street behind the would-be assassins might elicit at least some reaction from the two, but they seemed entirely unbothered. Ilan simply charged into the line, catching and breaking the spears with a swing of his massive sword. At both his sides, Vail and Serala also charged into the line, flipping through the air in an amazing show of acrobatics as they sailed between the spear points and into the enemy lines.

Tala looked on in wonder: the spaces between the spear rows were very narrow, and had either of the two messed up their jumps even slightly, they would have been impaled. He couldn't imagine how much training such a maneuver required.

The three were causing utter chaos in the mass of soldiers, who easily outnumbered them more than ten to one. In order to react to them, the soldiers had to drop their spears and draw the short swords they carried at their waists, lest they be slaughtered from behind.

Tala stayed out of the fight, keeping back with Nuri, Caida, and Alina while Dunlop, Lito, and Gazin shot forward to help the three fight. He watched Gazin run forward in shock, wondering what the man was thinking as he wasn't even holding a weapon. Upon reaching the melee, Gazin merely grabbed the head of the nearest soldier, who immediately dropped to the ground, dead.

Tala's mind raced frantically, trying to figure out what he had just witnessed. He had heard the same stories as anyone of how terrifying the Bodyland Hordes were to fight, of the massive quantities of Descendants of either Blood, Flesh, or Bone who were almost impossible to kill but could cause death themselves with a single touch. He supposed that last bit must have been what he had just witnessed: the ability of a Flesh Descendant to destroy the heart, lungs, brain, or any other organ of whomever they touched. He shuddered, recalling the feel of the man's magic in the mornings as it coursed through his body, relieving his muscles of their soreness. Even though he had heard the stories and knew at the time that the man supposedly *could* have killed him at any moment, actually seeing the ease with which he could do so was terrifying to witness.

Two soldiers surrounded the unarmed Fleshy, and, as he was looking at one, the other shoved his sword straight through his torso, looking elated at his success. Gazin merely half-turned around and grabbed the soldier's arm that was still holding onto the sword inside his body. Before the soldier could react, Gazin ripped the soldier's skin off of his body, sliding it out through his sleeve as he turned and slapped it at the head of the other. The mass of empty flesh wrapped around the second soldier's head and erupted into a gruesome array of countless fleshy spikes, easily piercing the unfortunate man's non-magic-enhanced skin, killing him instantly.

The man who Gazin had so smoothly flayed collapsed as a bloody corpse of bone and muscle, a sight that Tala was sure would haunt his dreams for years to come. The simple brutality that the generally peaceful, jovial man exhibited was almost as shocking to Tala as the acts themselves were.

The sword that was still in Gazin's belly seemed to be little more than a nuisance to the Flesh wielder, who simply put a finger on the tip and pushed it all the way back out of him until it fell to the ground. The man then stood still for a few moments before stretching briefly and jumping back into the fray.

Tala watched as the small battle finished, barely believing what had happened. All six of his allies were still standing, while every single one of the dozens of enemy soldiers lay dead or dying on the ground, despite greatly outnumbering them.

While his six companions were all covered in blood, none of it seemed to be their own, with the exception of Gazin, who only had a small spot of his own blood staining his shirt around the place where he was stabbed. Tala felt immensely relieved that they were all fine, and more so when Lito began calming down, no longer gripping his sword quite so tightly or looking around so wildly. Tala attributed that improvement to Alina's presence beside the boy, speaking quietly to him while she tried not to look like she was checking him over for injuries. A pretense she was failing quite miserably at.

After a quick assessment of them all from Gazin, ensuring that there were in fact no injuries that needed his healing, Vail commanded them to keep moving. They were getting closer to the northern gate, but still had a ways to go before reaching it. As the last of them crossed through the mess of corpses and blood, they began running again, going up the street and turning another corner.

Perhaps the fight with the Light spearmen had lasted too long, or maybe they were just unlucky, but as soon as Vail passed the corner to the next street, he dove to the ground as a spray of metal spikes shot through the air, narrowly missing the man. Instantly, Ilan charged forward, slamming a foot on the ground as he cleared the alley and created another large wall of earth, blocking off the street from the direction the spikes had come.

The Earth-Marked giant turned to the group, intending to speak with a fiercer, more intense look on his face than he had donned yet, but was interrupted as a human form smashed through the earthen wall, crashing into Ilan and sending him flying down the street.

Tala looked on in shock as the large, indomitable Ilan was so easily tossed aside, eyes turning to the figure that had done it. It looked like a man, taller and broader than Tala but nowhere near the size of Ilan. He looked strange, though: his skin was shimmering in an odd way, as though it was covered in some sort of strange metal.

Tala's eyes, first widened in shock, were now so in fear. To smash through the earthen wall and knock Ilan through the air like that meant the new arrival was most definitely a Metal Descendant.

Tala wasn't the only one who came to that conclusion, as the same concern he felt was mirrored on the faces of his allies. Alina—a Descendant herself, an Awakened one at that, he thought with relief—stepped forward, gesturing with her hands before unleashing a much smaller beam of light at the man than she had at the soldiers. Before she had even unleashed the light, the metallic sheen of the Metalborn's skin shifted slightly, looking suddenly brighter. As the beam of light made contact with the man, it bounced off his forehead, deflected into the sky.

The man grinned nastily and shot forward, faster than Tala could react. Dunlop tried to block him, stepping into his path with his shield raised and sword dropped on the ground, but was tossed aside as the man smashed through him, undaunted. The Metalborn reached Alina and swung his fist, smashing it into her midsection and throwing her into the wall of the alley, where she fell to the ground, unmoving.

Lito screamed in rage and swung his sword at the man in a wild, overhead smash, only for the man to grab the sword in midair. Immediately, the sword began to deform, looking to Tala as though it were melting, as the metal of the sword began flowing onto the man's hand and over his arm. It took only a second for Lito to be left with an empty hilt, the sword having been consumed entirely. The Metalborn laughed as he swung the back of his fist in an almost casual manner, hitting Lito in the head and making him crumple to the ground.

Tala looked in fear at the man who had already taken down half their group. As Lito had shown, normal metal weapons would be worse than useless here, meaning Nuri, Caida, and himself could do nothing. From the look of anger in Serala's eyes, he had a feeling there wasn't much she could do either.

He turned to Gazin, hoping that the skilled Flesh wielder would be able to challenge the Metal wielder. The dark look in the older man's eyes as he stared at their new enemy killed that hope. While he looked like he was waiting for an opening, if there was anything he could do, he would have already done it. From what little Tala knew of the different interactions between elemental wielders, Gazin would need to be touching the man's flesh to use his power, a hopeless endeavor as the Metal bastard was entirely covered in said element.

In a last bit of desperate hope, Tala looked toward where Vail lay. For all the mystery surrounding the strange man, he was clearly an incredible fighter, so Tala hoped that he had some way of dealing with a Metal Descendant. To his confusion, however, Vail wasn't there. There were chunks of rock and dirt from the Metal wielder's entrance, but no person, aside from the nearby Ilan, who was slowly crawling to his feet.

As Tala turned back to the others, he saw Serala looking at Vail's missing form the same as he had. She seemed to know what was going on, though, as she smirked and started taunting, getting the Metal wielder's attention. He began to stalk towards her. As he got close, Vail suddenly appeared right behind the Metal man.

To Tala's surprise—and slight disappointment, if he was being honest—all Vail did was swiftly kick his foot up, connecting firmly with the Metal man's genitals. To Tala's further surprise, there was a strange crunching sound, and the Metal wielder gave a keening wail as he collapsed to the ground, hands covering his groin.

Tala looked on in bemusement as Vail brought the man low with such a simple, juvenile attack. "Metal Descendant. Even Awakened can only cover their skin with Metal, can't easily go deeper. Doesn't do much against blunt force, especially down there. Won't work on a Blessed, though."

Tala could only nod, amazed at how simply Metal Descendants could apparently be beaten. That was… a very strange and unexpected weakness, and Tala wondered when, where, and how Vail had discovered it. Maybe this was the secret reason why Metal had become a trade-focused nation like Dust: because their Descendants could be beaten by such a simple trick. *No, that doesn't make sense. They could just add armor down there. And women would be immune by default.* As frustrating as Vail could be to talk to, Tala resolved that when he had an opportunity in the future, he was going to ask Vail about where and when he had learned that little trick. And if he knew any others. After all, if Metal Descendants had such a weakness, maybe Descendants of other elements also had glaring weaknesses so simple most people wouldn't even think of them! Tala himself had already discovered a massive weakness present in Fire *Blessed*. A sudden thought rushed into his head, one that he couldn't believe he had never thought of before, especially in the last few weeks: *was this why Arcane Research was forbidden? Because the Empowered have* weaknesses!? He was going to have to look into it more; if Tala was right, he might have just discovered a way to accomplish one of the Dissidents' absurd goals!

Vail, oblivious to the chain of thought he had inspired in Tala, was taking the time to properly deal with the downed Descendant, who was still writhing in agony on the ground. The enigmatic man had retrieved a small pouch from inside his cloak and from it pulled out a small pinch of some foul-looking brown mush. Flipping the squirming Metalborn onto his back, Vail shoved the mush into the man's mouth, holding it closed afterwards.

The man on the ground tried to spit the strange mush out, but he was in too much disorienting pain to put forth a proper effort. Within moments, his actions had slowed, and he began convulsing, causing Vail to release him as foam began pouring out of his mouth. After only a few seconds, the man had stopped moving completely; his eyes stared blankly as the metal began to flake off of his skin.

Tala stared on in a strange mix of relief and horror. While Descendants weren't quite as hardy as a Blessed, they were still well known to be more resilient than the average person. A poison that could kill a Descendant that quickly was a terrifying prospect. *Another weakness?* A part of Tala, the part that he often considered (in the privacy of his own mind) as his 'Researcher side,' was fascinated with everything that was happening: the weakness of (male) Metal Descendants;

a poison that could kill (at least Metal) Descendants; the weakness he himself had discovered of Fire Blessed. He felt like he was just now getting the first few pieces of a puzzle that he hadn't even known existed. A puzzle that his 'Researcher side' desperately wanted to solve.

Seeing his look (and interpreting it only half-correctly), Serala, who had walked up to stand at his side, explained. "Special poison from the Jungle. Poisonous plants specially cultivated by Plant Descendants can be quite... effective." She sounded quite pleased. Tala could only shake his head in wonder as he turned to the others who had been injured by the Metal wielder. If he survived the day, he could ponder his new ideas on Arcane Research later.

He found Gazin already treating their friends, having gone to Alina first as the one who had suffered the worst blow. She was standing now, seemingly recovered but with one hand holding the wall to steady herself. Lito was there also, fussing over her despite the massive bruise already spreading over half his face. Gazin had moved on to Dunlop, who was sitting on the ground rolling his shoulders as Gazin laid his hands on his back. Ilan walked up to the front of the alley, seemingly already recovered from his brief foray as a titanic rag doll.

As Vail finished looting the Metal man's corpse, he stood and signaled for them to continue onwards. They began moving slower than they had before, a lot warier of any other surprises coming their way.

CHAPTER 25

Finally, they turned another corner and saw that in a straight path, only a few blocks ahead of them, stood the northern gates of the city. Standing a half-block in front of it, though, was one last small square that they would have to pass through. A square that was filled with many hundreds of soldiers arranged in a semicircle facing away from the gate, clearly prepared for their arrival. The path to the gate, and the other two streets leading off of the square, were completely blocked by the hundreds, maybe even thousands, of soldiers. As far as Tala could tell, though, it didn't look like there were any Descendants mixed in, and he wasn't sure if he should be worried or relieved. But as things stood, while the guard force wasn't small by any means, from what Tala had already seen of his companions, he was confident that they wouldn't have much difficulty breaking through and escaping from the city. Hells, with two Descendants and a (former) Stone Knight and Wild Guard on their side, it would take an army much bigger than that to stop them!

He wasn't the only one who had noticed the lack of Descendants, as Vail, Ilan, and Serala all began calmly walking towards the great force awaiting them. The garrison—who had spotted the group as soon as they turned the corner—were rearranging their formation. As they got closer, Alina swept past Tala and the rest, hands already shining with a bright white light.

As she entered the square, facing off against the mass arrayed in a defensive half-circle against them, the glow from her hands spread to encompass her entire body. A hand suddenly grabbed Tala and turned him around, pushing his head down as Lito whispered urgently in his ears. "Head down, eyes closed!"

Without thinking, Tala followed the instructions, hearing the 'thwing' of dozens of arrows being released as he did so. Not a moment later, a loud cry came from Alina, and even with his back turned and eyes closed, Tala's vision became a sea of white. Opening his eyes as soon as the whiteness faded, Tala turned around, dreading the sight he was expecting. Instead, extended in front of Alina were the charred corpses of at least a couple hundred men and women.

Tala stared in blank shock, wondering why he was even surprised at this point. He had heard the stories of what Descendants could do, had spent his whole life hearing about how a single Descendant could change the course of a battle, face down an army. But to see it: to see hundreds of soldiers wiped out in an instant, their armor in slag heaps and their bodies charred black, a great arc of death in the middle of the forces arrayed against them…

He was startled out of his stunned thoughts as a massive form thundered past him: Ilan, the giant of a man made even larger by the layer of stone that was encasing his entire body. Moving faster than Tala thought such a large being had any right to move, the Stone Knight charged into the square, crashing into the surviving yet disarrayed left flank of the soldiers.

Hot on his heels were Vail, Serala, Gazin, and Dunlop. The first two charged straight into the bloody chaos that Ilan had created in the left flank, swords and dagger flashing into the eyes, necks, and every other vulnerable bit of the soldiers who were too distracted by the rampaging man to remember that he wasn't the only threat. Tala watched as swords and spears shattered and slipped off of the hardened stone as their wielders were bisected or had their heads or bodies crushed by his flying fists or feet, or were slain by the ridiculously quick brutality of his two accomplices. They truly were a majestic sight, if only in the most macabre of ways. The speed at which countless soldiers were reaped by their dancing blades made them appear to him as death incarnate. Even as part of him shied away in disgust, another part was mesmerized by the dark beauty that was their butchery.

On the other side, the right flank of surviving, panicked soldiers, Gazin had similarly jumped into the fray, although with more caution and tact.

That wasn't to say that the genial old man didn't make for a horrific sight himself, though, for while the soldiers were still recovering from the shock and blindness that had come from Alina's massive… whatever exactly she had done, Gazin had charged directly at two soldiers kneeling on the ground, their hands clasped over their eyes as they screamed in mindless pain, blinded by the immense light even if they had avoided being killed by it.

The Flesh wielder grabbed both men by their exposed faces and, barely slowing his pace at all, once again ripped their skins off, their flayed flesh sliding over their bodies and out their armor through the neck. He proceeded to utilize the two masses of stolen skin, forming them into horrific, nightmarish weapons. The skins' shapes were constantly changing, and each move Gazin made brought one of the skins into contact with a soldier, where they would die a brutal death: throats were slit by sharp-edged flesh, and eyes were pierced by needles made of magically enhanced skin. The worst of it was when Gazin would throw his flesh-weapon over a soldier. The pliable substance covered and encased their heads like a living nightmare devouring a meal. To make it even worse, when Gazin pulled his flesh weapon back, it had grown in size, and the bare muscle of his victim's faces lay exposed as their bodies collapsed, flayed by proxy without the Fleshmancer ever even having touched them. How did the soldiers of the Dust Wall ever manage to face Hordes of such beings!?

Even attacking the Fleshy was proving a futile endeavor, as he could wield his stolen flesh as shields just as easily as he could use them as the most macabre of weaponry: the man was moving faster than anybody Tala had ever seen, faster than any non-Flesh wielder could, he supposed, and every attempt to strike him with sword or spear was met with a shield of writhing, magically reinforced flesh which could instantly shoot out a spear of hardened skin into whoever had attacked it.

Right behind Gazin was Dunlop, who, to Tala's great relief, wasn't committing any such sort of unholy acts in the process of killing his enemies. The man was simply fighting with his mace and round shield, protecting Gazin's back and keeping the Fleshy from being swarmed. Despite his simplistic combat style, Dunlop was leaving a pile of bodies in his wake, the soldiers no match for the martial skills of the former Wild Guard. It was said that Wild Guards were a threat even to Descendants, and for the first time, Tala thought he understood why: this was a man who through sheer skill and experience was slaughtering his way through a force that outnumbered him hundreds to one.

A beam of light suddenly shot past Tala's face, startling a scared yelp out of him. The beam of light hit a soldier who had been trying to sneak behind Dunlop right in the side of the head, bursting straight through her temple and into the face of another soldier. Tala gulped and glanced backward to see Alina walking up beside him, small glowing balls resting at the tip of each of her fingers. Tala hadn't even realized that, as he watched the slaughter disguised as a battle, he had mindlessly walked right past her and into the square, getting closer so that he could better see his companions fight—*slaughter*—their enemies.

In the cacophony of combat and deathly wailing, Tala could swear he heard the unbridled laughter of Serala as she frolicked her way through the sea of soldiers. Her euphoric behavior contrasted sharply with the silence of Vail and Ilan. Yet the quick glances Tala got of Vail's face left him with the impression that the man was smiling, as though he were enjoying himself immensely.

To escape the onslaught, some soldiers left the battle and went after Alina, trying to stop her from picking them off from afar. They were quickly dealt with by her, and the few who got close were then disposed of by Lito. Some went after Tala, Caida, and Nuri instead, likely seeing them as easy prey given their complete separation from the battle. Those who did found that Caida and Nuri were far from helpless. The smuggler and seductress were not traditional fighters, but they worked together with an astounding efficiency: one would steal the attention of their target, and the other would attack them from behind, daggers making short work of their distracted prey. Their method of combat wouldn't have worked with multiple assailants at a time, but Alina and Lito were letting few soldiers make it that far, leaving those who did easy victims of the other pair.

Tala stood alone in the middle of the chaos, surrounded by intense, bloody combat, the likes of which he had never even imagined he would ever see.

Frustrated at how useless he felt and simultaneously relieved that he didn't have to take part in the fighting himself, Tala looked around the square, deciding that he could at least keep an eye out for any surprises that his allies might miss. The rest of the square was completely empty, though, aside from the combatants. A large, empty, stone square with four streets emanating from it: one behind him that led back the way they came, one that led to the northern gate, and the two that led east and west, parallel to the northern wall.

The one thing he could do was yell out a warning when he saw many, many more soldiers: masses wearing the artistic sun of the Light lands or the more simplified hammer-and-anvil of Metal as they came swarming down the side streets.

Somehow hearing his desperate call despite the roar of battle, Vail looked up and saw the soldiers coming down the streets. He shouted to Ilan, who also looked up, saw the reinforcements, and, with a loud cry, swung his giant sword in a circle around him, clearing himself a small space free of any (living) enemies. The moment his swing stopped, the ferocious man began charging towards the nearest side street, throwing aside any soldier in his path as though they weighed nothing more than a child's cloth doll.

Once he was close enough, the Stone Knight slammed his foot on the ground, raising another giant earthen wall and blocking out that street entirely. Out of position, he was immediately swarmed by the remaining soldiers. *A poor move,* Tala thought as all those surrounding the giant man were mowed down like wheat, his stone armor making him literally invincible to the weapons of the soldiers. One had even managed to jump onto Ilan's back and attempted to choke him, a brave but useless move as the stone armor on Ilan's throat proved as impervious as the rest of him. The Stone Knight somehow hadn't even noticed the man that had jumped on him until the soldier began scrabbling around Ilan's eyes in a desperate move to claw them out. Tala wasn't sure if the attempt ever even could work, for Ilan simply reached up with his free hand, grabbed the man's arm, and swung him over his shoulder onto the stone floor with enough force that Tala could *see* the man's body burst inside his armor. Ilan then fought his way forward, trying to carve his way through the fray to block the other street, before the earthen wall behind him, the one he had just created, exploded outwards, pelting Ilan and all those around him with debris.

Tala looked on as the dust cloud that had erupted with the wall's destruction began to clear, revealing what could only be another Metal Descendant. Although Tala couldn't quite see them clearly, he was sure that the new Descendant had locked eyes with Ilan, for the two paused for a moment before suddenly charging towards each other at full speed.

The Metal Descendant and Earth Marked collided with such force that Tala wouldn't have been surprised if the city itself had shaken. Ilan had stabbed his sword into the ground before charging and so met the Descendant in a truly magnificent body slam, one that the Metalborn had tried to reciprocate. Unfortunately, the Descendant had overestimated the strength of his Metal magics when compared to the sheer brute power of Ilan in his full stone armor and was blasted backwards.

Unfortunately, the blow didn't take the Descendant out of commission, and the man rose, charging at Ilan with renewed vigor. He stopped short of another full collision with the larger man and instead engaged in a battle of fists; both combatants threw punches with enough power to instantly pulverize any normal person.

The reinforcements that had arrived with the Metalborn wisely chose to stay far away from the two dueling titans, breaking off to charge against Vail and Serala, a move that was heartily met by the two, or towards Alina and the others.

What truly concerned Tala, though, were the forces that had arrived from the other street shortly after. They poured unfettered into the square, and moved equally toward the central combatants and Alina and Lito, who were pushed deeper into the chaos as they were quickly surrounded, even as Alina's barrage of light beams came faster than ever. Tala could tell that the sheer volume of magic the girl was using was taking its toll, able to see the exhaustion on her face before it was obscured by soldiers.

Wait. There were soldiers between him and Alina. Tala stumbled back, further away from the chaotic melee and looked towards the others. There were soldiers between him and Lito, Caida, and Nuri! He was cut off. Alone! Panic began to mount in Tala as he realized what had happened! All of the others were being pushed towards the center and surrounded, condensing into an ever-shrinking circle with only Tala and Ilan on the outside.

Tala, who could barely fight. Tala, who was now alone on the outskirts, on the side of the square, the only thing now saving him the fact that all of the soldiers were so focused on the incredibly deadly fighters that were his companions that they were ignoring him entirely. He wasn't a threat, so they couldn't care less about him. So far removed was he from the fighting that they probably didn't even realize he was there. All but one, as Tala noticed a lone figure staring at him from the eastern street.

It was a woman—he could see that—but she wasn't dressed as a soldier. No, she was wearing a chainmail vest, but under it, her clothes looked nicer and less military-like than a soldier's. She also wasn't wearing a helmet. Tala and the mysterious woman looked at each for a few seconds, neither moving, before the woman promptly turned and began striding towards him, a self-satisfied smirk growing on her face as the chainmail she wore began melting and flowing over her body.

Tala's eyes widened in fear as he realized this woman was another Metal Descendant. A Blessed wouldn't need to cover themself in metal, although that knowledge was of little comfort. As the Descendant bore down on him, Tala couldn't help but take a quick look when he heard an enormous roar come from the other side of the square. Ilan had beaten his opponent; the Descendant was lying dead at his feet, head broken open, but another had already charged the Earthen Marked and was engaging him in another fight. Ilan was starting to struggle. Faintly, through the swarm of soldiers, Tala could see another man, who was quickly becoming enveloped by a Metal coating, marching straight towards Ilan, clearly intending to fight the Stone Knight in a two-versus-one brawl, a brawl that Tala was not confident his companion could win.

With a sinking heart, Tala turned back to the Metal woman approaching him. A quick glance behind and Tala saw that the street behind him—the one that he had come from—was also full of soldiers making their way towards the square. He was trapped. He had nowhere to run, nowhere to hide, and a Descendant was bearing down on him. Trying to think through his growing panic, Tala sheathed his sword, remembering what had happened to Lito's when he tried to use it against a Metal wielder. The boy had had to replace it with one taken off of a dead soldier. *Think!* Tala yelled at himself in his mind. *Think, damnit! You killed a Blessed! Metal... bait her in, kick her in the balls! Shit! No!*

The one tactic Tala knew of that could work here was useless since his opponent was a woman. What could he do? He was dead! They both knew it! He could tell by the malicious smile on her face that she knew there was nothing he could do. He watched in terror as she bore down on him. When she was only a few meters away, a metal spike started growing out of her hand. Clearly, she was going to impale him on it. When she was only a couple feet away, so close that Tala could feel the specter of his impending death hovering over his shoulders, a wall of fire suddenly erupted out of nowhere, passing right in front of Tala and burning straight through the Metal woman, who barely had the time to make a short, agonized scream before the fire consumed her fully.

Tala frantically stumbled back from the wall of fire that had suddenly materialized in front of him, falling on his butt as he realized that the fire was surrounding him on all sides. As the flames died down, he caught a glimpse of the rest of the square and all the people in it—soldiers and Dissidents alike—staring at the ring of flame before the fire rose back up in a great burst. Fire flooded the square as it pushed outwards in all directions, leaving nothing but the melted, charred corpses of those who had been caught by it. Tala looked around in a panic, seeing that the entire square was now surrounded by a wall of flame easily as tall as the buildings behind it. All that Tala could see now was fire and death, the flames surrounding him in a box that he knew could only have one source, and the burnt, charred corpses that littered the square, sparing only Tala when moments before there had been hundreds.

Despite the heat that now surrounded him, Tala felt an icy shiver as his heart palpitated in despair. There was only one type of being he knew of that could create such intense flames and control them in such a way. In his mind he heard Caida's voice from earlier that day: "Both Fire and Light were allowed to have a Blessed enter the city. They're here now."

He spun around in circles, trying to look in every direction at once. He didn't know what he was looking for: he was trapped in the fire, and the Blessed controlling it could kill him at any moment, before he would even know what was happening. He stopped his spinning as he caught sight of something in the flames: a man calmly strolling through the worst of the blaze. Tala stared in terror as the man left the flames behind, entering into the square proper with a calm, relaxed, and absolutely confident demeanor.

He was well dressed, with very fine red clothing adorned with the symbol of the Fire Church emblazoned in orange on his left breast: a singular, flickering flame. He strolled towards Tala who, for the second time in his short life, found himself staring down a Blessed of the Fire God. *No, not any Blessed. I know that face. That—that's him. That's who they sent after me.* He would have cried if he hadn't felt so totally, absolutely broken. *That's the greatest Blessed in the world. They sent Anderas Anto to kill me.*

CHAPTER 26

Tala stared at the man sauntering towards him, cold sweat pouring down his back despite the intense heat surrounding him. He could feel his brain trying—and failing—to work. To think. To come up with something that could save him. There was nothing. Nothing except the man walking towards him. The man whose very name could cow nations. The man who had survived a fight with the Demon from Wind when he was still just a mere Awakened. The greatest Blessed alive. Anderas Anto. Fire's favorite son.

As the world's most famous man approached, Tala could do nothing but stare at him. Shock, fear, horror? He had no idea what look he had on his face. Hells, he didn't even know what he was feeling! He simply watched as the legendary Blessed came near, a look of calm curiosity on the man's face. His pace was even, measured, as though he was taking a casual stroll and hadn't just murdered hundreds of people.

That thought broke through the overwhelming... whatever that had consumed Tala: his friends were dead! The people who had saved him, who had risked their own lives to smuggle him not just out of the city but out of the entire country, who had just fought their way through a city for him, were dead! This man's power had killed multiple Descendants in a matter of seconds and swept over the square, annihilating all who were unfortunate enough to stand in its wake, friend and foe alike.

Tala's hand tightened on the hilt of his sword as a surge of despair and anger swept through him. His allies—his friends—were dead at this bastard's hands! The Fire Country's most beloved son had murdered them all! And not just them! Hundreds of soldiers, men and women, even Descendants, had just been killed by him! They were his allies, and he had slaughtered them without a second thought! And he left Tala alive, trapped in a cage of fire, trapped with the scorched bodies of hundreds of people! Why? Did he want to gloat? Was he planning to slowly torture and kill Tala in revenge for Ignis? He wouldn't give him the pleasure! As soon as the Blessed got close enough, Tala would attack. He let go of his sword's hilt: the weapon would be useless here. So would his fists, sure, but at least the Blessed would have to turn to fire to avoid being hurt. A fire that would burn—and kill—Tala quickly if not instantly. Better to die fighting than slowly tortured to death. Even if it would do no real good, he could at least die on his feet, honoring his friends' memories and refusing their killer his bit of fun.

Anderas stopped walking right in front of Tala, just far enough out of reach that Tala couldn't attack without the Blessed having time to react. Tala glared at him, daring him to take one more step forward. Just one more step and Tala could steal his final victory away! The Blessed just stared at him, unmoving, unabashed curiosity still written all over his face. After a few long moments of staring between the two, one in hatred and the other in curiosity, Anderas spoke in an infuriatingly calm, cultured voice.

"So. You're Tala. Killer of Ignis. You do look quite like your description, I must say. Didn't even bother trying to disguise yourself? Bold move. You inherited your father's looks, I believe?"

The question sparked a new round of fear and fury within Tala: what did this man know of his parents? The Blessed must have seen the fear pass through him, for he was quick to continue speaking, waving a hand blithely through the air.

"Oh, don't worry. Your parents are fine. They disappeared not even a day after you did. We have no idea where they are in fact, and finding them isn't exactly our number-one priority, you know?"

Relief flooded through him. Something about the non-chalance, the sheer disinterest in the man's voice convinced Tala that he was telling the truth. Besides, if he wanted to torture Tala, he wouldn't have said that; he would have told him his parents were dead, or worse. But then why *was* he telling him? Was it some sort of mercy? Letting him know that his parents had at least escaped before killing him?

"Of course, their disappearance made uncovering *your* identity quite a bit easier. Even with the chaos you caused, when two of our esteemed Researchers up and vanish like that, we do tend to notice. Not that that really mattered much anyway. We knew you were coming here regardless. A bit concerning,

if you ask me. You'll need to be far more clever, far more…
unpredictable going forward if you intend to survive."

Anderas spoke calmly, as though he was discussing the
weather. His words weren't making much sense to Tala, though:
was this some sort of sick game he was playing? Giving him
advice, acting like he actually had a future, trying to give him
hope of surviving before snuffing it out?

Tala didn't respond, trying to figure out the man's game.
After a few moments of silence, the man sighed and opened
his mouth to continue talking when a massive earthen wall,
larger than any Tala had seen yet, shot up in the middle of
the fire on one side of the square, disrupting the flames that
had been there. Tala felt a jolt of surprise—and hope—before
it was snuffed out as the flames instantly flooded the earthen
barrier, burning it away as if nothing had happened.

Seeing the surprise and hope on Tala's face, the Blessed
resumed, unfazed, his tone still light and conversational.
"Ah, yes, that Earth Descendant. Quite an impressive man
if I do say so myself. If he were a Blessed, that plan might
have even worked." As Tala's surprised eyes turned to him,
he chuckled and continued speaking. "Oh, yes, your Earthy
friend is still alive. All your little friends should be: I was
careful. I wouldn't have gotten involved at all if that Metal
girl hadn't shown up. Well, probably. You lot were struggling
quite a bit, impressive as your friends are. Tell me: that man,
the one in the cloak, who is he?"

Tala didn't answer, still trying to process what he was
hearing: not only had Ilan survived, but they all had? The
Blessed had intentionally, not only not hurt them, but had

saved them? What exactly was going on here? And Earth Descendant? Ilan was a Marked, not a Descendant. Somehow, it was relieving to realize that Anderas didn't quite know everything about them, even if it was obvious that he had been watching them. And the cloaked man had to be Vail. Why was he asking about Vail in particular?

"You know, it's rude to ignore someone when they're talking to you." Tala blinked and refocused on Anderas, the Blessed seeming more amused than angry at Tala's lapse of attention. "I asked you—"

Anderas whipped his head back towards the flame wall with such speed that his neck momentarily transitioned into flames, eyes wide, as the fire that made up that small portion of the wall suddenly began spluttering and died down so low that Tala caught a quick glimpse of what looked like his companions standing beyond it before the fire rose back up with a vengeance, burning higher and hotter than before.

Tala turned to look at Anderas, wondering what had just happened. Why had the man lowered the barrier? And why had he seemed surprised about it? What Tala saw was Anderas staring in stark disbelief at the wall, eyes wide and brow intensely furrowed. If Tala didn't know better, he would have said that the Blessed looked scared. Anderas turned back to Tala, stepping closer and leaning down so that their eyes met. There was an intense look in the Blessed's eyes that was a far cry from the relaxed, amused look that had been there prior.

"That man. In the cloak. Who. Is. He?" the Blessed demanded, his voice hitching slightly.

"I don't know," Tala blurted out, a sudden sense of primal terror making him answer on instinct. "He's just sort of… there. He doesn't really talk much. He's weird."

The two stared at each other in silence, Tala feeling like he was looking into the eyes of a large, particularly dangerous predator. He couldn't begin to guess what emotion it was he could see in the Blessed's eyes, but it scared him. The fact that the man had moved closer to him didn't even register, his earlier plan of a suicidal charge having fled his mind completely.

Anderas stared into Tala's eyes as though he were trying to read his mind. Seemingly satisfied with his answer, the Blessed leaned back, standing straight as he cleared his throat. "Right, well, maybe it's time we ended this." Tala tensed up at the words. Whatever game the Blessed had been playing seemed to be over now. If this was the moment Tala was going to die, he wanted to at least do so in a way he could be proud of. To his surprise, the Blessed wasn't paying attention to him anymore; instead, he was looking over the burnt corpses on the ground.

Tala watched him warily as the man moved over the bodies, examining them for something. Seeming to have found whatever he was looking for, Anderas picked up one of the corpses, holding it up by its throat. He looked between it and Tala, as though comparing the two, before nodding in satisfaction.

"This should do. Now, your friends are over there." He waved idly in the direction that the earth wall and fire mishap had come from. "The gates are right there too. You should all be able to get out easily. I'd appreciate you not telling your friends about me. Make something up. Tell them you played dead and snuck out while I was distracted looking through the bodies for you.

Also, I recommend stealing some horses from the stables right outside the gate. Light breeds fast horses—I'll give them that."

Tala continued staring at the man, who seemed more occupied with the corpse he had grabbed than concerned about Tala. It sounded like he was letting him go, but that couldn't be it! What sort of trick was he pulling? Did he want to kill him from behind? Get Tala to walk into the fire and kill himself? Spite him out of any sort of noble death? The Blessed looked at Tala with a raised eyebrow.

"Well? We *are* rather short on time here. Are you going? Oh, right. The fire. Let me just—" He cut off, looking behind Tala with a frown. "Shit. Make that out of time. I thought it would take him longer." Tala whipped around to look behind him, realizing too late that this might be a trick. His fear went unfounded and forgotten as he saw another figure burst through the wall of fire.

Unlike Anderas, who had casually strolled through the flames unbothered, this new figure had charged through them, head ducked low and hidden beneath crossed arms. He was also dripping large globs of something thick and heavy, forming steaming puddles on the ground. Tala almost laughed (or cried, he couldn't tell them apart anymore) when he realized that it was metal—hot, melted metal—dripping off of the new arrival. Unless Anderas had drastically reduced the heat of the fire wall, then that fire was hot enough to kill a Metal Descendant in a second. There was only one type of Metal wielder who could survive charging through those flames.

Tala glanced back at Anderas. The Fire Blessed was glaring at the dripping man with an irritated look on his face. His eyes flicked to Tala, and he spoke in a quiet tone. "Kid, just… don't *do* anything. I have to deal with this first."

What? Tala blinked in confusion. What the Hells was going on? Was Anderas actually serious about letting him go? That didn't make any sense! He was one of the most glorified people in the entirety of the Fire Church! He was *Anderas Anto,* Fire's favorite son! The most loyal, decorated, indomitable Blessed in the country! Letting Tala go was a betrayal of everything the man had spent his life serving!

"Lord Elidor! Good to see you! Had I known you were here, I would've lowered my flames for you!" Anderas called out, sounding perfectly relaxed and happy, all traces of irritation gone.

Elidor. Yep! Tala closed his eyes and took a deep breath. Elidor, the lord of Southtown. One of Metal's most distinguished Blessed. One of the few Metal Blessed who actually *had* a reputation, given the nation's neutral, trade-focused nature. A man who had been made lord of Southtown well over a hundred years ago because his abilities and brutal reputation were great enough to keep the contentious city that sat on the border of Fire and Light firmly under control. Despite the city being the only real point of contact between the two nations, no serious altercations had occurred between the two within the city since the earliest days of Elidor's rule.

Tala was now trapped in a cage of fire with not one but *two* of the world's most famous and powerful Blessed. Even if Anderas was planning to let him go, what were the odds that Elidor would? He took another deep breath before opening his eyes. He was getting tired of this.

CHAPTER 27

The Metal Blessed's form warped and shifted as liquid metal slid around, cooling itself from the immense heat it had endured. As he stopped dripping, the man rose to his full height, a bit shorter but much stockier than Anderas. As Tala got a good look at him, he couldn't help but note the differences between this man and the Metal Descendants he had seen before. Where they were covered in metal, and looked like it, this man looked as though his entire body was made of metal, inside and out. Which, at the moment, it was. The eyes in particular were unsettling: strange metal orbs that sat in a strange metal face. How in the Hells could the man see if his eyes were metal? Were his pupils still exposed? How the Hells did that even work? He was too far away for Tala to make out any details about his eyes other than their being metal. Maybe he'd manage to get a closer look for a few seconds before he died? Tala almost, *almost*, laughed out loud at himself: even facing imminent death—*again!*—he was a Researcher at heart.

"Lord Anderas," Elidor said casually, with a short nod to the Fire Blessed. "No need for that. Your fire doesn't hurt much." Tala couldn't help but look at the puddles of melted Blessed. Thankfully, the two men ignored him. "Would this be that boy you're after then? The one who killed one of us? 'Cause he doesn't look like much." His voice sounded strange, as though it was echoing out of metal pipes. Tala supposed that wasn't so strange, actually, seeing as his vocal cords were most likely made of metal at the moment. Not for the first time, he wished that the Researchers had been allowed to study the Gods' magics and how they worked. It would be fascinating to see how the Blessed could survive when their entire bodies were turned into distinctly not-living material.

"No," Anderas replied, shaking the corpse in his hands. "He's just some random lucky bastard. This was my target." Tala tried very, very hard not to react to *that*.

"Is that so? He looks an awful lot like your people's description."

"Merely a coincidence, I assure you," Anderas responded with his smooth voice. "I believe he's one of Light's men actually."

"Oh? Well… no reason to leave him alive then," Elidor said indifferently as he began walking toward Tala, who quickly backpedaled away next to Anderas as the man's whole arm transformed into a rather nasty-looking blade.

"There's no need for that, I'm sure," the Fire Blessed refuted. "One lowly nobody got lucky. Might as well reward his good fortune by letting him live, eh?"

The Metal man simply snorted in response, still bearing down on Tala. Anderas sighed in annoyance and—as Elidor raised his arm to strike—dropped the charred corpse he was still holding and thrust both his hands out towards the city lord, shooting two intense streams of fire directly into his face.

"Arrrrgh!" Elidor screamed, shielding his melting face from the inferno. His arms quickly shifted form into two large, wide, shiny shields that he held in front of the fire streams. Whatever new metal configuration he had shifted to using seemed far more heat-resistant than before.

With a guttural roar that reverberated oddly from his metal throat, the lord of Southtown charged at Anderas, who quickly dispersed into a wave of fire before reforming behind Elidor, once again shooting twin pillars of flame at his back. The sudden charge of an enraged Metal Blessed and subsequent flame-forming of Anderas beside him sent Tala tumbling to the ground in surprise. He sat up slightly dazed, wishing his instincts hadn't sent him to the ground quite so hard.

Elidor roared in pain and rage again, but, instead of turning around, his body seemed to morph backwards, his head and still shield-shaped arms suddenly appearing where his back had been and his legs reforming the same. In the blink of an eye, the man had gone from taking jets of flame to his back to charging at Anderas again with his arm-shields once more absorbing the fire. This time, though, he also launched blobs of metal forwards from his arm-shields, which flew through the air almost faster than Tala could see.

They were also too fast for Anderas to react to, for he didn't move as the metal blobs flew straight through his flames, splattering across his face and body. He roared in pain, his flames dying down as he reacted on instinct to the pain from the speeding metal, distracted enough that he failed to avoid

Elidor as the Metal Blessed slammed into him with his shields, catapulting Anderas through the air.

Despite his shock at everything that was happening, at what he was witnessing, a part of Tala was still analyzing everything it could. They couldn't avoid each other, he realized. Anderas was getting hurt by Elidor's attacks, and Elidor by his. A Blessed's automatic defense didn't work against other Blessed. Why not?

Oblivious to Tala's thoughts, Elidor stood there panting, his shields growing a field of sharp spikes across them. "What in the Gods' names are you doing, Anderas?" the man roared at his downed opponent.

The only response to his question was a pillar of flame bursting to life where Anderas had landed, the man himself rising to his feet in the center of the inferno. Without a sound, the pillar condensed into a sphere around him before he launched it at Elidor. The heat of the man-sized fireball was so intense it began melting the stones of the floor as it flew over them.

Apparently unwilling—or perhaps unable—to block the attack, Elidor quickly melted into a puddle, letting the fireball pass over him, where it continued into the fire wall that was still surrounding the square and vanished. The puddle reformed back into the shape of a man, who began screaming in agony as soon as his throat had finished forming. Despite dodging the attack, the sheer heat emanating from the fireball had still taken its toll on him.

Across from him stood Anderas, the Fire Blessed looking calm and composed despite the damage visible on his clothes. He strode towards Elidor, his hands and arms looking less like human limbs and more like twin pillars of white-hot fire. When he had crossed only half the distance between them, a new, feminine voice rang out across the square.

"Well now, what's this? Blessed of Fire and Metal, trying to kill each other? I'm shocked!" the voice said, sounding nothing but gleeful about the situation. Tala's head whipped around at the words. He had been so engrossed in watching the fight between Blessed that he hadn't even moved, still sitting where he had fallen after the fight had begun. He couldn't see anyone else in the square, though: the only people in the place were himself, the two Blessed, and the hundreds of corpses. It should have been easy to see anyone else within the square.

Then he noticed the light of the flames coalescing a short distance away, forming the rough shape of a person. The light-figure became more and more distinct until the light suddenly vanished, leaving a tall, lean woman in its place. Tala blinked in surprise, then annoyance, then fought the urge to laugh hysterically as he realized who she must be: the Light Blessed that Caida had told them had been allowed to enter the city in order to trap and kill him.

The two other Blessed stopped where they were and looked at the new arrival, Anderas in anger and Elidor in relief. Tala just stared at the three together, feeling like his mind was at its breaking point. One of the strongest Blessed in the world was actively trying to kill him. Another—who was *also* one of the strongest Blessed in the world—seemed intent on *preventing* his death, for reasons Tala couldn't even begin to fathom. And now *another* Blessed had arrived and in all likelihood was here to kill him too.

Hundreds had died, and three Blessed—from different Gods—were fighting to kill him. Two months ago, he had been an ordinary apprentice Researcher! For perhaps the first time, Tala really, truly wished that he was actually as dangerous as the Churches seemed to believe. Maybe then he could actually *do* something! To help Anderas, who *for some reason* was trying to *not* kill him. Anderas couldn't fight two other Blessed at once and win. Not when one of those two was Elidor. Even if he was the great Anderas Anto, that was a tall order.

"Annelore! This Fire bastard is a traitor! He's protecting the Blessed Killer! Kill him!"

Annelore? Why did that name sound familiar?

"Oh my! Is that true?" the woman—Annelore—asked Anderas in an amused tone, one eyebrow raised.

"Of course it's not!" he roared back. "That bastard killed one of my own! I was trying to kill him when Elidor got in my way! He's trying to take the kid for Metal! He's been planning to betray us both!"

The Metal Blessed roared in anger, struggling to get himself back into a proper form. Annelore looked between the two, still thoroughly amused.

"Well. That's not a bad idea, really. So how about I kill both of you and take the kid to Light with me?" she asked with a laugh before thrusting her hands out and shooting a blindingly bright, fast beam of light at the both of them. Elidor didn't move, the shiny metal that he was currently made of more than reflective enough for her attack to simply bounce off, even when slightly melted.

Anderas didn't have that luxury. His body burst into flames the instant the light beam hit him, passing straight through and eliciting an agonized roar from the man. Both beams eventually hit the buildings behind the fire wall in giant explosions.

Tala stared at the destruction—or as much of it as he could see, anyway—through the flame barrier. That attack was on a completely different level than Alina's were! He hadn't even known a light-based attack *could* cause an explosion! Light had no mass. How could it have kinetic force behind it? He looked at the three Blessed as they began fighting, finding a new, terrifying appreciation for the power of a Blessed. Light with enough force behind it to create explosions, a massive, superheated wall of fire that was being maintained even in the midst of an intense battle, and a man who was swiftly recovering from heat so intense it had left him more liquid than solid.

Tala watched in slack-jawed awe as the three began fighting. Seeing how useless her light attacks were against Elidor (the Metal man had again shifted the composition of his body's metal so that it reflected all light that Annelore threw at him), Annelore was focusing on Anderas, who hadn't noticed a mostly recovered Elidor charging at him from behind. With crushing force Elidor slammed into Anderas, continuing his charge toward Annelore.

The three tumbled to the ground, each morphing into their element before reforming on their feet in a triangle. Elidor's charge had brought the three into a strange sort of melee fight, where the lord of Southtown should have had the advantage, wielding an element that was mostly melee-focused already. But he was having trouble properly damaging either the Light or Fire Blessed, as they kept shifting into their respective elements before his attacks could land. It didn't help that Annelore was keeping a constant ray of light shining at his eyes, which seemed perfectly capable of blinding the man. Even as he shifted his eyes to appear elsewhere on his body, the woman was doing a remarkable job of finding and blinding each new eye, keeping Elidor too blind to do anything but get in the occasional hit while mostly swinging wildly and launching the occasional explosion of metal shrapnel out of his body. A body that was smaller than it had been when Elidor first appeared, Tala noticed.

He also noticed that, despite how much he was struggling, Elidor's attacks seemed to cause the most problems for the other two whenever they did land. Wherever they were struck stayed solid, open wounds that couldn't reform until his metal had left their bodies. This gave Tala an idea.

He shakily stood up and began looking around for something that would work as he kept one eye on the fight. Anderas might have told him to do nothing, but the man clearly hadn't anticipated the Light Blessed's arrival, and Tala would be damned if he was just going to sit there and wait to be killed by Elidor or captured by Annelore. *Earned herself a Blessing from it too. Her name's Anna-something.'* A half-formed memory began to whisper in his ears, but Tala shook it off: now was not the time! He looked back to the fight. He needed to see what was happening, needed to make sure his stupid, stupid idea could work.

CHAPTER 28

Anderas' attacks were easily the most problematic for Elidor as his super-shiny metal was constantly melting under the Fire Blessed's assault. And he was rapidly shifting around the metal of his body to reduce the effect as much as he could. A brilliant tactic even if it was probably excruciatingly painful at the same time. The fire attacks were also hurting Annelore, but the damage seemed to be rather minor, not causing her the same amount of trouble that Elidor's were. And there must be some reason the woman hadn't fled to throw attacks from range again, where the Light wielder clearly held an advantage.

Reaction speed, he realized. *Against Blessed, especially ones as skilled as those two, even the difference of a few feet can make a huge difference, no matter how fast she is. Even if the light itself is too fast to dodge, they can react to her movements. Harder to do when she's right there.*

Anderas was struggling the most in the fight. While not as injured as Elidor from the earlier battle, he was the main recipient of the others' attacks as he was clearly the biggest threat to them both. Even Tala's still rather inexperienced eyes could see that the man was faltering and at this rate, he would be the first of the three to fall. If that happened Tala's still developing, desperate plan would fail and he would certainly end up dead or worse in the hands of either of the other two.

Knowing his time was running short, Tala began to frantically search for what he needed. He had seen enough: his plan would either work, or it wouldn't, but there wasn't time to come up with another one. The three Blessed were so focused on each other that they seemed to have completely forgotten about him. So while still trying to keep from drawing their attention, Tala rushed across the square, looking for the shiny metal puddles that had melted off of Elidor and were still hot enough for his needs.

Most of the earlier puddles had already cooled enough that they were solid and useless for what Tala was intending. He followed the trail of puddles from the fight until he got to one that Elidor left right after he had charged the other two. Reaching it brought Tala far closer to the fight than he wanted. Thankfully, this puddle was perfect: it had been made after Elidor had changed his metal's composition to deflect Annelore's light. It was also rapidly cooling but still in liquid form. With a desperate prayer to… well, nothing, he realized with a snort, Tala unsheathed his sword and laid as much of the blade into the puddle as he could, swirling it around and flipping it over, trying to coat as much of the super-shiny Blessed metal alloy onto it as he could.

It didn't take long for the sword to become encased in a quickly hardening layer of Elidor's metal. It wasn't sharp anymore, but that didn't matter; he wasn't planning to use it to cut anything. All he needed was the metal from Elidor that had already proven itself capable of reflecting Annelore's light.

With his sword now little more than an oddly shaped stick of super-hard, super-durable, super-reflective metal, Tala turned back to the fight. All three Blessed were moving slower and slower, attacking less and less frequently. Anderas was clearly the worst off of the three, though, so Tala took a deep breath and steeled himself for the (likely suicidal) move he was about to make. He gripped his pseudo-sword in both hands and crept even closer to the fight.

Elidor and Annelore, seeing the weakened Anderas, had started teaming up against him, ignoring each other so as to get rid of him once and for all. This tactic caused them to both face him exclusively as they beat him down, leaving Tala at their backs. It wasn't until he was only a few feet from the battle that Anderas looked up from his frantic defense and saw what Tala was about to do, eyes widening in alarm as he opened his mouth to warn him away.

Tala merely grinned maniacally in response, the panic he felt and sheer absurdity of what he was about to do hyper-stretching his muscles well beyond the smile he had meant to give. Seeing the change in Anderas's demeanor, the sudden surprise and shock, Annelore began turning around to see what had caused it, but she was too late. She had only half-turned when Tala, sword held high, slammed the mass of super-light-reflecting metal into her head in the same downward swing that Dunlop had first taught him. He halted his swing earlier than usual, though, making sure the not-quite-a-blade stopped right in the middle of her head, where her brain would have been had it not immediately turned into a mass of light on impact.

With deep, panicked breaths, he held the hyper-reflective not-blade there, watching through squinted eyes, as though in slow motion, as the streams of light that her head had become shot outwards, reversed, and streamed back in, hitting the length of shiny metal and instantly rebounding away again, in an explosion of light that blinded Tala.

The sounds of battle faded as the two other Blessed were also blinded by the sudden onslaught of light. As Tala blinked rapidly to restore his vision, he saw the body of Annelore, Blessed of Light, lying on the ground, the entire top half of her head, everything above the jaw, missing. Long lines of gore—blood, bone, and brain matter—were splattered about, painting a disgusting picture that reminded him far too much of the similar scene after he had killed Ignis. The same scene that had first given him the fledgling idea that this just *might* work.

The other two Blessed stood where they were, gaping in uncomprehension at the headless body of their counterpart, eyes moving to Tala and back in disbelief and fear.

Tala wanted to laugh. Here he was: an ordinary, powerless person, little more than a kid, and he had just killed his second Blessed! A feeling of exhilaration—of achievement—began to fill him. He had done it! He looked at the two Blessed to see them staring at him, their former fight forgotten. They were both just standing there, watching him dumbly.

The first to come out of his stupor was Anderas, who raised his hands and began shooting as much fire as he could at Elidor. Even Tala could tell that the attack was much weaker than any of his earlier efforts, but thankfully, the Metal Blessed was also greatly weakened and was barely resisting. Even the great barrier of fire that Anderas had kept up since he first entered the scene was running low, the flames thinning and flickering enough so that Tala could vaguely see the shapes of people on the other side.

Elidor—who had been entirely unprepared for the attack and far too exhausted to react in time—screamed in agony as metal sloughed off him. Tala was forced back by the heat of the flames as they engulfed Elidor, shielding his eyes from both the heat and the light. When Anderas' attack finally ceased, Tala uncovered his eyes and looked up: Anderas was on one knee, panting, sweat pouring down his face. Elidor was in a similar position, though much worse off; the lord of Southtown was on both knees, but that was about as far as Tala could tell. The rest of the man was little more than a slumped pile of melted metal: his arms were… gone? Melted into his sides? Tala couldn't even tell. Even his face was gone; Hells, most of his head was gone! On top of what *might* have been the man's shoulders was a grossly misshapen lump of metal, dripping down in clumps with massive holes scattered around through which Tala could see what must have been the man's brain. It had clearly been partially melted—much like the rest of him—but was already, albeit very slowly, squirming back into shape. Even as he looked on, Tala could see the folds and squiggles of a brain reforming in the metal.

Elidor was still alive! How in the Hells was the man still alive? He couldn't believe it! He could see the man's brain—metal as it might have been—but the bastard still wasn't dead! He looked to Anderas to see him looking at his Metal counterpart from beneath hooded eyes, his whole body slumped in a way that screamed he had no more strength left. Elidor was going to live; he was going to win!

No! He can't! I refuse! Tala began to think, his mind racing with everything he knew, everything he had learned since that day with Ignis. *The brain. The brain is how he died. Air and water wouldn't let the fire reform where it was supposed to, so it formed anyway, wherever it was.* That had led to the man's head exploding around the alley. *Annelore: the reflective metal, designed to reflect the light of a Blessed. It didn't hurt her quite like Elidor's actual attacks did, but it still wouldn't let her light reform where it was supposed to, so it reformed where it could.* A grim display currently scattered around them, similar to the scene of Ignis' death. *But that won't work with metal. It can't be blown away like fire, reflected like light.* He had no other Blessed magic, or even Descendant magic, to use! What was he supposed to do against a brain of metal? One that was already reforming? *Reforming. Not formed, reforming. It doesn't have to explode. It just can't be allowed to reform. Not where it's supposed to, at least.* He glanced at his sword; it was made of metal. Worse, it was now coated in the Blessed's own metal. Sticking it in him would probably just heal him faster. He looked around frantically.

There! He rolled a charred body over, a wooden spear stuck under it, protected from the sea of fire when it had swept over the square. He grabbed the spear and stomped on the head as he pulled it up, breaking the metal bit off so he was just holding a long stick of wood. Elidor was weak, so weak his metal was barely moving. And his brain was already exposed. Metal it might have been, but it was as much a liquid as a solid at this point. Would it work? He didn't know, but he had to try. He tried with Ignis, and it killed the bastard. He tried with Annelore, and there were now bits of brain in his hair. Again.

Dropping his sword—since it was now too thick and mis-shapen to fit in its sheath—he grabbed the spear-stick in both hands and walked up to Elidor, right to one of the holes in his slowly reforming metal skull, through which he could see his brain. With one last breath, Tala braced himself and stabbed the wooden stick through the hole and into the liquified brain, shoving it so deep he saw it pierce through the other side of the man's head. The lump of a metal body shuddered, seized, jolted, and jerked, and went still. Slowly, the metal began to revert into flesh until there was a horribly disfigured, melted, grotesquely brutalized corpse left kneeling on the ground. The thing barely even looked like it had been human.

Tala panted, joy and disbelief warring with immense exhaustion within him. He looked up into the eyes of Anderas, still on his knees, too exhausted to even stand, staring blankly at him. With a slow blink, and another, Anderas' mouth slowly crawled up into a grin. He opened his mouth as if to speak before his eyes rolled back in his head and he collapsed to the ground, unconscious.

Tala stood still, staring at the immobile form of Anderas Anto, slowly realizing the full implications of what he had just done. He had survived an all-out fight between the Blessed of three different Gods. Not just survived, no: he was the victor!

The last one standing! The one who had personally killed two and now stood with the last unconscious at his feet! In a battle of three Blessed and one ordinary human, he had won!

Feeling as though he were in a dream, Tala slowly raised his arms to the sky, fists clenched in triumph as he roared his victory to the heavens. An impossible situation and he had survived! The sole victor of a battle between beings that could crush cities and slaughter armies on their own without even breaking a sweat!

As the heady feelings of *survival, victory,* and *life* began to fade, Tala slowly became aware of his surroundings. The grand walls of fire that Anderas had erected around the square had fully dissipated, leaving him surrounded by soldiers from all three nations on three sides: Metal to the west, Fire to the south, and Light to the east. To the north, standing just inside the open gates leading into the Lightlands, stood his companions, staring at the scene with eyes wide and mouths agape. Even the ever-stoic Vail looked to be in shock, a stronger show of emotion than Tala had ever seen from the man.

His mind quickly went over the last few minutes; when had the barrier fallen? It had still been up when Annelore died, if barely, hadn't it? It must have fallen completely just as he was killing Elidor, meaning that all those present—his companions and the hundreds of soldiers in the streets—had just witnessed him kill a Blessed, possibly two, before seeing a third collapse at his feet. Before seeing *Anderas bloody-fucking Anto* collapse at his feet!

Too tired to properly run, Tala turned towards his friends at the gate and began slowly walking towards them, trying to do his best to stand tall and confident instead of shuffling tiredly, stopping only for a moment to pick up his discarded, misshapen sword. By the way none of the soldiers moved, he figured he was doing a decent job of appearing strong. Or they were all just simply that terrified of the man who had defeated three Blessed at once, killing two of them.

Slowly, he walked out of the square and down the short bit of street that led to his companions. Too tired for anything else, he simply motioned for them to follow him as, without slowing his pace, Tala strolled through the gates, eager to leave that damned city behind him.

CHAPTER 29

Gazin stared in dismay at the raging wall of fire, his heart crushed. They had failed. Tala was dead. He didn't know how the rest of them weren't. Luck, he guessed. An oversight on the part of the Fire Blessed. And it had to be a Fire Blessed, to have made this flaming wall. To have had it burn through Ilan's earth wall instead of being smothered by it. To have maintained it even as Vail tried, and almost succeeded, to bring it down.

The way the fire had spread through the square almost seemed like it was pushing them out on purpose. Whoever the Blessed was must have been so focused on trapping Tala that they hadn't even realized they were saving the rest of the Dissidents. And a handful of soldiers too, but those were quickly dispatched by Gazin and the rest. For all their good fortune at the oversight, Tala was still lost. They had still failed.

A hand grabbed Gazin's shoulder, strong but comforting, as comforting as it could be, at any rate. He turned to see Vail, looking at him with as sad an expression as he had ever seen on his old friend's face. Vail didn't speak; he didn't have to.

Gazin knew that it was time for them to leave. Escape while they still could, for there was nothing left that they could do. Whoever this Blessed was that had trapped Tala was strong enough to even keep Vail out. Fighting back tears, Gazin gave one last look at the fire wall before turning around.

And double-taking back towards the wall. It was lower, weaker, flickering in its life. What was happening? A brilliant, immense light suddenly exploded from behind the fire, forcing Gazin to shield his eyes. He used his power to alter his eyes, forced his pupils wide the moment the light ended so that he could see what had happened without having to wait for them to recover on their own. It was a risky thing, for a Fleshy to manipulate the eyes, even their own: so much of the eye fell outside his power's domain (and in the domain of the Bloodies) that if he made a mistake, he might be unable to fix it. But he couldn't wait: he *had* to see what was happening, what had caused such a massive explosion of pure light. He was certain that the only person alive in the square after the fire had come was Tala, and the only people who could now survive entering that flaming barrier were Blessed. Was there a Light Blessed inside? What were they doing?

He looked up and, to his great surprise, saw that the wall of fire hardly even existed anymore. It was maybe a foot high, two at most. And what he saw he couldn't believe. The square was littered with burned bodies—that was hardly a surprise—and all three other streets that ran into it were filled to the brim with soldiers behind the wall of fire. That wasn't a surprise either.

He was surprised by the people alive in the middle of the square. One was clearly the Fire Blessed who had conjured the fire wall. He was crouched on one knee, but Gazin had seen the ending of the powerful stream of flames pouring out of his hands into the face of another figure, one he hadn't been sure was actually human, it was so… disfigured. Grotesque. It was a melted person! Made out of metal! By the Gods, that was a Metal Blessed! Why had the Fire Blessed been attacking the Metal Blessed!? Gazin's eyes quickly swept around, but he was the only one who had seen. All the others had been too blinded by the Light explosion to have seen the attack. What in the Hells was going on?

He looked at the third figure in the square, assuming it must be the Light Blessed he knew was there, only to feel his heart seize in shock: it was Tala! Tala was alive! But how!? And what was he doing? He was holding some sort of pole—a spear! Tala was holding a broken spear! Why? What was he doing with—Gazin was so shocked at the scene before him that he lost awareness of his body. A shock he wasn't the only one to feel as he heard gasps come from his companions. Tala, that naive, kind, unlucky boy, had just speared the broken shaft in his hands right through the head of the Metal Blessed. A Metal Blessed who began to spasm before growing still. A Metal Blessed whose horribly mutilated body was slowly transforming back into flesh and bone. Tala, that wondrous, ridiculous lad, had just killed another Blessed! A Metal Blessed! In front of hundreds of people!

So stunned by what he had just witnessed, Gazin barely even registered it as the Fire Blessed collapsed on the ground. His eyes were locked on the deformed body of Tala's latest victim, mind moving more sluggishly than it ever had before.

Even his brilliant brain, that he himself had spent a lifetime tweaking and improving, didn't know how to process what he was seeing. Never in his wildest dreams did he expect to see such a thing!

Movement caught his attention, and his eyes slowly moved to Tala as the boy raised his fists in the air and roared out into the sky. Never before had Gazin seen such a beautiful sight as this young man before him roaring out his victory after besting beings who might as well have been Gods compared to him. Tala's arms lowered, and his head slowly panned around, taking in the sight of the hundreds of soldiers and probably at least a dozen descendants who were surrounding him. None stepped forward. None dared to challenge the boy who had killed a Blessed right before their eyes. Gazin couldn't blame them. Even now, as Tala's eyes roamed over to him and the other Dissidents, Gazin felt a spike of fear shoot through him towards the boy. The kind, caring, inquisitive boy who he had truly believed wasn't—couldn't be—a threat to anybody.

Tala slowly began walking towards them, stopping only to pick up some strange-looking sword next to the body of a woman whose... head had exploded? What in the Hells had happened inside that giant, flaming prison!?

Ever so slowly did Tala finally approach them, not another person anywhere moving as they all stood stock still, watching the Blessed Killer, entranced by every small step he made, every breath he took, every tiny rustle of his hair. Finally, after seconds that felt like hours, Tala reached them. His eyes looked both more alive and more tired than almost any Gazin had ever seen. The young man didn't stop walking; he barely even acknowledged the rest of them. He just kept moving, giving a tiny nod of his head and a small, stunted gesture of his arm for them to follow him. Unspeaking, they all did.

As they walked through the north gate of Southtown, Ilan paused, letting the rest of them pass. Once they were all through the gate, the former Stone Knight turned around and, with barely a stomp of his feet, brought the great northern gatehouse crashing down in a massive heap of rubble. Nobody would be following them from Southtown tonight, even if any were willing after what Tala had done.

As they made their way over to the stables, the stable master and all his workers were nowhere to be seen. Not surprising: even outside the walls, they all must have had an idea of what was happening, and were likely barricaded in their homes, hoping to survive the night. With his mind still all askew, Gazin mechanically went about securing the horses that he thought would be easiest to handle and ran the rest off, making it even harder for any pursuers to follow them.

As they all secured some riding gear to the horses, Gazin kept an eye on Vail and Tala, the latter of whom was blankly staring off into the distance, strange, misshapen sword still clutched tightly in his hand.

Once the horses were ready (at least, Gazin hoped that they were all ready; they really had done everything as quickly as they possibly could), he watched as Vail and Serala helped get Tala onto a horse, taking some spare straps to make sure he was well and truly secure. That was clever of them; the lad really didn't seem to be all there at the moment, a dangerous mindset for his first time riding a horse.

The moment they were all set, and with a few extra horses tethered along just in case, they began riding north, as fast as they could go without exhausting the horses. Thankfully, Light horses were quite fast, so they were able to travel far from the city without having to run the horses into the ground. The Lightlands were composed of lots of empty plains, similar to much of the Firelands, and getting stuck without rideable horses would have put them in a terrible position.

It actually turned out to be the riders who grew too tired to continue, rather than the horses. After all the hiking through the hills and walking over the plains that they had done, one night's rest in a proper bed hadn't been quite enough, and that followed by a day of frantic running and fighting had left them all deeply exhausted. Even Gazin was feeling it, and he could easily go for days without rest when needed.

So when they finally broke for the night, they didn't even bother making an actual camp. They hobbled the horses and drove a few stakes into the ground to tie them to so they didn't wander off in the night. Gazin couldn't help but feel some amusement at the way they all collapsed onto their bedrolls afterwards, most falling asleep almost instantly. Lito hadn't even opened his bedroll; the lad was just lying on the grass using the bedroll as a pillow.

Gesturing to Ilan to get some sleep, Gazin set himself up to take the first watch. Tired as he was, he wasn't nearly as exhausted as the rest of them were. Perks of being a Fleshy. He had readjusted his eyes for good night vision while they had been gathering the horses, and now looked out over the plains as far as he could, in every direction. No signs of people anywhere for miles; that was good. The mountains were close, and looked even closer in that way mountains did, but he knew there were many miles between them. Satisfied that they were safe, at least for the time being, Gazin left the not-camp to forage for some fuel for a fire. With Alina asleep, it would be far too dangerous to light one while it was dark out, but he was sure his companions would appreciate having one come morning.

As Gazin passed the time collecting what fuel and food he could from the plains (he even managed to find some edible berry bushes, how fortunate!), his mind mulled over the events of the day. The previous day. Whatever. They had been fools to think that they would be safe in Southtown! It was the only good choice they had. Of *course somebody* in Fire had figured that out too. Soleil or Anderas probably, their immense skill with their magics wasn't the only reason those two were so famous, after all. There were a few others who were smart enough to have figured it out too: Sulien. That man was incredibly clever from everything Gazin had heard, and had quite the love for chaos. He wouldn't be surprised if he had been the one who figured it out and prepared such an elaborate trap. Ishaan too had probably quickly realized where they were going. He was one of the oldest Blessed alive and had been a Researcher before, like Tala. Although he doubted it was the ancient Blessed who told the Church where they were going. Gazin had personally met the man, after all, and he had been a great friend to the Dissidents over the many long centuries of his life. That was a secret belonging to few beyond Gazin and Hagan, though.

It didn't really matter, whoever it was that had figured it out. Southtown had been the best choice, in some ways the only good choice, and that made it the obvious one. An oversight that had very nearly cost them Tala. That *should* have cost them Tala. From what little Gazin had glimpsed of the events in the square, after the fire wall had died, he honestly didn't understand a thing about how the lad was still alive. Whatever Fire Blessed it was that had created that wall could have—should have—killed the boy easily. But instead, in that one little second that Gazin had seen, it had almost looked like the Fire Blessed had been working *with* Tala. He had certainly been trying to kill the Metal Blessed, the one who *Tala* had ended up killing. When had the Metal Blessed even arrived? And what had happened to the Light Blessed? There *had* to have been one. There had definitely been a Light Wielder in that square, who arrived *after* the fire wall had been put up, and even Alina wouldn't have survived that. So where had the Light Blessed gone?

Gazin was anxious for morning to come. He wanted, *needed*, to hear the tale from Tala. Find out what had happened. The boy had been practically catatonic during the ride, completely silent and seemingly oblivious to the others' attempts to talk to him! Gazin needed to know; they *all* needed to know. What little they did know was that Tala, somehow, had killed *another* Blessed. In full view of hundreds of people. In a month's time, the lad had killed two Blessed. He had done the impossible, and then *done it again*. And left a second Blessed unconscious on the ground. They *needed* to know how he had done it.

The Churches would be in an uproar like never before: what would they do? A Metal Blessed had been killed by Tala, a powerless boy from Fire, with the help of a Fire Blessed. How would *any* of the Churches react? Suddenly, the dominance of the Blessed over the world was under threat. This was no longer an isolated incident; a one-time, once-in-a-lifetime freak occurrence. The Dissidents *needed* to know everything that had happened.

They needed to plan, to prepare, for the future. Because the future was suddenly looking less certain than it ever had before.

CHAPTER 30

Tala awoke with a groan, sore in places he had never been sore before, the pain and discomfort in his legs and butt quickly reminding him of the events of the previous day. He lay still, thinking back on what had happened: running through the city, fighting and avoiding a seemingly endless stream of soldiers. The Metal Descendant, the ambush in the square, the Blessed. He rolled over, trying to stretch out his legs a bit.

Anderas: the undyingly loyal, beloved son of Fire, one of the greatest Blessed alive—maybe even ever—had been sent to kill him but instead saved his life. And the lives of his companions. Not only that, he had then defended Tala from Elidor, another one of the greatest Blessed alive, at great risk to his own life. The man even fought against the Light Blessed woman. Anderas nearly died, surviving only due to Tala's own actions to save them both. And who was that woman anyway, that Annelore? She had to have known who Anderas and Elidor were—there were few people who didn't—and she chose to fight them, both of them, anyway. And she kept up with them, as much of a danger in the fight as either of the two famous Blessed were. *Well, she's dead now.*

Thoughts returning to the present, Tala reached an arm out and grasped the hilt of his sword. Rolling onto his side, he examined the weapon for the first time in proper light. It… wasn't very pretty, he had to admit. The way the morning light shone off the Blessed metal in a rainbow hue was nice, sure, but the sword didn't really look like a sword anymore, not with the uneven, ragged metal coating the blade. *Not that a sword has to be pretty. It just has to kill. And this sword can kill Blessed. Well… Light Blessed, at least.* His grip on the sword tightened as a mix of pride and horror rushed through him: he had a weapon capable of killing Blessed! It might not work on other Blessed, but the fact that a weapon could exist—*did exist*—that could kill any Blessed at all almost beggared belief! He shifted his grip to the blade, running his thumb over where the edge would be. It was completely dull. Not surprising given how he had 'made' it. It might not really work as a sword anymore, but it should be damn near unbreakable at least. Blunt-force trauma could kill just as well as a sharp blade, after all. And it could kill Blessed!

With a groan, Tala released the sword and sat up, feeling his muscles protest the action. The fact that last night had been his first time on a horse, a night when he was too tired—and probably too shocked—to figure out *how* to ride a horse, was biting him in the ass. *Almost literally,* he thought as he rubbed his screaming cheeks. Hopefully, Gazin would be able to help with that like the Fleshy had when his underused muscles had ached from hiking.

Tala stretched as best he could as he looked around the not-quite camp. They had all been too tired by the time they stopped to set up a proper camp. To his surprise, Tala found that most of the others were still asleep. *Well, they did do all of the actual fighting yesterday.* All Tala had done was run and wait for them to stop fighting before running again. Even what happened with the Blessed at the end didn't really count as fighting. It was more akin to murder.

He shook his head clear, trying not to dwell on what he had done. Killing one Blessed, albeit by accident and in self-defense, was ridiculous enough. To have killed two more Blessed, intentionally and at (basically) the same time, was mind boggling! He wasn't sure what he should think or feel about what he had done and so, for the meantime, had decided to just not think about it.

Shaking himself again, he looked towards the two other people who were already awake: Vail and Ilan. They were sitting next to each other on the ground at the edge of the 'camp,' looking out over the empty plains of the Lightlands. Judging from where the mountain range was, they were facing south, towards Southtown.

The two were quietly talking to each other, but stopped as Tala approached them. He wasn't sure how they knew he was there, as there was nothing but short, soft grass that made little to no noise under his feet, but he had well learned not to be surprised by some of the amazing things this group could manage.

As he moved next to them, Ilan gestured for him to sit down and join them. He did, feeling slightly awkward; he had barely ever spoken to these two, and for good reason. The three of them sat there quietly for a while, with Ilan and Vail not really hiding the fact that they were staring at him. Tala ignored them, looking off into the distance. He had a feeling he knew what they were thinking, but if they wanted to know, they were at least going to have to act like normal people and ask him.

So he was surprised when, instead of asking about what had happened in the square, Ilan asked a different question.

"How are you?"

Tala blinked, not expecting the gentle question from the man. After a moment of silence, he responded, "I'm alright. I think. I'm not really… not really sure how I should be, to be honest."

The former Stone Knight nodded solemnly in response before speaking again. "That's understandable. Killing somebody for the first time. It's complicated. People react differently to it. There is no 'right way' for you to be feeling."

Tala was bemused; he hadn't been expecting this conversation. Or for the large, quiet man to be so… sympathetic. Understanding.

"It's not my first time. I killed Ignis."

"But that's different, isn't it? You can feel it, even if you aren't sure how or why." Tala nodded, unsettled. "What happened with Ignis was an accident. You were just trying to defend yourself and pulled off a miracle. This time it was on purpose. I don't know what exactly happened before, but we saw you thrust that spear into that man's head. Killing somebody on purpose is… very different."

"Two people," Tala muttered absently, thinking over Ilan's words.

"What?"

"I killed two people. That Metal guy you saw, Elidor, and the Light woman."

The two stared at him surprised, the shock barely visible, apparent only because of how utterly impassive their faces usually were. Tala wasn't sure how to feel about getting such a reaction from them.

"Elidor? You mean Lord Elidor?" Ilan asked slowly.

"Yep. Turns out if a Metal Blessed is practically dead already, a hunk of wood right in the brain will finish the job. Resilient bastard."

He was met with silence. Glancing again at his two companions, Tala saw that they were looking at him blankly again, much like they usually did. This time felt oddly different, though.

"Elidor. *The* Elidor. You killed a centuries-old Blessed, one of the most powerful in the world, with a stick to the brain?" Ilan asked again, even slower.

"Yep. Believe me, I'm just as surprised as you."

"Explain. All of it. *How?*"

"Uh, can I do it later? When everyone's awake? I don't really want to go through it multiple times."

The giant man stared hard at him before sighing and nodding. They devolved into silence again, once more staring out at the southern horizon. Except Vail, who hadn't shifted his gaze an inch from Tala, who promptly ignored him.

"Light woman?" Ilan asked aloud. Tala sighed to himself.

"Yeah. They called her Annelore. I don't know the name but she was a Blessed also. And she was keeping up with those two."

"…and you killed her?"

"Mm." Tala nodded.

"You killed two Blessed. Last night. Lord Elidor and Annelore, the Blessed Slayer?"

"Yep. Wait—Blessed Slayer?"

This time it was Ilan, who sighed as he gripped the bridge of his nose. "There is one Light Blessed woman named Annelore that I know of. She is called the Blessed Slayer because she gained her Blessing from killing a Lava Blessed when she was still a Descendant. And she's made a name for herself by killing more Blessed since. Mostly from Lava, but even one of her own, from Light."

"Oh! I remember her! Serala told me about her! I—uh… I didn't realize that was her."

"Mhmm. And how did you kill her, exactly?"

Tala sighed and stood up, ignoring his aching muscles screaming at the movement. Without a word, he walked over to where he had slept and picked up his sword, holding it out for Ilan to take as he sat back down with a grunt. "Smashed that into her brain."

Ilan took the sword, sending Tala a strange look as he did so. His brow furrowed as he examined the not-blade, running a hand along the blunt, uneven surface.

"What in the Hells happened to your sword?"

"I dipped it in a puddle of melted metal."

Both men stared at him, Vail in his usual blank manner and Ilan with his eyes half-lidded. Tala got the feeling that the large man was unimpressed with his answer. He also got the feeling that Vail was amused by it for some reason.

"And you were able to kill a Blessed with it?"

"Yep." Tala would've sworn that he saw the ghost of a smirk flash on Vail's face.

"No." A slight chill went down Tala's spine at Ilan's voice. The look he was giving him didn't help. Tala coughed and decided it might be in his best interest to stop doing that.

"Sorry. It was Blessed metal. When she showed up and started fighting, Elidor changed the metal of his body to reflect her light attacks. It worked well. He was basically immune to her. A bunch of his metal had been melted off during the fight, so when it looked like she might win, I figured that if a bunch of steam could stop Ignis' fire-brain from reforming properly and kill him, then Blessed metal made specifically to reflect her light would do the same. And it did. It was less messy than Ignis, too. A bit. I think. Maybe."

Ilan stared at him, disbelief written all over his face. Slowly, he lowered his head to look at the blade resting in his lap. "You mean… this sword… this can…"

"Kill Blessed? Yep. Light Blessed at least. I don't know if it'll work on any of the other types. She might've also been weakened from the fight, but honestly, I don't think that really mattered much."

"Gods, kid. I don't… Gods!" The man stared dumbfounded at the sword on his lap, completely still apart from his eyes, which watched as Vail grabbed the sword and examined it himself.

"Barely a month in and you've killed three Blessed and created a Blessed-killing weapon. Not bad, kid. Not bad at all."

"Uh… thanks?" Tala blinked. Vail just complimented him! Vail had spoken to him in full, coherent sentences!

Until yesterday when the man had suddenly taken charge over Serala, Tala had forgotten if the man was even capable of that! What the Hells?

"And what about the Fire Blessed? You haven't said anything about them yet," the strange man continued.

Tala subtly pinched his leg, making sure he wasn't dreaming. *Vail* was engaging *him* in conversation! Casual, non-urgent, non-life-threatening conversation! The topic might have been anything but normal, but this was way too weird! And what was he even supposed to say? He didn't even understand what the Hells had happened yesterday with Anderas! Everything that man had said and done left Tala dumbfounded!

"He, uh—he lived, I think. Passed out right after I killed Elidor. They—Elidor and Annelore—kind of teamed up on him. I killed her while she was distracted with him, and Elidor after he was already melted into a barely human-shaped pile of slag."

"Damn. Must be one powerful Blessed to have dealt with those two like that. I don't suppose you recognized him, being from Fire and all?" Tala fidgeted, not sure what was making him more uncomfortable: the topic or the fact that Vail was acting like a normal human being.

"I did, yeah. It was… it was Anderas. Anto. Him."

Ilan made a choking, coughing noise as Vail—who had still been examining the sword—snapped his head up, looking at Tala with an expression of unmistakable surprise. He was even showing emotions like a normal human. What the Hells was happening?

"Anderas Anto? *Anderas. Anto.* Hunted you down and you survived? You beat *Anderas Anto?*" The question came from Ilan. Vail was simply staring at Tala with an intensity he hadn't seen from the man since that first day they met, in the alley after he and Serala had pulled Tala away from Ignis' body.

"Yes? I mean, I didn't really *beat* him. That was those other two. I just kinda survived? He was actually winning until they both stopped fighting each other and focused on him."

"What the fuck, kid." Ilan had dropped his head into his hands. "What the fuck! You've killed three Blessed and survived Anderas fucking Anto! Do you know how many people have survived Anderas fucking Anto trying to kill them? Two! That Earth Blessed he beat when he was a teenager and… the Demon. That's it! And both were when he was still just a Descendant! In that man's entire life, almost 100 years, you are only the third person to survive him! The first since he became a Blessed over 20 years ago! Who the fuck are you, kid?"

"Nobody! I'm nobody! I wasn't even a proper Researcher yet: I was just an apprentice! I don't know why this shit keeps happening! Before Ignis, there was literally nothing special about me! Now I'm—I don't even know what the fuck I am anymore!"

"You're the kid who's going to change things," Vail said calmly as he passed the sword back to Tala.

"What?"

"Tell us, kid, how'd you know doing that to that sword would kill Annelore?" Vail asked casually.

"I—well, I didn't, really. I just figured it'd probably work because of Ignis. I told you that already."

"Mm. And what about Elidor? Continuous blast of steam to Ignis' face, sure. Makes sense. Special light reflecting Blessed metal into Annelore's head? Also makes sense. A normal stick into Elidor's head? Makes less sense. If it was that easy to kill a Blessed, we'd have been doing it for millennia. So how did you know that would work?"

"It was the same concept, kind of. He was weak. Like I said: Anderas had already melted him so much he was practically dead already. His brain was exposed, for Gods' sakes! But I could see that it was reforming. Slowly. I figured if he was so weak that even his brain was slow to fix itself, then sticking anything non-metal in it would be too much for it to handle. It's basically how I killed the other two: just don't let the brain reform. It wouldn't have worked if he wasn't so weak, though. Why?"

"Because we've been trying to find reliable ways to kill those bastards for thousands of years. And you've managed to stumble upon the answer."

"What? What answer? Are you telling me that none of you, in thousands of years, ever thought to just go for the brain?"

"Of course not. It's not about going for the brain—it's about *how* you did it. Finding something that will make them shift but not allow the one part they need most to reform. A steady and powerful stream of steam to disrupt fire, powerful hyper-reflective metal to disrupt light, a Godsdamned stick to disrupt metal too weak to dislodge it? I'll grant you that each of those are exceptional circumstances, circumstances we can't easily replicate, but in nearly 7,000 years of living under the Gods and the Blessed, you are the first to even manage that much. You've proved that it *can* be done. Multiple times. You've even managed to create a weapon that can do it. Even if it's limited, that sword of yours is probably the most valuable weapon in the world right now."

"But how?" Tala asked, flustered. "Ignis was just an accident! And the other two were just logic! Just simple reasoning! If that worked on Ignis, then maybe this will work on her, and this on him! How am I the first to figure that out? It's not exactly Arcane Research!"

"But it is," Vail said quietly. "That's exactly what it is. Why do you think you Researchers are forbidden from studying the Gods? The Blessed or Descendants or Marks? Oh I know what you've been told." The man held up a hand, stopping Tala from answering before he could even start. "You've been told that it's not for us to know. That the Gods and their gifts are beyond human knowledge, that we can't understand how their magics work and don't deserve to know even if we could. Right?" Tala nodded; those were exactly the reasons he had always been told. "What if that's not true, though? A lie like everything else?"

He stopped, clearly waiting for an answer this time. Tala thought about what he had said. "So what? Research into it all is forbidden because it can lead to discovering the weaknesses of the Blessed? That's—" Tala cut himself off. He had been going to say that was ridiculous, but that was just habit. It wasn't ridiculous, was it? He had already been starting to wonder that himself. And hearing it now, spoken aloud, it actually made a lot of sense: steam killed Ignis, the limitations of his Blessed ability to automatically transform into fire having worked against him. The same limitation that Tala then exploited to kill Annelore. And then, to a much lesser extent, Elidor. Had the Researchers been allowed to study the Blessed—how their magics worked, what exactly they could do—they would have discovered those same weaknesses! And more. Many, many more, he was sure. "That makes sense." He explained his thoughts to his two companions, who both nodded along.

"But that still doesn't explain why you think I'm so special! Just because I *may* have been the first person to kill a Blessed like that doesn't mean I'm the first to realize it could be done! Or that no one else will figure it out! I mean *anyone* could do that under the same circumstances!"

"No, kid, they couldn't. You don't realize just how different you are. Even as an apprentice Researcher, you're educated. Even if you've never studied the magics or those who use them, you know how elements interact: you knew that high-pressure steam—water and air together—would work against Ignis. You didn't know it would kill him because you didn't know about his ability's limitations, as you called it, but you knew enough to stumble on it by accident. You knew enough about how metal cools and light reflects to kill Annelore. The reason you're special is because of the education you've had. You know how the world works in ways that most people never do. And you were able to use that knowledge to become the Churches' worst nightmare. You're a living testament as to why it's so important to them to keep people dumb and uneducated, and why even the few that they do allow to study and learn about the world are so heavily monitored and controlled. The Church of Fire knew the risk that they were taking, all those thousands of years ago, when the Institute was first established. They knew that somebody with learning and knowledge could figure out that the Blessed have weaknesses, maybe even more than that, and they thought that by keeping you Researchers on a tight leash, they could prevent that from ever occurring. And for thousands of years, they were right, and became the dominant nation in the world because they took that risk. And things would probably still be going that way for thousands of years more if one dumbass kid hadn't decided to play the hero one day. So good job, kid: your idiotic heroics that day may just bring about the collapse of the world as we know it." Vail finished with a vicious grin, even going so far as to give Tala a pat on the back.

Tala stared at the man before turning to Ilan, who only gave him a helpless shrug and nod in return. He turned back to Vail, who was looking at him in blatant amusement, a smirk sitting solidly on his face.

"He's right, you know." A voice sounded from behind Tala, making him jump in surprise and spin around with his sword clenched tight in his fist, prepared to swing. He stopped as he saw that it was Serala, who had approached their little trio without making a sound. He had been so focused on their conversation that he apparently missed the rest of the camp slowly waking for the day, as the others were slowly beginning to bustle about.

"You're basically the worst-case scenario as far as any of the Churches are concerned. Especially Fire, since they're the ones who created the Institute and were supposed to keep somebody like you from happening. Also: what happened to your sword?"

Tala stared at her in surprise before her last question registered, causing him to sigh as he relaxed again. "I'll explain later. It's a bit of a story."

Later came sooner than Tala would have liked, as he was still uncertain about what exactly he should tell his companions about the events of the night before. Anderas'... request to keep the truth about his actions a secret was still ringing loudly in Tala's ears. But once everyone had woken, and were all sitting around him, eagerly awaiting his tale, he couldn't delay any longer. So with a deep breath and a prayer to nothing, he told them all the best (slightly edited) story he could, hiding only the truth of Anderas' traitorous behavior.

"Gods, lad. I don't—I don't even know what to say." Gazin's voice relayed his shock, a state mirrored on the faces of all their companions.

"And that sword, is it really capable of killing Blessed?"

"Light Blessed, at least. Or it should be. I've only tested it the once."

"Blessed Metal," said Dunlop reverently, who was closely inspecting the sword. "If we can get this sharpened, make it into a proper sword, it could be a weapon like you wouldn't believe. Hells, even Metal Descendants might be weak to this thing. It should be damn near unbreakable, and even their powers won't work on it. Not fast enough to save them at any rate."

"If it's 'damn near unbreakable,'" asked Lito, "how would we sharpen it? I'm pretty sure a whetstone would grind itself to dust before it even made a dent in that thing."

"Some Descendants might be able to. It would be slow, but if they're skilled, they should be able to mold the metal enough to at least smooth it out and sharpen it," the short warrior replied without ever taking his eyes off of the blade that he was lovingly stroking. Tala shared a look with Lito; the man was a bit of a weapons maniac, but he was acting a little too weird with the sword.

"And where are we going to find a Metal Descendant to do it? Pretty sure we won't be able to get into the mountains now. With Elidor dead and everything else that happened back there, they're going to lock their borders up tighter than a tick's asshole."

"Lightning," Serala stated. "There are some Metal Descendants who've left the mountains and set themselves up in other countries—Lightning, Light, Fire, and the Jungle, naturally. But we can't go back to Fire, and we can't stay in Light, not after he killed Annelore." Tala noticed that Alina's body sagged minutely when she heard that they wouldn't be staying in Light. Clearly, she was relieved that they would be leaving, not that he blamed her after what he had heard about her past. "And the Jungle is on the other side of the Metal Mountains, so we can't get there very easily either. So we head north and cross into Lightning once we pass the mountains. That border isn't hard to cross with both sides focused on fighting off Lava. Lightning should be a safe place for us to lie low for a while too; they're too busy holding their borders to pay much attention to anybody already inside."

"Wait," Tala spoke up. "I know I'm new to a lot of this, but how are there Metal Descendants just living in other countries? I thought foreign Descendants were all either killed or enslaved?"

"Aye, that's normally the case." Gazin nodded. "But Metal's different. So's Dust for that matter. As the trade nations, nobody is willing to piss them off by killing or enslaving their kin; Dust's trade network is too valuable, and Metal's goods are just too good to lose. And since Metal Descendants make the best metal craftsmen, for obvious reasons, the other nations are more than happy to accept them. The only real problem will be finding a Descendant willing to work with us who can be trusted. They're all heavily monitored by the other Churches, and turning you or that sword in to a Church could make them rich. Hells, lad, capturing or even just killing you at this point would earn an instant Blessing for whoever pulls it off."

"Oh. Great. 'Cause there's nothing I need more than a bounty on my head worth a Blessing."

"Oh, it won't be that bad, laddie. After what you've done, even Blessed will be right scared of you. Only the most desperate, arrogant, or insane folks will try to hunt you down."

"Oh thanks. That makes me feel much better," Tala deadpanned.

"Always happy to help, lad." Gazin grinned.

"Right. Tala's future as a psychopath's chew toy aside," Serala interjected to snickers from the others, "Alina, what can we expect to happen after yesterday's events? Large scale?"

The Light wielder frowned, brushing her fingers through her hair as she thought about her answer. After a minute of silence, she spoke up with an odd note in her voice.

"Honestly? It's hard to say. Normally, I would say war, a proper war, at least between Fire and Light." The group collectively perked up at that. Vail was the only exception: he had spent the whole meeting sitting quietly watching the clouds, seemingly oblivious—as usual—to the conversation going on around him. After his sudden leadership the day before and his mostly normal behavior that morning during their own private conversation, Tala was beginning to suspect that the man's behavior was an act: a character that he was playing. He just couldn't figure out the reason for it. Deciding to contemplate it later, he turned his focus back to Alina.

"It all depends on Anderas Anto, though, seeing as he survived. Metal will undoubtedly question him, and what he tells them will determine how the war unfolds. At least I can't think of anything he could say that would entirely prevent a war. If anybody could, though, it would be him." There were murmurs of disgruntled agreement at that; the man had proven himself a diplomat capable of wielding words just as well as he wielded the Fire God's gift. "Assuming he doesn't somehow stop a war, though, Light will almost certainly declare war on Fire. The fact that he survived when Annelore didn't, and she was killed by somebody from Fire, will mean they blame Fire; maybe even that Tala and Anderas conspired together to kill her. Either way they'll want reparations. Reparations greater than Fire will be willing to give."

Tala sat still, trying not to give anything away; that was far closer to the truth of what had happened than he was really comfortable with. At least until he knew what game Anderas was playing. Nobody seemed to be suspicious of him, though, letting him relax as his body untensed. He noticed too late that Vail, who he thought had been cloud-watching, was actually watching him from the corner of his eye. They made eye contact for a few long seconds before Vail turned his eyes upwards again, seemingly dismissing the whole thing. And did Gazin's eyes just flick away from him? Why would Gazin be suspicious of his story? No, he probably wasn't: Tala was just being paranoid about keeping such a big secret from them.

"Regardless, Anderas killed hundreds of soldiers when he conjured those flame walls, most of whom were from Metal or Light, and neither will be happy about it. With Elidor's death, I wouldn't be surprised if Metal decides to ally with Light against Fire. Of course, depending on what Anderas says, they may side with Fire and declare war on Light. From what Tala told us, it wouldn't be hard for Anderas to twist things and convince them that Light is entirely, or at least mostly, at fault. Especially because it was Annelore.

"If Metal sides with Fire, then very little will happen: Fire doesn't have the numbers to properly invade Light. Light would lose out on trade with Metal, which would hurt them, but it wouldn't be crippling. And it would only be temporary. Light is wealthy enough that they could just pay reparations to Metal after a while, and everything would go back to normal. The war would be short anyway: Metal has no real reason to invade Light. Nothing within the area they could take has much of interest to them. Even if Metal cut off trade permanently with Light just to spite them, it wouldn't matter too much. The only other consequences for Light would be a push from Lava and maybe Lightning due to the focus on their southern border. But Light's northern territories have been torn apart by that war to the point that they would only be losing some pride; that land is practically worthless now.

"If Metal sides with Light, though, then Light will definitely take some of Fire's northeastern territory. Earth and Mud will also push into Fire and probably take some land. Metal won't push too hard against Fire, though. Trade with them is too important. So, again, they will mostly be fighting for reparations. And since they'll be more reasonable than Light, Fire may pay reparations from the start, and they'll avoid the war entirely. Nobody will attack whoever Metal does side with and risk losing trade with them, except Lava of course, so that will probably be the end of things. Best-case scenario: Fire might lose some territory, and things will quickly go back to normal."

"Well, damn!" Nuri whined. "I was hoping for a bit more than that! A minor war? That's a tiny war! Gods!"

"What were you expecting? A great war like the old days?" the former noble asked condescendingly.

"Yeah! Wouldn't that be great? Blessed and Descendants dying by the dozens? I've heard the stories: our ranks were never larger or our jobs easier than when the Churches were all focused on killing each other instead of us! People were flocking to our cause on the daily!"

"Yes, and then we started causing so many problems that they began focusing on us, and we were nearly wiped out! And then the first Bodylands Horde showed up! Even the Churches—the central ones, at least—don't want a great war again! Not when they're so comfy with the way things are and the Bodylands are still a threat! Each new Horde comes with a whole new array of twisted abominations, and it's only a matter of time before they break through the Dust Wall again! The only way we'll get a great war is if Metal stays out of the conflict between Fire and Light entirely and doesn't side with either, not even to get reparations! Which is almost impossible! Especially with Anderas Anto alive! If I can predict all this, I promise you he can too!"

"How is she predicting all of this?" Tala whispered to Lito, curious. Everything the girl was saying made sense to him, but to come up with it all required a knowledge and grasp of world politics well beyond what even he, a former (apprentice) Researcher, had.

"She was being groomed to become the next High Priest of Light," Lito whispered back. "Between her family and skills, she was all but guaranteed the position eventually. Things kind of… changed, but she's an expert in politics and whatnot."

"Oh." Tala sat back, eyeing Alina in a new light. He had known the girl was considered a prodigy in her magic and was fiercely intelligent—he had noticed that part for himself during their blossoming friendship—but he hadn't realized just how intelligent she apparently was. Or just how grueling her childhood must have been with such high expectations placed upon her.

"How would Metal's non-involvement lead to a great war?" Tala asked aloud. Everything she had said so far had made sense, but he was missing the logic there.

"Because then there's no deterrent for the other countries to get involved," Alina replied swiftly. "Nobody will choose to fight against Metal for fear of losing their trade, except Lava, who doesn't trade with them anyway. Take Metal out of the equation, and Fire's neighbors will swoop in as soon as they can. Lightning might even invade Light. Light will still come out on top if they manage to seize some of Fire's territory, but Fire will be devastated. Having Light, Earth, and Mud invading at once? Fire will have to start deploying Blessed on the front lines just to survive. The Churches stopped doing that because they ran the risk of creating a chain reaction. The other countries will send their own Blessed to counter. Then Lightning, Dark, Steam, Ice, and the Jungle will use that opportunity to try to take some of their territory in turn. Even Mist will probably join in at that point. Gods know they've done nothing but build up their forces for the last few centuries. Either way the whole world would end up in a massive war with Descendants and Blessed on the front lines 'dying by the dozens'… But, again, that's unlikely to happen: There's no way Anderas Anto won't convince them to side with Fire unless they're already determined to side with Light. I don't see how they could possibly not get involved on one side. At least as a token effort to prevent a situation like the one I just described."

"Well, that is a pity, that is." Gazin sighed. "But take heart, lad. Even without sparking the first great war in millennia, you've managed to do more good than almost any Dissident in history: three Blessed dead and a minor war started!" Gazin laughed along with a few others.

After a few more cheers for Tala's—entirely accidental—achievements, Serala decided it was time to get moving.

"We're heading north to Lightning. Alina, what's the closest town in that direction from here?"

"Loastar, I think. It's a decently sized town, but unimportant enough that I don't expect there will be much of a force there. It's also too far from any of the borders to need much of a standing garrison. It should be ruled by a Descendant from a minor family. We shouldn't run into any trouble there."

"Good." Serala nodded. "We'll go there and resupply. We prepared to enter Metal, not go traipsing through Light, so we'll need more if we're going to make it to the border of Lightning."

With their new course settled, the group packed up what little of their camp they put out. As Gazin helped him saddle his horse, Tala asked the man a question that had occurred to him earlier.

"Gazin? Why is everybody so… relaxed this morning? After what happened, I would've thought that we'd be fleeing as fast as we could, like we did out of Fiahren?"

The man snorted in humor. "There's no need, lad, not right now. Last night, we moved fast because we were all worked up, and we wanted to get far away from that city, just to be safe. But the odds of anyone having followed us are slim to none. Hundreds of soldiers from Light are dead, not to mention all those from Metal and Fire who died, a few Descendants, and two Blessed dead with one unconscious. Those three Blessed specifically? Even if there were enough people free to chase us, with the means to, who would dare? After what you've done, I doubt even a Blessed would dare challenge us by themselves, not when it would mean facing you! So take heart, lad! However it may have happened, you're a man who even scares Blessed now!" He laughed heartily as he finished helping Tala and went over to his own stolen horse, while others nearby who had heard his words laughed along with him.

Feeling a bit disoriented at the thought of people being terrified of him—especially at Blessed being terrified of him—Tala mounted his horse, preparing for what would hopefully be a much calmer, nicer ride through the Lightlands. After all, if even Blessed would be scared of him now, how much trouble could the future really hold?

"Now then, Lord Anderas, would you care to explain to us just what happened the other day? From your own, ahem, *esteemed* perspective."

Anderas stared back at the Metal priests before him dispassionately, ignoring the obvious slight in the man's question even as his servants in the room bristled in irritation. They cared far more about him being shown 'proper' respect than he did. It was no more disrespect than he had been expecting anyway. Perhaps under better circumstances, they would have been subtler about it, but with one of their most prominent dead along with multiple descendants and hundreds of soldiers, their displeasure came as no surprise. He would allow them their petty jabs.

Anderas leaned back in his chair, observing the priests before him as he maintained the calm demeanor that he had perfected in his many long years serving the Church of Fire. They were looking back at him with poorly hidden disdain and distrust. The details of the events that had occurred only a few days prior were known to none but Anderas himself, and that boy, Tala, who had killed his fellow Blessed. He had to fight back a smirk when he recalled those moments: when Annelore's head exploded in a dazzling display of light and gore, and Elidor had been murdered shortly after by a stick—a stick!—right before Anderas himself had passed out from exhaustion.

Anderas looked the Metal priest dead in the eye as he began to speak. "I presume you already know about as much as I do in regard to what happened before my intervention, no?" He saw the man's eye twitch in irritation, as well as a few similar small movements from the four other Metal priests sitting at the table beside him.

"Yes, we do. We have heard repeatedly about our soldiers' failures in killing that boy or any of his companions," the woman on the leader's left bit out through clenched teeth.

Anderas' eyes flicked over to her briefly before returning to the leader of the Metal contingent. He saw the priestess' jaw clench in anger at his clear dismissal. These five were truly abysmal at masking their emotions. Their frustration at his own relaxed, calm demeanor was so obvious even his servants could see it. Whoever decided that these five were the right people to meet with him was clearly incompetent. Or perhaps they actually were the best that Metal had to offer? It wasn't a church known for its diplomatic tact, after all, despite its focus as a trade nation. Their whole culture was far too blunt and straightforward to produce skilled diplomats.

"We want to know what happened after! When *you* got involved and killed hundreds of soldiers! How did you *and* that boy survive when Elidor and that Light bitch died?" the man seated at the far left of the table roared out, fist landing on the table with a thunderous bang. Anderas' eyebrow rose, impressed at the durability of the table. Truly, the craftsmen of Metal were a skilled lot. That blow could have easily caved in a person's skull.

Unfazed by the aggressive act, Anderas pretended to ponder the question—to the further aggravation of the Metal delegates—before answering.

"Well, you can't really blame me for the soldiers' deaths. Or the Descendants that were there," he drawled out, the reminder of the Metal Descendants who had died making the priests' fists clench. "They were all dead already. They just didn't know it yet. A small group they may be, but that boy has some powerful people protecting him. I watched some of the battle before I intervened, and I must say I was quite impressed by them."

"Yes, we know," the leader bit out, doing a marginally better job of keeping calm than his companions, who were glaring daggers at Anderas. "A Flesh wielder, a Light wielder, an Earth wielder. And from the reports we've heard, the rest were capable enough fighters to hold their own as well. Some of the survivors said that that cloaked man was so terrifying that he may as well have been the Demon himself reborn."

For the first time, Anderas' fist clenched as he spoke in an icy tone. "Your soldiers know nothing about the Demon. Had that been him, half the city would've been razed."

The priests shifted uncomfortably, undoubtedly remembering just who they were talking to. With an awkward clearing of his throat, the head priest spoke again. "Then we can remain grateful that he died fighting the Bone Merc up in Lightning." Anderas' eye twitched. "Regardless, you still haven't explained how that group survived your fires, how that boy survived, or how Elidor or Annelore died!"

Anderas shrugged and relaxed his muscles, more than happy to move the conversation away from the Demon. "How that little group survived I can't begin to guess." *I let them go.* "None of us were even aware that there were Empowered amongst them." *Only a partial lie.* "So perhaps they have some other tricks we aren't aware of that allowed them to escape." *A certainty, my flames never falter.* He happily ignored the teasing voice in his mind that reminded him that his flames had in fact faltered once before.

Despite the nonchalance of his speech, Anderas was actually thinking quite deeply about what he had seen in the small group protecting that boy. He had spoken truly when he claimed to have watched some of their battle but was vastly underselling just how much he had actually seen. He had been following them in secret for a while before the battle in the square, since they left that inn in fact, and had been truly impressed by their prowess.

The Flesh Descendant had been a remarkably skilled combatant. He'd seen him remove the skin from the man who stabbed him, before weaponizing that same flesh to brutally murder other soldiers. The speed and skill he displayed with that act alone, much less everything else Anderas had seen him do, was frankly terrifying. It reminded him of the horror stories he'd heard about the Bodyland Hordes. *Either he's an Awakened, which shouldn't be possible this side of the Dust Wall, or he's truly gifted. Either way, how have I not heard of him before?*

He had been similarly impressed with the Light Descendant. He was positive the girl was an Awakened; her power was simply too great to not be, no matter how skilled she was with it. But where had she come from? An Awakened with such skill would have been known to the Churches. And when would she have joined the Dissidents? He wasn't aware of any known Light Descendants—Awakened or otherwise—who were missing that matched her description. Either Light was keeping secrets they shouldn't be—which truthfully wouldn't surprise him—or something else was going on. He'd have to investigate it later. Secretly.

An identity that was less mysterious—if no less interesting—was the Earth wielder. A man who Anderas had initially believed to be another Descendant, but had found himself reconsidering in retrospect. An Earth Descendant, even an Unawakened one, wouldn't have fought that way. They would have used their magic far more, and done far more with it than create barriers and stone armor. But all that left was a Marked, which could only mean that the man was a Stone Knight. Or a former Stone Knight. But there was only one missing Stone Knight to his knowledge, a man whose description did happen to match perfectly with the large, dark-skinned warrior he had witnessed beat down a Metal Descendant with sheer brute force.

But was that even possible? That the traitorous Stone Knight had joined the Dissidents wouldn't be a surprise—it had long been assumed after the man's bloody defection—but there had been no proper sighting of him for over 10 years! He'd been presumed dead, despite his fabled strength! How could a man such as him have stayed hidden for so long? Ilan of the Stone Knights had been famous, the greatest warrior in Earth, a man who, before his betrayal, had been believed to be on track to becoming a Blessed! For him to appear now at the side of the boy who had killed a Blessed? Three Blessed? A boy who—according to the Fire Church's investigation—had had nothing to do with the Dissidents before killing Ignis? How were the two possibly connected?

Anderas wasn't sure what to think of the rest of the group. The smaller, shield-bearing warrior had been exceptionally skilled. Frighteningly so. His fighting style reminded Anderas of the Wild Guards that Mud employed which, if true, meant that he was not someone to underestimate. The man didn't appear to be an Empowered, though, so he held low hopes for learning about him. The Churches rarely bothered keeping close track of their non-empowered assets. Mud tried to with the Wild Guards, but that was an impossible task: their lifestyle meant they could go years without having any contact with the Mud Church. They might not even know that the man had left their country! And the young man who had fought in defense of the Light Awakened had been a competent, if not particularly remarkable, boy. He certainly wasn't lacking in training or skill, though. And the two who had helped cover them—the dagger-wielding man and woman—were capable enough, even if he got the impression that they weren't normally fighters.

The last two, though, did weigh on his mind. The cloaked man wasn't the Demon from Wind; of that he was sure. Not only was the city itself still standing, but he had personally experienced fighting the Demon and, had he thought that man was him, Anderas would never have gotten involved, even if it meant letting that Tala boy die. Even now, as a Blessed, he wouldn't ever willingly relive that encounter. He'd sooner cross the Dust Wall and face the unknown horrors of the Bodylands before facing the Demon again!

But the cloaked man's fighting style had been eerily reminiscent of the Demon's, if much less… rampantly sadistic. And the girl who had been beside him had fought similarly, clearly the cloaked man's student from the way the two worked together. Although the way she laughed as she all but danced her way across the battlefield brought back memories that Anderas had long tried to forget. He spent a lot of time thinking about those two. Was it merely a coincidence that they fought that way? Or could that cloaked man be a former student of the Demon's? Had the Demon even had students? That was a bone-chilling thought. Or was he merely a product of… whatever had made the Demon? All that the Churches had ever learned about the Demon was that he was male and had come from the Eastern Ocean, the territory of the Wind Church. That he had arrived mere months after the sudden and inexplicable end of the Wind Raids had led to much speculation. The very thought that another Demon could have arrived—could even exist—sent a shiver down his spine. Anderas had long since accepted that he wasn't a good person, but the Demon was incomparably worse.

And there had been some sort of unknown trick that the small group of nine possessed, much like he'd told the priests. Something had disturbed his fire barrier, if only briefly, while he had been speaking to the boy. The earth wall had been a respectable, if futile, attempt to smother his flames, but what had happened after—that was far too reminiscent of the events that featured in his worst nightmare. It was unfortunate that the boy knew nothing about it.

Unbidden memories of his fight with the Demon rushed through his mind before he could stop them: the screams of his companions as their carefully laid trap fell to pieces around them; his fellow Descendants dying, slaughtered by sword and dagger and *burning to death!* Hundreds of soldiers suffering that same fate as laughter filled the air, contrasting sharply with the screams of the dying and the crackling of wild, *uncontrollable* fire burning through the city! His own horror, despair, his *anger* as his friends and allies burned and bled around him as hundreds—thousands!—of innocent civilians died in the raging fires that had been unleashed upon their small city. The Blessed who had panicked and fled from the one-sided slaughter!

And more than anything Anderas remembered the evil, soulless smile on the Demon's lips, the only part of his face that could be seen beneath his hood, as Anderas attacked him in a suicidal rage. He had fought a hopeless battle against an over-whelming opponent before the Demon suddenly spun around a corner and vanished, inexplicably leaving Anderas alive among his brethren's corpses, all alone in the heart of a dying city.

Mercilessly forcing himself out of his memories before the Metal priests noticed, Anderas continued.

"As for how that boy survived and Elidor and Annelore died? Well, that's both simple and quite complicated. Simple in that the boy killed them both." The reactions from the priests were about as he'd expected. They had undoubtedly heard it from the soldiers, but likely dismissed their claims as baseless rumors, the kind of wild tales that always sprung up during chaotic and traumatic events. To have them confirmed by Anderas himself was clearly not what they were expecting.

"How!? How—just how!?" yelled one of the priests, a question they were all clearly wanting answered.

Anderas arranged his face to look somber. This was where things were going to get tricky. "I don't really know," he said apologetically, while replaying their deaths in his mind. At the renewed looks of rage on the Metal priest's faces, he smirked internally and quickly continued, spinning the tale he had created with his servant's help.

"However the rest of them escaped my flames, that boy, Tala, was trapped inside with me, and he had no way out. I was using the opportunity to interrogate him before I killed him, naturally, when Elidor burst through my fire. That complicated things a bit."

"How did that complicate things? You were supposed to be cooperating!" shouted one of the priests.

"We were," Anderas responded calmly. "But you must understand I had orders of my own to follow. *If* I had the opportunity, I was to interrogate the boy about killing Ignis, and about those who helped him escape Fire; you know as well as I do how valuable information on the Dissidents is, after all. Of course, I wasn't supposed to share whatever I did learn with any of you. That's why Elidor's arrival made things… complicated."

The surprised looks on the priests' faces at his blatant admission almost made Anderas smirk. This would be the tricky part of his plan: manipulating these Metal morons into partly blaming the Church of Fire for what happened while still allowing him to leave the city alive. If he screwed up here, he might very well die, with three of the five priests before him being Blessed. If he was at full strength, he could easily take them—none of them were even close to the level of Elidor, after all—but he was still weak and tired from that night, far more than he showed.

"I share this with you now in good faith, as my personal apology for what transpired. Our relations with Metal have been good for centuries, and I never quite agreed with the order for this deception."

There was silence for a few moments before the lead priest spoke, suspicion clear in his voice. "Then why tell us of it now?"

"As I said, consider it my personal apology. We all lost in this scheme to kill the boy, but you lost the most. Elidor was a good man, and half a dozen of your Descendants died as well, to my knowledge."

The priests glanced at each other, suspicion still on their faces. The head priest spoke up however, cutting off the silent conversations the others were having. "We appreciate your… candor on this matter and accept your apology in the same good faith that you presented it."

Anderas relaxed considerably at those words, although he made sure to hide it. If the priest in charge of their emergency delegation accepted his apology, then he likely would be allowed to return to Fire unharmed. The consequences of this conversation, however, would not be so benign, and he wasn't quite done yet.

Anderas bowed his head and resumed speaking. "It makes me glad that we can still be civil with each other despite everything that's happened. To continue with my story, though, Elidor's arrival made my… more questionable mission complicated. The two of us spoke briefly about whether we should kill the boy or interrogate him together. That was Elidor's idea actually. He didn't know of my intentions. As I said, he was a good man."

The priests before him nodded solemnly, as though Anderas' words were true. He held back a sneer; they probably believed that Elidor had been a good man. He had been just as much of an evil bastard as any of the Blessed Anderas had ever met. Although he had been willing to cooperate with two other nations, even allowing a Blessed from both to enter his city. Anderas at least respected the man for that.

"I agreed to his proposal, and we were going to interrogate the boy together, but Annelore arrived. She was… well, not as good a person as Lord Elidor. When he suggested we three interrogate the boy together, the three nations who cooperated in catching him each benefiting equally from any knowledge he might have, she decided to turn on us. I don't know if it was her decision alone, but I suspect she had hidden orders as well, much like I did. Either way, she decided that if anyone was going to interrogate the boy, it would be Light alone. She attacked us, blinding us with a flash of light as she tried to steal the boy away. Elidor managed to intervene and stop her, and we began fighting.

"As much as I hate to admit it, I was far less useful in that fight than Elidor was. We Fire Blessed do have a rather prominent disadvantage when fighting Light Blessed, after all, which was thankfully offset by Elidor.

"Unfortunately, Annelore is—*was* quite experienced at fighting against Blessed. She has spent quite some time on the front lines against Lava after all, and she didn't gain the title of 'Blessed Slayer' for nothing. So despite outnumbering her, we were on the defensive more often than not. And things really got bad when she managed to weave an illusion around us, making me look like her and her me.

"I unfortunately had missed her doing that and so was caught by surprise when Elidor suddenly attacked me. He quickly realized what had happened, but a surprise attack from him of all people hurt me greatly. And I may have retaliated on instinct, which certainly did him no favors. So even though her illusion was short-lived, it hurt us enough that she gained a distinct advantage in the fight. And from then on we had to keep a careful eye on each other to make sure we didn't fall for that trick again, putting us at an even worse disadvantage.

"By the time that boy, Tala, got involved, I was barely able to stand. I was so focused on Annelore that I hadn't even realized my flame barrier was up, or that he was trapped in there with us. I was far too gone when he killed Elidor to know how he did that, and I was barely any better when he killed Annelore. I was seconds from fainting at that point, and my vision was blurry and starting to fade, so all I saw was him swinging something at her head. The last thing I can remember before I fell unconscious was her head exploding into light. Truthfully, I don't know why he didn't kill me as well. Perhaps he thought that I had died from the fighting? Or perhaps whatever means he used to kill them was limited and he couldn't use it on me? Or perhaps when my barrier fell with me, he decided escape was more important? I truly have no idea. But from there on I was entirely unconscious and so have no idea what happened, apart from the stories I'm sure you've heard."

"And that's everything?" asked the head priest.

"Everything that I can remember."

"I see," the head priest sighed in aggravation. "Thank you for sharing the details with us. There has been much speculation about what occurred. It is good to finally hear the truth of the matter. If you would return to your quarters, we must discuss this amongst ourselves before we make any decisions."

"Of course. By your leave." With those parting words, Anderas stood, and with a short bow to the Metal priests, he turned on his heel and walked through the door. The three servants he had been allowed to bring to the meeting followed behind him, and the two guards from his personal retinue that had been standing outside the door followed in turn.

They walked in silence through the halls of the great mansion until they returned to the set of guest rooms that Anderas had been given. The guards posted outside the doors opened them as he approached, and he entered the opulent sitting room, taking a seat on one of the fancy chairs spread in a loose circle. His two guards, as well as two of the three servants, took seats around him, while the third retrieved a jug of wine and cups for them all before joining them himself.

"Well, I'd say that went quite well," Anderas said before drinking deeply.

"Indeed, sir. It seems that they believed your story," said Uri, one of Anderas' most trusted servants.

"It would seem so. Now all that's left is to wait and see if they'll allow us to leave the city in peace," Anderas replied.

The small group drank in silent contemplation as they relaxed in their seats. Anderas observed his fellows in silence, contemplating them. To most in his position, they would barely even count as people. For him, though, these five were some of the only people in the world he truly trusted.

"And what of the coming war?" asked Abena, the female of the two guards. "Were you able to convince them?"

"I believe so. With nobody to contradict what I told them, they should place the majority of the blame on Light but won't side with Fire. They should declare themselves neutral, entirely uninvolved."

"So this is really it then? The beginning of a new great war?"

Anderas merely grinned in response.

"And what of that boy, Tala? He's about to become the catalyst for the greatest war seen in millennia. And he's killed *three* Blessed. What should we do about him?"

"I don't think we need to worry about him. At least, not for now. Those companions of his will keep him safe. They truly are an impressive lot," Anderas said simply.

"And what of that cloaked man with him? You said the way he fought reminded you of the Demon. And that something disrupted your fire. The Demon's body was never found after what happened in Lightning. Isn't it at least possible that they're one and the same?"

Anderas' eyes fell on Uri with a weight they rarely held, making the man shift uncomfortably. He held his stare, unblinking, before he spoke.

"Nobody has seen any sign of the Demon since that day. Even what happened in Mist all those years ago was merely a rumor. Whoever that cloaked man is, I doubt he's anything like the Demon. Not enough death and destruction. Too little chaos."

"Too little? How many are dead again?"

"Not enough."

His servants paused at the warning in his voice, nodding and moving on.

"What about the Bone Merc? Is there any news on him?"

"Not much," Abena answered. "He's up in Lightning last I heard. He still refuses to officially move against any of the Churches, regardless of pay. Can't say I blame him, really. He's got a good deal worked out."

"Pity. But Lightning? Tala's little group will likely be heading there soon, won't they? There's nowhere else for them to go. Maybe they'll run into each other," mused Uri.

"Just so long as the Merc hasn't accepted a contract for him. He's the one the damned Demon died fighting! I don't want to imagine what would happen if he went after that kid."

"That would be most unfortunate. No matter how strong that little group is, they wouldn't survive against the Bone Merc."

Anderas eyed his servants as they talked, quietly taking a sip of wine. The Bone Merc was as unpredictable as they came, and easily one of the two most deadly people that Anderas had ever faced, even if it had just been a friendly, and secret, spar. If that man got involved in the things to come, the world really would never be the same.